PRAISE FOR CASSIE HAMER

'Cassie Hamer is a merging of all that is wonderful about authors like Marian Keyes, Liane Moriarty and Sally Hepworth. With this, her second novel, she shows she's here to stay. *The End of Cuthbert Close* is a fabulous, fun, thought-provoking read.' *Better Reading*

'This well-crafted piece of commercial fiction is both warm and full of light ... a satisfyingly chunky and intermittently very funny beach read.' *The Sydney Morning Herald* on *The End of Cuthbert Close*

'Australia's answer to Marian Keyes ... [this] terrifically entertaining story is filled with the sort of people you need in your life—and the strain on relationships you learn to live with.' Chrissie Bellbrae, blogger, on *The End of Cuthbert Close*

'Hamer's approach is authentic, eye opening and intuitive, which ensures that the pages of *The End of Cuthbert Close* turn themselves.' *Mrs B's Book Reviews*

'Full of warmth, humour, friendships, mystery, delicious food, and highly relatable characters, *The End of Cuthbert Close* is a lovely read and highly recommended.' *Scatterbooker*

'A brilliant combination of wit and snark.' Debbish.com on *The End of Cuthbert Close*

'… captures Australian suburbia perfectly … Hamer's strength is in the slow, considered revelations that pepper the novel, making it difficult to put down … *After The Party* forces the reader to confront uncomfortable questions like, How far would you go to protect a child? How clear is the line between right and wrong? And, what does it truly mean to be a good mother?' *Mamamia*

'Everything I love in a novel – jam-packed with intrigue and humour. *After the Party* will keep you turning the pages into the early hours.' Rachael Johns, bestselling Australian author

'I guarantee you will recognise your child, your neighbour, your partner or yourself in this story … light-hearted and heart-warming … I can see it being passed from sister to sister, or from girlfriend to girlfriend, with a knowing look, an exasperated sigh and a genuine giggle.' Cass Moriarty, author of *The Promise Seed* and *Parting Words*

'… blending the relatable with the extraordinary, Cassie Hamer hits the sweet spot with her debut novel, *After The Party* …' *Daily Telegraph*

'In a very clever way, Cassie Hamer has intertwined several stories into one, almost forcing you to keep reading.' *Starts at Sixty* on *After the Party*

'Sharp and witty prose … well paced, funny, and appealing, and should delight anyone looking for fresh women's fiction this season.' *Word Mothers* on *After the Party*

Cassie Hamer has a professional background in journalism and PR, but now much prefers the world of fiction over fact. Her debut novel, *After the Party*, was published in 2019, and her second novel, *The End of Cuthbert Close*, in 2020. Cassie lives in Sydney with her terrific husband, three mostly terrific daughters, and a labradoodle, Charlie, who is the youngest and least demanding family member. In between making school lunches and walking the dog, Cassie is also working on her next novel, but she always has time to connect (or procrastinate) with other passionate readers via her website—CassieHamer.com—or through social media. You can follow her on Facebook, Instagram and Twitter.

Also by Cassie Hamer

After the Party
The Truth about Faking It

the end of cuthbert close

CASSIE HAMER

First Published 2020
Second Australian Paperback Edition 2022
ISBN 9781867208013

Published by
HQ Fiction
An imprint of Harlequin Enterprises (Australia) Pty Limited (ABN 47 001 180 918),
a subsidiary of HarperCollins Publishers Australia Pty Limited (ABN 36 009 913 517)
Level 13, 201 Elizabeth St
SYDNEY NSW 2000
AUSTRALIA

A catalogue record for this book is available from the National Library of Australia
www.librariesaustralia.nla.gov.au

Printed and bound in Australia by McPherson's Printing Group

To my three gorgeous girls — Ruby, Sasha and Lucy.
It IS possible!

CHAPTER ONE

Bring a plate!

The three little words sat so cheerily at the bottom of the invitation.

So simple, so innocuous, so friendly.

So deceitful.

Because it wasn't just a plate, was it, thought Alex O'Rourke as she removed a tray of shop-bought spinach and cheese triangles from the oven. After all, any old clown could turn up to a party with a piece of dining-ware. She had a million plates and platters that did nothing more than collect dust in her kitchen cupboard. They'd love an outing to a party!

She started stabbing at the formerly frozen pastries with a spoon.

'Hmmm … something smells good.' Alex's husband, James, sauntered into the kitchen and peered over her shoulder. 'Did you make these?'

He went to pick up a triangle and Alex tapped his hand away. 'Of course I didn't make them.' She stabbed again to make divots in the golden pillows.

'What are you doing? You're ruining them. They're perfect. Stop it.' James put out his hand to shield the defenceless triangles.

'They're *too* perfect,' said Alex. 'No one will ever believe I made them. Maybe if I just burn them a little …' She went to open the oven door but James stood in front of it, arms folded.

'No one cares if you bought them from a shop. You have twins. A full-time job. The neighbours don't expect pastry made from scratch.'

Alex looked at him. Her sweet, supportive husband, trying to be so millennial, while completely failing to understand that some things never changed, like the meaning of that god-awful phrase *bring a plate*, which meant today what it had always meant – that a plate of homemade food was to be produced (exceptions could be made for foodstuffs by a celebrity chef. A Zumbo cake, for instance, could be forgiven) and, as keeper of the social diary, the responsibility for such provision lay in the hands of the woman of the house.

Bring a plate was the phrase that time forgot.

'It's all right for you,' Alex grumbled. 'No one expects you to cook from scratch.'

'But I would have, if you'd asked me. Remember my meatballs?'

Alex nodded. 'Impressive balls.' She tapped her nose. 'And you've given me an idea.' She smiled and kissed his cheek.

'Glad to be of service.'

Alex set about loading the triangles onto a platter, humming happily.

'Er, so what is this idea?'

'I'll tell them that I specifically asked you a week ago to make the meatballs, but you forgot, so rather than having the neighbours go hungry, I ran out and picked up a box of spinach triangles from the supermarket.'

James frowned. 'But that's a lie. You never asked me. If you had, I would have made them.'

'They won't know that. And because you're a man, they'll think nothing of it.'

'But these people are our friends. Cara? Beth? They wouldn't judge you.'

Alex thought of the women who lived in the houses to their immediate right. Beth, two doors up, an incredible homemaker and mother extraordinaire, and Cara, right next door, who managed to be both strong and fragile as she negotiated parenthood all on her own.

'You're right. Cara and Beth would understand.'

'But the rest?'

Alex sighed. Her husband's desire to see the best in everyone was endearing and exhausting. 'They're neighbours. We smile, we wave, we say hello and we get together once a year. They don't know what happens in my house and I don't know what happens in theirs. The one little insight they get is through what I bring to the party. And you know what they see when a full-time working mum turns up with a plate of frozen pastry?'

'A woman with an actual life?'

Alex gave him a look. 'They see a woman who's put her work in front of her family, values convenience over health, is a little bit stingy, isn't quite coping, and doesn't really care if other people's arteries become clogged with trans fats.'

'They get all of that from a plate of pastry?' James looked crestfallen.

'You have no idea.' Alex wearily covered the steaming parcels with a sheet of aluminium foil. 'Here, you can carry them out. It'll look more like your fault that way.' She handed over the platter and checked her watch. 'Where are the boys?'

'They're out front playing with Henny.'

Alex whipped around. 'You left them alone, unsupervised, with a three-month-old guinea pig?'

James shifted his weight uneasily. 'They won't hurt her. They love her to death.'

'That's what I'm afraid of. Have you seen the way Noah hugs her?' Alex strode towards the driveway and cursed inwardly. How could she and James have been wasting time discussing pastry when their little boys were potentially monstering a poor, defenceless guinea pig? If any harm had come to Henny, Alex knew exactly which three little words to blame.

Bring a plate.

Beth Chandler poked the last of the licorice tails into a prune and stood back from the bench to survey her collection of edible mice. So cute, with those little musk lollies as eyes. Twenty-two, she counted – that would be enough for the kids of Cuthbert Close. What was the collective noun for a group of mice? A nest? Yes, nest. A nest of mice for the nest of kids in her street. Perfect.

'These aren't for the party, are they, Mum?' Twelve-year-old Chloe sidled up beside her.

'What do you mean? The prunes are seedless, if that's what you're worried about. None of the kids could possibly choke.'

'It's not that.'

'Then what is it?'

Chloe bit her lip. 'It's that they're kind of gross.'

'Rubbish. Kids love my mice. We had them at all your parties when you were little.' Beth wiped her hands on the tea towel.

'But that was before we knew they were made from prunes.' Chloe picked one up and held it between her finger-tips like a piece of toxic waste. 'Only old ladies eat prunes.'

Beth did a quarter turn and drew herself up. 'What rot. Prunes are for everyone. They're full of fibre and vitamin K and they're as sweet as a lolly.'

Chloe dropped the mouse back to the tray and wiped her hands down her sides. 'They're disgusting.'

'What's disgusting?' Ethan sat up from where he'd been lying on the couch and removed his earbuds.

'Mum's made the prune mice,' said Chloe.

'Yeah, sure.' Ethan went to put the buds back in.

'No, seriously. They're here.' Chloe wrinkled her nose.

'Oh, Mum, you haven't, have you? They are all shades of wrong.' Ethan leapt up. 'Remember the effect those things used to have on me? I'd be on the toilet for days after my birthday.'

Beth started to wash up the pots and pans that had accu-mulated during her preparations for the neighbourhood party. As well as the mice, she'd elected to make a range of other treats for the kids, figuring that as she was one of the few stay-at-home mothers in the close, she had the most time to give. And besides, she did enjoy cooking.

'That's a complete lie, Ethan Chandler. You were not.'

Her son came to the sink and put his hands on her shoulders. At seventeen, he'd well and truly outstripped her in the height department. 'Mum, please tell me there's going to be something else for the kids to eat at this thing. It's not just prune mice, is it?'

'Of course not,' said Beth in a huff, wriggling out of her son's condescending grasp and opening the fridge door. 'Look, there's fruit kebabs, mini quiches and cheese-and-vegemite sandwiches.' She'd even used her star-shaped cookie cutter. 'Healthy *and* delicious.'

Chloe and Ethan exchanged glances.

'Mum, it's a party. The food's supposed to be … like … good, you know?' said Ethan.

'Yeah, like chips and pizza – that kind of thing.' Chloe leant her elbows on the bench.

'I think I know what little children like to eat, thank you very much. I'm not sure if you've forgotten, but I actually raised two of them, and anyway, Cara's little Poppy loves my vegemite sandwiches and Alex's little boys will love the mini-mice. They look just like that new guinea pig of theirs.'

'You really think a kid wants to *eat* their pet?' Ethan shook his head and Chloe giggled.

'They wouldn't be— Oh look, never mind. It's too late now to do anything else, and besides, your father's going to be cooking up some sausages, so there'll be plenty of food if no one likes what I've made.'

Ethan exhaled with relief. 'Phew. Those beef ones are pretty good with heaps of sauce.'

Beth went to open her mouth but thought better of it. They'd find out soon enough that the sausages were of the chicken variety – so much lower in saturated fat than beef or pork.

'Speaking of Daddy, has anyone seen him?'

Chloe smirked. 'I think *Daddy* is in the garden.'

Beth glared and handed her the tea towel. 'Thank you, Chloe. You can finish the washing up for me.'

The near-teenager took it sullenly. 'What's the point in having a dishwasher if we never use it?'

Beth held up a finger. 'Ah, but that's where you're wrong. We have two dishwashers. They tend to moan quite frequently and they cost a lot of money to run, but we just can't bear to get rid of them. You never know, *one* day they might just do the dishes without an argument.' She went to kiss her daughter lightly on the forehead, but Chloe feinted and ducked.

'This family sucks,' she said under her breath.

Beth stopped, stung. This was not her sweet little Chloe. The child who, less than a year ago, had insisted on kissing her at least ten times a day and never walked anywhere without her hand slipped into Beth's. Where had it all gone so wrong? Hormones? Or something more ... Was this somehow Beth's fault? Maybe she'd coddled her children too much? Held them so tightly that now they were springing, like elastic bands, away from her. Beth hurried out of the kitchen and towards the front yard, hoping neither Chloe nor Ethan would notice the flush in her face or the heat in her eyes. But, of course, how could they notice, when her son was too busy nodding away to the music between his ears and her daughter was caught up in cursing the unfairness of her life.

Beth stood at the top of the steps, breathed deeply and repeated the mantra she'd started using when Ethan was only a few weeks old, though back then they didn't call them mantras, just sayings.

This too shall pass.

She closed her eyes. Usually it gave her a sense of peace.

This too shall pass.

But maybe that was the problem. Everything was passing, just too quickly for Beth to keep up.

She breathed deeply one more time and opened her eyes. Living in the 'bulb' end of the cul-de-sac gave her a good overview of the length of the street. The party was beginning to take shape. Lanterns and fairy lights going up. Neighbours pulling out deckchairs and tables.

She made her way towards the garage and stood at the door.

Inside, through the gloom, she could just make out her husband in the corner of the garage, frowning over his phone, the lines on his face accentuated by the screen's eerie glow.

'Oh, there you are. Everything all right?'

Max looked up, surprised, and quickly stuffed the phone back into his pocket. 'Oh, nothing. Just a couple of issues at work. Tony couldn't find some keys for an open house. No drama.' He came towards her through the dim light. 'Everything set for the party?'

Beth made a face and put her hands on her hips. 'Chloe and Ethan say the food I've made is all wrong and none of the kids will eat it.' As she spoke, her stomach contracted with nerves. Perhaps the children had a point. Maybe kids of today had different tastes. More sophisticated. Salmon sushi seemed to be a staple food from what she saw of children at the local food court.

'Just ignore them,' said Max. He turned away from her and began sifting through the gardening tools and sports gear. 'What does it matter? This party's more about the catch-up than the food. The kids probably won't eat anything anyway. They'll just scoot up and down the street like they always do.'

Beth folded her arms. It was all very well for him to tell her not to worry, all he had to do was wheel out a barbecue and throw some sausages onto it. The difficulty level of that was close to zero, certainly much lower than making mice out of prunes.

'I don't want the neighbours to think I don't care. I did promise to provide for the children.'

'And you are.' Max stopped ferreting about under the surfboards and stood still. 'You need to stop worrying. You always do this and you should know by now that it's always fine.' He glanced down again. 'Now where the hell did I hide the barbecue tongs.'

Beth coloured. Max had given her similar pep talks before every one of the kids' birthday parties, events that always brought her panic levels to fever pitch. For a stay-at-home mother, a child's party was a little like a performance review, or a grand final – the culmination of so many hopes and dreams, for the child, that is. But Max was so easygoing, he always treated it like just another day, albeit with a few extra kids involved. No biggie. Beth told herself it was good for her – the laissez faire approach. He was the yin to her yang. The ebony to her ivory. Usually, his pre-party spiels served to reassure her, but this one in the garage sounded more like a rebuke and she was glad of the gloom to cover her flush.

'Will you set up the barbecue on the Pezzullos' lawn?' The house at the end of the cul-de-sac had been vacant for months, thanks to George's job transfer to Singapore.

'Sure, whatever you think,' he said, still ferreting through boxes.

'I think it's the best spot, out of the way.'

'Hmmm …' Max murmured.

'Are you listening? I said—'

'Here they are!' Max held up the tongs with a self-satisfied grimace, like a dog holding up a bone. 'Now, we're set.'

'Who wants to try a chicken wing?' Cara Pope stopped at the doorway to the living room as two heads swivelled around to face her.

'Meeeeeeeeeee!' Her daughter, Poppy, leapt up from the piano stool and ran towards the kitchen.

'Hey, little girl, you come back here and finish your scales.' Cara's mother spoke with a rapid-fire delivery.

'Ma, please. It's been nearly an hour.' Cara entwined her fingers behind her back. 'She needs a break, and the party's about to begin.'

Joy bent down to collect her handbag and a pile of sheet music from under the piano. 'You are too soft with that girl,' she grumbled in Korean, which was what she always did when she didn't want Poppy to understand. 'Practice makes perfect.'

Cara bit her lip. 'Come and eat something.'

In the kitchen she found Poppy smacking her lips and wiping sticky soy sauce off her lips. 'Can I have another one?'

Cara smiled and picked up a tissue. 'Just one, or there won't be enough for the party.'

'Little girl, you should wait for your elders.' Her mother tapped Poppy on the shoulder before prodding at a wing.

'Try one, Ma,' Cara encouraged.

Joy picked up a wing and sniffed it before taking a small bite. 'Good,' she said, chewing. 'They need more gochujang.' Her mother went to reach for the fermented chilli paste.

'Wait, Ma. These are for the neighbours. The annual street party. Remember I told you? Poppy's going to wear the hanbok you had made.'

Poppy nodded. 'It's very pretty, Halmi. Thank you.'

Her mother let go of the chilli paste. 'Then it is okay.'

Cara exhaled. 'Would you like to stay, Ma? You're very welcome.'

'Will the lawyer be there?'

'Alex? Yes, and you know Beth, the one who's married to the real estate agent.'

Her mother cocked her head. 'She is the one who asks for my kimchi recipe?'

'That's her. She loves your kimchi.'

'She has a very clean house.' Her mother grunted with approval, her eyes flicking to the dishes piled high in Cara's sink. 'I will not stay for this party. Your father will die of hunger if I am not home to feed him. So hopeless.' She shrugged and sighed. 'What can you do.'

Cara suppressed a smile. Her father had been the one who suggested she stay for the party. *She is too much in this new house*, he'd complained on the phone. Joy always made him ring to let Cara know she was on her way for Poppy's piano lesson, as if she expected the little girl to be ready and waiting with hands poised on the keys for her arrival. *Your mother needs to get out more. She loves this place like a baby, almost like she loves that church. So much praying. I think she will be the first Australian-Korean saint.*

'Oh, okay, Ma. That's a shame you can't stay.' She paused and contemplated how to phrase what she was about to say. 'They'll be closing the street soon, and I would not want you to be delayed ...'

Her mother's eyebrows shot up. 'Closing the street? Woh, these people and their parties. So strange. Why would you want to eat in a street when you all have nice houses.' Her gaze went to the peeling wallpaper above the oven. 'Some are nice.' Clutching her bag more tightly, she patted Poppy on the shoulder and headed for the hallway. 'Goodbye, little girl. Practise your scales twice every day.'

At the front door, she went to remove her slippers and put her shoes back on.

'Need some help?' Cara bent down to pick up the shoes.

'Who do you think I am? An old lady?'

Ignoring Cara's outstretched hand, her mother instead reached for the wall to steady herself, putting her hand right near the wedding photo of Cara and Pete. Joy's gaze went to it, and she shivered, blessing herself, as she always did.

'Such bad luck.' She shook her head and gave Cara a look that asked her for the thousandth time why she chose to stay in the broken-down old cottage that was saddled with no dishwasher, and the curse of a death of a man in his prime.

Cara kept silent.

Shoes on, Joy was out the door in a hurry. No goodbye. No *I love you*. Not even a *See you next week*. Just gone.

'Bye, Ma. Thanks for the lesson,' Cara called, and her mother waved without turning around. Further down the street, she could see Beth and Max, setting up the barbecue on the Pezzullos' front lawn, and Alex's twins playing in the driveway with their new guinea pig.

Waiting for the little lawnmower engine of her mother's ageing Daihatsu sedan to come to life (Joy believed in good appliances over good cars), Cara allowed herself to shift focus from the street and back to the photo of her and Pete. She stepped closer, rubbing a speck of dust off his grey-green eyes, then flinched as the car emitted a tinny beep of farewell. Her mother's way of saying goodbye.

CHAPTER TWO

'More bubbles, ladies?' Beth started to pour, not bothering to wait for answers from her two neighbours, because she already knew exactly what they would say.

Alex would say *yes* because she always said yes to alcohol, and given the excitable nature of those twins, Beth didn't blame her. Cara, on the other hand, would say *no* because she was self-conscious of the flush that rose in her cheeks when she drank even one glass of champagne, something about Koreans not having a certain type of enzyme? Beth wasn't certain of the biological reason but always assured Cara it was virtually unnoticeable.

She passed a full glass to Alex.

'You could at least *pretend* I might have said no,' she protested, then took a sip. 'God that's good.'

Beth held out a small glass to Cara. 'Are you sure you won't have just a little more?'

Cara pressed her fingers to her cheeks. 'I look like one of those scary porcelain dolls, don't I? Like I let Poppy put blush on me or something.'

'Not at all,' Beth patted her arm. 'It's like you've just had a brisk walk.'

'Or, you know, a shag.' Alex took another gulp.

'Alex!' said Cara and Beth in unison.

'What? It's true. And it's less offensive than saying you look like a *doll*,' she snorted.

'But there are children around.' Beth's eyes zoomed to Poppy, Noah and Jasper, flying up and down the close on their scooters.

'... Yes, hanging off our every word, aren't they,' said Alex drily. 'Personally, I think we could all do with a little more shagging in our lives. At least Cara *looks* like she's getting some. These days, the closest James and I get to sexy-time is watching Nigella cook a chocolate cake. The way she licks her fingers ...'

'A bit unhygienic, really when you think about it ...' Beth trailed off, trying to remember the last time she and Max had had 'sexy-time', as Alex put it.

'Oh, no.' Cara shook her head. 'I love Nigella.' She sat forward in the chair, her eyes bright. 'My mum doesn't like cooking at all but she used to watch when her English wasn't so good. You don't need to know the words to follow what's happening.' Cara drew her knees together and clasped her hands. 'But I just think she's amazing. So sensual. So ...' She looked skywards. 'So ... free, and loose with a dash of this and a pinch of that. No recipes and exact measurements, just pure instinct. I would never have gone into food styling if it wasn't for Nigella ... and Pete, of course ...'

Beth gazed at the younger woman beside her, still looking towards the heavens, caught in her memory. She lightly touched her hand. 'Speaking of your mother. Where is she? I thought I saw her car earlier.'

'Oh, she had to go home.'

'Probably just as well.' Alex rested the flute on the arm of the chair. 'No offence, but she doesn't seem a street party kind of person.'

'Oh, that's true,' said Cara.

'I suppose she's had more important things to worry about in her life. Such a strong woman.' Beth returned the champagne bottle to the ice-bucket at her feet.

'Very strong,' Alex nodded. 'I'm not sure she approves of me.'

'Oh, no, you're a lawyer. She loves all lawyers.'

'I don't know why. Most people think we're money-grabbing bastards.'

Cara gave a small smile. 'You're supporting your family. She likes that.'

'Then she must really disapprove of *me*! I don't support my family at all.' Beth tried to keep her voice light.

'Oh, no, you give your *life* to your family. That's important too, as much as money.' Cara paused. 'And you make kimchi. That's most important of all.'

The three women laughed. Food, again. Somehow, their conversations always came back to it.

'Oh, I always love this party,' Cara remarked, settling back again in her chair.

The three of them fell silent and tuned in to the sounds of chat, laughter and music coming from the sixty or so people dotted in groups about the close. The young couple at number six had brought out their portable speaker and made a special playlist of laid-back summer beats that were electronic enough to appeal to the kids, but not too heavy to turn off the adults. Someone had produced bats and a ball for a game of backyard cricket at the southern end of the close and shouts of *howzat* and *got 'im* punctuated the music. Each one of the twenty-five houses in the street had strung either lanterns or fairy lights along their front fences and they were starting to twinkle with the sun now nearly set behind them. Beth had even put them along the Pezzullos' empty home, just to maintain consistency in the bulb of the cul-de-sac. A light breeze tickled at the fig trees, making them sway and murmur, but the night was otherwise balmy. Like stepping into a warm bath. No one was quite sure who'd begun the tradition of Cuthbert Close's End-of-Summer Street Party. Beth thought it might have been the old couple at number three, who'd moved out in the early 2000s when the wife died and the husband developed dementia. Such a lovely family; their children, now fully grown adults with families of their own, still turned up each year to the party – the last Saturday in February – to reconnect with the neighbours they remembered as kids. That was the thing about Cuthbert Close, once you'd lived there, you never really left.

'It's calm now, but I hope the butterfly hasn't flapped its wings.' Alex gestured to the white wall of cloud building far away in the south, the setting sun appearing to line it with gold thread.

'What do you mean?' said Cara, curious.

'You know, the butterfly effect. Chaos theory. A butterfly flapping its wings in the Amazon causes a tornado in Texas. Last thing we need tonight is a storm.'

'Just ignore it and look the other way.' Beth inclined her champagne glass towards the sky directly above them, which was completely clear and resembled a pastel colour-wheel of pinks and purples. The clouds didn't worry her. She'd checked the forecast. The southerly wasn't predicted for hours yet, by which time the party would well and truly be over, and while some people made a habit of never relying on weather forecasts, Beth tended to have more faith. She trusted people, even meteorologists.

'That sky looks good enough to eat,' said Cara, following Beth's gaze.

'Like sherbet,' said Beth.

'Or a grapefruit martini,' said Alex.

'A berry-swirled Eton mess,' said Cara.

'Is that the one with crushed-up meringue and cream?' asked Beth.

Cara nodded. 'I do a version with raspberries, blueberries and blackberries folded into the cream. And a little dash of Cointreau.'

'Fat, sugar, and booze? All food groups covered. You win.' Alex tapped her champagne glass in applause.

'You should put it on your website thingy,' said Beth, reaching beneath her chair to produce a tray of cheese and crackers.

'It's called Instagram, Beth, and Cara's got a gazillion followers last time I checked,' said Alex. 'Ask your kids. I'm sure they're on it. Every teen is, maybe not for the gastro-porn though.'

Beth made a face. 'I know they're on Instagram, but they tell me it's all about Snapchat now. I can't keep up.' She offered the tray to Alex. 'Truffle cheese?'

'Thank god the twins are too little for it all.' Alex cut herself a wedge. 'That said, a couple of their school friends already have their own iPads. Five and six years old. Ridiculous.' She passed the tray to Cara. 'Poppy doesn't have one, does she?'

Cara shook her head. 'Oh, no. But she helps me a little with the Insta posts. Holds the lights and things when I'm styling new dishes in the shed.' She pulled out her mobile phone and started tapping away. 'I need to text myself a reminder about that Eton mess. I don't think I've done it yet.'

'But don't call it Eton mess,' said Alex. 'Call it something different.' She gulped her champagne. 'Like Summer Sunset.'

'Sounds more like a cocktail than a dessert,' said Beth, looking towards the sky for inspiration. 'Summer Fling.'

'*That* sounds more like a cocktail than Summer Sunset. And very adulterous.'

The women fell into a thoughtful silence.

'Oh, yes, maybe I have it.' Cara clicked her fingers. 'Summer Street Party.'

'Summer Street Party,' said Alex slowly. 'Berries, cream and meringue. A party in your mouth. I like it.'

'Maybe we could do it for your anniversary, Beth?' said Cara.

Beth's stomach flipped a little at the mention of the party. Six weeks to go until she and Max would celebrate twenty years of marital bliss in front of eighty family and friends. Cara had agreed to help with the catering but Beth had started to wonder if she was biting off more than she could chew, or cook.

'Twenty years, Beth ...' Cara trailed off in admiration.

'That's more than you get for murder,' remarked Alex.

The women laughed and settled in to chatting companionably about their all-time favourite desserts. After five minutes of discussing chocolate fondants, artisan gelatos and trifles, Alex's stomach let out a large growl.

'Is it time to eat yet?' She patted her belly. 'It may not look empty but I can assure you it feels it.'

Beth checked her watch. 'How about I rustle everyone up and ask them to put their platters out? Let's hope we don't have twenty trays of party pies, or spinach triangles.'

'What's wrong with spinach triangles?' said Alex stiffly. 'Your note said to *bring a plate*. You didn't say anything about not bringing spinach triangles.'

'Spinach triangles are absolutely fine.' Beth patted her shoulder. 'Did you make them?'

'Of course not. James was supposed to make his world-famous meatballs, but he forgot, so I raced out this afternoon to the supermarket on an emergency spinach-triangle mission.'

Beth couldn't hold back a tiny sigh of relief. Even by her own admission, Alex was a terrible cook and Beth had almost considered issuing her with a version of the invitation that omitted the request to bring a plate. The poor woman already had enough on hers. 'Excellent, excellent. And Cara's done her chicken wings, so we'll definitely have *some* variety.'

'Perfect. I'll get the serviettes and the paper plates,' said Cara.

But as the women went to rise collectively from their deckchairs, a thunderous, mechanical rumbling came from the end of the street.

'Goodness, what is *that*!' said Beth, craning to see.

It was a removal truck, turning with a dinosaur-swing into Cuthbert Close.

'If that guy thinks he's coming down here, he can think again.' Alex put her hands on her hips and surveyed the over-sized vehicle, looming at the entrance to the close, the top of it scraping against the lower hanging branches of the figs as it paused at the corner. 'Must have taken a wrong turn. I'll set him straight.' Alex started striding down the street.

'I'll send Max up. He's got the closure permit,' called Beth. Apart from co-ordinating the food, she'd volunteered her husband to organise the council permit allowing them to officially block the street to traffic for the night, not that there was strictly any need. After all, a dead end meant no through-traffic, and all the neighbours would be in atten-dance at the party with no need to drive anywhere. Still, better to be safe than sorry.

Beth hurried through the crowd to locate her husband, eventually spotting him deep in conversation with Alex's husband, James, both of them oblivious to the commotion at the end of the street.

'Max, we need you,' said Beth, a little breathlessly. 'Sorry to interrupt, James.'

Her husband pulled a face. 'Can it wait five minutes? James was about to tell me what brand of sneaker I should get for the marathon.'

'No, it can't wait,' said Beth with as much patience as she could muster. 'Didn't you hear the truck? It's trying to get in, and Alex has gone down to stop him but she might need the permit.' She pointed up the street to where Alex was gesticulating animatedly at the truck driver.

'My wife will sort him out, quick smart, don't you worry about that,' said James in an admiring tone. 'She is a force to be reckoned with.'

'Yes, of course, but still I'd like to have the permit handy, just in case. Max?' asked Beth. 'Where is it?'

'Well, I, um ...' Max dropped the tongs to his side and his expression went from one of irritation to one of embarrassment. 'Ah, well, you see ...'

'Max, where is the permit?' Nervously, Beth put her fingers to her lips. 'Please tell me you got it.'

'All right, so, when you asked me to organise the street closure, things were going crazy at work and it got to a couple of days beforehand and I thought how about I save everyone a few bucks by not getting the permit? It's not like we ever really need it.'

Beth's heart sank. He hadn't organised it. She knew her husband. To him the glass wasn't just half full, it was consistently as full as an Alex-sized glass of champagne. As a real estate agent, he was expert in putting the most positive spin on everything. Derelict houses were 'an opportunity to capitalise', apartments that looked straight into a brick wall 'offered complete privacy and seclusion', and gardens that never saw sun were 'low maintenance' because nothing ever grew there.

'Well, we do need it,' said Beth.

'I can fix this. Leave it with me,' said Max.

James shifted awkwardly. 'I'll give you a hand. Make sure my wife doesn't punch someone.'

Max drained the last of his beer and went to hand the empty bottle to his wife. 'Could you please, Beth?'

'Take it yourself, Max.' Beth turned and stomped away towards the truck, not bothering to wait for her husband. Along the way, Cara snuck in by her side.

'What is happening? You're upset.' Cara linked her arm into Beth's.

'Max forgot the permit.'

Cara sucked in a breath, then let it out again before speaking. 'Oh, I'm sure it's all a misunderstanding, as Alex said. After all, who would move house on a Saturday night?'

From a distance, they heard Alex's voice, rising above the truck driver's. 'Look, I don't care whose house in this street you have to deliver this furniture to, you cannot do it tonight because we have a permit that says it's closed to traffic from 4 pm until 11 pm.' At that moment, Alex turned and spotted James, Max, Beth and Cara. 'Ha! And here comes the man with the paperwork. Show him, Max. Show this man that he is not allowed to drive his ridiculous truck into the middle of our street party.' Alex folded her arms and stuck out her chin.

'G'day. Max Chandler's the name.' He thrust out his hand and gave his best real estate agent smile to the driver. 'Seems we have a little problem here.'

Max started talking quietly to the driver and Alex sidled up to Beth and Cara. 'What is he doing?' she hissed. 'Why hasn't he thrown the guy out already?'

'Oh, we don't actually have a permit,' said Cara in a low voice.

'Why the hell not?'

'Because my darling husband forgot,' said Beth tightly.

As Alex opened her mouth to speak, Cara briefly shook her head in warning, before squeezing Beth's shoulder. 'We'll sort it out.'

'Cara's right,' said Alex. 'This bozo driver will not ruin the party.'

'Max! Max Chandler! Is that you?' A woman's bright and breezy voice came from behind the truck.

'Who's that?' asked Alex.

'No idea,' said Beth, watching as a tanned blonde woman dressed in a long and strappy white linen dress floated towards them from the equally white and shiny SUV parked behind the removalists' truck.

She greeted Beth's husband with a warm handshake. 'I thought it was you.'

'Charlie, welcome to the neighbourhood. And this must be Talia, is it?' Max offered his hand to the teenager who'd sidled up behind her mother. Beth took in the girl's jeans and t-shirt. Freckles, wide cheeks, spectacles. Twelve, maybe thirteen, at a guess.

'Charlie Devine, meet my wife, Beth. And our next door neighbour Cara, and Alex and James O'Rourke, who are two doors down.'

'Pleased to meet you all.' Charlie gave a dazzling smile and peered past them, down the street. 'I hope we haven't interrupted anything.'

'Well, actually you have,' said Alex with an equally dazzling smile. 'It's our annual street party, and usually we get a permit to shut the street to traffic but it seems someone forgot this year.' She glanced sideways at Max. 'Then again, we don't often get people moving in on a Saturday night.'

Charlie's eyebrows furrowed while her lips remained in a smile. 'Yes, we had planned to be here much earlier but the truck had some mechanical trouble in Brisbane.'

Beth clasped her hands. 'You've driven all the way from Queensland? In one day? Oh, you poor things. You must be exhausted. Come and sit down. Have something to eat. A drink perhaps? We're just about to have dinner.' She gestured to the tables set up further down the street.

Charlie shook her head. 'Thank you, Beth. That's so kind, but we really need to get this lot unloaded.'

'Of course. Maybe we can help.' Her brain did the calculation. There was only one empty house in the street. 'You're moving into twenty-five, I presume?'

Charlie confirmed with a tight nod. 'We're going to be neighbours, I seem to recall Max telling me when we signed the lease.'

'Wonderful.' Beth hid the small hurt in her voice. Max had been trying to sell the Pezzullo place ever since they left for Singapore. Clearly, they'd changed tack, renting it to the Devines, but why hadn't Max mentioned it?

'Is that … is that a barbecue on my lawn? I can get my removalists to help clear it all away, your tables, too, if you like?' Charlie looked over her shoulder to the burly men, leaning quietly against the truck and enjoying a smoke. 'And we'll take down those fairy lights, obviously.'

Her voice was friendly enough but Beth had a sense that she was being told what to do, rather than asked.

'Mum, why don't we let the guys have a break and something to eat, and we'll unload later.' Talia Devine hooked her hand through her mother's arm and Charlie's smooth face collapsed into worry lines.

'Are you sure, darling?' The woman fingered her ear lobe, drawing attention to a massive set of diamond earrings. Beth had never seen bigger. 'I thought you'd want to get settled straight away, set up your room.' The concern in Charlie's voice was genuine, and Beth softened. Of course a mother wouldn't think twice about driving through the middle of a party to get her child settled into a new house. Relocating a teenager was a huge wrench, especially when it was to an entirely new city.

'I don't mind waiting, it's cool,' said Talia.

'All right, sweetie, as long as you're okay with it.' Charlie patted her daughter's hand. 'That's really thoughtful of you.'

A little bit over the top, thought Beth, then scolded herself. Who was she to judge? She was a stay-at-home mother who'd made a life, a good life, out of servicing her children's needs. She could barely criticise others for doing the same. And it *was* nice of the daughter to offer to wait.

'Thank you, Talia. That would be wonderful. One hour, okay? That'll give us just enough time to serve up the dinner and clear out of your way,' said Beth. 'And I'll have to introduce you to my Chloe. She's just started high school at St Therese's.'

Talia smiled. 'Oh, cool. That's where I'll be going, too. But I'm fourteen, so a couple of years ahead … Year Nine,' she explained, and Beth hid her surprise. Talia was older than she'd thought. Just small for her age.

'We meant what we said about joining us for dinner. You're more than welcome,' said Cara.

'There's enough to feed an army,' said Alex. 'Beth always does an incredible job getting us all organised.'

'Thank you but I think we passed a supermarket near here, so we might go there and pick up some supplies,' said Charlie smoothly.

'Oh, please don't,' said Beth. 'I can give you some milk and bread for the morning, and I probably have a cheese and bacon quiche in the freezer somewhere for tomorrow's lunch if you'd like.'

Max cautiously put his arm on Beth's shoulder. 'My wife declares a national emergency if there's no food in the house.'

National emergency … That's a bit much.

Charlie paused. 'That's very sweet of you, but we follow a strict kangatarian diet.'

'Sorry?' enquired Beth.

'Vegetables and kangaroo meat, and a little fish sometimes. If it's wild caught.'

'That's a new one,' muttered Alex, soft enough for only Cara to hear.

'Talia's kangatarian as well?' asked Beth.

'Mostly.' Talia grinned. 'But bacon is pretty hard to resist.'

'Oh, you are so right,' said Cara.

'Maybe I could bring one round for Talia, then?' asked Beth.

Charlie exchanged glances with her daughter. 'Whatever she likes.'

'That would be awesome, thanks, Mrs Chandler.'

'Wonderful, but please call me Beth. Now, come and have something to eat, and meet the rest of the Cuthbert crew. There're some sushi platters, somewhere. Salmon and tuna, that might be suitable for you, Charlie? Or green salad?'

The woman gave a tight smile and started to follow Max down the close, her arm around Talia's waist.

Beth, Alex and Cara fell in behind them.

'Who does this woman think she is, barging into our party with her ridiculous truck and her made-up eating habits?' hissed Alex.

'Kangaroo meat is actually very low fat and high in iron, so it could be very healthy,' said Beth. 'Provided you include legumes.'

'I think I know that woman from somewhere,' said Cara, producing her phone.

'Now that you mention it, she's kind of familiar to me too.' Alex squinted into the distance.

Cara held her phone up. 'Here she is. Charlie Devine – wife of the Primal Guy, Ryan Devine.'

'The primal who?' Beth peered at the shot of a muscle-bound couple doing something that looked like tight-rope walking no more than a couple of feet off the ground between two trees. *Slack-lining is how we chill,* read the caption.

'Oh, he's a lifestyle guy. All about the hunter-gatherer way of life. Lots of meat, kangaroo, I suppose, and veg. No grains. No carbs. Crazy intense exercise. He's huge on Instagram and he sells green smoothie powders and that kind of thing. I think his wife is in the business too.' Cara tapped at the screen. 'Oh, yes. Here's a better shot. The Primal Wife. Former dancer, and now wellness educator.' The next photo was a close-up of Ryan and Charlie, arm in arm, with matching sixpacks.

Alex took the phone. 'I know that guy. What a goose. The daughter seems nice. Poor thing, with parents like that.'

'Don't be too harsh, Alex. Give the woman a chance,' said Beth.

'I wonder why the Primal Guy isn't with them,' remarked Cara.

'Maybe moving house doesn't quite fit the brand. Bit too mundane. He's probably off building a grass hut somewhere,' said Alex.

'I'm going to sign up for his newsletter,' said Cara, typing away.

'Sign me up too. I love cyber-stalking the neighbours.' Alex checked over Cara's shoulder.

'I'm sure, in time, all will be revealed,' declared Beth. 'After twenty years of living in this street, I've learnt that it's almost impossible to keep secrets from your neighbours.'

'I don't know. I reckon most people in this city would have no idea of their neighbour's first name,' said Alex.

'Oh, but that's not true for us,' said Cara. 'I can't imagine ever leaving this place.'

'They'll have to carry me out of here in a box,' said Beth. 'I've told James that if he wants to move, he'll either have to divorce me, or get me fired so that the bank repossesses.'

Walking in the middle of the trio, Beth linked her arm through Cara's, and then through Alex's. While she made a point of being friendly with everyone in Cuthbert Close, the two women by her side were special to her. In so many ways, they were different. Different ages. Different marital status. Completely different in fashion. Yet, they clicked. They balanced each other. It was chemistry, and perhaps a shared love of bundt cake.

'Even if I'd had a choice, I could never have picked two more lovely neighbours.' As Beth spoke, a strong breeze blew up the close, causing her skirt to flap around her legs and threaten to fly higher, into her face. She let go of Alex and Cara to pull it down. 'Oh my goodness, where did that come from?' Just as she'd settled herself, there was another gust, more powerful than the first. Leaves skittered across the bitumen and a couple of small branches tumbled to the ground.

'Holy shit, that southerly blew up fast,' said Alex, looking skywards.

Beth walked ahead, quickly. 'I think we'd better hurry with the—'

The wind interrupted her. Howling up the close, the turbulent air buffeted the women, causing them to stumble. There were shrieks from the kids as tablecloths and lanterns went flying. In the distance, Beth saw Max put a protective arm around Charlie as a beach umbrella came flying towards her. Meanwhile, James threw himself over the trestle table to stop it from becoming airborne, Alex's twins cowering under it along with little Poppy. A flock of squealing cockatoos flew across the sky and the trees let out groans as they were battered sideways.

From above came a cracking rumble of thunder. Beth turned. Mountainous clouds loomed behind her, thick and grey and pregnant with rain. Lightning forked across the sky, white with heat, and the ground almost sizzled as big, fat raindrops started to fall.

Spotting Ethan and Chloe taking shelter near the garage, Beth started to run. 'Don't just stand there, take what you can,' she yelled to them, filling her arms with platters and cutlery, whatever she could grab off the tables. Out of the corner of her eye, she spotted Alex and Cara doing the same.

'Take it all to my house,' she shouted over what was now driving rain, sweeping over the close in thick, heavy sheets.

Ten minutes later, saturated, but at least indoors, Beth despatched Ethan and Chloe to the shower, and distributed towels to her drowned-rat neighbours, now dripping onto the floorboards. They quivered silently in a huddle near the French doors, gazing out onto the now deserted street, the houses across the road barely visible through the fog of rain.

'Such a shame. All that effort everyone put in. I feel awful,' said Beth, sensing that as chief organiser of the food, she was also somehow responsible for organising decent weather. Just as Max had failed to get the permit, she'd failed to get the sunshine. But who would have anticipated such a freak storm? In twenty years, she'd never known the Cuthbert Close End-of-Summer Street Party to be rained out before. The last weekend in February was always guaranteed perfection.

'There's always next year, I suppose,' said Alex gloomily.

'Mummy, can't we go and jump in the puddles, please?' the twins beseeched her.

'Absolutely not.' Alex folded her arms and watched as the removal truck started to make its way down the street. 'Well, the Devines got what they wanted, at least.'

'They won't try to unload in this, will they?' James put his arm loosely on his wife's shoulder.

'I suppose I should give them a hand.' Max came up beside them.

Beth patted his arm. 'Wait till it's settled a little. I'm sure it will blow over soon.'

'I hope the cottage won't leak like last time.' Cara raked a finger through her daughter's rain-flattened curls. 'This rain is so violent.'

They stood and watched, the stunned silence in Beth's living room broken only by the beep of the reversing truck and the loud beat of torrential rain.

Across the way, Charlie Devine ran out to the truck under the cover of a pristine white umbrella.

Like a moth, Beth thought. *But prettier.*

A butterfly.

ThePrimalGuy.com.au

From: The Primal Guy

Subject: Moving On

Hey Prime-Mates,

So, I know you're already down with the idea that the first humanoids had a rad diet and exercise regime. But did you also know that they were mad travellers? And when I say mad, I mean crazy, like wandering from Africa to Alaska kind of crazy.

Sounds batshit insane, right? I mean why leave the fertile grounds of the African savannah to go off to the freezing cold of Alaska?

Well, obvs, it's cos that's what we crazy cats called humans love to do. We're built to move. We go where the wind takes us. To seek out the food. Explore. Find the nectar and suck the life out of that shit. And if that means trekking to Alaska, then that's what we do, man.

You see where I'm going with this, yeah?

The Primal Guy is on the move! Yep, I'm headed for new pastures. New horizons. Places where they've never even heard my name.

But that doesn't mean I'm going to forget you guys. No way, no how. You know what? I'm actually gonna take you on my journey, thanks to the wonders of this thing they call the interweb.

Now, I've gotta plan, and it's going to get a little hairy, but you gotta stick with me okay?

As the great man, Bob Dylan, once said, 'Chaos is a friend of mine.'

Or, as the Primal Kid, Talia, would say, 'Chaos is a *BFF* of mine.'

Peace out, dudes.
Ryan (AKA the Primal Guy)

PS Super-awesome two-for-one offer going on for our uber-popular Smash It! Green Smoothie powder. Promo code 2SMOOTHIE4U

CHAPTER THREE

Her fingers clenching the steering wheel tightly, Alex pressed the button for the garage door and wondered why the fuck she'd elected to pick the boys up early from after-school care.

'I can do twenty-two,' said Jasper.

'I can do fifty,' retorted Noah.

The twins were fighting about who could do the most burps in a row.

'Well, I can do forty-five.'

In the rear-view mirror, Alex saw the boys straining against their seat belts. 'Jasper, you do know that forty-five is actually less than fifty.'

The boys continued to squabble and Alex tuned out. The garage door was open, yet her foot stayed firmly on the brake. Driving *into* the garage meant she would have to get out of the car, unstrap the boys, get their bags out of the boot, carry them in, unpack them, organise some afternoon tea, shout at them to do some homework, then get a start on dinner and check her emails to tie up a few loose ends from work.

It would just be easier to stay right here and let them argue about burps.

'Mum,' whined Jasper. 'Where's our arvo tea? Daddy always brings it to eat in the car.'

'Yeah, we're starving,' said Noah.

Other mums raved about mindfulness and meditation, but Alex found selective deafness far more useful. She wasn't listening to the burp conversation, or the demands for food. Not at all. She was sitting there, peacefully admiring the view of her home and, while studiously ignoring the twins, she was also paying no attention to the other little voice telling her she would never quite feel at home here.

Where was the fibro? The wire-mesh fences? The rusting letterboxes and weeds growing out of concrete?

Wasn't *that* how kids grew up? It was how she'd grown up, all those thousands of kilometres away in Perth. Nothing like this beautiful street that today looked as classic and fresh as a crisp, white shirt, thanks to the Sunday afternoon working bee, unofficially co-ordinated by Beth, to clear the storm damage.

You earned this. You deserve this. You worked for this.

Well, not quite. Officially, the bank owned most of their house. The mortgage was eye-watering, but provided Alex kept working, they could keep their heads above water, just. Still, the oversized debt didn't exactly alleviate her sense of being an impostor, like a troll doll that accidentally found its way into the Barbie mansion. Not that Alex had ever owned either as a child. Not like her sons, who had everything.

'Mum, c'mon. I'm hungry. Why aren't we moving?' said Jasper.

'Yeah, Mum, come on,' said his little echo, Noah, younger than Jasper by only ten minutes, but it may as well have been ten years.

'Okay, boys. I'm moving, I'm moving.'

She swung into the garage and set her little lion cubs free from their cage.

'Mum, can I play with Henrietta?' Noah leapt out and stopped at the door.

'Course you can,' Alex opened the boot and leant in. 'But come and get your bags first.' Silence. She leant out again. The garage was empty. The boys gone. Alex sighed and surveyed the load for a second, trying to work out how she could best use her two arms to carry six bags, including two backpacks. How did James make it look so easy?

'Would you like some help?'

Alex turned quickly. That new girl in the street. What was her name? Tanya … Dara … Dahlia. No. Talia. That was it.

'Oh, hi, Talia. Thanks for offering.' Helpful *and* mature. Potentially A-grade babysitter material. Alex was always on the lookout as they tended to go through a lot of them. 'That would be wonderful. The boys have run off to play with our guinea pig.' She handed a backpack to Talia. 'Do you have any pets?'

The teenager grimaced. 'We have a cat and she gets out all the time. Mum didn't want to bring her here. She said pets don't like being moved and it's better to have a clean start.'

A clean start. What did *that* mean?

'What about your dad, does he like animals?' Alex kept her voice casual to obscure what a judge would have dismissed as a leading question.

'He said we had to bring Banjo or the pound would put him to sleep. He loves animals.' Talia beamed, then the smile faded. 'He's in America at the moment … On business.'

The Primal Guy in the USA. That made perfect sense. They'd wet themselves over his nutty ideas.

'Mum, Henny's not back in her cage yet.' Jasper was back and panting, little tendrils of hair stuck to his damp forehead.

'And the hutch is still open,' added Noah.

'Well, I wonder whose fault that is?' The boys had a habit of playing with Henny and forgetting to put her back. But she was such a timid little thing (probably traumatised by the boys) she generally tended to return herself to the hutch.

'Not mine,' said Jasper quickly.

'Not mine,' said Noah, not quite as quickly.

'Look, she's probably somewhere in the garden, or maybe at one of the neighbours'. Go and start looking. Quick.' She shooed the boys away, regretting for the one hundred and fiftieth time that she'd ever been talked into getting a pet.

'I thought I saw something earlier, it was little and furry, near our place. It might have been your guinea pig. Maybe I could help look?' said Talia.

'Thanks, Talia, that'd be great.'

Alex smiled tightly through the prickle of fear in her stomach. The boys would be devastated if anything happened to their beloved guinea pig.

'Hen-yyyyyyyy. Where are youuuuuuuuuu? We miss youuuuuu.' That was Noah. Heartfelt and sincere.

'We've got food, Henny. Come quick or you'll miss out,' called Jasper, irritated. Always strategic.

Through the garage door, Alex could see that the twins had moved beyond the garden onto the footpath, with Talia close by. Alex watched as she took Noah's hand and spoke gently to him.

'Let's look in our front garden. I thought I saw a little rat there earlier but it might have been your guinea pig.'

Alex resumed her focus on the mountain of bags in the boot.

'Only five years old. And they come with so much *stuff*,' she grumbled to nobody in particular, reaching in to collect another bag.

She had her hand on the strap, when a piercing shriek made her jerk up so quickly that her skull banged into the door of the boot which, in her laziness, she hadn't quite lifted to its full height.

'Muuuuuummm!'

Ignoring the thumping pain in her head, she dropped the bags and ran. Was it Noah or Jasper? Please god, don't let them have fallen and cracked their heads open like Noah had done when he was three years old and decided that he really *was* Superman and needed to test his powers by leaping off their balcony onto the concrete six feet below. Or the time Jasper decided the Alsatian at the local dog park was a pony that he could ride, and the Alsatian very much disagreed and bit him deeply on the ankle to tell him so. Please let it not be one of those very awful, very traumatic and very time-consuming accidents that required every ounce of compassion she could muster, not to mention two days' leave from work. Please not that. Rushing towards the Devines' front garden, Alex saw Noah's shoulders heaving behind the low brick wall, and Jasper's arm around him.

'What? What is it?' Alex raced to Noah's side. 'Are you hurt? Is something broken? Did Jasper do something to you?' Jasper pointed and Alex followed his finger to where Talia was wrestling with a ball of fur in the corner of the garden.

'No, Banjo!' she cried. 'No, you can't. Naughty cat. No.' She stood with a very fluffy, very squirmy white cat in her arms. Her face was distraught. 'I'm so sorry.'

At Talia's feet was Henrietta – the cute, fluffy little guinea pig that Noah and Jasper had wholeheartedly embraced into their lives, even though it wasn't the puppy they so desperately wanted. Five weeks, and they'd managed not to squash or step on her.

'Oh dear,' whispered Alex, drawing the boys in close. 'I think something very bad has happened to Henrietta.'

For a start, she wasn't moving, and Henrietta was never not moving. Then there was the fact that her legs were in the air, and seemingly frozen in that position, and her eyes were open. Wide open, and very much not blinking.

'I'm so sorry.' Talia shifted her weight from side to side. 'He's never done anything like this before. I mean, he gets out, but he's not a killer.' At that moment, the cat screeched and squirmed in the girl's arms as if he wanted another piece of the little dead guinea pig on the grass. Noah and Jasper huddled into Alex's legs.

'I think you better take him inside, Talia. I'll deal with Henrietta.'

Talia nodded and half-ran, half-walked towards her front door, castigating the cat as she went.

'Is Henny frozen? She looks frozen. Maybe she's playing statues? To trick us or something.' As he spoke, Noah kept a tight hold on his mother's leg, while Jasper eased his grip to take a closer look

'C'mon, Henny. Wake up. We're home now. It's okay, we'll look after you.' Jasper touched Henrietta with his toe.

'Boys, I'm very sorry to say this.' Alex took a breath. 'But I think Henrietta is dead.'

'No, Mummy,' cried Noah. 'She's not dead, she's just playing a trick on us, aren't you, Henny?' He knelt down beside the unmoving guinea pig.

'I'm sorry, darling. I really am. But I think she's dead.'

'Should we try saving her? I've seen ambulance people breathe into someone's mouth to get their hearts going again.' Jasper, ever the practical one. 'There's got to be something we can do.' He got down beside his brother, opened his mouth and went to put his hands on Henrietta.

'No, Jasper!' said Alex quickly, kneeling down next to her sons.

'What? What's wrong?' said Jasper.

'I don't think it's a good idea. Let's leave her in peace.'

'But why did she have to go and die?' wailed Noah, burying his head in his hands. 'Why?'

'It was the cat.' Jasper looked towards the Devines' house. 'He was probably trying to eat her.'

'Nooooooo,' sobbed Noah. 'Mummy, did Banjo really attack Henny?'

'Maybe,' said Alex. Noah wailed harder. 'No, I don't mean attack. I think the cat thought Henny was something to play with. That's what it was. Just play. But Henny probably got a bit of a shock at something so big trying to play with her. I don't think it was painful, though,' she went on quickly. 'Look at her. Not a scratch and certainly no sign of a struggle.'

The boys peered closely.

'Sometimes, bad things happen to good pets. It's part of life,' said Alex. 'One day you're alive, and the next you're not.'

Noah wiped his eyes and peered at her. 'You mean, I could just wake up one morning and die?'

'No, no, of course not. Not you, sweetie. You're not a pet. You're a human. You won't die for a long, long time.' She opened her arms and let Noah crawl into her lap. Damn those people who said getting a pet would be the best thing that ever happened to the boys. That it would teach them valuable lessons about life and death. Where were those people now? Huh? She wanted to have a stern word with them. Pets were just another parenting con. It wasn't the animal that taught the child anything about life and death, it was the poor parent left behind to deal with the inconsolable child.

'Do you think Henny's in heaven now?' Noah sucked his thumb. Ordinarily Alex would have demanded he take it out, but given the extreme circumstances, she let it go.

'Yes, definitely,' Alex said. 'She was certainly a very well-behaved guinea pig, so I'm sure God has chosen her to be with him.'

Still on her haunches, Alex wobbled a little, feeling slightly dizzy. One hour ago, she'd been in a boardroom, representing one of the firm's biggest clients in a messy fight over a hostile takeover. Now, here she was, explaining guinea pig heaven to her five year olds. Her brain was spinning. No wonder she suddenly felt unwell. Queasy, in fact.

'So, you think God killed her?' Jasper put his hand on Alex's shoulder. 'Because when Jack's grandma died, our religion teacher Mrs Appleby said God had chosen her and he should be happy. Like what you said.'

'No. That's not what I meant. I meant that God would choose her to be in heaven. Not choose her to die. God doesn't work like that.'

'Mrs Appleby says God knows everything we think and do and he forgives everything we do wrong, as long as we say sorry,' said Noah.

So, *this* was what they were learning at school. Too much God and not enough basic mathematics. Well, that needed to change. After all, God wouldn't be the one marking their final exams and giving them a job. Maybe she should put them into the ethics class.

'I'm sorry, boys. I can see you're really upset. But believe me, Henrietta did not suffer. I can tell.'

The boys nodded gravely, and Jasper looked up at her, eyebrows raised.

'So, when can we get a new one?'

'Jas, Henny hasn't even been dead five minutes yet. Let's just give ourselves a chance to be sad. Noah especially.' Alex stroked her sensitive son's blonde hair.

'Yeah, Mum, can we get a new one?' Noah twisted and smiled up at her. 'Please, pretty please?'

Ah, children! So *present* and *in the moment* that it rendered them almost sociopathically unsentimental.

'Maybe,' Alex sighed and lifted Noah off her lap.

Jasper held up a stick. 'Can I poke her?'

'No, you may not poke Henrietta with a stick.'

At that moment, the Devines' front door opened. Charlie, grim-faced and Lycra-clad, jogged down the front steps, followed by a tearful-looking Talia.

Alex took a breath and forgot Henny for a moment to appraise Charlie Devine's ridiculously perfect body. Not a skerrick of fat. Abs like a rock. A thigh gap you could drive a small car through. And this was in all-white Lycra, which was notoriously fattening. Perhaps there was something to be said for restricting one's diet to one half of the national emblem.

'Talia says there's been some kind of accident.' Charlie's long ponytail swung jauntily and her insanely large diamond earrings sparkled in the sun. Were they real? Possibly … the Primal Guy was worth a squillion.

'Well, actually, it seems your cat must have attacked our guinea pig, and now …' Alex began before Charlie put her hand up.

'Oh, I'm so, so sorry.' She put a hand to her chest. 'Let me understand this. Banjo came over to your place and got into the hutch and attacked your guinea pig? That's appalling. I can't even imagine how he got into it?' She frowned, and Alex's inner lawyer stirred. Much as she felt the aggrieved party in this guinea pig death, there *were* such things as facts, mitigating circumstances and the presumption of innocence.

'Well, not exactly. You see, the boys were playing with Henny this morning before school, and we were in a bit of a hurry when we left, so we don't know for sure if she got put back in the cage. But Cuthbert Close is usually such a safe neighbourhood …'

'So she wasn't in her hutch for the whole day?' Charlie delivered the question in a neutral tone as if she was simply trying to ascertain facts but Alex glimpsed what she thought was a raised eyebrow, lifted so slightly as to be almost imperceptible.

Has she had Botox? Is that why I can't tell if she's judging my pet-care skills?

When it came to passive aggression, Alex had a particularly highly tuned antenna. There were only two things that threw it out. One of them was Botox, and the other was genuine sincerity, which Alex found very difficult to pick, mostly because it was so rare.

'Well, yes, she was out of her hutch,' conceded Alex, feeling a prick of discomfort. 'But, like I said, this is usually a very safe neighbourhood and normally she doesn't wander off. Anyway, when we got home we started looking and Talia offered to help, and we found her here, dead on your lawn, with Banjo nearby.' Alex was babbling. Charlie had said nothing. Her face was surgically inscrutable.

'So I suppose it was probably our fault in a way that we didn't properly secure her before we left. We don't normally let her wander the streets …' Alex trailed off.

'But you saw Banjo attacking her? How awful for the boys!' This time, the frown in Charlie's forehead was deep – no Botox then – and everything in her face spoke of genuine concern. Yet Alex couldn't help feeling that she was somehow being played. She'd seen this in courtrooms, how brilliant lawyers could make innocent witnesses look incredibly guilty by asking what seemed like guileless questions but were in fact incredibly astute and cunning ones. It was a skill – one that Alex hadn't quite mastered … yet.

'Well, I didn't actually see it happening,' Alex admitted. 'Banjo was in Talia's arms by the time I got there.'

'Boys, did you see the cat actually attacking your guinea pig?' Charlie's gaze narrowed.

The twins shook their heads. 'Mum says she probably died of shock, but she's in guinea pig heaven now,' volunteered Jasper.

'That's speculation,' Alex muttered.

'Boys, I'm very sad about your loss,' said Charlie solemnly. 'I know you'll say some lovely prayers for your guinea pig when you bury her in the garden.'

Burial? Who has time for a burial? These boys have homework.

'I don't think we'll …' Alex was cut off from talking by Noah and Jasper pulling on her arm and bouncing up and down.

'Yes, Mummy, can we have a burial?' asked Noah.

'I'll dig the hole,' volunteered Jasper.

What's wrong with rolling Henny up in a plastic bag and putting her in the garbage?

'Sorry, boys, but we don't have a shovel, we might just have to …'

Charlie cut in. 'We can lend you one, if you like.' She took a few steps around the side of the garage and returned with a small spade. 'We haven't quite put everything away properly yet,' she added, by way of explanation.

'Oh, fabulous,' said Alex, straining to sound enthusiastic. 'I'll use this to carry her home.'

'All right then, we'll leave you to it. Good luck,' Charlie smiled, put her hand on Talia's shoulder and directed her gently towards the house. Alex watched them. At one point, the teenager looked around and gave her an apologetic nod. Charlie, on the other hand, didn't look back at all.

'Thanks for the spade,' called Alex, as the front door closed solidly behind them.

'You could at least have said sorry,' she muttered under her breath. Admittedly, the evidence was slightly circumstantial and the fact of Henny being on the loose was a mitigating factor. But any fair judge would also find the case compelling beyond reasonable doubt. Charlie Devine's cat had killed Henrietta, yet Alex was the one saying *thank you*!

'Okay boys, let's get Henny back to our place.' Reverently, the twins stood by as Alex put the spade under the guinea pig's lifeless body. As she lifted it, she was struck by the most terrible wave of nausea that rose from her bowels and right into her throat.

Alex paused and swallowed hard.

Get a grip. It's just a guinea pig.

Gently, she carried Henny across the road, down the side of their house and into the backyard to a shady spot under the jacaranda tree. There, she laid her down and started digging a small hole, letting the boys each have a go until there was a Henny-sized space in the soil.

'I think that's deep enough,' sighed Alex. 'Let's cover her up.'

The boys didn't move.

'Aren't you supposed to say something?' With his free hand, Noah clutched at his groin, which was what he always did when he was scared, nervous or just bored.

Jasper nodded furiously. 'Like a prayer, or a speech. You have to, or she won't go to heaven, right?'

'All right.' Alex smoothed down her skirt. 'We are gathered here today, to mourn the passing of our dearly beloved guinea pig, Henrietta Jane O'Rourke. She was so kind and loving, and so, so furry. She never bit, or clawed anyone,

and she was the best guinea pig we could have asked for.'
Alex bowed her head. 'Boys? Anything to add?'

Jasper cleared his throat. 'God. Please let Henrietta into
guinea pig heaven because she doesn't eat much, and her
poo is tiny.'

Noah made the sign of the cross and clasped his hands
together. 'Amen.'

'Lovely words, boys. Now, you cover her with the dirt,
while I just duck inside to the toilet. Mummy's not feeling
so well.'

As Alex took one last look at Henrietta's stiff little body,
another wash of bile filled her mouth and she half-walked,
half-ran into the house, fumbling with the keys in her haste
to get inside to the bathroom.

In front of the mirror, she gripped the sides of the basin
until the nausea subsided again. What the hell was going on?
A virus? She had been feeling even more exhausted than usual
lately and her tummy had been funny for the past couple of
days. Alex sat on the toilet seat to think. She'd had this queasy,
pit-of-the-stomach feeling before. A bit like having a hangover, but it couldn't be that. Sunday and Monday were her
alcohol-free days. Her tired mind ticked over. Think. Think.

She snapped her fingers. Six years ago, when she fell pregnant with the twins. That's when she felt like this. Shocking
all-day sickness for the first twenty weeks.

Oh goodness. Morning sickness.

She couldn't be, could she?

No, no, she couldn't. Her obstetrician had stated cate-
gorically that she would never ever be able to fall pregnant
naturally. Conceiving the boys had taken ten rounds of

IVF and a substantial wad of savings that could have gone towards the mortgage. Not that she begrudged the cost. Not entirely. She was thrilled to have the twins and had come to accept that they would be her one and only experience of birth. After that, contraception seemed a waste of time, and besides she and James were always too tired to make love.

So when? How? When did we last …

Ah! She had it. There had been that one occasion, after her big win in the Cormack matter, where Beth had taken the twins for the evening and Alex celebrated by taking James for a spontaneous night at a five-star hotel in the city. That was it! Their dirty weekend away.

Alex looked around the bathroom before leaping to her feet to run upstairs to their bedroom. There were some old pregnancy testing sticks somewhere in her bedside drawer. She'd bought dozens of them when she fell pregnant with the boys to keep checking it was real, and she'd never got around to throwing them all out.

She held up the packet and turned it over. Six months past the expiry date.

Whatever. At this point, a slightly inaccurate result would be more useful than none at all. She went into the ensuite and sat down. Took the stick out, did a wee, and waited.

She tapped the packet and listened. The boys weren't even talking, let alone fighting, which was usually what happened when they were left alone for two minutes.

Pulling out her phone, Alex set the timer and started scrolling through work emails. At the three-minute mark, her phone buzzed and her stomach clenched. Fingers trembling, she picked up the stick and inhaled.

Only one pink line. Not pregnant after all. What a relief!

Must be a stomach bug, then.

Alex exhaled and put down the stick. It certainly wasn't the right time for them to bring another little O'Rourke into the world. Actually, there would probably *never* be another right time. Alex had sold all the baby gear on eBay in expectation that it would never be needed again. They had neither the time nor the money for any more IVF cycles. The remaining embryos had been donated to science. Her job was far too demanding for her to squeeze a baby into the mix and the mortgage meant she couldn't afford to stop work. Thank goodness for the single line.

She stood in front of the mirror and squinted. Gosh, she looked tired and haggard. Dark shadows underscored the redness of her eyes and the crow's-feet at the corners seemed at least a half-centimetre deeper. Alex picked up the pregnancy test that she'd left sitting near the tap.

Thank goodness it's negative! Imagine how much older I'd look with all those night wakings for a baby.

She stopped, still holding the stick between her fingers.

What the fuck …

She brought the stick closer to her eyes, so close it was almost blurry. Oh god, now she probably needed reading glasses. Slowly, the test came into focus. The first pink line was there, strong and vibrant as it had been when she first did the test. But now it had a little friend, almost like a shadow next to it. Faint, but unmistakably there.

Alex blinked, thinking maybe it was simply a case of seeing double, which occasionally happened when she was exceptionally tired.

But no matter how many times she opened and closed her eyes that second pink line wouldn't go away.

Alex closed her eyes, clutched the stick to her chest and let the thump of her heart pulse through it, as if channelling the little being within her.

Voices filtered in from outside. 'Give me the spade!'

'Mum gave it to me.'

'No, she didn't.'

'Get back away from me or I'll hit you over the head with it.'

Alex opened her eyes.

They're about to hurt each other. Run! Stop them!

But she didn't run, like she normally would have. Instead, she walked slowly to the window and looked down onto the garden. The boys had the spade between them in a tug of war. Back and forth it went. Only one of them had to let go and it would send the other sprawling.

Can I put a baby into the midst of that?

Alex's gaze shifted. There was a flash of movement from the garden next door. It was Cara, dragging an easel out into the backyard with her daughter, Poppy, in tow. Painting was something they often did in the afternoons – Cara said it was when the light was best. Alex watched them set up, Cara clipping the paper into place and pointing out a rainbow lorikeet while her eight-year-old daughter set out the brushes and paints.

Oh, to be the kind of mother who did art and craft with her child, and actually enjoyed it!

Last week, after a particularly difficult afternoon of frantic work calls and emails, Jasper had asked her what she actually did that was so important she couldn't stop for a quick game of soccer with them.

'Well, I help people, I suppose,' she'd said, momentarily lifting her head from the laptop to look into his deep brown eyes.

'But help them do what?' Jasper insisted.

'Well, you know, when people own a business, sometimes it's really popular and they get enough money to buy someone else's business.'

He nodded in understanding and Alex went on.

'But that other person might want to keep their own business, so then they have to go to court and a judge works it out.'

'So a court is where you do the fighting?' Jasper squinted. 'Like a boxing ring?'

'More like a conversation fight, and a judge who decides the winner.'

'They should just have an arm wrestle. That's what Noah and me do when there's a toy we both want. What a silly job,' he said, cocking his head and smiling at her with pity.

Alex bit her lip. It was her silly job that paid for the roof over his head, the clothes on his back and the food in his belly. In fact her job was so silly it brought in three times the money that James did as a chiropractor, and until that changed, she was stuck with it, and possibly a baby on top.

A baby. How the hell would she manage that?

Alex blinked and blinked again to try to get rid of the tears forming in her eyes. She wiped them away and the movement must have caught Cara's eye, because she looked up and waved.

Alex waved back and cleared her throat.

From her own backyard came another piercing shriek. She looked down. Poor Noah was splayed across Henrietta's grave, and Jasper stood over him with the spade.

'I'm lying on a dead thing.' Noah's eyes were scrunched shut and Jasper prodded at him with the spade.

'You've-got-dead-guinea-pig-germs. You've-got-dead-guinea-pig-germs.'

Alex leant against the window sill and closed her eyes.

CHAPTER FOUR

Cara smoothed down her paint smock. Seeing Alex hadn't exactly helped her nerves; if anything, they'd redoubled. Her poor neighbour. So pale and ghostly. Cara almost regretted waving. Alex looked so startled, though it was not surprising given the noise coming from the O'Rourkes' yard. The twins certainly had a lot of energy. Cara didn't know how Alex did it, on top of such a demanding job. Maybe she would invite her over later for a cup of nokcha, once all the children were in bed. They could both do with a calming green tea.

Cara turned her attention back to her daughter. 'Now, Pops, remember that Mr Parry will be here in a minute for the inspection so we may not get time to finish.'

Could her daughter hear the slight quiver in her voice? Cara hoped not.

'Okay, Mum. Have you made the kkulppang?'

'Oh, of course.'

Their landlord, Mr Parry, had made no secret of his love of the deliciously sticky honey donuts, filled with a tart yuzu curd that her mother dismissed as being 'no good' because it wasn't the traditional red bean paste. But Mr Parry said the little sweets reminded him of the sweet pumpkin scones made by his wife, Norma, who'd passed on a few years earlier. She used to serve them with cream and a tart ginger jam, he said. *Just to be a bit different, you know.*

Cara did know.

'Okay, sweetie,' she said. 'What's it going to be this afternoon? The frangipanis or the gardenias?'

Poppy screwed up her face. 'What about bottlebrush?'

'Oh, good choice. Sketch first or paint?'

'Sketch, I think.' Poppy hopped up from the stool and relocated herself closer to the bottlebrush tree. Cara watched her daughter, her cherubic-haired child sitting among the late summer blooms of their back garden. It was as if the flowers had inhaled the late February sun so as to blast out one final, glorious burst of colour and perfume. The bougainvillea had climbed around the shed like a red velvet curtain while the crisp white of the gardenia bushes fringed one corner of the garden like a bride about to make her entrance. In the other corner the frangipani tree dripped sunshine and tropical fragrance.

Perhaps the pipes inside the house were a little noisy and a few broken tiles made the bathroom floor a bit of a tap dance, but the garden more than compensated for the flaws of the run-down old house. For Cara and Poppy, Cuthbert Close was their stability and sanctuary. It was the only home Poppy had ever known, and Cara intended to keep it that way, especially now she was at school. Hopefully, Mr Parry would agree.

From the back garden, she heard the doorbell ring.

'That'll be him, Pops.' Cara got to her feet, swallowed the knot of nerves in her throat, and dusted off the knees of her capri pants. 'I'll bring him out here for afternoon tea.' She kissed her daughter on the head where the afternoon sunlight glinted off her curls.

Halfway down the side passage, she stopped. Through the slats of the gate, she could see the man at the front door wasn't the rotund, white-haired old fellow she remembered. This man was much younger and slimmer, with dark brown hair and his hands thrust into his suit pants.

Cara opened the gate and the man took his hands out of his pockets.

'Hello, can I help you?' said Cara.

'Yes, I'm looking for Cara Pope.'

'Oh, that's me.'

The man looked her up and down. 'You're Cara Pope?' His forehead crinkled, doubtful, and Cara registered a flick of annoyance. He wasn't the first to imagine Cara Pope as a blue-eyed, blonde Aussie.

She smiled and nodded. She'd given up explaining that Pope was her married name. It opened too many doors that she didn't have the energy to walk through.

'I'm sorry, forgive me, I was … Well, never mind,' the man stammered. 'I'm here for the house inspection. I'm Will Parry. Steven's son.'

Mr Parry had mentioned his children. Three of them. Two sons and a daughter, if Cara remembered correctly. All grown up and at least two of them with children of their own. Certainly, Will had his father's twinkly hazel eyes, but clearly not his grace or manners.

'Pleased to meet you.' She shook his hand. 'We were expecting your father today. Is he well?'

Will's face clouded and his forehead creased. He dropped his eyes. 'Look, no, he's not ... Look, there's no easy way to say this ... He died ... two months ago.'

'Oh my goodness. I'm so sorry.' Her knees weakened as old feelings began to stir. Grief. Fear. Sadness. All the things she'd tried so hard to leave behind. 'He was such a sweet man.' Her voice cracked.

'It was a heart attack.' Will cleared his throat. 'Very quick in the end. He'd rung me to say he wasn't feeling well, and I went around straight away to see him but he was gone.'

'That's awful. Truly, I'm so, so sorry.'

'Why? It's not your fault,' said Will, then softened. 'He didn't suffer, which is the main thing. Not a bad way to go, really, when you think about it. I hope I'm as lucky.'

Will gave a tight smile and Cara curled her fingers into a fist. Lucky? Death? Never. 'Still, it must have come as an awful shock. To pass, just like that, without any chance to even say goodbye. He seemed so ... robust.'

Will rubbed near his temple. 'Look, I'm sure you're probably busy so if you wouldn't mind, I'll just take a quick look around and get on my way. He'd written this appointment down in his diary, just your name and Cuthbert Close, no phone number that I could find or I would have called you.'

Cara stood back from the gate. She would deal with her feelings later. Have a good cry in bed. 'Oh, please, come through.' She gestured towards the back garden.

Will didn't move. 'Is there something wrong with the front door?' He inclined his head towards it.

'Oh, no. It's just that Mr Parry, your dad, was only really ever interested in the garden, so I just automatically assumed.' She stopped. 'But, of course, you want to see the house.' She passed Will, close enough to smell his aftershave, woody and musky, and opened the door. 'Come in.' He followed her down the hall of the narrow cottage and into the kitchen. 'Would you like a cup of tea?' she called over her shoulder. 'I made some special Korean sweets as well. They were your dad's favourite.'

'Thanks, but no,' said Will. 'I'm on a bit of a schedule.'

'Oh, okay then,' said Cara. 'I'll leave you to have a look through.'

He headed towards the bedrooms. 'I won't be long.'

She knew he wouldn't. The cottage was a tiny two-bedder with a cramped bathroom and a lean-to out the back that housed the kitchen. But from the beginning, Pete had seen the potential – a second storey with master and ensuite, and a back extension to make an open-plan living space that led into the garden. They'd even talked, informally, with Mr Parry about buying the place, but that was before Pete started coughing. By the time they found themselves in an oncologist's office, peering into a lightbox with Pete's lungs splayed before them like butterfly wings, the idea of buying the cottage had been completely forgotten. Cancer? How? He'd never smoked, not really, maybe tried one or two cigarettes as a teenager. *Just bad luck*, the doctor had said, shaking his head. *I'm so sorry.* Into the light, Cara and Pete had squinted at the white shadow, haunting his lungs like a tiny ghost.

From the kitchen doorway, Mr Parry's son cleared his throat. 'Ah, thank you for letting me look through. Seems like everything's in order.'

'Of course, it's no trouble at all.'

'I'll be off then.' He made a move towards the hallway.

'Oh, are you sure you won't stay for a cup of tea? Please, there's so much food.' She gestured to the platter of sweets.

Will raised an eyebrow.

'He usually took some home as well,' Cara confessed.

'Mum! Where are the cakes? I'm starving.' Poppy's voice was high and insistent, and from the kitchen window, Cara could see her standing in the garden, hands on hips.

'That's my daughter. The ravenous Poppy.' Cara turned back to Will. 'Please come and have afternoon tea with us, or she'll eat most of the plate.'

'And then won't eat any of her dinner.'

'Oh, yes, exactly. Do you have children?' Cara collected the tray and headed towards the back door.

'No. Just nieces and nephews.' Will stopped by the table. 'Do you need these teaspoons? And the milk?'

Cara stopped. In a bid to perfect the arrangement of the tray, she'd had to remove a few items which she'd then forgotten to find a place for. 'Yes, thank you.'

Her daughter was at the back door. 'Where's Mr Parry?' she demanded.

'Poppy,' her mother admonished. 'Where are your manners? This *is* Mr Parry – it's his son. Please make him welcome.'

The little girl bowed her head. 'I'm sorry. Hello, Mr Parry, my name is Poppy. It's nice to meet you.' She thrust out her hand and Will took it awkwardly.

'Call me Will,' he said gruffly.

'Where's the *old* Mr Parry?' Poppy made eye contact.

'Poppy,' her mother said sharply.

'No, it's all right. He was old.'

Poppy's eyes narrowed. 'What do you mean *was*? Where is he?'

Cara thought quickly. 'He's gone away.'

'Where?'

'A holiday.'

'Where to?'

Cara turned in panic to Will.

'Italy,' he said firmly. 'Venice for the canals and Rome for the Colosseum.'

'All right.' Poppy nodded. 'Can we have the kkulppang now?' She took two and raced outside. 'I'm gonna eat them in the tree house.'

They moved into the garden. Cara tried to catch Will's eye to give him a nod of thanks – he'd just saved her an evening of questions and tears about death, and whether Cara was going to die and leave Poppy all alone, and why did Daddy have to die before she even got to meet him. In short, a night for which Cara didn't have the energy.

But the man was too busy looking about the colour-bomb that was her backyard. He whistled softly.

'It's so … so …'

Pretty? Colourful? Lively?

'So … chaotic.' He frowned.

Cara stiffened. 'Oh … your father always said the garden was his favourite part of the house.'

'That figures …' Will set the tray down. 'I mean, the house is rubbish, isn't it? A knockdown job from what I can tell.'

Cara cringed. 'I'm sorry. I've tried my best to take care of the place.'

'I'm not saying you haven't.' He stood in the garden, arms folded, surveying the lean-to. 'It's just ... really old.' Will's nose wrinkled in distaste.

'Oh, I think it's charming.'

'You do?' He looked at her quizzically. 'I think most people would take one look at this place and run in the other direction. Especially in this part of town. I mean, it's hardly a gleaming white box, and that's what everyone wants these days.' There was a hint of bitterness in his voice.

'Not everyone.' She paused. 'Your father and I had an understanding. He was very good to Poppy and me, and so, when things broke or needed fixing, I tried not to bother him.'

'Maybe you should have bothered him,' said Will. 'It's in a real state now. I wouldn't even know where to begin.'

Cara handed him a cup of tea. 'My neighbour, Max Chandler, is a real estate agent and he's always saying it's preferable to own the worst house in the best street. A house can be changed, but the location cannot.'

'That's what we're banking on ...' Will muttered.

'Excuse me?' Cara set down the teapot and sat.

Will cleared his throat. 'We're selling ... We *have* to sell.' He clasped his hands and looked down.

'Oh, but you can't!' The words were out before she could stop them.

Will's face darkened. 'Like I said, I am sorry, but I think you'll also find that under the terms of my father's will, the decision *is* between me and my brother and sister. They say they need the money, so that's it, end of story.'

Cara moved to the edge of her seat and lowered her voice. 'Oh, no, it's just that we love this place. Your father loved it too. It's the only home Poppy has ever known and I thought that one day we might buy it from your father. We have friends here, good friends, and Poppy has her school …'

'Well, why don't you buy it? I'm sure my brother and sister would be willing to sell to you, at the right price. Might save us all a lot of hassle.' He looked at her with what seemed like hope.

Cara shook her head. Easy for him to say, nearly impossible for her to do, as a single mother on a freelance food stylist's income. 'I appreciate the offer, but I know I can't afford this place.'

In the decade since she'd moved there, homes in Cuthbert Close had nearly doubled in price. The Parry family would expect at least $1.5 million for the run-down cottage.

She took a kkulppang and munched slowly, hoping the sugar might prompt a sudden bolt of inspiration. 'Perhaps we could pay more rent? Mr Parry was extremely generous, and I'm happy to repay his generosity.' She stopped eating. 'This cottage could be an excellent investment for your family—'

'I'm sorry but we have to sell.' Will raked his hand through his hair. 'Ben and Sarah say it's the only way.' He looked away. 'Private schools and ski holidays aren't as cheap as they used to be …'

'So, you're not convinced?' said Cara, feeling a small glimmer of hope.

'No, no. They're right. It's the best idea.' He fixed her with his gaze. 'We have to move on. It's just a house. Just a crappy, old house.'

Cara took a second to swallow the anger in her throat.

'See that little tree house.' She pointed to the casuarina in the back corner of the garden. 'Your father built that when your mother fell pregnant with you. You remember that scar on your father's hand?'

He nodded.

'That's where the saw slipped. Six stitches in the hospital. But it was worth it, he said, in return for the hours you spent pretending the cubby was a pirate ship.'

Will raised his eyebrows. 'I didn't know that.'

'You probably just don't remember.'

He gave a noncommittal grunt.

Cara splayed her fingers in her lap. 'When we moved in, the tree house was falling down, and my husband was a builder, so he fixed it up because I was pregnant with Poppy …' She clasped and unclasped her hands. There was more, but her voice was already thickening with emotion. 'My own parents moved around a lot when I was a kid, and this cottage was the first place that really felt like home.'

She stopped, and Will didn't speak, the silence broken only by the sound of Poppy, humming gently to herself from the cubby house.

'It's more than just a house.' She looked at Poppy, sitting in the doorway of the tree house and swinging her legs. She was as rooted to this place as the old casuarina beneath her, the exact spot where Cara had sprinkled some of Pete's ashes – grey, like moon dust. Was that why Poppy spent so much time there? Cara had never told her about the ashes but wondered if she somehow sensed Pete's spirit, nurturing the soil and giving strength to the foundations of the tree house. This cottage was their rock and their refuge. It was everything she'd never had as a child, but was determined to provide for Poppy, particularly in Pete's absence.

Will rubbed his temples. 'There's really nothing I can do.'

'I think there is …' Cara began but Will glanced at her sharply.

'Please, don't tell me what I can and can't do. I've already told you – there's no choice.' He went to rise and Cara put her hand out.

'Oh, I'm sorry, please don't think I was trying to tell you what to do. What I know is that your father loved this place and he would want you to think carefully about what you do with it.'

'So now you know my father better than I did?'

'I only meant that I know what it's like to lose someone you love. It's sad, and confusing, and there are so many decisions to be made and you feel like you have to make them all at once and people are tugging you this way and that.' Cara's mind flicked back to Pete's funeral, her mother telling everyone that of course Poppy and Cara would leave Cuthbert Close and live with her and Sam. In times of hardship, family needed family. Her daughter couldn't possibly cope alone.

Will lifted his head. 'Okay.' He nodded. 'I'll talk to Ben and Sarah. Try to buy some more time … But I'm telling you it's a waste of effort. Their minds are made up.'

Cara exhaled and sat back in her chair. With the sun inching slowly towards the horizon, a raven flew overhead and let out a mournful cry of farewell to the day.

CHAPTER FIVE

Beth was in her happy place – mortar in one hand, pestle in the other, and the exotic aromas of lemon grass, chilli and coriander wafting into her nose, making her mouth water.

Pound that coriander! Smash that garlic! Grind that lemon grass! Release your flavours, or else!

She always began her curry pastes in a fit of frustration, and ended them on a nirvanic high. In what other activity could you collect such a chaotic mix of ingredients, then grind and smash them together to make something totally delicious? That's what cooking was: making order out of chaos, and there was no bigger devotee of order than Beth Chandler.

She raised her head for a moment and puffed through her mouth to blow away the stray hairs that had come loose from her low ponytail during the wild pounding. Her eye was drawn over the fence to the two heads bowed together in discussion. One of them was her neighbour, Cara. The silken black hair was a dead giveaway. But who was the other person?

A man. She craned her neck for a better look. A rather handsome one too, by the looks of his smart business shirt and luxurious dark hair.

Beth let out a small sigh of satisfaction. Even though the age gap between them was only fourteen years, there was a fragility about Cara that made Beth feel extra specially motherly towards her. She was too young to be on her own.

For a moment, Beth observed them talking intently, then Cara stood and shook hands with the mystery man. Both were frowning.

Not a budding romance, then. Beth let her tight grip on the pestle go slack.

As the pair passed out through the garden and into the house, Cara caught Beth's eye and waved. Startled by having been caught watching, Beth waved back quickly, forgetting she had the pestle in hand.

CRACK! The sound was extraordinary as the pestle dropped to the tiled floor of the kitchen, rattled around for a moment and promptly split in two.

Beth bent down over the grey shards of granite and picked them up. Her precious pestle. It was one of the few wedding gifts she'd actually ever used, and oh! the curry pastes, pestos and chermoulas it had produced, with such utter reliability, unlike the blender given to them by cousin Judy, which had conked out within the first year of her married life.

Nearly made it to twenty, thought Beth wistfully as she pressed the two halves together.

Everything breaks eventually, I suppose.

'Mum, what was that? Are you okay?' Ethan stood over her, concerned.

He's not really that tall, is he? Maybe it's because I'm on the floor.

She scrambled to her feet and still found herself looking up into Ethan's solar plexus.

He actually is that tall. Goodness, how am I now the mother of a near-adult?

'I'm fine. Just dropped the pestle by accident.'

He smiled and shook his head in that pitying teenage way. *Ugh, parents. Can't they do anything right?*

'Well, it was pretty ancient after all. Better to get a new one, right?'

'It was a wedding gift from Aunty Marg.'

'Is she the one who did that tofu cookbook? And doesn't believe in deodorant?' He made a face.

'Aunty Marg is a wonderful woman. She brought us the mortar and pestle back from India when no one in Australia had ever heard of them. Cost her a fortune in excess baggage.'

Ethan sniffed. 'Cooper's mum has a two thousand-dollar blender that cooks things too. It makes the best bolognaise in, like, twenty minutes.'

Any cook worth their salt knew that a good Italian ragu took at least four hours to make, but Beth bit her tongue. In the past few years, she had learnt two things about teenage boys. The first was that there existed an inverse relationship between their *actual* understanding of the world and their level of confidence about that understanding. The more they *thought* they knew, the less they actually *did* know. The second was that they absolutely hated this being pointed out to them, and denied it with confidence bordering on vehemence.

Still, in this moment of pestle tragedy, Ethan was being relatively restrained. At least he was helping her to pick up the remaining tiny shards. She watched. Maybe a new, more mature Ethan was emerging. Look at him, all dressed up in a collared shirt and those horrible beige chinos that young men insisted on wearing, tight in the leg and baggy about the crotch.

Hang on. Why, exactly, was he so well dressed given it was a Monday night and he was supposed to be hard at work, studying for his English assessment?

'You're looking pretty sharp for a night with the books,' she said. It didn't pay to go in with all guns blazing. Teenage boys fought fire with fire.

'Just going round to Dylan's to hang out for a little while. It's his birthday,' said Ethan, equally casually.

'On a Monday night? How many others are going?' Having despatched the remnants of the pestle to the rubbish bin, she now turned her focus back to cooking the curry. At least the mortar and its delicious contents had survived.

'I dunno. It's not a major gatho.'

Gatho was shorthand for gathering, that much Beth knew. She ignited the gas hob and heaped spoonfuls of paste into the fry pan, along with a glug of oil.

'So, how many usually attend a *minor gatho*?' The paste started to sizzle and release its mouth-watering aroma.

'Maybe twenty or so.'

'And will there be alcohol?' She could hear it in her voice, how the casual tone had been replaced by something distinctly more antsy. She focused on the paste.

Breathe, calm. Stir three times in one direction. Then three times in the other. Be at one with the curry paste.

'Mum, he's turning eighteen! He's allowed.'

A piece of lemongrass popped, along with something inside of Beth. She turned to him. 'But you're seventeen, so you're not allowed, and it's a school night and you've got an assessment tomorrow, remember?'

'It's only English and it's only worth ten per cent of our overall grade.'

'That ten per cent could be the difference between you getting into engineering at the university you want, and not getting in at all.'

Ethan folded his arms. 'I'm thinking of taking a gap year.'

Beth clenched the spoon. 'Oh, really? What will you do?'

'I don't know. Take a break. Travel maybe. It's so full-on, all this final-year study stuff.'

But you haven't actually done any study! she shouted internally, her fingers going white around the spoon.

'I'm not even sure I want to do engineering.' He paused. 'I don't even know if I want to go to uni at all. Seems like a waste.'

The curry paste was now fizzing and spitting and Beth felt herself heating inside and wanting to fizz and spit at her son. What was Ethan saying? Where had this come from?

'Ethan,' she said, her voice more brittle than burnt toffee. 'University is not a waste of time. It will set you up for life. And if you think your father and I will pay for you to sit around for a year doing nothing, then you are very much mistaken.' She pointed the spoon at him and noticed a faint quiver in it from the tightness of her grip.

'I knew you wouldn't understand.'

'You're right. I don't understand why a bright child like you would want to throw it all away.' Now she was shouting, on fire, lit beneath by a flame that she had no hope of extinguishing.

'Look at yourself, why don't you.' Ethan flung his palms out.

'What are you talking about?'

'You went to university and your life is terrible.'

'What are you talking about? My life isn't terrible.'

'You don't *do* anything!'

'I look after you and your sister, and dad. That's what I do.'

'But you don't need a PhD in nutrition to do that, do you?'

Beth opened her mouth, but no words came out. She waved the spoon. She contemplated hitting Ethan's backside with it, but in seventeen years she'd never laid a finger on him and now didn't seem the right time to start. Besides, there was turmeric in the paste and it would stain his chinos – a stain she would have to scrub. Instead, she brought her other hand to the spoon and thought about trying to snap it in half. Aunty Marg's voice sounded in her head. *It's breathing. That's all it is. The key to life and getting through it is breathing.*

Beth turned back to her curry, which was now on the verge of burning, and breathed.

In, out. In, out. This too shall pass … But when? How?

As Ethan shifted his weight nervously, Beth turned the gas to low and felt her anger ebb away to a dull flicker. Silently, she added chicken, coconut milk and vegetables to the pan.

'Mum? Aren't you going to say anything?' Ethan thrust his hands into his pockets. 'Mum?'

She didn't know where to begin. Yes, she had given up her career to be a full-time mother, but she'd never regretted the decision because her children and her marriage were her life, and it was a good life. Certainly, it wasn't glamorous or exciting, at times it was downright tedious and extremely menial, but it felt worthwhile. How could Ethan not understand that he was worth it?

'Mum, I'm sorry.' Ethan crossed one leg in front of the other. Five years old again. Nervous. Needing a wee.

'Hey, what's going on here? We could hear you from outside.' It was Max, collar unbuttoned and jacket slung over his shoulder, and Chloe, peering out from behind him, her wet hair dripping onto the floor.

'Where's your towel, Chloe? I only mopped the floor today,' said Beth, going to remove the schoolbag from her daughter's shoulders, where she would inevitably find a wet swimming towel squashed over her school uniform, which would now be damp and chloriney and in need of a wash as well.

Max slung his jacket over a dining chair.

'Please don't put that there. I'm about to serve dinner,' Beth snapped, rubbing vigorously at Chloe's hair.

'Well, hello to you too.' Max picked up his jacket.

'Ow, Mum. Stop. You're hurting me.' Chloe shimmied free.

'I'm going,' said Ethan, starting for the door.

'Oh, no, you're not.' Beth glared at Max. 'Do something,' she hissed. 'He's got an exam tomorrow and he's going to a party.'

Max slung the jacket over his shoulder and thrust the other hand in his pocket. So infuriatingly casual! 'Ethan, mate. Slow down, buddy. I haven't even had a chance to say hello.'

Ethan stopped. 'Hey, Dad. I'm just off to Dylan's for a little while. No biggie.' He shot a look at Beth.

'What's all this about a test tomorrow?'

'I've done heaps of study, honest. It'll be fine, I won't be late home. Promise.'

Max nodded and slapped his son's shoulder. 'All right, then. Have fun, mate.'

'Bye, Mum.' Ethan strolled out the door, while Beth, seething, stomped over to the cupboard and flung open the door to find a half-empty bottle of cab sauv – the one she'd used in yesterday's coq au vin.

'Is there one for me?' said Max as Chloe scuttled out of the room. For a twelve year old, she was as accurate as a barometer in gauging a pressure change between her parents.

Beth slammed the cupboard door shut. 'Get it yourself.'

'What is it now?' Max sighed, going to the cupboard.

'You let him go to the party, just like that! After I told him he couldn't go.'

'What else could I do? He's seventeen. I can't actually stop him. Ethan's a sensible kid. He's done his study and he'll be home early. You heard him.'

'And you actually believe that?'

'He's my son, I raised him after all, and I like to think the best of him, where you want to think the worst.'

Beth flinched. 'Beg your pardon? *You* raised him? I think you'll find it was a joint effort.' Even *joint* was generous. The division of labour in the Chandler household was quite clear – Max was chief financial provider and Beth was chief household manager, which meant much of the parenting over the years had fallen to her. Not that Max was a uninterested father. Not at all. He was more loving than most, but he simply wasn't around as much as Beth. Houses didn't sell themselves, as he so often reminded his clients.

Children didn't raise themselves either.

'You're right,' said Max. '*We* have raised a son who is now seventeen years old. It's time for us to let go a little. Let him off the leash and get our own lives back.'

'He *is* my life, he and Chloe, and I don't want it any other way!'

'Don't you see that if you hold on too tight, you'll only lose him.'

'So, we just have to stand by and let him get drunk before exams? I'm sorry, I can't do that.'

'You don't have a choice. He's going to make mistakes, and all we can do is be there to help pick up the pieces.'

'I don't see why we have to let him break to begin with. It just seems ... careless.' She picked up the mortar off the bench, and moved to the sink to wash it up. Careless, she'd been careless with her treasured wedding gift, and look what happened. She wouldn't make the same mistake with her family. Max was wrong. All wrong. Now was the time to hold close. Stay tight. Keep focused. She hadn't worked on her son for seventeen years to throw it all away now.

'I'm going upstairs to change,' said Max, eventually, shifting off the bench. Beth didn't turn around, but listened to him clump slowly up the stairs. She was alone now, the curry bubbling away. As she drained the sink, her anger emptied away with the water, and was replaced by guilt. She hated fighting with Max, and in the course of their marriage it had happened rarely, at least up until the last few months. Beth put the increased friction down to the stress of having two high-school-aged children in the house. What was that saying? Small people, small problems, big people, big problems. Max's strategy seemed to be one of denial, which, in Beth's view, wasn't a strategy at all.

She snapped off the washing gloves, lifted the garbage bag out of the cupboard under the sink and headed for the door. Outside, the sky was glorious, crimson as the bougainvillea spilling over the fence from Cara's, and Beth stopped for a minute to appreciate the view. Lights had come on in a few of the houses and through the leadlight windows that typified the federation homes of the close came an inviting amber glow in the approaching dusk.

'Evening, Bethy,' called Ian from number seventeen, the elderly gent with his equally elderly golden retriever, Rex, walking haltingly at his side.

'Hello, Ian. Beautiful evening, isn't it? Nice to see the sun again today.' Beth waved her hand into the warm air.

'It's always beautiful in Cuthbert Close – rain, hail or shine,' he replied, moving tortoise-like towards his house. 'The family well and happy?'

'Never better.' She gave a bright smile. 'And Paula?'

'Ah, she's grand. Sitting up and sipping a sherry as we speak.' Paula, Ian's wife of fifty-two years, had advanced dementia. There was a carer who came twice a day for bathing and toileting, but eighty-one year old Ian did the rest.

'You've just reminded me – I've got a lasagne in my freezer that didn't get eaten at the street party. How about I pop over tomorrow with it?'

Ian beamed. 'Ah, you're a wonder. No doubt about you, Beth.' He turned for the house. 'Best be getting back.' He clapped his hands gently to summon Rex. 'Off we go, old boy.'

'Give my love to Paula, and tell her I'll come round for a cuppa tomorrow.'

Ian waved over his shoulder and Beth waited to make sure he got inside safely.

Once the door had closed, she lifted the lid on the wheelie bin.

Completely full. Plastic cups and plates from the party, along with all the detritus from the storm.

'He could have at least mentioned it,' Beth muttered under her breath. Garbage was usually Max's job.

Beth closed the lid, dragged the bin into position for collection and looked about the quiet street. Where to put the extra bag of rubbish? There'd be someone in the street with an emptyish bin. But who? House by house, she went down the line until her gaze settled on the Pezzullos'.

Not the Pezzullos', but the Devines' now.

They'd only been there two days. Surely *their* bins couldn't be full. Did they even know it was collection night? Beth squared her shoulders. Excellent. A chance to be neighbourly *and* find a home for her rubbish.

Garbage bag in hand, she strode over, cutting across the lawn. Nearing the Devines' door, she could hear voices coming from inside. Good, they were home. At the front step, she stopped. They weren't just voices, they were *raised* voices. An argument. Beth leant in. Not eavesdropping, she told herself, just trying to gauge if it was a bad time. The words were indistinct but Beth could swear she heard the word *neighbours* repeated at least once, then there was silence.

'Hi, Mrs Chandler. Everything okay?'

Beth jumped back in surprise as Talia peered from around the door, her face pale and wan.

'Of course, Talia. Everything's fine. Sorry, I was just about to knock but I thought it might not be … Never mind. Are you all right?'

She nodded. 'I'm making sure our cat doesn't get out again. He's been a bit naughty today.'

'New street, new home. It's to be expected, I suppose.' The Chandlers didn't have pets. Beth found the children enough work as it was. 'Well, I just wanted to let you and your mum know that tonight is rubbish collection night … and I was wondering if I could put a bag into your bin. Ours is full,' she explained.

'I'm sure it's fine. Mum's a bit busy at the moment.'

'Talia,' came a weary voice from down the hallway. 'Where's all the medication? You unpacked the box, didn't you?'

The girl looked nervously over her shoulder. 'Mum, Mrs Chandler's here,' she called down the hallway.

Beth put up her hands. 'No need to bother her …'

A second face appeared around the door.

'Oh, Beth, hello.' Charlie Devine smiled but there was a tone in her voice that Beth couldn't quite pick. Annoyance, perhaps? Obviously she'd interrupted *something*. The smile didn't reach her eyes, which were … They were cold, Beth realised with a start. And there were dark shadows underneath that hadn't been there yesterday. The fatigue of moving, no doubt.

'I'll go check on Banjo.' Talia disappeared, and Charlie took her place in the doorway, blocking Beth's view down the hall.

'I'm sorry I've caught you at a bad time, but I was just letting you know it's bin night, and Talia said it might be okay for me to pop this in yours?' Beth held up the plastic bag.

Charlie's nose wrinkled and she fingered the collar of her satin shirt, which formed one half of a very glamorous, pure-white pyjama set – the kind of outfit Beth would have stained in five seconds flat. Hopefully, Charlie wouldn't notice the splodge of curry paste on her jeans.

'Sorry, it's a bit whiffy from last night's lamb chops,' Beth apologised.

'No, it's fine. Go ahead,' Charlie said, waving her hand tiredly.

Beth paused. 'I know that moving house can be overwhelming, let alone moving interstate, so if there's anything I can do to help, please don't hesitate to ask. I mean that,' she added.

'Thank you, but really, we're fine.' Charlie went to close the door, and stopped. Her eyes flicked over Beth dispassionately. 'I know you mean well … but, look, what Talia and I need right now is space and time to get ourselves settled. Do you understand?'

Beth stepped back from the door. Charlie's slow and deliberate delivery had made the words sound almost like … like a warning. 'Yes, yes. Of course,' she stammered. 'I completely understand.'

Charlie nodded, and closed the door.

Feeling the flush of a rebuke rising up her neck, Beth scurried down the front path. The Devines' bin was on her left. Should she still put her rubbish in? Or would that be crowding them?

'Don't be silly. It's just rubbish. Not a marriage proposal,' Beth muttered to herself, swinging open the bin lid.

She peered in, and stopped. What was that? Was it what she thought it was?

She looked more closely.

It was! Her quiche, sitting in a smashed pile at the bottom of the Devines' bin. The one she'd taken over in the pouring rain after the ruined street party.

But why? Why throw it out?

Talia had seemed so happy to receive it. Perhaps Charlie decided it was against their eating principles. Perhaps she saw it as Beth interfering or dismissing their dietary choices? Oh, dear. She'd only been trying to make them feel welcome. Should she apologise? Yes, she should apologise, and make them see.

Beth pivoted and started back up the path towards the house. Her eye was drawn to a sudden lift in the curtains. It was Talia at the window, and she was shaking her head.

Don't come in, she seemed to be saying, her eyes large and sorrowful. *Don't get involved.*

Beth stopped and took a breath. Max's words about Ethan pinged in her head, about holding on too tight. She saw it as caring. He saw it as crowding. Was that what she was doing to the Devines? To Ian and Paula? Even Cara and Alex? Maybe they were just too polite to tell her? All except Charlie, that was.

Retreating quickly down the path, Beth dumped the rubbish in the Devines' bin and scurried back towards home.

At the front door, she stopped and looked back over her shoulder, but Talia had gone from the window, like she was never there at all.

ThePrimalGuy.com.au
From: The Primal Guy
Subject: Black Swans

Dear Prime-Timers,

Okay, so don't drop your phones when you hear this, but, I have news! I've been reading. I mean, I'm always digesting the latest and greatest in food and nutrition. But this was an actual book, by my home-boy Nassim Nicholas Taleb. That dude is like the Jesus of the new millennium. You know he predicted the big crash of 2008? Seriously. The guy's a freak.

Anyway, in his book, he goes back a few hundred years to when the first white dudes turned up in Australia and discovered this crazy looking bird. It was a swan, but it was BLACK! What the freak? The only swans they'd ever seen were WHITE. They couldn't believe their freakin' eyes. It was insane. Hectic. I mean, who'd have predicted it?

But, that's life, right? Shit happens, and we never see it coming. It's so predictably unpredictable. Jobs, love, fire, floods, accidents, death – who knows what's around the corner.

All we know is that we don't know what's coming. And, boy, am I learning that. This trip is pushing me so far on the inside I can almost see my own a-hole, and it ain't so pretty, even with an a-bomb diet.

But here's the thing – if you know that shit never quite goes how you want, you're already ahead. If you're quick and agile and strong, you can cope with any black swan that flies your way. Disasters aren't the time to bunker down, they're the time to get moving.

You just gotta be ready to be brave, reach out, grab those wings and fly high.

Peace out,
Ryan (AKA the Primal Guy)

PS Introduce a new Prime-Mate to the crew and get 50% off a pack of our super-awesome Chicken and Jalapeno Primal Meal Bars, packed with 100% natural chicken and 0% gluten. You know you want it!

CHAPTER SIX

Alex stared at the basket of washing in front of her, hoping that if she looked at it for long enough, it might actually fold itself. Wasn't that the theory of visualisation that she'd learnt about during a break-out session from a two-day corporate law conference last year? That if you imagined something hard enough, it would come to fruition?

The facilitator had made them use the technique during trust falls, visualising themselves landing safely in the arms of their colleagues before they actually went ahead and did so. True, no one was dropped, though there were a few wobbles when it came to catching the pompous barrister with the personal hygiene issue, and perhaps, as corporate lawyers, they might have been better served imagining piles and piles of money. After all, that was the core business. Falling successfully into the arms of colleagues and opponents wasn't exactly a key performance indicator at

Macauley Partners, where Alex had worked for twelve years.

She closed her eyes and imagined the twenty pairs of underpants, four school shirts, three business shirts, umpteen socks and two pairs of school shorts all neatly ironed, folded and put away. She squeezed her lids and clenched her fists. In her mind she saw razor-sharp folds and starched collars. She squeezed more tightly, then opened.

Nothing. The clothes hadn't moved.

She pulled out her phone and scrolled through emails. Nothing urgent from work. A bit of spam from travel and clothing websites that Alex couldn't remember using. A new one from The Primal Guy. She opened it and read through. Another slightly unhinged rant about life and black swans. Actually, this one wasn't quite as bad as the others. He had a point about life throwing up the unexpected, like a baby for instance.

Alex yawned and visualised herself falling successfully into bed. She ached for sleep. At least the boys were out cold and the house was quiet. James had a couple of late clients but he'd be home soon and she would need to talk to him about the baby. Or at least the potential baby.

Would he be happy? Only yesterday he'd commented on how nice it was to be working again, properly, with the boys now in their second year of school. Only one thing was certain. He'd be surprised about the (possible) pregnancy.

Alex picked up the first pair of underpants, and her stomach sank. Another certain thing about a baby was that the washing load would at least double when it came along. Babies, or at least Alex's babies, puked enthusiastically after every meal, which was possibly testament to the calibre of her cooking but certainly made for an endless round of changing and washing. At one point, she remembered dressing the twins in nothing but singlets and nappies for weeks on end because she simply didn't have time to wash the puked-on clothing, and they never left the house anyway, so what was the harm.

Alex sat at the dining table, fished out a couple of the boys' shirts from the basket, and laid her head on them. *Just for a minute*, she told herself. How she longed for a glass of sauv blanc. Anything to ease the knot of worry at the pit of her stomach. But that second pink line made alcohol out of the question. She could stomach the anxiety better than the guilt. *Just a short, short rest. Until the desire for wine passes.* Next thing she knew, James was gently squeezing her shoulder.

'Alex, Alex,' he said softly. 'You fell asleep.'

She lifted her head quickly and swallowed hard. Her mouth was like sand. James got down on his haunches and used his thumb to wipe her chin. Drool, she realised, which would explain the dry mouth.

'Shit, what time is it?' Alex groggily checked the clock on the oven.

'It's just after nine.' James stroked a piece of hair off her forehead. 'You were out like a light.'

She yawned. 'The boys were asleep, and I felt so exhausted I thought I'd put my head down for a minute and then get to the washing and—'

'You don't need to explain to me.' James rose and wandered towards the fridge.

'There's one of Beth's lasagnes in the fridge, if you want to throw that in the microwave. I ate with the twins.'

James opened the fridge door. 'How were they this arvo?'

'Oh, fine.' Alex resumed folding the washing. 'Henrietta died.'

James turned quickly. 'Who died?'

'Henny … the guinea pig.'

'Oh, shit. Already? She was only a few months old, wasn't she?' James covered the lasagne with cling wrap and set it in the microwave.

'The boys didn't put her back in the hutch this morning and when we went looking this afternoon we found her at the Devines'. Their cat killed her.' She thought back to Henny's taut little body, Talia's dismay and Charlie's ambivalence. 'You know, Charlie Devine didn't even apologise.'

'Well, it's not her fault that Henny wandered off. She really should have been in her hutch. It's our fault more than hers.'

'Look at it this way,' said Alex. 'If one of the boys ran out onto the road and got run over, you'd blame the driver, not the child.'

'I'd blame the parent for not supervising the child.'

Alex groaned. 'Why do you have to be so reasonable all the time? It's annoying. Charlie Devine should have said sorry. That's what neighbours do.'

'How'd the boys take it?'

'They were fine … A bit too fine. They sort of seemed to *enjoy* it.'

The microwave pinged and James brought a steaming plate of lasagne to the kitchen table. 'Good lesson in life and death for them, I guess.'

Life and death. Perfect segue. Tell him about the baby, Alex told herself. But she couldn't. Her mouth was watering so badly, the words couldn't make their way past the saliva.

Beth's lasagnes were the perfect balance of rich tomato ragu and creamy, cheesy sauce. Even Alex's fussy boys loved them. The first time Beth turned up on the doorstep with a casserole, Alex barely knew her at all but kissed her right on the spot. Having moved into Cuthbert Close just one week before her due date, she was still surrounded by packing boxes and the only room that had been properly sorted was the twins' nursery. Neither she, nor James, had eaten a proper meal in weeks. Beth was a godsend, though she claimed to simply be *doing the neighbourly thing and welcoming them to Cuthbert Close.*

As James tucked into the lasagne, Alex found her mouth moving in time with his. Nearly six years after that first casserole, Beth was still supplying the family with meals – two every week, for which Alex insisted on paying $30 to at least cover the ingredients. She had to put the money into Beth's letterbox, as her neighbour found it too embarrassing to accept it in person.

'Would you like a bit?' James pushed the plate towards her.

Alex took the outstretched fork. 'I'm famished,' she admitted.

Tell him why you're famished. Tell him.

'But, actually,' she held the fork in the air, 'I need to tell you something first.' She slid the plate back towards James, who quickly resumed eating, perhaps worried Alex would change her mind and want more. Beth's meals were too good to share.

'I … I think I'm pregnant.'

James started coughing. The fork clattered out of his hand and he clutched his throat.

'What is it? What's wrong?' Alex leapt out of her chair and thumped her husband on the back as he struggled for breath.

'Is this helping?' She struck a few more blows between his shoulder blades. 'More?'

'Please,' James croaked. 'Stop hitting me.' He cleared his throat a couple of times and took a large gulp of water. 'What did you say?' His eyes narrowed.

'What? Before you started choking?'

'I wasn't choking. It just went down the wrong way, I think.'

'Yes, probably, I mean, I've never heard of anyone choking on pasta, it's so soft …'

'Alex,' James interrupted, his cheeks flushed and his hair now a little skew-whiff after the near-choking. 'What did you just tell me?'

She sat down again and clasped her hands in her lap. 'Well, as you know, we got home this afternoon and found poor Henny, dead, and then I felt like I was going to throw up and—'

James put his hand over his wife's. 'Are you pregnant?'

She nodded slowly and whispered, 'I think so.'

He pushed himself away from the table. 'But how? I don't get it. I mean, the doctors told us it would never be possible, except with IVF again.' He sat back and ran a hand through his hair. 'It's a miracle. I can't believe it. Another baby,' he said in wonder.

'Possibly another baby,' said Alex.

'What do you mean *possibly*?' His eyes zeroed in on her.

'The pregnancy test I used was out of date, so it might be a dodgy result.' She stood and emptied the contents of the washing basket onto the bench.

James drummed the table. 'Not possible,' he said confidently. 'You can get false negatives from these things but false positives are pretty unheard of.'

Alex blinked. She wasn't surprised at his knowledge. Throughout the IVF process and the pregnancy, he'd read obsessively about anything related to conception and birth. Once, she'd caught him commenting on a post for InVitro-Mums, the go-to website for IVF mothers.

'It's meant for women, you know,' Alex had pointed out.

'It doesn't say that anywhere,' said James peering at the screen.

'It's not called InVitro*Dads*.' But James had continued to comment as LuvBubs007, in honour of his James Bond obsession.

Alex picked up a random sock from the washing pile. 'I guess I'm pregnant then.'

'Shit. I mean, wow. I can't believe it.' James came around the table to take Alex in his arms. 'Another baby.'

The amazement in his voice made Alex drop the sock. She turned to hug him properly and buried her head in his shoulder.

'I'm scared,' she said quietly.

'What? That you'll miscarry? That's normal, babe. You can't do anything about that.'

'It's not that. I'm scared I won't be able to cope.'

James pulled back. 'You've never not coped with anything in your life. *We'll* cope together like we always do.' He took her hands in his. 'You said this about the twins, remember? That you didn't know how you'd do it.'

'Yes, but that was because I didn't know what was coming. But now I do know what's coming, and I'm even more frightened. I mean, look at me, still folding washing that's been sitting at the bottom of the stairs for five days. I barely ever cook a meal and I can't even remember the last time I read a book.'

'Read a book?' James raised an eyebrow.

'It's something I used to do all the time before we had the twins. Now, I'm lucky if I read a page before falling asleep.'

'Book reading isn't exactly essential though, is it?'

Alex started flinging folded socks back into the basket. 'It is to me,' she said huffily. 'You could barely get a book out of my hands as a kid and now the only time I really get to read is when I'm doing it to the kids and I'm sorry, but stories about dorks and farts and treehouses aren't exactly my literary cup of tea.'

James stood by her side and quietly started re-coupling the socks that Alex had been flinging. 'You could quit your job, you know. Take a break for a year or two.'

'And do what?'

'Have the baby. Spend more time with the boys.' He nudged her and smiled. 'Read books.'

'It's a lovely idea.' Alex sighed. 'But there's this thing called a mortgage and ours has a scary number of zeros in it.'

'We could live on my wage for a while.'

'How? By treating food and electricity as desirables rather than essentials?' James looked hurt, and Alex patted his arm. 'I appreciate the sentiment, babe, but given our debts, I just don't see how it could work.'

'It could if we moved out of the city. Maybe up north? It'd be closer to Mum and Dad.'

Alex snorted. 'I'd rather die than move up there. Actually, I probably would die … of boredom.'

Every year, James, Alex and the boys made their annual pilgrimage four hours north, to visit James's parents in their seaside retirement village. While it was fun to play half-court tennis and lawn bowls for the week, Alex was always more than pleased to see the gabled roofs of Cuthbert Close coming back into view. The perfect thing about where they lived was that it gave them the best of both worlds. If they wanted peace and tranquillity, they could stay home and laze about the backyard, but if they wanted a little culture or excitement, the city was only twenty minutes away, and you could barely set foot outside the street without falling over a cute new restaurant or boutique.

Or at least, that was the theory.

The reality was that ever since the twins could walk, the backyard had been a war zone, and because of work, Alex never had the energy to attend a concert or even a dinner.

Had they lost their reasons for being there? She paused and fingered a hole in one of Noah's school shirts. Why exactly were they running themselves so ragged? Slaves to a mortgage that never seemed to get any smaller?

Maybe the pregnancy *was* a sign that something had to change?

James had said nothing, and from the hunch of his shoulders, Alex could tell he was hurt by her disparaging comments about his parents' hometown.

She squeezed his shoulder. 'I'm sorry, babe. It's not the worst idea.'

'I know it's not. The kids love Porpoise Point. They never want to come home.'

But their idea of a good time is doing forty-five burps in a row. Alex resisted the urge to remind him.

'I'm just not sure what *we'd* actually do there?'

'I could set up a practice,' said James. 'The coast is crying out for health professionals.'

Mostly because everyone who lives there is nearly dead.

'I'm just not sure what *I'd* do there? I know I could spend more time with the kids, which would be fantastic. But I also know I'd need more.'

'More than a new baby?'

Alex nodded sadly. 'I know myself. I'd go crazy. Even though our lives here aren't exactly exciting, I think I'd feel trapped if we lived in such a small town.'

'Don't you feel trapped here? In your job?'

Alex opened her mouth but no words came out. She sat down, suddenly overwhelmed with exhaustion.

Living in Cuthbert Close was supposedly about giving themselves freedom and options. But the mortgage made it a type of imprisonment, albeit one that came with charming federation houses and hundred-year-old fig trees.

'Well, what if we asked *your* parents to come over from Perth for a while to help us out?' James folded one of her bras, the elastic completely gone. It looked almost as tired and saggy as Alex felt.

'Have you forgotten last time?'

Alex's own memories of the period were hazy. The twins had only been a few weeks old, after all. But she did remember her mum and dad, skulking about the house like cats around water. Her mum, too nervous to touch the convection stove, despite Alex's repeated assurances that it would not burn her, and her dad, who, after inspecting James's fridge full of craft beer, confessed that all he wanted was a VB.

'You've got to get over this chip on your shoulder.' James placed her bra on the pile.

Alex stiffened. 'You have no idea what it's like.'

If James's and Alex's childhoods were cuts of meat, hers was mince, and his was rump. She wasn't ashamed, far from it. Who didn't love a meatloaf? No, happiness hadn't been the problem. Growing up, her parents had sacrificed everything for her education, and it had worked. They were the little rockets that could – propelling her into a privileged planet of university and a high-paying job, everything they'd all worked for, except now they lived on different sides of the universe and it was awkward. She'd offered to help, financially, to get them out of working in their corner store and into retirement – a little closer to Alex's own privileged planet – but they wouldn't hear of it. *Just give those little boys everything you never had. That's all we want.*

James kissed her head. 'I know, I know. You're scotch fillet, and they're mince, and my parents are rump, and our kids are junior burgers.' He smiled. 'But we're all cut from the same cow, aren't we?'

'You're an idiot,' said Alex affectionately.

'Well, I'm a piece of meat, after all. But seriously, whatever we decide about this new little beef pattie, it doesn't change the fact that I am absolutely over the moon and one hundred per cent there for you. Even if it turns out to not be a pregnancy at all.' He whispered in her ear, 'But I secretly think you're a better miracle worker than you realise, and we'll work something out … together.' He rose, his arms full of neatly folded washing. 'Now, I'm going to put this lot away. You just relax.'

He closed the door softly and Alex felt tears beginning to pool in her eyes. Oh hell, she must be pregnant, crying at the drop of a hat over everything. But James! What a lovely, lovely man. She had absolutely won the lottery of husbands when she married him, to the point where she sometimes felt that the union was perhaps an unequal exchange. He always referred to her as the brains of the marriage, and proudly declared his status as a 'kept man' to anyone who'd listen.

But Alex knew the truth.

It was James who was the glue of the whole shebang. He was the one who got the boys off to school, and mostly picked them up from after-school care. Whatever he did it was seamless – no guinea pig funerals required. He made the lunches and kept across the school admin and was generally more patient with the boys than Alex could ever hope to be. In fact, he was so capable that she occasionally felt redundant in her own family. She was the main breadwinner, yes. But apart from the money, what did she actually contribute, apart from an extra layer of guilt?

She wiped her eyes using a pair of Noah's Spider-Man underpants that had gone unnoticed in James' collection of the clean washing, and went into the kitchen to switch on the dishwasher. At the sink, she paused. The light in Cara's shed was still on. She must be out there, working, which she often did after Poppy had gone to bed.

Wiping her eyes, Alex suddenly felt very wide awake. Crying always did that to her. Maybe Cara would be up for a chat? Despite being younger than Alex by quite some years, she was always a source of calm and wisdom, probably because of everything she'd been through with her own husband. Grief had a habit of making people grow up very quickly.

She checked her watch. Nearly 9:30 pm. Normally at this time, she'd be getting into her pyjamas and removing her make-up. But not now. Now she felt wired and in need of conversation. She needed to talk this through and find a solution. Cara would be a perfect sounding board.

She scribbled out a note to James and left it where he would see.

Popped over to Cara's for a bit. Back by 10. Xx

CHAPTER SEVEN

Cara squinted at the computer screen, her eyes burning with fatigue. Her search had yielded no results. Probably because she didn't quite know what she was searching for. Money, essentially, and that meant extra work. But in her industry, jobs weren't advertised like they were for accountants or lawyers. Styling work came through word of mouth or a nebulous thing called 'exposure' – the number of followers and 'likes' you had. She'd scoured through her social networks, looking for any clues regarding opportunities, new food sites or magazines. She'd even reached out to a couple of former clients who she hadn't heard from in a while.

Nothing.

She scrolled through emails, quickly glancing through the latest Primal Guy newsletter. Oh, dear. The chicken bars sounded disgusting. Who would buy such a thing?

There was a minor crackle on the baby monitor and Cara turned up the volume to make sure it wasn't Poppy, or a robber.

Nothing. All quiet.

Usually, the hours after her daughter went to bed were her creative time in the she-cave that Pete had built for her – mini photographic studio at one end with a couple of lights and a white wall, and a mini-kitchen at the other with sink, microwave, a small oven and double-gas burner. She called it 'moodling' – making things, doodling, playing around, basically. Failures went in the bin, successes went up on her Instagram account 'Sweet Alchemy'. To Cara, that's what baking was – a form of transformational magic. Last night she'd concocted a dessert 'burger' with a disc of candied beetroot, a firm chocolate mousse as the patty, a square of yellow jelly as the cheese, and all of it sandwiched in a sweet brioche bun. The photo had attracted three thousand 'likes' – not that Cara was particularly driven by the adulation, but she could see its use in terms of reaching potential clients. The magazines she worked for certainly loved it and made much of her 'reach'.

She replied to a couple of comments on the burger, then returned to the flashing cursor in her search engine.

Jobs that make you a lot of money quickly

She clicked and held her breath. When the results came up she exhaled. No suggestions of drug dealing, thank goodness, or any other illegal activity. She clicked through to an article titled 'Fifteen Jobs that Could Make You an Instant Millionaire'. The list was fairly predictable – doctor, surgeon, investment banker, software architect – all things that required specific skills that a food stylist simply didn't have. Then there were the ones that required a huge dose of luck, like writing a bestselling novel, or becoming a YouTube star or blogger.

'Yes, because it's so easy to make yourself go viral,' Cara commented to herself.

On the last page she stopped.

'Entrepreneur, inventor, online seller, create multiple streams of income,' she murmured, and leant back from the screen.

She was creative. She was inventive. Not in a gadget type of way, but over the years, through countless food shoots, she'd learnt that she saw things in a different way to other people. She had a knack of composing objects and patterns so that they seemed fresh and surprising, but totally right. Didn't everyone see the world like that? Wasn't it obvious there was a right and a wrong way to make a group of objects look their best? Apparently not, given the way people oohed and aahed over her culinary compositions and told her they'd never thought to do it *like that*.

But Cara didn't know any other way. It was simply what she felt. Instinctive. In recent years, her work had taken a darker turn that had only served to make it even more popular.

Surely that could be translated into a new line of work?

At the tap on the window, Cara startled. Poppy? A bad dream perhaps? But she would have heard her on the monitor, if that was the case.

Cara hurried to the shed door and scraped it back to find her pale and frowning neighbour standing behind it.

Beth.

'What's wrong? Are the kids all right?'

She shook her head. 'No, they're fine. Everyone's fine.' She touched Cara's arm. 'I know I shouldn't have bothered you, and it's nothing. I'll come back in the morning.' She turned to leave.

'Oh, no, stay, please stay. Actually, you are just the person I wanted to see.'

Beth's laugh was brief and high-pitched. 'You're the only one to say that to me all day.' She walked tentatively into the shed and perched on a stool, her fingers tightly entwined in her lap. 'Cara, I need you to answer a question honestly – do I crowd you? You and Poppy?'

'Crowd us? How do you mean?'

'Oh, you know. Meddle in your lives. Come around too much. Force myself upon you.' Beth looked at her anxiously. 'Tell me the truth. I won't be offended. Truly.'

Cara took the stool next to Beth. 'Oh, no, you're wonderful to us. We're so lucky to have you as our neighbour. Your advice, your recipes, the way you worry about Poppy like she's your own child.' She cocked her head. 'You know I think of you as the aunty I never had. Where is this coming from?'

Beth waved her hand in the air. 'It's silly, really, you'll probably laugh when I tell you.' She paused. 'Tonight, I went over to the Devines', just to say hello and tell them about bin night, and see if I could add a little of my rubbish to theirs … Anyway, when I went to put my bag in their bin, I found my quiche at the bottom of it.'

Cara's eyes widened. 'The whole thing?'

Beth nodded. 'Every bit of it. Virtually untouched, as far as I could tell.'

'They just threw it out?' Her hand went to her chest. All the love and care that Beth put into those quiches – pastry made from scratch, free-range eggs, naturally cured bacon. Cara had begged for the recipe, hoping to recreate the magic. Poppy loved it, and while Joy moaned about the lack of garlic and chilli, even *she* would never have contemplated not eating it. The offering and taking of food was a matter of respect and ritual. You couldn't throw *that* in a bin.

'I know I'm probably overreacting. It's just a quiche after all, and actually it's not so much the food I mind, but it's the way Charlie spoke to me. I think I crossed a line.'

'By giving them a quiche? You were welcoming them to the neighbourhood, being friendly,' Cara burst out.

'Well, I suppose it's not compulsory to be friends with your neighbours. Like Max says, sometimes I do come on a bit strong. Perhaps I need to let go a little. Be *cool*, as the kids would say.' Beth gave a twisted, sorrowful smile. 'Sometimes I wish they were little again, like Poppy. All they need at that age is love and food and a roof over their heads.'

Cara flinched. *A roof over their heads.*

She should tell Beth about the visit from Will Parry. She would know what to do.

As Cara went to speak, there was another knock at the door, and both women jumped.

'Hey guys, I saw the light on and thought I'd pop in for a chat.'

Alex stepped into the shed and stopped, her gaze going from Beth's worried face to Cara's extremely sombre one. 'Oh shit. Have I interrupted something? I'll leave. It's fine.' She backed away into the dark night.

'No, no, you're very welcome here. Right, Beth?'

'Certainly.' Beth nodded vigorously. 'I think we could definitely use another wise head in this conversation.'

'Well, I don't know about a wise head but I do come bearing gifts.' From behind her back Alex produced a block of 70% cacao chocolate.

'Oh, perfect,' said Cara. 'Exactly what we need.'

'I would have brought champagne, but I have news.' Alex paused and shuffled her feet. 'I'm pregnant ... I think.'

There was a beat of silence as Cara and Beth digested the news and then gasped with excitement.

'That's wonderful, I'm so happy for you.' Beth rose and folded the younger woman in a warm hug.

'Oh, so amazing,' said Cara, kissing Alex on the cheek. 'And you said a third child would not be possible.'

'It wasn't, actually. This is all a bit of a shock.' She took the stool next to Beth's.

'Well, it's exactly the good news I needed to hear. How far along are you?' Beth asked.

'Only a few weeks, I think, so it's probably a bit silly of me to be saying anything. And the test might be a bit dodgy.' Alex fiddled with her hands. 'But I knew I could trust you both.'

'We won't tell anyone until you tell us it's okay.' Cara unwrapped the chocolate and broke off pieces for Alex and Beth. 'Cheers!' She held hers up.

'To the baby,' said Beth.

'Cheers,' said Alex, choking on the words.

'Sweetheart, what is it?' said Beth.

'I'm happy,' sighed Alex. 'But I'm also secretly freaking out because as much as I want this baby, the twins are so full-on ... and then there's my job ... and James thinks we should move up the coast and I don't want my brain to die.' Her voice started to break.

Beth rose and began to rub Alex's back. 'There, there, honey. It's going to be okay,' she soothed. 'You'll make it work, whatever happens.'

Alex accepted the tissue box offered to her by Cara. 'I'm sorry. I really didn't come here to burden you with my problems.'

'No, poor Cara here has really copped the lot tonight,' said Beth.

'How so?' asked Alex and Beth proceeded to fill her in on the quiche incident.

'Pardon my language, but what a bitch! You know something else? The Devines' cat killed our guinea pig, and she didn't even apologise,' Alex huffed.

'What? Little Henrietta? She was so cute!' exclaimed Beth.

'Oh, Poppy will be devastated. She loved Henny,' said Cara, wondering how she could possibly avoid telling her.

The women collapsed into glum silence and Beth bit off a large chunk of chocolate. 'Well, that's two of us who've had run-ins with the Devines. What about you Cara? Anything to tell us? Bad news tends to come in threes.'

Cara flexed her fingers and took a breath. 'I think Poppy and I are going to be evicted.'

'What? No, you can't be,' said Beth, sitting up straighter on the stool. 'But why? You keep this place so beautifully. The old owner loves you two.'

'Oh, it's so sad. Poor Mr Parry passed away. His son came to see me today. It was very sudden. A heart attack.'

'Ah, so that's the man I saw here this afternoon. Very handsome.' Beth dropped her eyes. 'Not that I was watching ... so sad about his father,' she murmured.

'Yes, very sad,' said Alex perfunctorily. 'And now they want to sell, don't they. We see it all the time at the firm. Offspring who try to flog everything before the body is even cold in the grave. But you know they have to wait for probate to be granted, which can take months, and in that time they might change their minds. In ten years, this cottage will be worth twice what it is now, the way prices are going. Get Max to help you put the figures together. Convince them to hang onto it.'

Cara thought of Will. The set of his mouth, so straight and firm. Arms crossed defensively. His eyes, critically appraising the cottage. 'He seemed quite definite. His brother and sister need the money...' She trailed off.

Beth crossed her legs and leant forward. 'Didn't you and Pete talk to Mr Parry about buying the cottage at one stage? As I recall, he was pretty agreeable.'

'Oh, he was, but now, financially ...' The words fell away. Money was her least favourite topic, probably because it was one of her mother's favourites.

'Of course, of course. It's hard enough for a working couple to buy something, let alone a single mother,' said Beth, flustered. 'You don't have to explain.'

'No, no. You are friends ... Pete did leave some money. His superannuation and life insurance. I've been saving it for Poppy. But it's not enough anyway.'

'Could your parents help to make up the difference?' said Alex. 'I know if it was my boys I'd do whatever it took.'

'Oh, maybe,' said Cara, feeling a little defensive. She knew her neighbour meant well, but her forthrightness could be unnerving. Not everyone was lucky enough to have a kitchen with a double oven and smart-fridge, and no doubt parents who could give them half a million dollars. 'Mum and Dad have an embroidery business, and they're comfortable … but they don't have much to spare, if you know what I'm saying. They've always rented.'

'My parents have run a corner store for thirty years and never taken a holiday,' said Alex matter-of-factly. 'I know exactly what you're saying.'

Cara coloured. So much for her assumptions about Alex's background. 'I will ask them.' But would Joy and Sam understand her need to stay in Cuthbert Close? Her mother thought the cottage was a dump and didn't understand the idea of an emotional connection to a home. No wonder Cara's childhood had been a continual round of moving from one apartment to the next. For Joy, the promise of something slightly better was reason enough to uproot their lives.

She looked from one woman to the other, shoulders hunched, frowning and silent. She stood and clasped her hands together. 'I think we should cook.'

'What? Now?' Beth checked her watch. 'It's nearly ten o'clock.'

'I do my best work after ten,' said Cara, busying herself with pots and pans under the bench. 'I've got an idea that I've been wanting to test out for ages, and your chocolate has just reminded me.'

'Ah, Cara.' Alex raised her hand. 'You're forgetting that I'm a complete disaster in the kitchen. I'm also thirty seconds away from falling asleep.'

'This is going to be super quick and easy. Promise. You'll be in bed by ten thirty and all you need is to be able to work a spatula,' said Cara.

'What's a spatula?' asked Alex and the three of them burst out laughing.

'Right, we need flour, cocoa powder, butter, milk, peanut butter, brown sugar, vanilla essence and cream. Beth, you get the ingredients, and Alex, you start breaking up the chocolate, but put on one of these so you don't mess up your work clothes.' Cara retrieved three aprons from a hook on the shed wall and handed them out.

'Yes, sir.' Alex saluted.

'Sorry, I can get a little bossy in the kitchen.'

'It suits you, in a crouching-tiger kind of way.' She stopped. 'Sorry, that's cultural stereotyping, isn't it.'

'Maybe, but just wait for my hidden dragon,' Cara joked.

Beth started sorting through the mini-pantry under the bench. She'd helped Cara in the shed a few times when she'd needed a kitchen hand for a particularly tricky recipe.

'What are we actually making?' said Alex, watching the flurry of activity as Beth whipped out ingredients and Cara produced an array of measuring cups and spoons.

'It's one of those cakes you make in a cup in the microwave.'

'Oh yep, I've seen packet mixes for those at the supermarket.'

'A packet mix for a mug cake? But they're so easy.' Beth stopped working for a second to look at Alex.

'The twins think every cake comes out of a packet, and I'm inclined to let it stay that way.'

'Well, you can't get a packet mix for this one.' Cara got out her notebook and started scribbling. 'This one is going to be a muddy chocolate sponge with a gooey peanut butter centre and a hot butterscotch sauce to top it all off. And maybe a scoop of vanilla bean ice cream to finish.'

Alex groaned. 'Sorry Cara, but you are turning me on right now. Not sure about you ladies but when I'm pregnant, the words *chocolate* and *butterscotch* are like foreplay.'

'I guess we better get a move on then, so we can get to the climax,' said Cara.

Alex stared at her. 'Um, where has my friend Cara Pope gone? And who replaced her with this saucy minx?'

The women took roles. Cara scribbled and issued directions for the steps, while Alex smashed the bar of chocolate and Beth did the mixing. Within ten minutes, the microwave pinged and out came three steaming mugs of delicious chocolatey goodness.

Alex held up a spoon. 'Can we eat? Now?'

'Just a second.' Cara whipped a container of vanilla bean ice cream out of the small freezer and placed three scoops over the chocolate sponges. Quickly, she poured the butterscotch sauce over the three mugs so that it dripped decadently down the sides and onto the tray below. As a final flourish, she took a vegetable peeler and shaved delicate chocolate curls on top.

'Now?'

'Nearly.' Cara flicked on the bright photography light, carried the tray over to the table in front of the white wall, picked up the camera lying nearby and started snapping.

'This is excruciating,' whispered Alex to Beth, watching Cara intently.

'She's always quick.'

True to Beth's word, the photo shoot was done in a minute. With the ice cream starting to melt and puddle with the butterscotch sauce, the cakes looked even more delicious.

Alex's stomach growled audibly. 'The baby needs food.' She patted her tummy and Cara handed one mug to Alex, who started to eat hungrily, and another to Beth, who was more tentative, smelling first before taking a small mouthful that she rolled about her mouth, like a critic in a restaurant.

'It's really very good.' Beth inspected the spoon. 'I would never have thought to use peanut butter at the centre. So clever.'

Cara took up her camera again and started snapping photos of the pair of them eating.

'Oh jesus, it's out of this world. And I don't even care if those photos make me look like a pig.' Alex spoke with her mouth full and her eyes closed in ecstasy. 'It's like I've died and gone to a heaven that's filled with melted Snickers.'

'Oh, that's perfect.' Cara lowered her camera. 'I'll call it Melted Mug Snickers. Thank you,' she said to Alex.

'Ha! All I did was eat the damn thing. You made it up.' Alex spooned another mouthful of the divine concoction towards her lips. 'Aren't you going to eat some?' She gestured towards the third mug.

'In a sec. Just want to post these while the inspiration's fresh. Why don't you have it? Eating for two and all.'

Alex looked at Beth. 'How about we go halves? We've both had a tough night. It's the least we deserve.'

'Too true,' Beth agreed.

For the next few minutes, the only sounds were the clinks of metal on ceramic, the occasional groans of ecstasy and Cara tapping away on the computer.

'Beth, Alex, come and check this out.' Cara was seated at the laptop, her face lit by the screen. 'The post is already going crazy.'

Beth and Alex looked down at the screen.

Mummy's Magnificent Mess …
So, what do you do when life gives you lemons?
You make chocolate cake, that's what! At least, that's what I did tonight with two of my dearest friends. Believe me – we deserved every morsel of this indulgent concoction, which I am calling my Melted Mug Snickers. Recipe below.
Happy eating, my friends.
#dessertgoals #chocolatefix

Cara clicked through to show them the photos she'd posted. The first one featured the mug cake in all its gooey glory, but the second one was a close-up of a spoon, piled high with cake, butterscotch sauce and ice cream, about to enter a very wide and clearly delighted mouth. The red lipstick was a pop of luxurious colour against the browns and caramels of the cake.

'Holy shit. That's me.' Alex peered closely. 'It's kind of hot.'

Cara tapped again. This one was a close-up of someone's eyes, scrunched closed but clearly in ecstasy. Just to the side was a spoon, smeared with chocolate, the person clearly just having had a most amazing mouthful.

'Gosh, I look really happy.' Beth stood up. 'But a bit old … those crow's-feet.' She tapped the screen.

'They're not crow's-feet, they're evidence of smiles,' said Cara.

'Whatever they are, people are loving them. Look at the likes! Seventy-six already.' Alex pointed.

'Is that a lot?' asked Beth.

'It is when it's only been up for three minutes,' said Cara.

Alex scanned the comments. 'LadyBaker83 says *I'll have what they're having.*'

'Oh, like that line from the movie with Meg Ryan and Billy Crystal.' Beth clapped her hands together. 'I love that movie.'

'Refresh the screen,' ordered Alex. 'Let's see how many likes now.'

Cara tapped a button.

'254 likes and forty-two comments! Oh, man,' breathed Alex. 'Look at this comment from FoodDude – *Home delivery? Ladies included?*' She chuckled. 'Cheeky bugger.'

'It's quite the response. Must have been the gorgeous models I used,' said Cara, swivelling on the stool to face them.

'I hardly think so,' said Beth. 'It's your beautiful photos more likely.'

'You know.' Alex cocked her head to the side. 'This has given me an idea …' She tapped the spoon on her temple. 'I got a newsletter from The Primal Guy, and even though I think the guy's a douche, he did have an interesting theory about making the most of unexpected events.'

'The black swan thing?' said Cara. 'I only skimmed it.'

'Sounds like I need to subscribe.' Beth pulled out her phone. 'I'll do it right now.'

'It's worth it, just for the laughs,' said Alex. 'But anyway, he was saying how unexpected catastrophes are actually the best time to take action, to launch a new business. Capitalise on the turmoil.'

'I am all ears,' said Beth.

'Me too,' added Cara.

'Beth here is an amateur MasterChef, and Cara, you are a recipe genius who can make food look even more beautiful than it actually is.' Alex leant forward. 'So, how about you join forces?'

'I'm not following,' said Beth.

'As in, what if you cooked meals and delivered them to people?'

'Like those diet delivery businesses, Lite n' Easy or something?' said Cara.

'No.' Alex shook her head. 'Not like that at all. I mean creating delicious, home-cooked meals for time-poor mums that you deliver straight to their door.'

'But would people actually pay for that? I mean it's not that hard to whip up a dinner. Surely mums wouldn't pay for someone to do that seven nights a week?' asked Beth.

'Ah, I would.' Alex put up her hand. 'And I already do, remember?' She patted Beth's arm. 'I couldn't survive without your meals.'

'But I do that because you're my neighbour, and I hate you paying me, you know that,' Beth protested. 'Besides, I don't think I'd have time. There's the children to think of ...'

'Haven't you been saying for a while how little they need you, and how you now have time for more in your life? This could be it.' Alex tapped the table with her index finger.

'It's actually a great idea,' said Cara. 'But a business like that could take ages to make a profit and I'm sort of desperate.'

Alex nodded. 'I know it won't make you a million overnight, but it's a start. Every dollar will count, after all, and it's not like you'll need extra equipment to begin with. Between us, we have three kitchens, which should be more than enough to get you going. And Beth has her deep freezer for storing meals. C'mon, you should at least think about it.'

Cara took in Alex's eager face, her shining eyes. Her neighbour had such faith, such confidence.

Squid ink pasta.

The thought popped into her head. People were like dishes, in Cara's view – a dash of this and a pinch of that, which, when mixed together, made a complete dish. Alex was brave and challenging. Also surprising. Silky black pasta. Of course.

Beth gave her a sympathetic glance. 'Cara already has a lot on her plate, what with Poppy, and her own work. She might not have the time.'

Beth? Beth was a bowl of hearty pumpkin soup. Deceptively simple, always comforting.

'I'll think about it.' Cara went to collect the near-empty mugs, which now contained nothing more than little pools of muddied vanilla ice cream. A meal delivery business wasn't the worst idea. Far from it. But just how quickly could she get it up and running? Not quickly enough to buy Cuthbert Close from the Parry family, but perhaps enough to start paying higher rent. Absentmindedly, she dipped in a spoon and licked at the remnants. She loved that aspect of cooking, how it was the chef's prerogative to lick the spoon, scrape the bowl, dip a finger. All the secret tastes. Everything and nothing.

I am not one particular dish … I am the bits and pieces that are left behind.

In the years since Pete's death, she'd prided herself on her strength. Her resolve. Her commitment to being there for Poppy and avoiding useless self-pity. She had her way of handling things and that way was through cooking. It was the perfect distraction from her emotions because it required total focus. Complete immersion. No doubt that's why she'd suggested making the mug cake to Beth and Alex. It was a diversion from having to deal with the fact that death had once again stalked into her life and threatened the stability she so desperately craved.

Picking up the scourer, Cara started scrubbing the mugs in the sink while the other women chatted behind her. She would think about it later, once they were gone.

CHAPTER EIGHT

Alex settled in to the waiting room chair and tried to relax. Thanks to a last-minute cancellation, Dr Vin had managed to squeeze her in at short notice, which was nothing short of remarkable. She was an incredibly popular doctor and what Alex remembered of the waiting room from when she was pregnant with the twins was that it had been consistently full of bumps and babies.

Oh, how she had looked longingly at the neat little basketball bellies that other women grew, and the sweet, doll-like babies that emerged from them. Surely, after the emotional and physical roller-coaster of IVF, Alex deserved one of these perfect, pretty pregnancies and a set of matching cabbage-patch babies?

Sadly, the fertility gods hadn't agreed and had gifted her with a body that bloated beyond recognition and two little boys who were skin and bone, consistently ravenous, and very cross about it too.

Alex shivered. Nothing about this waiting room had changed. Bumps and babies abounded, all against the background of mint green. Chairs, carpet, the walls, the reception desk – everything tinged in a colour that was no doubt supposed to be soothing but only served to remind Alex of baby puke after pureed peas. A gentle yet twisted sign to the mums-to-be of all they had to look forward to.

Alex sat across from the only other splash of colour in the room – a poster on the wall that read 'Are you getting enough folate?' and featured a food basket, overflowing with bread, broccoli and various legumes.

She made a mental note to buy more supplements and started flicking through her phone to the emails she needed to forward to Cara and Beth. After the cooking session with the girls, Alex had gone home completely buzzed. A catering business was the perfect solution for her neighbours. At 11 pm, Alex had sent out an email to the other working mothers she knew through the twins' school, asking if they'd be interested in having a meal delivery service that was healthy, delicious and wouldn't cost the earth. She'd barely finished typing before the responses came flooding back. One mum was finishing off her son's make-a-rocket project for school. Another was ironing shirts and one of them was up to her eyeballs in vegemite sandwiches for the week ahead. They were IN! When would it begin? Could they sign up straight away?

Since then, there'd been more. Twenty-eight affirmative responses that Alex forwarded to Cara and Beth with the shouty subject line: I TELL YOU, THIS IS A THING!

The receptionist was off the phone. Alex closed her email and stood to let her know she was there.

'You're back!' The woman beamed at Alex.

'You remember me?'

'Twin boys, six years ago, correct?'

'Yes. That's amazing. Do you remember all Dr Vin's patients?'

'Only the memorable ones.' She said it with a smile but Alex couldn't help feeling that the word *memorable* wasn't necessarily a compliment. She recalled her last visit to the obstetrician's office, when the twins were a mere six weeks old and Alex had hit a personal rock-bottom in terms of personal hygiene. She couldn't remember the details of those early days, but she could remember how they smelt – and the words *overripe blue cheese* were the ones that came to mind.

Was that what this perky blonde receptionist was remembering? The cheesy aroma of her?

'How are the boys?' asked the receptionist, leaning her elbows on the desk.

'Oh, they're great. Beautiful.' *Noah told me this morning that I had a hairy bum, while Jasper ate his toast into the shape of a gun and fired it at me.*

'Do you have a photo?'

'Of course!' Alex opened her phone and started scrolling. 'Sorry, um, looks like one of them took a few selfies.' Bloody Jasper and his obsession with photographing his own nostrils. Alex kept scrolling. Fifty-three photos of a hairy black hole later she came to a shot of the boys standing arm in arm on the first day of school. She'd had to bribe them with a chocolate bar to do that.

'But Mummy, you always say no lollies before 9 am,' Noah had said with a worried face.

'Today is special, honey. Your first day of Year One. It's okay on special days,' *and when Mummy is heartily sick and tired of scrolling through her friend's pictures of perfectly pressed, shiny children.*

Alex held up the phone. 'Here they are.'

The receptionist leant in. 'They're exactly like you.' She leant back and even though her mouth was in the smiling position, there was a definite furrow between her eyebrows.

'Well, thankfully not in all ways.' Alex laughed and took a seat, discreetly sniffing her armpits. She was quite certain she'd put on deodorant this morning. Or was that yesterday? Whatever. There was definitely perfume on her wrists and no hint of blue cheese, of that she was quite sure. She picked up a well-thumbed magazine and tried to concentrate. *The Primal Guy's Top Ten Tips for LGN (Looking Good Naked!).*

Ugh. What a bore. Alex could count on one hand the number of people who saw her naked and she gave precisely zero shits about impressing them. Noah and Jasper watched her in the shower like she was a museum specimen, while James was nothing less than grateful for any nudity he received. No, it was the people who saw her clothed that she was more concerned about. Like the receptionist.

'Alexandra?' Dr Vin stood at the doorway to the surgery. She was always immaculate. Pearl earrings set off beautifully by her deep brown skin. Ladder-free opaque tights beneath a chic grey skirt suit. And she always called Alex by her full name, which made her feel like she was possibly in trouble.

Dr Vin briskly closed the door behind her.

'So, are we here today for babies or pap test?'

'Babies, I think,' said Alex.

Dr Vin raised her eyebrows. 'You think?'

Alex poured out the story, including the parts about Henrietta and Banjo. At this, Dr Vin's nose wrinkled, which Alex liked to think was an expression of judgement over Charlie Devine's appalling manners. Ugh! That woman. This morning, Alex had ducked behind the bushes as she sprinted past in all-white activewear. White Lycra. Bizarre. Didn't she worry about sweat patches? Or people seeing her pubes? But even more weirdly, it actually looked good on her. No doubt, she was headed off on a lengthy run to ensure she still *looked good naked* for her husband.

'Anyway, we buried Henny and the test was positive, even though you said I'd *never* get pregnant naturally,' Alex finished.

Dr Vin smiled. 'A doctor never says *never*. I simply told you it was highly unlikely, given your LPD.'

LPD. Luteal Phase Defect. In layman's terms, a too-short menstrual cycle that meant Alex's embryos could never develop naturally. Or, at least that was the theory behind why she couldn't get pregnant. No one was *exactly* sure. There was so much still unknown about pregnancy and conception, said doctor after doctor, as if this was somehow reassuring. More than once, Alex had been tempted to suggest that it was possibly because pregnancy happened to *women*. You could bet your bottom dollar that if men had to be pregnant that science would have discovered everything there was to know about it.

'And when was your last period?' Dr Vin opened a folder on her desk.

'It was … um … not long ago, I think. A couple of weeks at most, I'd say. They happen so regularly it's a bit hard to keep track.' Alex pulled out her diary and flashed through the pages of the last few weeks looking for the tell-tale P, with a circle around it. 'Where is it, where is it,' she muttered as Dr Vin waited..

'Here it is,' said Alex triumphantly. 'January 2.'

'Eight weeks ago.' Dr Vin looked at her. 'So you've missed two periods, then.'

Alex stared at her diary. Two periods missed without her even noticing. 'It's been a busy couple of months,' she mumbled.

'Up to the table then. Everything off below the waist.' Dr Vin stood and pulled back the curtain around the examination table. Alex undressed quickly and placed a small white sheet over her knees to protect her modesty, even though Dr Vin was better acquainted with her genitalia than even James was.

'I'm ready,' she called, and Dr Vin stepped inside the confines of the curtain.

'Bring your knees together, then let them relax to the sides. I'm going to touch the inside of your leg, and then I'll conduct the internal examination. Let me know if it's too uncomfortable.'

Alex closed her eyes and waited for the inevitable discomfort. She opened them again to see Dr Vin looking into the distance and frowning.

'Eight weeks is about right,' she said, directly, and snapped off the rubber glove.

'Really? I'm *that* pregnant?' said Alex. How had she got to eight weeks without realising? With the twins she'd felt sick from the minute she conceived. She'd budgeted on being four weeks, at most, with this one.

'Let's check on the ultrasound. If it's twins, that might be changing the size a bit.'

'Oh, shit,' Alex breathed. Her pulse picked up tempo and she felt a small sweat breaking out in her armpits.

'It's possible.'

Alex raised her top and startled at the cold of the ultrasound gel. She held the bed sheet as Dr Vin used the flat-headed probe to spread the jelly-like substance over her abdomen. Both their faces turned to the screen above the examination table. Grey and grainy at first, then from out of the blur emerged the clear outline of a misshapen kidney bean.

'Your uterus,' said Dr Vin, manipulating the angle of the probe.

Alex's eyes narrowed on the screen. There was definitely something inside the kidney bean. Something that resembled an overgrown tadpole. 'Is that the head?'

'Yes, that's baby number one, and here is—'

Dr Vin pressed another button on the machine and Alex curled her toes.

'The baby's heartbeat.'

From the machine came the *whoosh, whoosh, whoosh* that sounded more like a snorting bull with a terrible cold than a tiny foetus.

'One heartbeat?' Alex held her breath.

'Just the one that I can see,' said Dr Vin, frowning at the screen. 'Let me take some measurements.' She flipped the probe again and started tapping at the keyboard. 'Head,' she murmured. 'One arm, second arm. Leg number one.' She shifted the wand. 'And leg number two.'

Alex stared. The creature on the screen bucked and jerked.

'Hiccups,' commented Dr Vin, still tapping notes into the computer.

The little tadpole stilled, and a second later bucked and jerked again.

'And I can't feel a damn thing,' said Alex in wonder.

'Because it's the size of an olive, and it's buried beneath layers of muscle.' Dr Vin went to remove the probe and stopped. 'It's waving at us.'

She was right. The tadpole's miniature arm, more like an oversized ear than an actual limb, waved back and forth on the screen.

'Hello baby.' Dr Vin used her other hand to wave, her face breaking into a smile. That's what her patients came for – the little flashes of brilliant humanity that occasionally bolted out from behind the stethoscope and starched white coat. 'Always amazing,' she murmured and flicked off the screen.

Alex felt her eyes growing hot and itchy. 'Thank you, Dr Vin,' she said in a shaky voice.

'I'll give you a minute.' With that, she rose from the stool and whooshed the curtain open and shut behind her.

Silently, Alex dressed, her eyes never leaving the screen with her little foetus frozen on it.

Having paid and scheduled another appointment, Alex stepped out into the busy city street. Usually, she rushed through the CBD, conscious of racing against a ticking clock to get through her work by 6 pm so she could be home in time to see the twins before bed.

Today, she dawdled, still caught in the heady cloud of post-ultrasound wonder.

Stopped at the crossing, all the suits and heels rushing about her, Alex looked up at the skyscrapers leaning against the blue sky and cutting the sun into blocks and right angles. It was the same view she saw every day, but after her visit with Dr Vin, it seemed the angle of everything had tilted ever so slightly.

Her phone buzzed and Alex reached in to her handbag. Twenty-nine unread emails, two missed calls from the office and one text message from James.

She opened it.

How was Dr Vin?

Alex tapped back.

Professional and lovely as ever.

You know what I mean! Don't keep me in suspense.

All right. Yes. Dr Vin is still wearing the opaque tights that you used to find such a turn-on.

ALEX!!!!!

OK. Here's your baby. Turns out you're right. When it comes to expiry dates, pregnancy tests are not like lamb chops.

To the text message, Alex attached a photo from the ultrasound of their baby in profile, its tiny bump of a nose like a miniature ski jump.

Holy shit. That's the cutest baby ever. Well done you miracle Mum! I told you so. Celebration tonight? Xx

Alex smiled.

James's enthusiasm was infectious, and she was starting to feel it too. Of course she still had no idea how she would juggle a baby and the twins and her job. But she would. There was an actual little human being inside of her. You couldn't dread a tiny tadpole thing that waved at you. You could only love it, and, if she was being completely honest, there *was* a part of her that felt she had unfinished baby business. The process of conceiving the boys had been so fraught and difficult that even when the tenth round had succeeded and the twin embryos 'stuck', Alex had felt nothing but fear. What if she miscarried? What if there were birth defects? At no point had she been able to relax and enjoy the process, certainly not in the way that other women seemed to revel in it, with their Insta-bumps, beatific smiles, and #blessed posts.

This baby was her chance to make things right.

Definitely! Let's crack out the Jatz!

He'd smile at that. No party in the O'Rourke household was ever complete without the little round crackers. Her mother was a woman of the seventies after all, and it seems James had adopted her jazz for Jatz, plus the mandatory cheese cubes.

The lights changed. Alex clicked the screen off, but the phone buzzed again.

Where r u? Boss asking!

Oh shit. It was Brianna – her secretary-come-paralegal – starting to panic, by the sounds of it. For a young person, she was quite a stress-head about work, which Alex liked, because it meant she was taking it seriously.

Coming. 5 mins.

Alex scurried through the city streets, collected a take-away coffee (decaf – such a waste) and allowed the glass doors of her office tower to swallow her up. Waiting at the lift, she removed her jacket and slung it over her arm to cover her small handbag. She didn't carry a large one any more. It was such a giveaway. Carrying it to and from the lift, she may as well have emblazoned the words I AM JUST ARRIVING/LEAVING on her forehead. This way, with the bag hidden, anyone who saw her would think she'd just ducked out for coffee, not that she was more than an hour late for work. In the afternoon, she always walked out with a file in her hand, as if she were just off to a meeting, and not racing home to kiss the boys goodnight.

The lift was empty and Alex urged it through the floors.

When it pinged, she rushed out and straight into Brianna, nearly spilling coffee over the both of them.

'Jesus, what are you doing out here?'

Brianna only left her desk for fire drills and Friday afternoon drinks in the boardroom, and only because both were somewhat compulsory.

'Martin's looking for you. C'mon.' Brianna took her jacket and bag, and motioned for her to start walking. Long-legged and with what seemed an almost unfair amount of long hair, she walked the corridor like a thoroughbred and Alex had to trot to keep up. 'There's a huge matter that's just come in and he's thinking about giving you the brief. I didn't want you to miss out.'

You mean you don't want to miss out.

That was fine. Brianna was smart and ambitious, and, judging by how often she brought her lunch, not rich. She was paying her own way through law school. Alex admired and respected that. She understood it. Brianna was herself, before children. Focused, and with texta-free clothing.

'There are some letters on your desk that need signing.' Brianna hung Alex's jacket and slipped efficiently into her workstation while Alex flopped into her seat and sighed.

Made it. She swivelled to face the window for a moment. Gathering herself for the work ahead.

'Ah, so you are here.'

It was Martin – her boss – standing neatly in the doorway. Everything about Martin was neat. He was English and reminded Alex of a squirrel with his little buck teeth and jerky movements.

'Yes, of course. Been here for hours. Just popped out for a coffee.' Alex held up the cup.

'Right, well, a large matter has just come in. Rather huge, I'm afraid. Terribly complicated.' He smiled, teeth over lips, like a squirrel nibbling a nut.

'How … exciting,' said Alex, with forced enthusiasm.

'Indeed. Would you have a moment?' Martin rose up and down on his toes, which was another of his odd little habits. Alex thought he did it to make himself appear taller, while Brianna thought he was strengthening his calf muscles. He cycled for six hours every Saturday. 'Imagine him in Lycra,' Brianna would comment in a tone of disgusted wonder while Alex tried very hard *not* to. The visual image of her squirrelly boss in genitalia-revealing bike pants wasn't pretty. Nuts. Bleurgh.

'Of course.' As Alex gestured for Martin to take a seat, her phone buzzed, and she surreptitiously looked at the number.

The boys' school.

It stopped, and Martin began droning on about a big takeover that the firm was being asked to handle. What a complex case it would be. How much work would be involved. Yadda yadda.

No message on her phone. Phew. Mustn't be anything serious. Probably a mislaid hat, or grazed knee.

The phone started buzzing..

Alex glanced sideways.

The school. Again.

This time, her stomach dropped.

Martin was still prattling on. *Bid ... takeover... stakes... shares ... hostile.*

Nervously, Alex tapped the darkened screen. Again, no message. She slipped the phone into her hand and held it just under the desk.

Her palm vibrated. Alex looked down.

The school.

'I'm sorry, Martin, but I'm expecting a rather urgent call from ... from opposing counsel in the Acton matter. Would you mind if I take this?' She stood in a rush and held up the phone.

Martin peered at the screen. 'The caller ID says *School.*'

Shit. Of course. 'Oh, yes, right ... Ah, that's my nickname for him. He's very conscientious.'

Martin gave a doubtful nod. 'All right then. We'll continue our chat later. I want you taking the lead on this one.' He rose and, with another little bob, was gone.

Alex dived on her vibrating phone. 'Hello, this is Alex speaking.'

'Good morning, Mrs O'Rourke, it's Annabelle Ryan calling,' said the cool voice at the end of the line.

Mrs Ryan. Shit. The principal. Alex's eye twitched. 'Is everything all right? Are the boys okay?'

'The boys are here with me in the office. They're fine.'

In the background she heard one of them yell out, 'Hi, Mum. We're okay now.'

'Jasper, quiet please while I'm on the phone.' That bit was muffled. Probably Mrs Ryan putting her hand over the receiver. 'Mrs O'Rourke, the boys are physically unharmed. But there has been an …' She paused. 'An incident. I'd like to meet with you and Mr O'Rourke as soon as possible. Today, ideally.'

Alex thought of the twenty-nine unread emails waiting for her, and the brief for the Acton matter that still required a mountain of work to get through, and now this takeover thing that Martin had just landed on her. The visit to the obstetrician had already set her so far behind that a visit to the school would make the day a complete write-off. Besides, if the boys were talking and breathing, it clearly wasn't an emergency.

'Mrs Ryan, I'm sorry but I have several work commitments today that I am obliged to attend to. Could we possibly meet tomorrow morning, before school?' Alex attempted her solicitor-addressing-the-judge tone. Authoritative, yet accommodating.

'I'm sorry, Mrs O'Rourke, but this issue cannot wait. I'm happy to fit in with your work commitments but it really must be today.'

Alex tightened her grip on the phone. 'I'll be there as soon as I can.'

'And Mr O'Rourke too?'

'I'll do my best.'

Alex hung up, pushed herself out from behind her desk and paused. How could she do this without being spotted?

She rose, slipped her phone into her pocket and dug a credit card out of her wallet. It was all she needed. It would be cab–school–cab–work. She collected a file from her desk and approached Brianna, whispering urgently.

'I have to go to the boys' school. There's been an emergency.'

Brianna nodded and kept typing as if Alex had simply told her to dig out a file. On many occasions, she had declared that she would never have children – and she said it with a certainty that made Alex feel both amused and envious.

Holding the file as if off to a meeting, Alex marched down the hallway to reception, and kept on going right into the lift. Out on the street, she flagged a cab, gave the driver the directions and dialled James.

'Hey there. Everything okay? The baby?' She heard the worry in his voice.

'It's fine. All good, but I could murder a Macca's chocolate sundae right now,' she joked.

'Well, you must be pregnant then.'

She heard the smile in his voice. 'I guess so. But, uh, listen, um … I just got a call from the boys' principal, Mrs Ryan.'

'Which one of them is it? Leg? Arm?' he said in a rush.

'No. No. She said they're physically fine. But she needs to talk to us straight away.' Alex cradled the phone and reached into her pocket, where she'd been known to stash her lipstick when her tiny handbag was too full.

'Oh, no.' He sighed. 'They must have hurt someone. Another kid or something.'

'The boys? No. They wouldn't hurt a fly. Noah cried this morning because I accidentally squashed the daddy-long-legs in his room that he'd nicknamed Alfred. They probably just graffitied something, or said the f-word maybe.'

'You really think they'd call us in for that?'

'I don't know. Maybe. It's a school. The boys got in trouble for wearing the wrong coloured sneakers, remember? Anyway, I'm going to be there in twenty. Can you come?'

'Sure. My next patient's not till 12,' said James. 'But I don't like the sound of this.'

Alex ran a slash of red lipstick around her lips, the colour she always wore when she wanted to project confidence. 'Hon, it'll be fine. Seriously. They're alive and breathing. How bad could it be?'

But as she hung up the phone, Alex asked the taxi driver to pull over. Into the gutter she quietly heaved up her breakfast.

Getting back in, she cursed herself.

Now she'd have to redo the lipstick.

CHAPTER NINE

Beth swung into Cuthbert Close, but instead of feeling the warm sense of comfort that usually came over her when she drove into the street, she experienced a prickle of irritation. Why hadn't the school rung earlier to say the sewing bee for the upcoming production of *Cats* was cancelled? The art teacher had been apologetic. Terribly sorry. But no one else had been available to attend the daytime session because they all had jobs. Didn't she get the email from the school saying it had been postponed to an evening next week?

No, she hadn't. She didn't check her email every day. At that revelation, the art teacher – dressed in a caftan and jewelled turban – had looked at Beth in wonder, like *she* was some kind of strange and exotic species. Or a relic.

Perhaps she was.

When the kids had started school, it hadn't been difficult to find other full-time stay-at-home mothers like herself.

Drop-offs and pick-ups were a social event. But over the years, the number had dwindled. Friends returned to work, and then there was the nature of high school. Larger and more anonymous. The kids didn't want her anywhere near the school gate. There was, generally, less need for parental involvement.

No, that wasn't quite right. Chloe and Ethan definitely needed her. Look at this morning for instance. Ethan, scrabbling around for his tie, which Beth eventually found stuffed behind the dirty clothes basket, and Chloe with her sudden, urgent need to produce ten plastic bottle tops for a recycled-art work. Max was no help. He'd swanned into the chaos, fresh from his morning run, and swanned straight back out again to the shower. Had Beth been rushing off to work, there would have been no way she could have helped the kids, and Ethan would have gone tie-less. Chloe, bottle top-less.

But now, driving down Cuthbert Close, the day stretched out before her like a yawn. Four and a half hours until the kids got home. She crawled along the curb, wanting to somehow extend the drive so as to eat up a few extra seconds.

Hang on. Wasn't that Max's car in the driveway? Yes, it was. Her spirits started to climb. He would understand. He would talk to her. Console her. Agree with her over the school's lack of consideration. It could be a small chance for them to reconnect after the distance of the last few months. Strange, though, he hadn't mentioned anything about coming home. Was he sick? He'd been perfectly fine when he left that morning. Then again, there was some kind of gastro bug doing the rounds.

She pulled quickly into the drive and hurried inside.

'Max, Max, I'm home,' she called into the silence.

Nothing. Just the hum of the fridge.

She dropped her keys on the bench and walked through the house, calling Max's name.

Fishing out her phone, Beth dialled his number.

'Everything all right?' He sounded breathless.

'Yes, fine. Where are you?'

'At work. Where else would I be?'

'Well, I'm at home and your car is here, but you're not.'

A slight pause. A woman's voice in the background. 'Ah, well, I'm actually just over at the Devines'. There's a couple of … um … problems with the house that need attention, so, I'm … uh … attending to them.'

'You're next door?' Beth went to the front windows.

'Yes, just finishing off now.'

There he was, walking out the door, phone jammed between his neck and his ear as he wrestled to put his suit jacket back on. No tie. Top button undone. Was that how he'd left for work?

'I didn't know you were going to the Devines'.'

'I mentioned it, but you were rushing to get to school.'

Was that true? It was plausible. The mornings were a whirl of activity, trying to get Ethan and Chloe moving, the lunches made, and this morning, the added drama of the missing tie and the desperately needed bottle tops. Was she really so busy that she couldn't even listen to her husband? Guilt nudged at her.

'Would you like some lunch? There's roast chicken in the fridge. I could make a salad?'

His face broke into a smile as he walked down the Devines' drive. 'That'd be great.'

Beth headed for the kitchen and tried to recount the events of the morning. In the maelstrom of tie-finding and bottle top-scavenging, had she even kissed her husband goodbye? Beth had no specific recollection of it. In twenty years of marriage, it was normal for her memory of these things to blend and fog. But remembering this one suddenly seemed important. Had he told her about the Devines? She felt sure that any mention of the name would surely have piqued her interest, given the quiche fiasco – an incident she hadn't divulged to Max. Beth still felt a sense of shame that Charlie had tagged her as a meddler and she knew if she told Max he would dismiss it as a storm in a teacup, which wasn't helpful at all. It was all right for him. Management of neighbourly relations wasn't his job. It was hers. Though, in the case of the Devines, the lines were blurred. With the Pezzullos overseas, Max was effectively Charlie's landlord. She couldn't afford to tell *him* to butt out. She needed him.

'Hey there.' Max sauntered into the kitchen, a bundle of junk mail in his hand. 'Aren't you supposed to be at school? The sewing thing?'

'Cancelled,' said Beth. 'No one else could make it, so it's been postponed to an evening next week.'

'And they didn't tell you?'

'There was an email …' Beth trailed off and Max nodded briefly, before turning his attention to the catalogues and pamphlets in his hand. 'Maybe I should get a job.'

Max looked at her, head cocked. 'I don't follow.'

'I'm like a dinosaur at that school. All the other mums have jobs, except for me.'

'You do a lot of work for the school.'

'Not as much as I used to. I think I could do more.' She paused. 'So, do you think I should get a job or not?' she said in a rush.

Max regarded her, folding his arms. 'Only if you want to. It's not like we need the money, and Chloe and Ethan do need someone to drive them around everywhere, which would limit a bit what you could do.'

'So you think I shouldn't get a job?'

'I'm not saying that … I just haven't really thought about it.' He went back to sorting the mail. Beth bit her lip.

'How was Charlie? Any problems?' She kept her voice light and avoided Max's gaze by going to the fridge to get out the salad ingredients.

He paused and she felt his eyes on her. 'Just minor stuff. Dishwasher on the blink. Remote for the aircon missing. Sticky window locks.'

'Don't the junior agents normally handle that kind of thing?' Beth focused on the two plates before her, laying a bed of rocket, then pieces of roast chicken. 'You don't want Charlie to feel like you're watching her.'

She looked up briefly. Max leant against the bench, arms folded. 'Seemed silly to send another agent when I'm right here.' He shifted. 'I think Charlie actually appreciated it.'

Beth cut wedges of avocado, enjoying the feel of the knife slicing easily through the creamy flesh. 'Did she say when her husband's coming to join them?'

Max despatched the junk into the recycling box. 'I don't know what's happening there.'

'You think there's a problem?'

'He's not on the lease, but that doesn't necessarily mean anything.' Max pulled out his phone. 'Just need to send a couple of messages.' He walked slowly into the living room, head bowed, and Beth finished the salads with a glug of olive oil and a dash of balsamic vinegar.

'But lunch is ready,' she called after him. Her husband's habit of disappearing when a meal was about to be served was legendary, and annoying.

'This will only take a minute.'

And now she had nothing to do. Beth looked about the kitchen and her gaze settled on the iPad. Emails. Yes, she should check them. Confirm the school had not forgotten her entirely. She brought the screen to life. Yes, there it was. *Sewing Bee Postponed.*

She made a note of the new date and time and replied to confirm her attendance. There were a couple of RSVPs for the anniversary party. An email from The Primal Guy. Beth read it and pressed 'delete'. Chicken bars and black swans. What a strange man. She went to her favourite recipe website. The anniversary party was getting closer, and now that her day was devoid of activity, perhaps it was time to start planning the menu.

Up came a message on the iPad.

So what time tomorrow?

A bit odd, she thought. But probably just one of those annoying pop-up things. She went to close the box and stopped. There were ten numbers above the message and they looked quite familiar. Aha! It was Max's mobile. She looked up to see him fiddling with his phone. They must have accidentally synced up, the iPad and his phone. She was about to tell him when up popped another message, this one from a number she didn't know.

5:30 pm suit you? Really excited about it.

Beth paused. Who exactly would be telling Max that they were *really excited* to meet up with him? It wasn't the kind of language you'd expect from a work colleague, and it clearly wasn't from one of his existing friends. She waited, her heart moving from a slow plod to a modest trot.

That's good for me. Never done this before …

Don't worry babe. Everyone freaks out about their first time. But after you've done it once, you'll want to come back again and again. It spices up your life like nothing else. Promise! Xx

Beth inhaled sharply. Was Max really part of this conversation? Quietly, she padded to the doorway between kitchen and living room. Silently, she watched her husband, tapping away and frowning at the phone in his hands.

Ha! I hope I can keep up with you. I'm a little out of shape these days.

Well, that was a complete lie. Max was the fittest he'd been since they were married. He would turn forty-five in September and was in training for a half marathon, his first, which meant rising every morning in the dawn light to pound the pavements around Cuthbert Close for nearly an hour, conveniently arriving home just as the kids headed off to school. He was doing it for charity, he said, and had set up a fundraising page to which he invited all their friends to contribute. So far, he'd raised $100 (donated by Beth) which seemed a paltry amount over which to risk a heart attack. She would pay him $100 not to do it.

How big are you?

Big enough, I think!

I think we'll be a perfect fit! See you tomorrow! Xx

Max looked up and caught Beth staring at him. She juggled the iPad and put it behind her back.

'Ready for lunch?' she said, too brightly.

He rose and jammed the phone into his pocket. 'Sorry, but I'm going to have to get back to the office.'

'Oh. All right.' She stood still, unsure what to say next.

'I'll put it in a container, shall I?' He looked at her, expectantly.

'No, no. It's all right, I'll do it.' Cheeks flaming, Beth scurried back to the kitchen and busied herself opening and shutting cupboard doors and drawers.

Max was back on his phone again, not watching her, thank goodness. Her fingers trembled and the rocket leaves quivered on the spoon.

Finally, she pressed the container into his hands. 'Here you go.'

'Thanks Bethy. See you tonight.'

With that, he was gone and the house was again silent.

She stood at the front windows and watched him reverse out of the driveway and take off out of the close in a hurry.

It was then that it struck her. He hadn't kissed her goodbye.

CHAPTER TEN

Alex paid the driver and climbed wearily out of the cab. He sped off before she even had time to close the door and her 'thank you' was sucked up in the squeal of spinning wheels.

'I'm pregnant,' she shouted uselessly into the gassy fumes left behind. At least she'd had the decency to puke *outside* of the vehicle.

Alex straightened her skirt, turned on her heel and walked straight into James coming the other way.

'Hey there.' James caught her arm. 'Are you okay? You're really pale.'

'Gee, thanks, you look terrible too.' She kissed him on the cheek. 'I'm okay. Just a bit of morning sickness, that's all.'

'So what's all this about then?' He took her hand and they walked towards the school gates.

'I suspect the principal has called us in to tell us the boys are too clever for Year One and need to be accelerated into Year Two.'

James looked at her, eyebrows raised. 'You really think that?'

Alex stopped. 'No, of course I don't but it's better than the alternatives.'

'A positive attitude,' said James, with approval. 'I like it.'

They stopped at the wrought-iron gates. The school itself was a red-brick monolith built in the fifties, designed to last well into the next century and intimidate all who passed through its doors.

Alex took a breath and walked forward.

Inside, the principal's secretary asked them to take a seat in the hall near Mrs Ryan's office. Alex sat and shifted uncomfortably.

'Did you see the look she gave us?' she whispered to James.

'What look?'

'That look, like *oh, you poor people*.'

'Maybe that's just her normal look?' James leant over and squeezed her knee. 'What happened to trying to think positive?'

'I gave up on it.' Alex crossed her legs with effort. The chairs were just as she remembered school chairs to be. Hard and plastic and designed to encourage excessive sweating of the legs.

The door swung open.

'Mr and Mrs O'Rourke?' The principal smiled grimly.

Alex peeled herself off the seat and wiped a sweaty palm against her skirt before offering it to the composed woman before her. 'Please, call me Alex. And this is James.'

Mrs Ryan nodded briskly. 'Thank you for coming at such short notice.' She closed the door behind her. 'I think it might be best if we conduct this in the boys' classroom with their teacher, Miss Douglas. All the children are at lunch.'

'Of course,' said James agreeably.

'This way.' Mrs Ryan set off down the hallway.

Following her, Alex noted the sensible court shoes and nude pantyhose, wrinkling a little above her heel. *She wouldn't like that*, Alex thought. Mrs Ryan struck her as the kind of woman who liked things to be smooth. Professional. She ran Prince's Park Primary as a tight ship, Alex had observed, not that she'd actually spent *that* much time at the school, much to the twins' disappointment. They were always going on about how all the mums did tuckshop except for her, and how lots of them volunteered to come in and read with the kids which, again, Alex never did. She came to the big things – the swimming carnival and the Mother's Day breakfast – where she usually snuck in, made a big fuss of saying *hi* to the boys before promptly sneaking out again.

Mum, did you see me in the 15 metre backstroke?
Of course I did, darling, you were wonderful!
But I came last!
You did your best, and that's what counts

Alex absolved herself of the guilt by laying blame at the school's feet. It was quite ridiculous, the degree of parental involvement it required. There were book-covering bees for the library, bake sales to raise money for the sister school in India, second-hand uniform shop sales, costume-making sessions for the annual show, barbecue attendants for the Father's Day breakfast, not to mention the annual spring fair – an extravaganza of cake, sausages and giddying rides.

Alex was happy to contribute. As long as the contribution was money. But the school only wanted her time, and that was something she simply didn't have. Her own parents never once set foot on *her* school grounds and she survived Hunter High just fine. Came second top in her final exams, a fact that Alex liked to use as evidence that parental involvement was not in fact critical to student success, as the boys' school would have had them believe. They were forever going on about the teachers educating 'in partnership' with parents, which Alex found disingenuous. She was a mother, not a teacher. She could read books to the boys, but not teach them how to read.

What's this word, darling?

Is it 'dog', Mummy?

Really? Look again. You really think it's a D?

Is it an X?

How about I just read the book to you?

The principal turned down another hallway and sounds of the playground filtered down the corridor. High-pitched squeals of delight, thudding basketballs and the occasional whistle pierced through it all. Alex pictured the twins in the thick of it. There was nothing they loved more than the rough and tumble of the playground at lunchtime.

Mrs Ryan stopped in front of the classroom door. 'Now, as I said on the phone, the boys are fine, but there has been some ... damage, you might say.'

Alex's stomach catapulted. Damage to what? Damage to who?

Mrs Ryan opened the door and Alex's eyes flew to the sight of her two sons, sleeves rolled up and washcloths in hand. To her surprise, it was Jasper who looked up first and launched himself across the room and into her arms.

'Mummy, I'm so sorry,' Jasper sobbed. 'I tried to stop him, but he wouldn't.'

'Shush, it's all right, darling. Mummy's here,' Alex crooned, and hugged the little boy tightly. Over his shoulder, she could see Noah, dawdling by the desk and clutching his crotch.

'Noah,' James called softly and crouched down. 'Everything all right, mate? Come here.' He opened his arms, but the little boy stayed resolutely by the desk.

Alex and James gave each other a look. That was strange. Usually it was Noah who came running for cuddles while Jasper was the tough guy.

'I'm Miss Douglas, the boys' teacher.' An earnest young woman in her late twenties thrust her hand forward in Alex's direction. 'It's lovely to meet you, finally.'

She disentangled herself slightly from Jasper's embrace and shook the teacher's hand. *Finally*? It was only March, which meant the boys had been in the class for less than six weeks!

'I tend to meet most of the parents at the school gate in the afternoons,' she said, as if reading Alex's mind. 'Hello, James. Good to see you.'

'Hello, Giselle,' said James, rising off his haunches.

'Now, I think it might be best if I take the boys outside for a minute while Mrs Ryan has a quick word with you both. Jasper? Noah?' She held out her hand. 'Let's go and find some extra cleaning cloths.' The two boys meekly folded themselves into their teacher's floral skirt, and trailed out of the room. Only Jasper looked over his shoulder, at which point Alex noticed the bruise on the side of his face, and a number of buttons missing from his shirt. Noah didn't turn around once and, for the first time since entering the school gates, Alex felt real fear.

What the hell is going on?

She went to follow the twins but James reached out to gently hold her back.

'Please take a seat.' Mrs Ryan gestured to two small chairs.

Alex sat, and nearly swallowed her knees. With as much dignity as she could muster, she sat up taller to give off an air of confidence that she certainly wasn't feeling.

Mrs Ryan straightened the already neat folder in front of her. 'There was an … incident this morning, as you can probably tell.' With an expression of distaste, her eyes roved about the room.

Alex had been too focused on the boys to notice the classroom, but as she looked around, she took in the chaos. Chairs upended. Picture books tossed about. Rorschach-test paintings of butterflies half-ripped from the walls. A large jar of paint spattered over the wall and dripping onto the carpet.

What had happened to this place? Or, more precisely, *who* had happened to it?

'Jasper,' she said, more to herself than anyone else.

'Actually, no,' said Mrs Ryan. 'This is all Noah's handiwork.'

'Really?' Alex shook her head. 'That can't be.'

Not her precious, sensitive son, the twin who'd followed his brother into the world and had been following him ever since. Noah never did anything without his brother doing it first. When they were toddlers, she'd discovered the nursery smeared, wall to wall, in nappy-rash cream, with Jasper holding the pot. The same went for the time they discovered the Nutella and thought it was make-up just like Mummy wore. Then there was the period, as four year olds, where Jasper decided they were running away and ended up dragging Noah to the end of Cuthbert Close before Alex offered them a lollipop to come back home. Jasper was first back in the door, just as he'd been first to leave.

Noah didn't trash classrooms. Not unless Jasper did first.

Mrs Ryan cleared her throat. 'We have witnesses who saw them.'

'Who are these witnesses?' Alex leant forward.

'Miss Douglas, for one. And several of the other children, too. They all say that Noah was doing the damage and Jasper was the one trying to stop him. That's how he ended up with the black eye and the ripped shirt. His brother attacked him.'

Attacked him.

The words fizzed about the classroom.

'No, no, no. You've got it all wrong.' Alex raised her palms, the comments still buzzing in her head like a mosquito. 'This is ridiculous.'

'Annabelle, I think what my wife means is that this is very out of character for Noah,' said James. 'Of course, whichever one of the twins did this, it's extremely disappointing. But we could perhaps understand it more if Jasper were responsible.'

The principal clasped her hands. 'I know this is difficult to hear, but in this case, there is no doubt. Noah was responsible for this, and, to be frank, both Miss Douglas and myself think this behaviour has been building for a while.'

Alex felt disquiet mounting inside of her. These people didn't know her sons at all. They'd barely taught them anything. Noah still couldn't spell his own surname. How dare they tell her that her dear little son wasn't the boy she knew. Alex prepared to unleash the vitriol inside her, but felt James gently squeeze her hand.

'How so, Annabelle? Because I have to say that Alex and I really haven't noticed anything amiss.'

So damn reasonable. Alex wanted to scream.

'At first, we weren't sure.' For the first time in the meeting, Mrs Ryan looked awkward. 'A few weeks ago, another child reported an envelope with some money for a book order being taken from his bag. We found the money in Jasper's locker, but he denied it and we put it down as a mix-up. But then, there was another occasion where paint was poured into another child's desk drawer. Noah came to Miss Douglas and told her Jasper had done it, but again, nothing was conclusive.' Mrs Ryan paused and pulled out an artwork from her sheaf of papers. 'The children were asked to draw a picture of their families. This is Jasper's.'

She handed it over and Alex and James studied the picture. It was the four of them, standing in a circle with their arms linked, and the house in Cuthbert Close behind them. The likenesses were rather good. He'd given James his trademark curly hair, while Alex had a big smile and her favourite red dress, right down to its bright gold buttons. The house had its gabled roof and he hadn't missed the small crack that existed in the front window. *My family*, he'd scrawled in big letters across the top, and below, *I love my family because they make me feel safe and happy.*

Alex couldn't help but give a small smile. On the outside, Jasper was all rough and tumble, but inside existed a kind and loving little boy. She handed back the artwork to Mrs Ryan.

'It's lovely,' she remarked.

'Yes, and it's exactly what we would expect for a well-adjusted child of that age.' She paused. 'And here is Noah's.'

In silence, Mrs Ryan handed over another piece of paper. The drawing was mostly in blacks and browns. Noah had drawn himself at the top, with his parents beneath on either side in a triangle formation. In the picture, Alex held a phone to her ear, and her mouth was turned down in a frown. She squinted. In the lower right corner there was a tiny figure. Jasper, she supposed. There was no house. Just blank white space behind them. At the bottom, there was written scrawl, from which Alex could only make out the words *Mummy* and *lollies.*

Watching them, Mrs Ryan spoke. 'I think you'll find it says *I love my family because my mummy gives me lollies when she's on the phone.*'

'Really?' asked James, peering more closely.

'Years of correcting children's work,' said Mrs Ryan. 'Makes you very good at reading the illegible.'

Alex cleared her throat. 'So, he's a little behind in his writing. We can fix that, can't we? Hire a tutor?' She handed back the artwork.

'It's not so much the handwriting that worries us. It's the actual depiction of the family.'

Alex thought back to the words Noah had written. 'Anna-belle, I'm sure you understand that I work full-time, which means I am sometimes on the phone when the boys are around but I can assure you that I don't bribe them with lollies. You know how children tend to exaggerate.'

Mrs Ryan shook her head. 'That's not it either.' She paused. 'When Miss Douglas asked Noah to explain the picture, he said that the figure at the top was Jasper, and that he, Noah, was the little one at the bottom.' She waited. 'That's highly unusual. At this age, we expect a child to depict themselves as the major figure in their families, or at least one of the major figures. It's normal to see themselves as the centre of their own universe. If anything, they need it this way because it gives them confidence. Self-assurance.' She held up the artwork again and pointed to the small, sad figure at the bottom. 'Here, Noah's showing us that he feels small. Overshadowed by his brother.'

'But it's just a picture,' Alex protested. 'He probably didn't even think about it. He doesn't even like drawing. He probably just wanted to finish it quickly. Small figures, less time, after all.'

'Perhaps,' said Mrs Ryan. 'But in the context of the other behaviours, and certainly from what we saw today, I think Noah is trying to get our attention.'

'By framing Jasper as the naughty boy, and him as the good one,' James continued. 'Interesting.'

'Interesting?' Alex exploded. 'It's not interesting. It's rubbish.'

James put his hand over Alex's. 'I'm sorry, Annabelle. My wife's had a bit of an emotional twenty-four hours.'

Alex whipped her hand away. 'Don't patronise me,' she snapped. 'I might be pregnant, but I haven't lost my mind.'

The principal looked from James to Alex. 'Congratulations.' She said the word with a slight upwards inflection, as if it was almost a question.

Alex seethed. The outburst was a poor move on her part, but everyone was being so ridiculous. She couldn't help it. And now, that principal was sitting there in judgement of them. Her face said it all. The down-turned mouth. The doubt in her eyes. The expression that read, *You two can't even parent the children you have, and now you're having another one?*

James cleared his throat. 'It's, uh, early days, but our fingers are crossed that everything works out.'

'All right then,' said the principal, rearranging the papers in front of her. 'Given this ... happy news ... I think it essential we address Noah's issues before there's any further deterioration in his behaviour.' She clasped her hands and looked Alex directly in the eye. 'We think he could benefit from being put into a separate class from Jasper.'

'That's an interesting idea,' James mused.

Interesting. That word again. Alex suppressed a growl. David Attenborough documentaries were *interesting*, miso soup was *interesting*, the last conference she'd attended on corporate law was *interesting*. But this? This was challenging and confronting to everything Alex wanted for the twins. She wanted the boys to be best friends and soulmates. To have that special 'twin thing'. Not to be forcibly separated from each other.

'They need to stay together,' said Alex. 'They need each other. This is probably just a testosterone spurt from Noah, and I'm sure it will pass. Anyhow, I don't see how it could work – there's only one class.'

The principal hesitated. 'Noah and Jasper are quite young for the class. Turning six later this month, yes?' She pretended to consult her file. 'Given that, along with Noah's social immaturity, we think he might be better off going back and repeating kindergarten.' Seeing Alex about to interrupt, she held up a hand. 'Now, I know what you're going to say. That he won't have any friends, or the other children will make fun of him, or that it might further accentuate any feelings of inadequacy he may have in comparison to Jasper.' She paused. 'But in our experience, children at this age are very accepting. It's one of the joys of working with them. They haven't yet acquired prejudices in the same way as adults.' She smiled at Alex, who shifted uncomfortably and resisted the urge to take a paintbrush and swab a large slash of yellow paint right down the front of the principal's sensible black suit. Was she insinuating Alex was prejudiced? The cheek! The only people she didn't tolerate were cyclists, charity-muggers, and people who tried to ruin her children's lives. No wonder Noah had attacked the classroom like it was his own Pro Hart project. The principal clearly had no idea what she was talking about. She was probably a cyclist, like Martin.

Alex crossed her legs and tried to restrain her fury. 'Let's say you're right. Let's say it works for the first year or two. But as we know, school goes for thirteen years. What about when Jasper leaves school and Noah's still a year behind? It would devastate him.'

Mrs Ryan shrugged. 'It's what happens with most siblings. They all finish school at different times.'

'But they're not just siblings, they're *twins*,' said Alex.

'Not identical, though. The way I see it, they're brothers who happened to be born at the same time and we need to acknowledge them as separate little boys who are very different to each other and have vastly different needs. We're trying to do what's best for them, as individuals.'

And Alex wasn't? She went to collect her handbag. There was no point to being in this room any longer. She had better things to do than argue with people whose sole intention seemed to be to misunderstand her children. 'Thank you for your suggestions, but I think we're done here.'

James cleared his throat. 'Thank you, Annabelle, for taking the time to meet with us.'

Alex glared, but James continued. 'You've given us a lot to think about. Can we get back to you next week about what we think is the best course of action?'

Bloody James. She wanted to kick him in the shins. Make him angry, like she was. Their children were under attack, for heaven's sake!

'Would you like to say goodbye to the boys? I'll find Miss Douglas and send them in.' The principal rose and Alex waited until she was out of the room before turning to her husband.

'Don't tell me you agree with all of this?' Alex hissed.

James studied her. 'You know how you hate those climate-change deniers.'

Climate-change deniers, yes. She did have one more prejudice. People who couldn't accept the science of climate change. Ignorant fools, in her view. The evidence was clear. 'What has climate change got to do with Noah and Jasper?'

'The way I see it,' said James. 'Mrs Ryan has presented us with the evidence. We can see for ourselves what's happened.' His eyes wandered over the dishevelled classroom.

'And we – or at least I – have seen similar things happening at home.'

'What's that supposed to mean? That I'm not around often enough to know my own two sons?'

'No, that's not what I mean.' James shook his head. 'You work so hard, at your job, at being a mum, and you're so caught up in the everyday stuff that it's impossible to see a bigger picture.'

'So now I can't see straight?' Alex felt a sting, like little bitey ants, nibbling at the corners of her eyes. It was bad enough for the principal to cast aspersions over her parenting, but not James, the one person she thought always had her back.

'You're deliberately misunderstanding me,' he said. 'This actually isn't about you at all.' Excellent. So now she was self-obsessed as well. James went to take her hand but Alex snatched it away. Childish, she knew. But the last thing she wanted was for him to touch her.

He sighed. 'You see everything through a lens of guilt. Even though you have nothing, nothing at all to feel guilty about. You're amazing. But our boys need help. And we can either argue about it while things get worse, or we can *do* something, however uncomfortable it makes us feel to admit there's a problem.'

Before she had a chance to respond, the door opened again and through it came two very subdued little boys, followed by Mrs Ryan and Miss Douglas.

Jasper went meekly to James, while Noah sidled up to Alex and took her hand.

'Mummy, now that you're here, could you stay for tuckshop?' He looked up at her with wide, hopeful eyes.

'I'm sorry darling, but I have to go back to work. I've already missed rather a lot today.' She knelt down and pulled him close.

He whispered into her ear. 'I'm sorry I was naughty, but I'm happy you came to see me. Do you like our classroom?'

Alex made a show of looking around. 'I'm not sure about the paintwork.' She winked. 'But yes, I like it very much. Do you?'

'I like it when I'm naughty because then I get to speak and everyone listens, even Jasper. And today I was so naughty that now you're here.' He grinned. 'And you never come to school.'

Alex leant back and fought the urge to admonish him. Her sensitive, complex little boy. Every fibre of her being wanted to scold him, tell him that breaking the rules was never acceptable, that if he continued to do it the school would separate him from his brother. Instead, she kissed him on the cheek.

'Yes, my darling. Here I am.'

CHAPTER ELEVEN

Cara squinted out the windscreen at the neat row of brand-new blond-brick townhouses, stacked along the street like a line of morning-coffee biscuits. The one in front of them appeared to have two pairs of shoes lined up neatly at the front door. This had to be it. Her parents' new home.

'C'mon, Mummy. What are you waiting for?' Poppy's voice was in her ear and Cara's fingers went to the keys in the ignition.

'Oh hey, I haven't switched the engine off yet. You should still be in your seat. It's dangerous.' Cara put the car into park. 'Please don't do that again,' she said sharply, then immediately felt guilty. It wasn't her daughter's fault that Cara's stomach was a ball of nerves. She hated asking anyone for help, and what she was about to ask of her parents went well beyond asking them to babysit or give her daughter piano lessons.

'Sorry, Mummy, I'm just so excited. I can't wait to see Halmi's new house,' said Poppy.

'Okay, could you pass me the gwapyeon.' The Korean fruit jellies were her father's favourites and Cara enjoyed making them for the way they made the cottage smell like a strawberry patch at the height of summer.

'Here you go.' Poppy handed over the tray, which had been sitting on the back seat next to her, then bounced up and down. After forty-five minutes in the car, she was like an over-excited puppy with the zoomies. 'She says there's a pool nearby.' Poppy craned her neck. 'But I don't see it.'

Walking up the front path, Cara balanced the tray in one hand and gripped her daughter's fingers with the other. Poppy kept up her chatter.

'Halmi says there's a room just for the piano and another one where you and I can stay, but only if I promise not to take any textas into the bedroom because she wants the walls to stay perfectly white.'

At the door, Cara stopped and fought the urge to scurry back to the car. It was silly to react so strongly against a place she hadn't even seen yet. This was not her home, it was theirs. There would be no new school for her, no nearly wetting her pants because she couldn't find the toilets, no sitting by herself at recess and lunch for weeks on end, no having to explain which country she was *really* from, no having to defend her *smelly* food.

'Why does Halmi move house all the time?' Poppy looked up at her, wobbling on one foot as she attempted to remove her shoes.

'Because she likes new things, I guess.' *And she always thinks there's something better out there.*

'I wish we could move house.'

'No you don't.'

'Why?'

'Because you'd have to leave your school and all your friends. All the people in the street. Aunty Beth, Aunty Alex, and all the kids.'

'We could make new friends.'

'It's not the same.' She leant down to eye level. 'By the time I was your age, I'd been to three different schools.'

Poppy's eyes widened.

'One time, I wet my pants because I didn't know where the toilets were.' Cara took her daughter's chin in her hands. 'Believe me, it's not fun.'

The door swung open.

'Halbi!' Poppy flew into her grandfather's arms.

'My wild Poppy.' Cara's father hugged the little girl tightly, his eyes seeking out hers. *Is this right?*

Cara nodded imperceptibly. Her father had never hugged her like that as a child but he was nothing if not conscientious and, over time, he'd come to understand, even embrace, the Australian fondness for physical affection.

Cara stepped into the cream-coloured hallway. The walls were bare, except for a crucifix at the end of the hall, and a framed certificate hung near the front door. Cara cringed. A bachelor's degree in accounting was hardly deserving of front door status, yet it had taken pride of place in each of the six homes her parents had lived in since she graduated.

'Oh, Appa, really?' She gestured to the gilt-edged certificate.

'Talk to your mother,' he muttered in Korean.

'What did you say?' demanded Poppy.

'Nothing, little girl. Are you still doing your Korean classes?'

Poppy wriggled out of his arms. 'I can count to ten *and* do all the days of the week.' She smiled proudly.

'I am impressed.' He pinched her nose. 'Soon you will speak better than me.'

'She certainly knows things that I don't,' Cara volunteered, with a mix of pride and guilt. At Poppy's age, she'd been so determined to erase all Korean from her vocabulary that she pretended she couldn't hear her parents when they spoke in their first language. Now, here she was, sending Poppy off to Korean classes for three hours every Saturday. The irony wasn't lost on her, but fortunately it was on her parents. For them, there was nothing ironic about education.

'Would you like to take a tour of our new home?' Cara's father stood aside and gestured with an open palm down the short hallway. 'The kitchen is this way.'

In a second, Poppy was gone, heels flying, while Cara ambled, trailing her finger along the pristine walls. She rapped lightly with her knuckle and the reply was hollow.

At the end of the hall, she paused. 'Appa, should we make a bet? I'll take two years and three months.'

Every time her mother and father moved to a new home, Cara made a bet with her father about how long Joy would last before getting itchy feet again. Her father always pre-dicted at least five years, while Cara never forecast much more than two, though this place certainly was nicer than some of the others they'd rented. Cara always won, though it was money she didn't enjoy pocketing.

'Certainly, daughter.' He folded his arms and looked to the ceiling. 'Twenty years.'

Cara gasped. 'You may as well give me your money now.' She took his outstretched hand, his skin warm and papery, and shook it.

'Why are you standing like strangers around the front door?' Joy had Poppy's hand in her grasp, and used her free one to shake a finger at Cara and her father.

'Sorry, Ma.' Cara pressed the plate of foil-covered gwapy-eon into her hands.

Her father went to take one but Joy tapped his hand. 'Later, old man. You want to get diabetes?'

'I think the sugar has already gone to his head. He says you will live in this house for twenty years,' Cara exclaimed, expecting her mother to immediately pooh-pooh the idea and dismiss it as being a fate worse than death.

But Joy grew still and looked at the ground. If Cara didn't know any better, she would have said her mother was almost *reluctant* to speak.

'Your mother has had a change of heart,' said Appa triumphantly. 'This is our forever home.'

Joy shuffled her feet and Cara looked back to her father. 'What do you mean?'

Her parents were obsessed with property shows – derelict homes being overhauled in a week, and befuddled English couples buying crumbling French chateaus. Appa must have learnt the phrase *forever home* from one of them.

'This is our castle. Our home. We bought it.' Her father swivelled about the hallway with a flourish. 'They will carry me out of here in a box.'

'Sung-soo,' said her mother. She didn't often use his Korean name, but a joke about death was not to be tolerated.

'Sorry, sorry.' Her father bowed his head, then raised it and smiled. 'But I am a happy man. Now, I can retire.'

'Oh, really? You're giving up the business as well?' This was all too much. Buying houses? Quitting their jobs? Who were these two people standing in front of her? 'Umma?' said Cara.

'Oh, you are such a fool, old man.' Joy shot her husband a withering look. 'Your father said he would get a divorce if we did not settle in one place, and I did not want to lose my place in choir at church, so I said yes. We will retire in five years. Not before.'

Cara swallowed heavily. 'Congratulations,' she croaked, overcome with confusion about how she should feel. Happy that they had decided to settle? Miffed that they had not thought to consult with her? Angry that they had not done this thirty years ago and given her the stability that every child deserved?

Her father stood at another door in the hallway. 'There is something to show you.' He paused, before opening it grandly. 'It's for you and Poppy.'

'Whoa, Halbi. This is for us?' Poppy breathed and stepped into the room.

'So you can come and stay whenever you like.' Sam stood aside to let Cara through. The room contained two single beds, one of them covered with a pink love heart–emblazoned doona, the other with a pale blue chambray-style bed cover. Between the beds was a whitewashed bedside table and lamp, and above it was a pink framed inspirational quote. *Without change, there would be no butterflies.*

In the corner was a small bookcase, stocked with what Cara could see were some of Poppy's favourites, and a couple of recipe books, presumably for her.

'Look, Mum, it's your wedding day.' Her daughter picked up a small picture frame from the bookcase and handed it over. Cara studied the photo. Her head thrown back in laughter as the breeze caught her veil, the golden light of the setting sun catching Pete's face as he grinned adoringly at his new wife.

The photo was half the size of her university degree, Cara noted with a smile. Still, lucky it was there at all, given Joy's angst over the day. Marrying in a garden? With only fifty guests! People from church would think they were poor. That they didn't care. But Cara was firm. This was what she and Pete wanted. A cookie-cutter wedding hall with 400 guests wasn't for her, though Pete would have gone along with it had she insisted. He would have done anything to make her happy. Her father understood this and quietly played peacemaker. Pete was a good man. He would take care of Cara. So what if he was Australian? So too was their daughter.

Cara placed the frame back on the bookcase.

'I love this room!' squealed Poppy, leaping onto the bed and hugging the heart-shaped cushion on the pillow. 'Can we stay tonight? Please, Mum? Please?'

'Oh, sweetheart, we didn't bring your pyjamas,' said Cara.

Her father coughed. 'I might have bought you some pyjamas when I was at Kmart getting the other things.'

Poppy dived under the pillow. 'He did!' She held up a star-spangled pyjama set. 'Look, Halmi,' she squealed as Joy went over to the bed to inspect.

'There are some for you too,' her father whispered. 'No stars.'

Cara nodded and coughed to clear the lump in her throat. It was so sweet of them, well, of her father at least, to try to make them feel so welcome in this new home of theirs.

She blinked, but as she went to deliver the thank yous, there was a knock at the front door.

'I will answer. Don't you go.' Her mother leapt off the bed and scurried out of the room.

'Are you expecting someone?' said Cara.

Her father shrugged. 'Your mother is always up to something.'

There were voices in the hallway – her mother's and a man's.

'Sam, Sam,' she called. 'David is here.'

Who's David? Cara mouthed to her father.

He shrugged again and left the room. Cara followed.

In the hall standing with her mother was a short, dark-headed man, dressed in a full business suit and tie. A briefcase in one hand, and a basket of fruit in the other.

'Sam, you remember David from church.' Joy was bright-eyed. Her movements animated.

'Hello, Mr Kim.' David from church bowed deeply

'Call me Sam.' Her father shook David's hand.

'And this is our daughter, Cara, the one who I was telling you about. She has the accounting degree. Same as you.' Her mother smiled sweetly, though Cara could tell her teeth were clenched.

'I'm actually a food stylist.'

'Oh, that sounds interesting.' David cocked his head. 'Korean food?'

'All types. There's not really enough work to be so specialised.'

'I eat mostly Korean food.' David seemed disappointed, but then brightened as he spotted the gwapyeon on the hall table. 'Your mother is a great cook. She brings sweets to practice all the time.'

'Oh, please. Have some.' Joy picked up the tray and put it under David's nose.

Cara shot her mother a look. So *that's* where all the sweets were going. Lately, Joy had been asking Cara to make them more often, and she assumed it was for her sweet-toothed father, not to feed the slightly chubby young man before her. Personally, Cara didn't much like the strange texture, which was like chewy jelly.

David popped one into his mouth and chewed loudly. 'So good,' he said with a full mouth.

Had Joy mentioned this guy? Possibly, though she tended to tune out when her mother started talking about choir practice.

Gwapyeon. That's how she would remember him. Chewy jelly.

'Who are you?' Poppy had silently sidled up behind her mother and she pushed her sturdy little body into Cara's.

'Little girl. Respect your elders,' said Joy sternly. 'This is Mr Kok.'

Her daughter giggled.

'Poppy, manners,' said Cara, adopting her mother's firm tone.

Poppy pursed her lips. 'Hello, Mr Kok.'

David's nose twitched. He looked at Cara with a slight frown. 'You have a daughter?'

'Surely my mother told you all about her.' *She told him about the accounting degree but failed to mention Poppy? Her only grandchild?*

'Of course I did,' her mother cried and tapped David on the arm. 'You just forgot ... So much happening at choir, you know, always so noisy ...' Joy trailed off. 'Let's eat,' she said brightly into the awkward silence, and beetled off down the hall without waiting for an answer.

The kitchen was small, open-plan and immaculately clean. Beyond it was a dining space, just large enough to accommodate her parents' six-seater round table. The food was already laid out. How many people was Joy expecting? Their weekly family dinners were usually modest affairs – rice, a bowl of kimchi, a soup and one or two side dishes, the *banchan,* to add flavour. Tonight, Cara counted at least eight bowls on the table, including a spectacular whole roasted fish. Her mouth watered.

'Looks delicious, Ma. And what a lovely kitchen.' She waited for her parents to sit before taking a place next to her father, with Poppy on her other side. David sat by her mother.

From this spot, Cara could see out over the cosy living space, dominated by her parents' leather lounge. Through the sliding doors was a small patch of lawn. No trees or plants. Just grass.

They would be happy here. It was modern and low maintenance. Everything Cara never wanted. She took a sip of water.

'How much did you pay for this place?' David's eyes darted about the room.

Cara nearly spat out her water.

'Seven hundred and forty-nine thousand,' said her mother proudly.

David nodded grudgingly. 'Good price. You got finance?'

'No need,' said her father gently.

Oh, gosh. No debt? Every last dollar of her parents' savings must have gone into this place. Her heart sank. She could never ask them to help her with Cuthbert Close. Not only was the cottage nearly twice the price and in need of one hundred times the work, there was simply no possibility of them having any money left to help her buy it. No way was she going to force her parents into debt when it was clearly something they'd tried desperately to avoid.

Cara busied herself, serving food onto Poppy's plate, then her own. To swallow her disappointment, she took a bite of the roasted fish.

'Oh, Ma. It's delicious.'

'I think it's too salty. David – what do you think. Too salty, right?'

The guest chewed thoughtfully. 'It is a little salty,' he conceded. 'My mother uses low-salt soy sauce. I think I am used to this.'

'I will ask for her recipe.' As she spoke, Joy kept her eyes downcast on the plate. When Sam lightly touched her hand, she flinched, as if zapped by an electric shock.

'It's extremely tasty.' He covered her hand with his own.

Cara cleared her throat. 'So, what type of accounting do you do, David?'

'Actually I'm more of an executive financial planner these days. Helping rich guys get richer.' He laughed.

'They must appreciate you so much,' said Joy.

'How do you do it? Make the money for them?' Cara leant forward.

'When you have money, it's not hard to make money.'

'But what if you don't have so much money?' Cara persisted.

'Why? You need money? Maybe I could find a job for you.'

Joy held her spoon in mid-air. 'That would be wonderful. You are so thoughtful, David. Her house needs so much work.'

'The big fish are fun, but sometimes it's nice to help the small fry too.'

Cara dropped her spoon. The man was insufferable. 'Thank you, David.' She fought to control her voice. 'But I've actually just started a new business, so I really don't think I'd have the time.'

'A new business? What kind?' Her father cocked his head, his eyes gently enquiring.

'Yes, sorry. I meant to tell you but it's all happened in a bit of a hurry …' She stammered at first, but felt a flicker of confidence building with each word she spoke. 'It's a catering business, for time-poor mums. I'm going to cook and deliver meals to them, for their families. Healthy and delicious. Save them, you know … having to do it themselves.'

Joy shook her head. 'Ah, these women, too busy to cook. Too busy to clean.'

Cara sucked in a breath, refraining from pointing out that despite the lavish spread in front of them, Joy hated cooking and had also employed a fortnightly cleaner, a friend from church, for at least a decade. If it was good enough for her, surely it was good enough for others?

'Sounds like hard work,' said David. 'Financial planning is much easier. Maybe you should take over your parents' business. Let them retire.' He leant back and tugged at his belt.

Joy raised her eyebrows in agreement but kept eating.

'Our daughter is too talented for embroidery,' said her father. 'What is the name of this business?'

'It's uh ... um.' She looked desperately at the plates of healthful, delicious food before her. 'It's called *Nourish*.'

'*Nourish*?' Her mother frowned. 'What is this word?'

'You might want to rethink that name,' said David. 'There's no point if people don't understand it.'

'It means to give life. To give someone good food to make them healthy,' Sam explained.

Cara felt a flush rising in her cheeks. Had she really committed herself to starting a new business and lied to her parents, just to spite the odious man sitting before her? She rose from her seat. 'Just need the bathroom,' she mumbled.

'First door on the left,' her mother called after her.

In the bathroom, she leant over the basin, and rested her head on the cool ceramic.

Her pocket vibrated and she fished out her phone.

A text message from Alex.

Hey Beth and Cara, feel like a drink at The Snowden tonight? Need to debrief with you about so much stuff. Got loads of leads on the cooking idea too. Say 8:30 pm? After the kids are in bed? Xx

It was a sign, and Cara believed in signs.

Oh, yes. Wonderful. See you there.

Quickly, she splashed water on her face, wiped her hands on the towel and went back to break the news to her parents that she would be leaving early.

CHAPTER TWELVE

Alex looked longingly at the drinks on the table – Beth's tangerine-hued peach Bellini and Cara's chilled chenin blanc, like liquid, silky gold, levitating in the oversized balloon glass. Even the condensation looked delicious and Alex had a sudden urge to lick the glass.

Instead, she reached for her lemon, lime and bitters. Perhaps if she just *pretended* it was alcoholic …

'Mmmmm … delicious,' she said, wincing at the sweetness.

The pub was a terrible idea. Awful. Whose stupid idea was it?

Oh, right. Hers.

After the horrific meeting with Principal Ryan, she'd thought a quiet debrief over a sauvignon blanc was exactly what she needed. Preferably, in a venue far, far away from her too-reasonable husband and two less-than-reasonable sons.

It was only once she sent the text to Beth and Cara that Alex remembered something. The baby. No drinking. Not even one. An officious pamphlet from Dr Vin's had informed her (with some glee, it seemed) that as little as one drink could affect her unborn child. What happened to one or two being quite acceptable? In the six years since Alex was last pregnant, it seemed the medical fraternity had gone and made a difficult nine months into a torturous one. Soon, pregnant women would be allowed nothing but air and vitamins. For a pregnant lady, organising a catch-up at the pub was as sensible as a gambling addict hosting a bingo night.

'This is such fun! Great idea, Alex. We should do this more.' Beth enthusiastically drained the last of her cocktail. 'Ah.' She exhaled. 'I think I'll have another. No one relying on me to be home in a hurry, after all.' Her laugh was high-pitched and brittle above the growing buzz of the bar.

The Snowden was getting busy. And everyone was so thin and glamorous and young. It wasn't the dim and dingy place Alex remembered from her last visit, but that was some time BC – before children. Now, it was like drinking in an IKEA catalogue. All blond wood, clean lines and happy, smiling Viking-type people.

'Oh, good point.' Cara gulped her wine. 'I might have another too. Poppy's with my parents for the night,' she explained.

Alex looked from Cara to Beth. Usually, they barely drank anything at all. Were they rubbing it in? 'We're here for a business meeting, not to get plastered,' she grumbled. 'Has something happened? What's going on with you two?'

'Nothing,' mumbled Cara.

'Everything's great!' Beth studiously avoided Alex's gaze.

Never mind. Whatever was bugging them, she would find out eventually.

'All right then, let's discuss this catering business idea that I need to talk you into doing, both for my sake and the sake of all culinarily challenged sisters, everywhere.' She held up her phone. 'This thing is bursting with emails from women like me who can't stand cooking, don't have time for it because they're working their arses off, and yet feel ridiculously guilty for serving up frozen lasagne every week because it tastes like cardboard and is making their kids fat ... well, that, and devices ... but don't get me started on screen-guilt. It's a whole other therapy session.' She took a breath.

'I'm in,' said Cara 'I'm going to do it.'

'Me too,' said Beth. 'If you'll have me.' She raised her eyebrows at Cara.

'Oh, of course!' Cara clasped Beth's arm. 'What do you think of the name Nourish for the business? I just thought of it while I was at Mum and Dad's.'

'It's wonderful!' exclaimed Beth. 'Nourish sums it up brilliantly. Healthy, comforting food for the whole family. Perfect.'

Alex sat back and watched her two neighbours talk animatedly about recipe ideas, the equipment they might need and how to go about getting the necessary food preparation licence for their kitchens. Her eyes narrowed. Before, they'd been so unsure about the idea. So uncertain. Now, they were talking like it was going to be bigger than McDonald's.

'Because I sometimes use the shed for shoots, I've actually already got it set up as a licensed food premises,' said Cara.

Beth clapped her hands. 'Excellent! I've got a deep freezer in the garage for storage, and I'll get a permit for my kitchen as well.'

'Include mine too,' Alex joined in. 'Someone may as well get use out of the double ovens.'

Cara and Beth looked at her and blinked, like they'd forgotten she was there. The meeting was her idea! And while she'd done it on the pretext of discussing the business, what she really needed was their input on the twins and what to do about them. Cara and Beth were two of the most devoted mothers she knew. They would understand the gravity of what Annabelle Ryan was suggesting. They would be shocked, appalled and no doubt sympathetic.

'Sorry, I know you're excited about this, but I need to tell you about my terrible day,' Alex announced.

Beth sat up straight. 'Is it the twins? The baby?'

'The baby's fine.' Alex began. 'Well, apart from the timing... but it's the twins' principal. We met with her today, and she seems to have Noah pegged as a psychopath in training.' She paused. 'She thinks he should go back and repeat kindy.'

'Oh,' said Beth. 'That is bad.' She paused. 'But it's not the *worst* thing in the world. They'll still be at the same school. It's not like they'll never see each other again. It's not like they're ... *breaking up*.' She choked a little over the words.

Alex glared. 'Actually, it is a very big deal.' She stabbed at the ice in the bottom of her stupid soft drink. 'Noah and Jasper *need* each other.' Stab, stab. 'I've always felt that God or Allah or Buddha or whoever it is up there gave me twins because they knew I'd be a bit shit at being a mum.'

Cara frowned. 'I don't understand. Having twins is hard. You do an amazing job, with your career and everything.'

'Have two kids of *different* ages is hard, let alone two at once. I don't know how you managed in the early days of the twins. The logistics of it all ...' said Beth in wonder.

'Well, yes, it was a bit tricky at first, but the thing I kept telling myself was that it was okay to be a bit shit at it because the boys had each other, so that's why I dressed them the same, put them in bunks, the same preschool, all of that ... I wanted them to be close. I needed them to be close. To look after each other, when I couldn't.' She stopped. 'And now they won't be, and there'll be a baby, and I'll have even less time for them.' The force of her final stab at the ice caused the straw to buckle in the middle.

'Oh, honey.' Beth put her hand on Alex's forearm. 'Don't be so hard on yourself. They'll still be at the same school. They'll have each other. It's really not that bad ... Not like ...' She took a breath, her brow furrowed. 'Max has been sending strange text messages to someone I don't know. A woman I think.'

Alex and Cara exchanged glances.

'What?' said Alex. 'What are you talking about?'

Beth fished out her phone. 'Here,' she said, handing it over. 'I took a photo, just in case.'

Alex leant over Cara's shoulder to read the messages. 'How did you find them? Were you snooping?'

'They just popped up on the iPad.' Beth threw her hands up. 'I don't know what to make of it all.'

Alex reread them. Time, place ... *how big are you?*

She'd seen enough family law disputes go through Macauley to know a philandering husband when she saw one. But Max Chandler? Sure, the guy had that easy charm about him that most real estate agents did, but she didn't pick up a flirtatious vibe. If anything, he'd been a bit less friendly lately. A little more withdrawn. 'It doesn't look good.' She handed back the phone. 'Did you ask him about it?'

'We haven't exactly been seeing eye to eye lately. I didn't want to make things worse. Like you say, it's not really conclusive, is it? It might just be a new friend—'

Ding-dong. Ding-dong. Alex blinked to get rid of the alarm bells in her head. Poor, sweet Beth. Men were such shits. Noah and Jasper wouldn't do this to a woman, would they? If they did they'd probably blame her … *Our mother was always on the phone. She gave us lollies to be quiet, and then, in Year One, she separated us AND had another baby! Of course we were destined to cheat on sweet, unsuspecting women.*

Alex shook her head. 'Hey, Pope, you're awfully quiet over there.'

'Oh, I was just thinking how bad news always comes in threes.' She let out a small sigh.

'Don't tell me your life's gone to shit as well?'

Cara regarded them both. 'My parents can't help me with the cottage. They've bought a place of their own, with a room for Poppy and me.'

'For you to live?' enquired Beth.

'I think so. And they want me to marry a financial planner.'

'Not the worst idea,' said Alex. 'Given your situation.'

Cara shot her a look, and Alex flinched. If she had to compare her neighbour to a foodstuff, as Cara herself had told them she often did, she would describe her as a chocolate-covered hazelnut – soft and sweet on the outside, but with true grit at the centre that you didn't quite know about until you bit into it and nearly broke a tooth.

'I can't live with my parents.' She shuddered. 'And I don't want to marry anyone, especially not the financial planner.'

'Not anyone, ever?' said Beth, wide-eyed. 'But you're still so young, and … gorgeous. You deserve happiness with someone.'

'Yes, because marriage can be *such* bliss,' said Alex.

'It doesn't have to be marriage,' said Beth. 'But to close yourself off to love … that's sad. Especially when there are lovely men out there, like that one, near the bar, who's been watching you all night.' She nodded in the direction of the bar and Alex craned for a better look. Blonde. Checked shirt. Heavy suede boots.

'Shit, he's hot, Cara. You should definitely go for it.'

The Viking winked and Alex gave a low wolf whistle.

'Please, stop,' whispered Cara vehemently, staring into her lap.

'What? Just because I'm married doesn't mean I can't look, and you're not married, so you can look. Actually, you can do more than look.'

'I don't want to,' said Cara.

'Please explain?' said Alex.

Cara paused and placed two protective hands at the stem of her wineglass. 'You'll think I'm silly,' she said in a low voice.

'Yesterday, I held a funeral for a guinea pig. I will not judge you.' Alex pressed a hand to her heart.

'I think I have bad luck.' Cara lowered her eyes. 'Like, a curse.'

'Okay, sorry – I can't not judge that, because that *is* utterly ridiculous,' said Alex.

'Why do you feel that way, Cara?' said Beth. 'Is it Pete?'

Cara nodded. 'My parents liked him. Well, my dad liked him, and my mum put up with him. She wanted us to marry in a church, and … as you know, we did not.'

'Your wedding was beautiful!' Beth protested. 'You should have seen her on the day.' She nudged Alex. 'She was glorious … And Pete, so handsome.'

'I've seen a photo. Total spunk.' Alex nodded.

Cara gave them a weak, appreciative smile and continued. 'When Pete got sick, Mum prayed for hours every day, for forgiveness … and a miracle … but …' She flexed her hands. 'There was nothing to be done,' she finished flatly.

'Forgiveness? Your mum thinks Pete died because you did something to offend God?' asked Alex.

'In Korea, it is considered unnatural for the offspring to die before the parent.'

'Well, it *is* awful. No one should bury their own child …' murmured Beth.

'But you mean it's more like a curse?' said Alex.

'Yes.'

'You know that's not only really silly, it's also quite damaging.'

Cara shrugged. 'She is my mother.'

Alex's muscles tensed. Mothers really knew how to fuck up their kids, even if they didn't want to. Ugh. Everything was shit. Her back was sore, her toes were being pinched by her heels. Cara's and Beth's personal lives were down the toilet. And she was in a pub, pregnant.

'Do you think anyone would notice if I took off my shoes for a minute?' Without waiting for answer, she went to bend, but found her bottom being shoved firmly in the opposite direction. She clutched the bar table to save herself from falling.

'What the—'

The woman behind Alex, the one she'd presumably bumped with her own bottom, turned on her heel. 'You made me spill my drink,' she said crossly.

She was angry? She'd nearly made a pregnant lady fall over! Alex righted herself to eye level and stopped. Her insides shifted. 'Charlie?'

Of course it had to be her neighbour. Looking amazing, as usual, in a sleek white sleeveless jumpsuit. Those arms! So sculpted they'd make Michelangelo weep.

'Alex,' Charlie said coolly, starting to dab gently at the small wet patch down her front. 'Wherever she goes, chaos follows,' she muttered, so quietly Alex wondered if she heard it at all.

'Was that me? Gosh, er, sorry Charlie. Let me get that for you.' Alex took a serviette from the bar table and started to dab. What was it about this woman that made her feel like a bumbling, apologising idiot? Was it the chic, all-white clothing? Or the sparkling diamond earrings? No, it was more than just her appearance. It was the general air of perfection she gave off. The sense that she had all her shit, not just her clothing, well and truly together. Unlike Alex. Was that remark about chaos a reference to the guinea pig incident, or the street party? Alex bristled. Neither was entirely her fault.

'I've got a wet wipe here somewhere,' volunteered Beth, searching her handbag.

'I could get some soda water from the bar,' offered Cara.

'No, don't.' Charlie held up a hand. 'All of you, stop. It's fine. It was only mineral water.'

'At least let us buy you another drink,' said Beth.

'No need, my friend is at the bar.' She tilted her head in the direction of a very tall, very good-looking man at the bar, who seemed to sense they were talking about him, and turned around to wave.

'He's looking at investing in the business,' said Charlie, as if reading Alex's mind. 'This is a business meeting.'

'Riiiiiight,' said Alex. 'We're having a business meeting, too.'

'Really? I thought it might be a neighbourhood watch get-together,' she said with a smirk.

'Oh, no, we don't have that,' said Beth. 'I mean, we used to, back in the nineties, but—'

'Beth, she was joking,' said Alex. 'Actually, Charlie, you might be able to help us. Cara here is setting up a business that's all about health and nutrition. Beth's going to help her.'

'Shakes or supplements?' Charlie's eyes narrowed.

'Oh, no,' said Cara in a deferential tone, as if shakes and supplements would be far too challenging. 'We're actually doing real food. Wholesome dinners for time-poor mums.'

'So, home-cooked food, and that's it?' said Charlie. 'How very … retro of you.'

Not quite as retro as eating like cavemen, thought Alex.

'Oh, yes, I suppose it is when you think of it,' said Cara, who loved anything vintage and accepted the comment as a compliment, rather than a veiled insult. 'Anyway, it's a very different space to yours, but we'd love to replicate the success of your online marketing presence. Any tips?'

Charlie fixed her gaze. 'You want my honest advice? Make sure you know who you're working with because a business will change and test that relationship in ways you never expected.' She paused. 'You have to fight for it.'

There was a beat of silence.

'Oh, okay. Thanks for that,' said Cara.

'Ladies, I'm sorry, I didn't know Charlie had friends here. Let me go back to the bar for you …' It was the 'investor', holding a beer in one hand and a champagne in the other.

Business meeting, sure.

'There's a free table over there. Shall we?' said Charlie to her investor.

'Bye, Charlie. And sorry again about the drink.' Alex stopped herself. Why did she keep apologising to this inscrutable woman? Always so cool and collected. The kind of woman who didn't take 'no' for an answer. A woman whose all-white clothing seemed to repel catastrophe, and stains. She would never let a primary school principal walk all over her. Her child wouldn't be allowed to fall behind. Charlie Devine was an achiever. She'd do something. Act. Put on her white Lycra and diamond earrings and summon her inner primitive force, or whatever it was that The Primal Guy crapped on about.

Alex collected her bag. 'Sorry, ladies, but I need to call it a night.'

'So soon? I was just about to buy more drinks. This is fun!' said Beth, looking about the bar like a prisoner recently released from jail.

'Maybe one more for me.' Cara pressed her cheeks. 'I'm not too red, am I?'

Alex kissed her lightly on the cheek. 'You have a rosy glow, like you've just had the most wonderful fuck with that hot guy over there.'

'Alex!'

She took in Beth and Cara's appalled faces and grinned. So what if she didn't have rock-hard abs or buns of steel?

She had spunk and fight and attitude. Perhaps she'd come to the bar for pity from Beth and Cara, but she was leaving with resolve, thanks to Charlie. The woman had annoyed her into action.

'Bye, ladies. Don't do anything I wouldn't do.' Chin up, Alex went to stride away but spotted Charlie and her supposed investor, heads bowed together closely.

Alex tapped her on the shoulder. 'Night, Charlie. And thanks for all your help …'

'All what help?' The woman looked confused but Alex was already halfway to the exit, head held high.

You're not the only one who can be inscrutable.

Near the door, she paused and looked back over her shoulder to enjoy Charlie's confusion one more time.

Yes. Got you!

Alex turned quickly, triumphantly.

And, bang, walked straight into the door.

CHAPTER THIRTEEN

The GOAT Club was not named after a noisy and destructive animal, as Beth learnt from Cara on the way inside, but in fact stood for Greatest of All Time. Very promising, and it was also conveniently located right next to The Snowden.

'Isn't this fun!' cried Beth, discarding her jacket as she wove her way through the crowd towards the dance floor.

'I hope Alex's nose is okay,' Cara shouted over the din. 'I really think we should be getting home.'

'Just half an hour, okay?' Beth yelled back, holding up her phone. 'Alex has messaged me and she's fine. A little bruised, but the blood's stopped.'

Her neighbour had looked rather forlorn, getting into the Uber with oodles of tissues stuck up her nose. Normally, Beth would have jumped into the car right beside her. Told her to keep pinching her nose and tilt her head forward, not back, so the blood didn't run down her throat.

But Beth didn't want to go home and play nurse.

She wanted to dance – in a real, proper nightclub with flashing lights and booming music.

'Dance as if no one is watching,' shouted Beth to Cara, standing at the edge of the dance floor and holding her handbag like a safety harness.

'Nobody *is* watching.'

Beth looked around. The dance floor was heaving. Gyrating sweaty bodies flung themselves about with incredible energy and no one was paying the slightest attention to the middle-aged woman about to dive in.

Cara checked her watch again. 'I'm going to the toilet, and when I get back I really think we should leave. Okay?'

'All right.' Beth waved and slipped into the mass of bodies moving about her. The music infused her arms and legs until she was dancing as energetically as everyone else. Joy surged through her veins.

Max didn't understand how anyone could love dancing. *It's so pointless.*

It's not. It's fun.

I look like an idiot.

It doesn't matter how you look, it's how it makes you feel.

I feel like an idiot.

In the whole of their relationship, Max and Beth had danced together once, and once only. Their first date, twenty-three years ago, when he'd taken her for dinner at a gorgeous little neighbourhood Italian and they'd both emerged so engorged with pasta carbonara that Beth insisted they find a nightclub to dance away some of the calories.

'I could think of another way to burn off the energy,' he'd suggested with a cheeky smile while grabbing her around the waist.

'Then you better find another girl.'

They'd met at a housing inspection where he was showing groups through a dilapidated bungalow, five minutes' walk from the university. After, they'd talked on the phone, firstly about the house, but then about other things – trivial subjects like music and movies they'd seen. He'd gently mocked her love of musicals. 'Imagine if I burst into song and dance at a housing inspection. People would think I was insane.'

When he'd asked her for dinner, she'd said *yes*, figuring it would at least help with her lease application, but then he came to pick her up in an actual car, rather than meeting her at the restaurant or dinking her on a bicycle, which was what one particularly impoverished uni boyfriend had suggested, and she began to think he might be more than just a one-way ticket to getting the house. He complimented her dress, opened the door for her, and followed her suggestions about what to order. He was charming. Perhaps a little too charming for her liking, as if he just *knew* that if he stuck around long enough she would fall in love with him.

But at the nightclub, after she'd twisted his arm into going, he'd stood at the bar and watched her, and for the first time in her life, Beth felt self-conscious on the dance floor.

Dance as if no one's watching.

She'd turned her back. Closed her eyes. Tried to lose herself in the music. Then she felt a tap on the shoulder, and it was him. Max. And they had kissed like it was the only right thing to do. They'd kissed, and kissed, until the dance floor disappeared from under her feet, and the music went silent, and it was just them, rocking slowly from side to side, kissing and rocking until the sun came up.

'Beth, please. It really is getting late. My parents are dropping Poppy back quite early tomorrow.' Cara stood before her, the only person not moving. The lights on the dance floor started to strobe and Beth spontaneously swirled her arms. It was such a gorgeous effect. Like being a butterfly.

'You go. I'm going to stay just a little while longer.' Beth fluttered. She couldn't stop herself.

'I can't leave you here alone.' Cara folded her arms.

'Yes, you can. I'm a forty-six-year-old woman. I can look after myself.'

Cara took her shoulders to stop her from moving. 'At least promise me you'll get a taxi home.'

'I promise.'

Cara kissed her on the cheek and squeezed her hand. 'Be careful, okay?'

'I will, *Mum*,' trilled Beth, letting go and backing away into the seething cauldron of people. Cara gave her a worried wave, a frown, and she was gone. It was strange, this role reversal, and for a moment, Beth felt a flick of guilt. Normally, it was *her* giving practical, motherly advice to Cara, on where to buy the best value school shoes for Poppy and whether it was acceptable to include the words 'drop-off welcome' on party invitations.

Beth was abandoning her duty, and while it was an odd sensation, it also felt absolutely wonderful!

She inhaled the sweet smell of smoke from the fog machine. Her feet had disappeared into a white cloud. She was dancing on air. Flying. She was no one's wife. No one's mother. No one's domestic help. She was a Dancing Queen. Da-dum. Da-dum. Dum-dum.

She stumbled slightly. All right, a slightly tipsy Dancing Queen. Only forty-six.

A pair of strong arms righted her.

It was the handsome young man from The Snowden who'd spent his whole night making eyes at Cara.

'It's you!'

His hands clasped her waist. 'Are you okay?' he called into her ear, tickling it with the vibration.

'I'm fine. Possibly one too many Bellinis.' She patted her forehead. He really was rather gorgeous. Those blue eyes, blue as that fluid she used to clean the toilet. 'What's your name?'

'Adam.' He gave her a crinkled smile that made Beth's stomach fold in on itself. 'What's your name?'

'I'm Beth.' She took his hand. 'I wish we'd met five minutes ago when my friend was here.'

'Who?'

'My friend Cara. The one you were looking at all night. Dark hair. Petite. She just left, actually, or I would have introduced you.'

Adam shook his head. 'I wasn't looking at your friend. I was looking at you.' His smile widened.

Beth threw her head back and laughed. 'Me! Ha! You're very funny, Adam, I really do wish you'd met Cara.'

Adam clasped her hands. 'I'm serious. You're gorgeous.'

'I'm ancient!'

'You're experienced.' He gave her a look that she felt right in her most private of places.

Beth shook herself. *Snap out of it. He's making a fool out of you.* 'How old are you?'

'Twenty-four.'

She nearly choked. 'I'm old enough to be your mother.'

Adam regarded her. 'You don't dance like a mother. C'mon.'

'I don't know if this is right,' Beth protested. 'I told my friend I'd go home.'

He took her hand, led her further into the crowd, turned her round and started to move. He could dance. Really dance. Smooth and sexy. He reminded her of Justin Timberlake, but without the funny-shaped head. Song after song, they drew closer and closer until Beth could feel the heat radiating off his skin as he moved about her, his hands skimming around her body but never quite touching. It was exquisitely excruciating. Her body tingled. She wanted to feel him. Oh god, did she want to feel him. It was shocking, and wrong. Her, craving the touch of a man who wasn't her husband. Desire pulsed through her veins and she fixed her eyes on the side of his neck where the blonde curls dissolved into fine hairs and petered out into skin. Oh, did she want to feel that part of him!

Reaching out, she curled a lock of Adam's hair into her fingers.

'Kiss me.' She tugged gently and suddenly his mouth was on hers, hot and wet and utterly delicious. She closed her eyes and kissed him back. It seemed only right, given she was the one who'd asked for it.

So this is how it happens, she thought. *I love my husband very much. I adore my family and I am risking nineteen years of marriage for this one kiss.*

Beth pulled away and Adam gave her a lazy, sexy smirk. The kiss was lovely. There was nothing wrong with it all. It was perfect. But in that moment, she realised she wanted nothing more from him. Breaking the kiss was like waking from a dream. He was gorgeous, but so completely wrong for her. This would be a kiss and nothing more, a 'pash and dash' they'd called it back in the day. It was lust. Pure and simple. It reminded her of the passion she'd once had for Max, before she became 'Mum' – the woman who held the bucket for the kids to puke into, made sure they ate their vegies every night, and cut the crusts off their sandwiches. Long gone was the young woman who'd once had sex in her parents' toilet at their thirtieth wedding anniversary party because she and Max were a little bored and horny as goats.

Or so she'd thought.

As her fingers still tingled from the touch of Adam's lovely neck, a picture flashed into her head – the one of the earth's crust in Chloe's geography book. All those different layers of rock and sediment, but hot, molten lava at its core, just waiting to explode to the surface, with who knows what consequences. That was her. At her core, she was still hot lava, but the passing years had seen that centre of passion covered over by a crust of ageing and motherhood.

She covered her mouth, and without a word to Adam, fled the dance floor, bumping shoulders and bottoms as she scurried towards the exit and into the street.

Outside, she breathed deeply. The air was cool and calming. A balm to her tingling skin.

There was a taxi rank fifty metres down the road. Beth set off towards it and felt a tap on her shoulder.

'Hey, are you okay?'

She wheeled around and Adam stood before her, hands jammed into his pockets. 'What happened back there?'

Beth bit down on her lip. 'It's fine, I'm fine. I just realised that I … left the oven on.'

He raised an eyebrow. 'The oven?'

'Yes. And I'm worried the house might burn down.'

Adam took a step closer. 'It was just a kiss, Beth.'

'I know.' She couldn't look at him. 'And it was a very nice kiss. Very nice. But I think I need something else right now.'

'Something else?' He grinned wolfishly. 'We can do something else if you'd like.'

'No, no, sorry, that's not what I meant.' Beth fidgeted with the strap on her handbag. 'I think I need to go home, that's all. I'm sorry.'

Adam cocked his head to the side. 'My mum does that too.'

'What? Kisses random young men in nightclubs and then runs away?'

'No,' he said seriously. 'Apologises for things when they're not her fault.'

'A mother thinks everything is her fault.' Beth went to kiss him on the cheek. A chaste, motherly kiss. 'But thank you.'

'Hang on, I'll get you a cab.' The street was empty, save for a single taxi pulling up slowly at the rank. 'Do you mind if we share? I'm buggered.' He stood by the passenger door and held it open for her.

'Of course not.' She hopped in. 'What kind of work do you do?'

'I'm a sparky ... electrician.' He slid smoothly into the seat beside her.

Sparky ... indeed.

The idea of him rewiring her house caused her cheeks to redden.

In the cab they were silent. Adam scrolled through his phone, while Beth looked out the window at the houses passing them by. Their unblinking, window eyes, sharing nothing of all that lay behind them.

The cab pulled up to a stop in Cuthbert Close.

'This is me.' Beth leant forward to pay the driver but Adam took her hand.

'Let me take care of it.'

Before Beth could thank him, Adam had jumped out of the car and jogged around to open the door. His manners really were refreshingly impeccable.

If only Cara was interested. If only Chloe was ten years older. If only I wasn't married and old enough to be his mother.

'Thank you.' Beth stood awkwardly next to the taxi. She wanted to say something to explain herself, to make him understand why she'd wanted to kiss him, how attracted she was, to make sense of her own madness.

She leant in. 'You're a lovely man ... A real credit to your parents,' she whispered in his ear and immediately cringed. She'd always been terrible at sexy-talk. That bit certainly hadn't changed.

Adam gave her a final crinkly smile and kissed her on the forehead. 'Night, Beth.'

On the footpath, Beth stood and waited until the red lights of the cab faded out of Cuthbert Close. Gosh, she was tired. All the alcohol and dancing, she supposed. And *kissing*.

She shivered. Leant against the gate. She needed to compose herself. What if Max was awake?

The moon was bright, and it shone particularly brightly on her house. Her home. A little worn about the edges now. Could probably do with a new paint job. Houses were a lot of ongoing maintenance. Bit like marriage really.

Beth tiptoed through the gate, which seemed to squeak more loudly than usual when she opened it. Or maybe it was just the contrast against the silence of the night.

She stopped. From the corner of her eye, she saw a curtain fall closed at number twenty-five, the Pezzullos' old place, or rather, the Devines' now. She checked her watch. 1:30 am. Was Charlie still awake? Maybe she'd only just got home herself. Beth waited for further signs of life, a light, or something, but none came. The house was dark and still. Beth continued towards her own front door. She must have been seeing things. It was probably just a trick of the light, not really what it seemed at all.

ThePrimalGuy.com.au
From: The Primal Guy
Subject: Reinventing Yourself

Hey Prime-Numbers,
A stack of dudes (and dudettes) come to The Primal Guy because they wanna reinvent themselves. They say 'Ryan – how'd you do it, bro? How'd you go from being a douche-bag soft-arse pen-pusher, to being a lean, mean, pre-historic fighting machine?'

You know what? I could give them a bunch of BS about how I was miserable in my job, and felt like I wasn't living my best life, and you know, crack out the violins and cry me a river.

The truth is this – I wanted to look at myself in a mirror, and like the way I looked in the buff. That's it! I wanted to look good naked, and I wanted others to admire me. I mean, can you get more superficial than that?

But hey, it worked. 300,000 followers can't be wrong, right? We're all pretty surface-level, when you get down to it.

Now I'm in this new place. And I'm having to re-invent myself all over again. Sometimes, it's tiring, you know. Sometimes, I wish I could just be the tired, grumpy, lazy dick that's still hiding inside me, some-where.

But no one wants that guy. They want the Primal Guy. Actually, they want Primal Guy 2.0. The 'evolved' paleo guy. And hell, I can do that. I'll dance however they want me to dance. 'Cause at the end of the day, it doesn't matter which way you get there, it just matters that you get where you want to go.

Peace out,
Ryan (AKA the Primal Guy)

PS Buy one smoothie bottle, get one free for this week only! So great for shaking up smoothies Mon–Fri, then cocktails for the weekend. Hey! A little cheat every now and again is okay by me. No one's perfect, right?!

CHAPTER FOURTEEN

Alex scooted around the kitchen bench to the fridge where she expertly withdrew the milk from the door with maximum efficiency and lobbed a dash into her tea, all without spilling a drop.

She was on fire this morning. Already, she'd shot off emails to a soccer academy and a jujitsu club, asking for the twins to be enrolled as a matter of urgency. She'd also made enquiries with a tutoring service that ran three-hour classes on Saturday mornings for five year olds. Socialisation and academic support – that's what Noah needed.

Her Fitbit buzzed. One thousand steps and it wasn't even 7 am. Her wrist vibrated in celebration. She'd even managed to not burn the twins' toast. Already, they were dressed and ready for school and playing outside. This was her day. She. Had. This.

Tea in hand, Alex perched on a stool across the kitchen island from her husband, busy eating his cornflakes.

'I Spy a woman on a mission.' He winked.

'With a capital M.' Alex blew the steam and sipped. 'Now, you be Martin and I'll be ... well ... I'll be me.'

'Martin ...' he mused. 'That's the Pommy one, isn't it? Looks like a chipmunk.'

'More squirrel, I'd say.'

'Right.' James munched thoughtfully.

'Okay ... so, here's what I'll say.' Alex took a breath. 'Martin, thank you for taking the time to meet with me.'

James cocked his head. 'Awright, geezer. What's up wiv ya. Know what I mean?'

Alex snorted and tea flew out of her nose. 'He's not the Artful Dodger! He's more ... Prince Philip.'

'I see.' James straightened and looked down his nose. 'Top of the morning to you, Dame Alex. How can one be of service on this fine-looking day?'

'Can you please take this seriously.'

James slurped the dregs of his cereal. 'I don't know what you're so worried about.' He rose and came around the bench to kiss her but Alex recoiled and pointed to his chin.

'You've got a cornflake.'

James popped the offending flake into his mouth and chomped on it. 'You're completely entitled to ask for flexible work arrangements. It's the law. And contrary to your fears that cutting back to three days will leave us destitute on the street, I can assure you they are unfounded. So really, what's the worst that can happen?'

Alex tightened her grip on the mug. 'That Martin says no, questions my commitment to the job and starts giving me minor matters that even Brianna could do with her eyes closed, so then I'm stuck doing a job that sends my brain to sleep.'

'A lot of people would love to sleepwalk through their jobs. Actually, a lot already do.' He paused to look right into her eyes. 'Don't sell yourself short. You're great at what you do. They love you there.' Breaking eye contact, James put his bowl into the dishwasher and closed the door with a firm shove as if he were quite finished with the conversation.

'Could you please be more gentle with the dishwasher. They cost a fortune to fix,' she said tightly.

'Yes, sir.' James gave a mock salute and smiled.

Ugh. So annoying. He didn't get it. The guilt. The feeling that she was backing away from everything that she and her parents had worked, and sacrificed, for. They didn't give up years of family holidays just so she could turn around and back off when things got a little tough.

Alex drained the rest of her tea into the sink. 'I've got to run. You're okay to drop the boys?' she called over her shoulder, collecting her keys and bag as she sailed towards the front door.

James stood in the doorway behind her. 'Hey! You forgot something.' He pointed to his cheek. 'Kiss?'

Alex stopped, eyebrows raised. 'Really? I have to go.' She looked at her watch.

He nodded and took a few steps towards her. 'I'm sorry about the dishwasher.' He deposited a soft kiss on her cheek and whispered in her ear, 'I'll be more gentle next time.'

As her husband held his lips against her cheek, Alex felt her frustration ebbing. It wasn't his fault that he'd had the kind of childhood where money was never a problem, where he could go out to dinner and have his own drink and his own dessert. That's what she wanted for the boys. Choices. No fears or worries.

'I'll see you tonight.' Alex withdrew and hurried out the door. The boys were in the Devines' front yard with Talia, sitting and stroking a white ball of fluff.

'He loves a scratch just behind his ears. Like this,' said Talia, demonstrating.

'Like this?' Noah pumped his hands up and down on the cat's head. 'Look! He loves it!'

'Boys, I'm going,' Alex called. 'Come and give me a kiss.'

'Hi, Mrs O'Rourke.' Talia rose and waved. 'Go on, boys. Say bye to your mum,' she urged.

The boys hurled themselves into their mother's legs, kissed her somewhere near her hip and bolted back to the cat. Alex went to hop into her car, but stopped with her fingers on the handle. 'Say, Talia. I don't suppose you'd be interested in babysitting for us sometime?'

'Yay, you could bring Banjo!' Noah's eyes shone.

The cat that murdered your guinea pig?

The girl beamed. 'Sure, Mrs O'Rourke. I'd love that.'

'Call me Alex, please.'

'I'm not sure that's a good idea.' Twenty feet away, in the shadow of the front door, stood Charlie Devine. Arms folded.

'Oh, sorry Charlie. Didn't see you there.' Alex shielded her eyes and Charlie walked closer, dressed as usual in her all-white, form-fitting activewear. The woman's penchant for such a pure hue verged on … well, it was almost like a uniform, like a cult leader might wear.

'Talia's never babysat before.'

'Mum, I'll be fine,' said Talia.

'I don't mind if she doesn't have experience. Everyone has to start somewhere,' said Alex. 'The boys really seem to love her, and that's all that matters to me. And I'm sure the extra cash for Talia wouldn't hurt.'

Charlie glared. 'We're not *that* desperate for money and I don't believe in child labour. Talia has everything she needs.'

Alex tensed. There was nothing wrong with teenagers having a part-time job. She'd worked all through her high-school years to buy the things she didn't entirely need, and her parents couldn't afford. Brand-name jeans and Doc Martens, for instance.

'Please, Mum. Please,' Talia begged.

Ignoring her, Charlie tapped her very fancy-looking smart watch. White, of course. 'It's getting late. You need to come inside now and get ready for school.'

'Boys, you too. Time to brush teeth. Dad's inside to help you. Let's go. Scoot,' Alex ushered them in the direction of the house.

'C'mon, Banjo.' Talia collected the cat and trudged inside, her mother's hand in the small of her back. Alex watched from her car. At the door, the girl stopped and waved wanly, her freckles now more pronounced against the backdrop of her pale face.

What is going on inside that house?

Alex was transfixed.

Charlie followed Talia, and as the teenager went inside Alex had the sense of her being pushed by her mother towards a dark, cavernous hole.

Charlie paused and looked back at Alex, an expression of … was it anger? Shit, she'd made her neighbour cross, again, for what seemed like no justifiable reason. All she'd done was to suggest Talia do some babysitting. What was wrong with that? If anything, Alex should be the one who was angry – all that judgement about kids not working. It was offensive.

The door slammed, cutting through the quiet of the morning. Yes, definitely angry. Alex flinched, and started to move. She didn't have time to worry about Charlie Devine. She had a meeting to get to.

CHAPTER FIFTEEN

Beth woke with a gasp, her head pounding. She sat bolt upright, and her hand searched for the glass of water she always kept by the bed. Her mouth was as dry as a chip and a feeling of doom sat heavily in her chest. What a terrible, terrible dream! What had happened in it? Her brain sifted slowly through the fragments. Yes, that's right. She'd been in a nightclub, dancing, and then she'd kissed another man. Actually kissed him on the lips. There might have been tongues. Then Max had turned up with a gun and waved it around at this nice young man even though Beth was shouting at him that it had just been a kiss and nothing more, and there was no need for anyone to be shot, especially when Max himself was sending strange text messages. What were they about? He had to tell her before shooting anyone.

There'd been a bang.

That's when I woke.

That sound had been terribly real. What was it? Beth lay still, the house silent. From outside came the sound of light footsteps on their front path. She sat up in the bed to see out the window. There was Ethan, his arm slung around Chloe's shoulder. The bang must have been the front door closing. On the street, Max's car idled at the curb. He must have agreed to drive them to school.

Beth felt a pang of guilt as she watched them trudge towards the gate, with Chloe clutching tightly to a bag that Beth recognised as her swimming gear.

Swimming. That was odd. Today was Wednesday, wasn't it? Beth fought through her brain fog to remember. Yes, yesterday was definitely Tuesday, which meant today was Wednesday the fourth of March, if her memory served correctly. There was something about that date. Something she had to remember. Something important. She closed her eyes and had nearly drifted off again when it came to her.

The swimming carnival. She clapped her hand to her forehead and checked the time. 8:20 am. Ten minutes until she was due at the pool, twenty minutes' drive away, for the sports teacher Miss Liu's pre-carnival briefing. She threw on clothes, pulled a comb through her hair and raced downstairs for her keys and wallet. She stopped at the fridge. There was a note, in Ethan's handwriting.

Hi Mum, the question I wanted to ask is – are you still coming to the carnival today? Chloe really wants you there.

Her heart twinged again. The poor kids. Why hadn't they woken her? Oh, wait, they had. Or, at least they'd tried. Now she remembered. They'd both come into the room, separately, tiptoed to her side, and breathed, watching her.

At one point, she'd sensed Ethan about to speak and she'd held up a hand, without opening her eyes.

'Please, don't.'

Away he'd crept.

And what of Max? He'd gone to boot camp, presumably, as he always did on a Wednesday at the crack of dawn. Normally, she would have woken with him and had her first cup of tea. The close was always so beautifully still and fresh at that time of morning, like a newly washed sheet.

But this morning, when the bed had creaked, she'd rolled the other way. She'd barely slept a wink after the club. Instead, she'd stared at the Uluru shape of her husband in the bed and wondered how a person could be so close and yet still so far away.

Oh, goodness. 8:23 am.

Beth popped a couple of Panadol, scurried to the car and took off down the close at a speed she would never usually have approved of.

Turning the corner, she slowed. Wait. Was that Talia Devine dawdling on the footpath? She was definitely going to miss the bus from school to the carnival. Would Charlie mind if Beth gave her a lift? Was that interfering? She checked her rear-view mirror before slowing down.

'Morning, Talia.'

'Hi, Mrs Chandler.' The girl gave her a friendly wave.

'Would you like a lift? I'm headed to the pool for the carnival.'

Talia bit her lip.

'It's fine, hon, if you think your mum wouldn't like it, I understand. It's just … I think you've missed the bus and you might be stuck at school.'

'Thanks, Mrs Chandler. That'd be great.' Talia scampered towards the car.

'It's Beth, remember. Chloe and Ethan's friends all call me Beth.'

Talia grinned and did up her seatbelt. 'Thanks ... Beth. Really appreciate it.'

'No problem, Talia. It's what any neighbour would do.'

Except Charlie Devine, she thought darkly, and then felt immediately guilty.

You live next to each other. You have to get along. Try to understand her.

'Your mum busy this morning?' asked Beth lightly.

'Not really. She's gone out for a run.'

'She's very fit. I guess it's part of her job, really.'

'I suppose so.'

The car fell silent. Beth flicked on the indicator. She didn't like silences in the car. 'We ran into her last night, actually. Alex and Cara and I. She was having a business meeting.'

'At the pub. I know.' Talia delivered this with a sigh, as if it had happened many times before, and she didn't quite approve.

'Actually, the girls and I were having a business meeting too. We're setting up a food business to make delicious meals for time-poor parents. It's called Nourish.'

Talia nodded slowly. 'I think that's a great idea. That quiche you made was really delicious.'

Beth looked at her sideways. Covering for her mother, perhaps?

'I'm glad you think so.' Beth clasped the steering wheel. 'Not everyone thinks it's such a great idea.'

'You mean Mum?' Talia was looking out the window, which meant Beth couldn't read her expression. 'Don't worry about her. She's very competitive.'

Beth gave an uncertain laugh. 'I'm not worried. Your mum has nothing to fear from us. No pills or powders, I promise.'

The car was quiet again.

'I don't think she likes this place,' said Talia, still staring out the window. 'She doesn't seem to like the people.' Beth felt Talia's gaze turn on her. 'Except for your husband. He's helped us a lot.'

'That's my Max,' said Beth. 'Always helping.'

'He's *really* helpful,' said Talia, in a voice that was disapproving, the same tone she'd used about her mother going to the pub.

Beth kept her eyes on the road while her stomach rose into her mouth. 'Is there something you're trying to tell me, Talia?'

The girl paused. 'Nope. No.' Now, her voice was airy. 'He's just a really friendly guy. That's all. Reminds me a bit of my dad, actually.'

'Oh, really. I'd like to meet him,' said Beth, the wheels of her brain struggling to turn under the weight of her hangover.

'He's amazing,' said Talia. 'Seriously, he's the best. He'll be here soon, I promise.'

They were at the pool now. Talia unclicked her belt and got out of the car, the door still open.

'Thanks so much for the lift.'

'Hey, Talia, just before you go, would you mind sending me your mum's phone number? I think I should let her know that I gave you a lift today, and it might be handy for the future. We can carpool, maybe.' Beth squeezed her thighs together. She hated lying to the poor child, but it was only a half-lie. She really did want to text Charlie, but she also needed to know if she was the woman that Max was texting.

'Sure. I'll text it to you. What's your number?' Talia produced her phone and Beth recited her number. A second later, her phone buzzed.

'Thanks, sweetie, and good luck today.'

She waited until Talia was out of sight before quickly tapping her phone to bring up the messages.

Sucking in a breath, she opened the contact card and her eyes raced over the numbers. She read them once, then again.

It wasn't her. Max wasn't texting Charlie Devine.

Relief swept over her, but it was as brief as a breeze because Talia was back and tapping at the window. Beth nearly dropped her phone.

'I forgot to say – don't worry if it takes Mum a while to respond. She's got a new phone and a new number and she's still working out how to use it.'

A new phone number? Why would she get a new number?

'Thanks, sweetie ... When did she get the new phone? Recently?'

Talia gave her a strange look. 'Uh ... I don't know. Maybe yesterday?'

'Okay, hon ... well, thanks for letting me know.'

Beth wound up the window and gave her a friendly toot of farewell. Damn! Now she couldn't check for sure if it was

Charlie who Max was messaging, and she'd also promised to text the woman to tell her about giving Talia a lift to the carnival, and god knows how she would react to that.

With a feeling of dread settling uneasily over her nausea, Beth started typing.

CHAPTER SIXTEEN

Alex's fingers paused over the keyboard as she reread the email to her boss.

Hello Martin,

Could you spare a few minutes this afternoon to catch up? It won't take long, but it's quite important. Twenty minutes at the most.

Best, Alex

Her hand quivered over the send button.

'Knock-knock.' Brianna stood at the door to Alex's office, looking particularly svelte and gorgeous as she leant casually against the handle, 'Partners would like a quick word.'

'I'll be one minute.' Alex's finger rested on the mouse. To send or not to send.

She pressed send, took a breath and waited for Brianna to leave before standing to zip up her skirt all the way. Walking to the conference room, she felt a flutter of nerves. It wasn't unusual for the partners to ask for an informal update on a matter during their regular Wednesday morning meeting, but still, Alex had the sense of having been summonsed to the principal's office. Again.

She paused at the door to the conference room and tapped lightly.

'Come in,' came the sonorous voice of Rex Macauley, managing partner and founder of Macauley Partners. Alex stepped timidly into the room and ten pairs of eyes swivelled towards her, all but two belonging to men over the age of fifty.

'Alex, thank you for coming,' boomed Rex.

'Of course. How can I help?'

'Sit, sit.' He motioned to the empty chair at the end of the boardroom table. That was strange. He never asked her to sit during the partners' meeting. Seats at the conference table were for partners only. Underlings gave their updates and skedaddled.

'Oh, I'm happy to stand … Really.' Alex was flustered. She didn't want to sit, and because of the tightness of her skirt around the little bean in her stomach, it wasn't actually possible. Unless she wanted to crack a rib.

'Alex, sit.' This time it was a command. She sat and felt her waistband crush her middle.

Sorry, baby.

She tried to catch Martin's eye to see if he could convey some inkling of what was going on, but he was studiously fiddling with some papers and refusing to glance in her direction.

What was going on?

Oh god. Had she made some grievous error in her work? She'd heard of one poor junior solicitor being called to the conference room, on Valentine's Day last year, only to be sacked on the spot for misuse of the company credit card. There'd been a security guard at the door, ready to escort her off the premises. She wasn't even allowed to return to her desk to collect the huge bunch of roses that had been sent by her wildly successful property-developer boyfriend.

'Would you like a tea? Coffee?' Rex gestured to the cups and saucers on the table.

This was getting seriously weird. Alex felt panic rising in her throat. Why were they being so nice to her? The partners weren't nice. They were tough and brilliant and hardworking. But *nice* certainly wasn't part of the job description. Perhaps there'd been a tragedy? Were they softening her up for some really terrible news? Not about her job but about something else far more important. Had someone died? Was it James? No. Even the partners weren't cruel or cowardly enough to deliver tragic news as some kind of group therapy session.

Rex cleared his throat. Alex gripped her chair.

'I still the remember the day you started with us, Alex. Twelve years ago, when the firm was a third the size of what it is now. You marched into our offices and declared to me that you would be the best solicitor this firm had ever seen.'

A couple of the partners chuckled.

Christ, was that really what she'd said? What a brazen little upstart! How had she not been fired on the spot, or at least killed by all the other talented solicitors already working at the firm? They must have hated her. Then again, that confident (and naive) young woman would never have quivered before the partners, feeling an urgent need for the toilet. That woman would have squared her shoulders and stuck out her chin.

'A bold, but perhaps not entirely inaccurate, prediction.' Alex laughed and locked eyes with the managing director. She straightened in her chair and felt the button that was securing her skirt's zipper go *pop*.

Great. Now she couldn't stand up or her skirt would fall off.

Rex clasped his fingers. 'For some time now, the firm has been thinking about taking on a new partner. Some fresh blood, you might say.' He gave a knowing look to the other partners at the table. 'We want someone with integrity, someone who excels in managing client relationships and, moreover, someone who puts the firm first.'

The partners murmured in agreement.

Alex flexed her fingers and clenched them again as Rex droned on about the importance of renewal and genera- tional change and a few other corporate buzzwords like *open kimono* and *synergies* and *blue-sky thinking*. Words that had inspired her and Brianna to think up a new game, Buzzword Bingo, where they passed the minutes in particularly boring meetings by counting up the number of times a particular client or partner used them. Rex was a renowned offender.

'So, Alex … Alex?' Rex rested his elbows on the confer- ence table.

'Yes, sorry, Rex.'

'Tell us your thoughts.' He sat back.

'Well, ah …'

'What value could you add to Macauley's stable of partners?'

'Wait, what? Me?'

Rex tilted his head in amusement. 'Yes, Alexandra. We want you to join us as a full partner in the firm.'

Her mind went blank

'Well, uh, obviously I'm very flattered,' Alex began. The partners around the table nodded encouragingly. Martin was trying to smile but managed to look more like a squirrel trying to crack open a nut.

'It's a huge honour to be invited into such esteemed company.' More head nodding. Alex rotated slightly on the chair and it creaked loudly. 'I'm, ah … quite overwhelmed, actually.' If only her parents could see her now. The mere thought of them made her eyes grow hot. Surely they'd be proud? It might take a bit of explaining, the significance of becoming a partner, but if she told them the salary, they'd soon get it.

Alex sat still. 'Rex, you have an incredible memory, and you are quite correct in saying that when I came to Macauley all the way from little old Perth it was my ambition to become the youngest female partner ever appointed at the firm.'

But I was young and highly ambitious and didn't have children back then …

'In those days, the firm took up only half of this floor and I knew everyone's name, from the receptionist to the mail-room clerks.'

And now it's a sprawling, three-level corporate beast where the office Christmas party involves me getting drunk at the bar, with Brianna holding my hand and the two of us turning to each other every five minutes to say, 'Who are these people?'

'The growth in this company is testament to you, Rex, and the commitment of all the partners. It's astonishing, really. Quite an example.'

Half of you are divorced. Most of you have children you never see. You have houses you never get to enjoy. But you do have money. Piles and piles of it. This is definitely what I want. To never have to worry about money ever again. To buy a smart little unit for Mum and Dad. To clear my mortgage.

'Thank you, Alex. We understand this is a critical step. No doubt you have many questions, which Martin will be happy to answer, and we'll have paperwork drawn up over the next few weeks for you to sign. But can I be the first to say—' Rex stood. 'Welcome to the family.' He started applauding, and one by one, all the partners followed suit until Alex was the only one not standing or applauding. Now they were walking over to her, to shake hands. Oh bugger, she would have to stand up and shake hands and god knows what was going to happen to her skirt.

My stomach's about to explode. My younger son is turning into a sociopath. I desperately need to cut down my work hours. But this is actually everything I've ever wanted.

With uncertainty, Alex rose to her feet and as she went to shake hands with Rex, she felt her skirt sliding down.

She was about to be exposed.

CHAPTER SEVENTEEN

For the eighty-second time that day, the starter's gun fired and for the eightieth time that day, Beth jumped. Hell, as she'd discovered, wasn't full of fire and criminals. It was packed with teens in swimsuits, smelt of chlorine, sounded like continuous gunfire and tasted of fermented peaches.

Hell, in other words, was fronting up to a school swimming carnival with a gigantic Bellini-triggered hangover.

'You look like you could do with this.' Marianna Hardacre, mum to one of Chloe's best friends, pressed a coffee into her hands.

'Thank you so much. You're a life-saver,' said Beth, resisting the urge to kiss Marianna violently on the lips. She could murder a coffee. She could hug it. But first she would drink it. Scull it, in fact. She brought the cup to her lips, closed her eyes and drank, and drank.

'Mrs Chandler! Mrs Chandler! Are you ready?'

Beth opened her eyes to find she was getting an icy glare from Miss Liu. 'We cannot begin the race until all marshals are ready. Are you?'

Yes, ma'am. Beth nodded. The young sports teacher was frighteningly efficient. She blew the whistle and Beth's head pounded in sync with the piercing noise. The painkillers really should have kicked in by now. She'd taken two Panadol before leaving home, and followed up at 10 am with two Nurofen – a terrific little tip she'd learnt from a GP when Chloe was five years old, running a temp of nearly 40 degrees and limp as a sock. *Alternate*, the doctor advised. *Controls the pain far more effectively.*

Why wasn't it working? Bloody swimming. Damn Chloe for being so good at it. Why couldn't she be average, like Marianna's lovely little Mia, who nearly drowned over the 50 metre freestyle but was a complete dynamo on the netball court. Netball was so easy. No pre-dawn starts. No endless squads. And no starter's gun.

Bang.

Beth jolted and stood to attention. The girls' 50 metre butterfly was underway. A thrashing mess of arms and mermaid-kicking legs made its way steadily down the pool. Her job was to identify the second place getter, pass them a red stick and direct them to the appropriate area to collect their ribbon.

Queen of Number Twos.

Last year, Miss Liu had put her on the marshalling desk to record the results – a position of some responsibility that Beth felt was a small acknowledgement of her capabilities and length of service. This morning, she'd been ten minutes late to the volunteer briefing, which had earned her a demotion into giving out second place sticks to kids who either seemed delightfully surprised by their placing, or bitterly disappointed about not winning

Get used to it, she wanted to warn them. *Life is full of second places.*

The race was over. She issued the stick to a bedraggled little girl who looked up at her with her yellow cap and foggy goggles like a tiny exhausted Martian.

'Well done, sweetie. Over to the marshalling area for your ribbon.' Beth offered a hand, but the shriek of Miss Liu's whistle in her ear made her startle enough to let go, which sent the little girl tumbling back into the water. The loudhailer squealed.

'Attention all volunteers: There is to be no interference with swimmers until they have cleared the pool. IS THAT UNDERSTOOD?'

Miss Liu glared and dropped the megaphone back to her side. Another ear-splitting whistle signalled the swimmers to get out.

'Sorry,' whispered Beth, as her little second placer swam limply over and under the lane ropes to the side of the pool.

Beth felt a tap on her shoulder. *Please, not Miss Liu.*

'Mum, can I have three dollars to get a donut.' Chloe put her hand out. Next to her was Talia Devine.

'Oh, hello again, Talia. Enjoying the carnival so far?'

'I'm a hopeless swimmer.' Talia grinned. 'Not like Chloe.'

'Mum, can I have the money? Talia's going to the tuckshop too.'

'For a donut as well?' Beth winked conspiratorially as Talia smiled broadly. 'I won't tell.' Poor child, having to sneak around. So what if she ate a pastry every once in a while? It wouldn't kill her. After eight years of nutrition studies, the sum total of Beth's knowledge could be boiled down to one fairly simple piece of advice. Everything in moderation. No fads, no fasts. No silly diets. Especially not for children.

'Girls, you really shouldn't be here. If Miss Liu sees you she'll be very cross.' Beth stepped sideways to shield Talia and Chloe from the hawk-eyed sports mistress.

'Then just give us the money. Quickly.' Chloe jutted out her hand again.

'Chloe, manners,' Beth admonished, reaching into her pocket. 'Are you sure you should eat before you've finished all your races? You might get a stitch.'

Chloe made a face and crinkled her nose, which carried a stripe of green zinc – the colour of her team. 'Please. I'm starved. I barely had any food because you were asleep this morning.'

Beth shifted uncomfortably. Chloe was like a heat-seeking missile when it came to locating her mother's guilt button.

'I'll faint if I don't eat and that's worse than getting a stitch.'

'All right.' She felt too liable and too tired to fight. 'Here you go.' She handed over the coins. 'Can you get one for me too?'

She hadn't eaten a kiosk donut in twenty years, but it was exactly what she felt like. Her headache was starting to ease, but her stomach was still dreadfully queasy.

'Thanks, Mum. You're the best.' Chloe trotted off, followed by Talia. 'And Dad's here,' she called over her shoulder.

'Wait. What? Where?' called Beth.

BANG!

Sweet jesus. Another race. And now her phone was buzzing. She set her coffee cup down.

'No food or drinks on the pool deck,' barked Miss Liu, swiping the cup from under Beth's feet.

'Sorry,' she offered, and waited for the teacher to stomp away before discreetly answering her phone.

'Hello,' she whispered.

'Beth. Are you okay? I can barely hear you. Just wanted to check you were all right? I came over this morning to make sure you'd got home safely but the kids said you were still in bed.'

Cara. Her voice full of concern.

Beth felt a flicker of irritation. One sleep-in and suddenly everyone assumed there was something tragically wrong with her.

'I'm fine,' she said curtly to Cara. 'I don't know why everyone's being so dramatic. I slept in. I'm allowed to, aren't I?'

A pause. 'Did something happen after I left?'

Beth breathed in. She had decided to forget all about Adam and keep him as her little secret. 'Why would you say that?'

Cara began in a small voice. 'Beth, it would be entirely understandable if you felt a little … lost, given what you showed us on your phone … about Max.'

'I'm not lost, I'm at the St Therese's swimming carnival,' Beth snapped. The next race was drawing to a close, and she clenched her fingers around the second place stick in her pocket.

Cara paused as if contemplating whether to challenge Beth further or not. 'Oh, right, good to hear then … I also wanted to see if you might have time to chat about Nourish, and get the menu started. I thought we could have a launch party in the close, test out a few of the dishes and get the neighbours on board with it all.'

'Sounds terrific,' said Beth. 'How about a cuppa after school?'

'Perfect.'

As Beth hung up, a little head bobbed up from the pool. 'Excuse me. Did I come second?'

'Oops, yes. You did, sweetie. Well done.' Beth rushed the stick to the child. 'Now, just wait till Miss Liu gives the signal for you to exit the pool.'

Beth rubbed her stomach. She'd forgotten that awful gnawing that came with hangovers, like your stomach was eating itself. She felt a hand on her waist.

'Special delivery.' It was Max. Frowning at her and holding a pink-iced donut

'But I sent Chloe …' Beth blustered.

'And I ran into her at the kiosk, so here I am. Donut delivery man.' He held it out and Beth involuntarily gave a little moan. It smelt so good. Sweet and deep-fried.

'What *did* you get up to with the girls last night?' Max folded his arms, watching her devour the donut. 'The bedroom smelt like an alcoholic sweet shop this morning.'

Beth's stomach lurched. 'Oh, nothing. Just trying to sort out some of Cara's and Alex's problems. Misery loves company and all of that.' She tried to sound casual, but it was proving difficult with a load of icing and sweet dough in her mouth.

'I can't remember the last time you ate a donut.'

'Probably before I studied nutrition and realised just how bad they are for you.' Beth wolfishly took another mouthful. She couldn't help it.

Cassie Hamer

'The kids said you wouldn't get up this morning.'

'It was one little sleep-in. One! Anyone would think I'd run away to the circus the way you're all carrying on,' she protested through the sticky sweetness.

Max regarded her. 'What's going on with you?'

What's going on with you!

'Why does everyone keep saying that?' Beth huffed. 'Last time I checked, it wasn't a crime to sleep in or eat a donut.'

Max's eyes narrowed on her. 'No, but it's not like you.'

'I wouldn't read too much into it.'

'All right.' He shrugged, and looked over her shoulder to the pool. His eyes narrowed. 'Hey, is that kid okay?'

Beth whipped around. While she'd been talking to Max another race had begun. Most of the kids were about to finish and Beth scanned the lanes for the person coming in second.

'That kid there.' Max pointed further down the pool. 'I think they're struggling.'

Arms flailing. A little head going up and then disappearing beneath the surface. Beth searched the crowd. Miss Liu was in the grandstand, making notes on her clipboard. Too far away to call out to. Everyone else's eyes were glued to the end of the pool where four swimmers were locked in a tight contest for the finish line. The crowd was going crazy.

'I'll go.'

Before Beth could say a word, Max was striding off down the pool deck, loosening his tie as he went.

'Help,' she called out lamely. 'Help. I think that child's drowning.'

Perhaps it was the word 'drowning' that cut through the noise, but somehow, over all the cheering, Miss Liu looked in her direction. As Beth pointed down the pool, the teacher's face went white and she took the stairs two at a time, shouting into the loudhailer. 'Emergency. Emergency. Life ring required in the pool. Repeat: emergency.'

Beth started running. During the pre-carnival briefing, Miss Liu's second briefing *for the latecomers*, the sports teacher had made a point of identifying the life ring's location. Beth had paid full attention. Easier to think about life rings and timekeepers than peach Bellinis and handsome electricians.

She got to the life ring and stopped. The crowd roared behind her. Max had not only leapt into the pool, almost fully dressed, he was now swimming to the side of it with a sobbing child clinging tightly to his neck. Beth met them both and offered her hand to the panicked boy to help him out of the pool.

'Oh, you poor love.' She scouted about for a towel to throw around him.

'He's fine,' panted Max over the quivering child. 'Just a bit of an anxiety attack, I think.'

Miss Liu took the young boy by the shoulders. 'Rory, are you all right? Slow breaths in and out. Have you swallowed water?'

'No, miss.' The little boy shivered, teary. 'I got a cramp and I couldn't go any further. I'm sorry.'

Miss Liu's face softened. 'Come with me to the first-aid tent and we'll get you warmed up.' She gave a grateful look to Max before leading the little boy away.

Beth touched her husband's shoulder. He was trembling. 'Are you okay?'

Max swept a hand through his hair. 'I'm good. I just hope the kid's okay.'

She squeezed, feeling a sudden tenderness towards him. 'Let's get you a towel.'

'Here's one,' said a voice from behind them. 'He can borrow Talia's.'

Charlie Devine, dressed in a flowing white cheesecloth skirt and a matching singlet top that didn't quite cover her taut stomach. With the sun behind her, the skirt was completely see-through and the rays sparkled off her diamond earrings, forcing Beth to squint.

'Oh, thanks Charlie but I think I've got a spare in my bag somewhere,' said Beth, making a move to leave.

But Max was already unbuttoning his shirt and, as he took the outstretched towel from Charlie's hands, Beth noted their neighbour's eyes flit quickly over her husband's naked torso.

'Thanks, Charlie.' Max rubbed himself briskly.

'That was quite the heroic act you pulled off there.' Charlie folded her arms under her breasts which, Beth couldn't help noticing, helped to lift them enticingly higher in her skin-tight top. 'Very impressive.'

'Anyone else would have done the same.' Max shrugged and turned his attention to Beth. 'Any chance of a lift home to get a change of clothes?'

'Sorry, but I'm on duty until 2:30 pm. Where's your car?' Any tenderness Beth might have felt towards him in the aftermath of his daring rescue (though really, how daring was it to jump into a pool where he could stand up?) had evaporated, thanks to Charlie Devine.

'I caught a cab down.'

'Why?' She stared at him. Max was *always* in his car. It was like a fifth limb. Last year, he'd bought himself a fancy

little Mercedes with a price tag that had made Beth feel sick
to the stomach. He'd justified it by saying it was where he
did most of his work, with inspections and the like, and
it was also a good way of inspiring confidence in the customers, something along the lines of 'Well, if he drives an
expensive car, he *must* be good at selling houses'.

Beth thought clients weren't quite so silly.

'I had an appointment in the city and the parking's awful
there, so I just cabbed it.' He shrugged. 'No big deal.'

'Who was the appointment with?' Beth demanded. Max
didn't sell real estate in the CBD.

'Ah … just a client who works in the city. I needed to talk
to them about auction strategy.'

In person? Why not on the phone?

If the car was Max's fifth limb, the phone was his sixth.

'I can give you a lift,' said Charlie, innocently lifting her
eyelashes. 'After all, Beth, you brought Talia to the carnival,
it's the least I could do.'

*Is that a little passive-aggressive nudge? What happened to
staying out of each other's lives?*

'That would be great, thanks,' said Max easily.

Too easily.

It was like they were trying too hard to act noncha-
lant. There was a familiarity that Beth couldn't quite put a
finger on. What was going on between them? Talia was right.
Or perhaps half-right. Was it Max being overly friendly? Or
was it Charlie?

'Hey Dad, nice work with the kid.' It was Ethan, and he
draped his arm around his father.

'Dad, are you all right?' Chloe's little face squeezed
through the gap between her father and brother.

'All good, guys.' Max stroked Chloe's hair. 'Nothing to worry about.'

'Are you staying for the championship race? I've qualified fastest. It's happening pretty soon. Please.' Chloe clasped her hands together.

'Of course I will.'

Could all competitors in the under-13 age championship make their way to the starting blocks. And all marshals, back to your positions. NOW!

'That's me,' Chloe squealed and darted off.

'Good luck,' called Max and Beth together.

The crowd had hushed. Beth looked up into the grandstand. She spotted Ethan, then Max next to him, deep in conversation with Charlie Devine.

Beth's stomach clenched.

BANG!

She stood on tippy-toes to see Chloe in lane four. Doing well. Swimming steadily and smoothly. Beth allowed herself a small swell of pride. Her daughter really was a beautiful swimmer and seeing her do what she loved and was so good at was all the compensation Beth needed for the early starts.

But wait. What was happening? The kid in lane five was catching her.

'C'mon, Chloe,' Beth muttered under her breath. 'Dig in, sweetie. Dig deep.'

But with every stroke, the other child was making ground. Wearing her down. Only ten metres to go. The crowd was going bananas. Max and Ethan were on their feet, fists in the air and screaming words of encouragement. Even

Charlie was standing and had her hands raised in a prayer position, kissing her fingertips.

'C'mon, Chloe. C'mon,' said Beth, clasping tightly to her second place sticks.

With a final thrashing of arms and legs, the race finished. The crowd was silent. Who'd won? It was too hard to tell. On first instincts, Beth thought it a dead heat. She looked for Miss Liu. There she was, holding her clipboard and frowning at the pool. In extremely close races, it was the sports teacher who made the final call on placings.

'Lane four,' she called. 'Second place, and lane five, first. Marshals,' she barked, eyes focused on Beth. 'Issue the placings.'

Beth trudged towards her daughter, the little red stick feeling like a burning poker in her hand. As she got closer, she saw tears running down Chloe's face, and she hurried the last few steps.

'I got a stitch,' she sobbed.

Beth knelt by the pool. 'Sweetie, second place is wonderful. It was so close. I'm so proud of you.'

Chloe's tear-stained face turned towards her. 'It's all your fault,' she cried. 'Why did you make me eat that donut?'

'I didn't. I told you not to. It was *you* who insisted.'

'But you gave me the money. I hate you!'

Beth felt slapped.

Silently, she placed the second place stick by Chloe's lane, and walked away without looking back once.

CHAPTER EIGHTEEN

Bugger.

Alex cursed and sucked on her thumb. Stupid needle. Stupid button. Stupid fingers that wouldn't stop quivering. In her mouth, the metallic taste of blood triggered a tidal wave of saliva. And she was nearly done too. Final stitch.

'You can't go in there.' From outside her closed office door, Brianna's voice was firm. Still, Alex's heart fluttered. Plenty of lawyers at Macauley – mostly the sexist has-beens, of which there were plenty – had a bad habit of disobeying the secretaries.

Alex looked down. She'd had to remove her skirt in order to fix the button – Brianna had an emergency sewing kit in her top drawer, god love her – and here she was, in her undies and a blouse, blinds drawn, with Brianna under strict instructions to not let anyone through the door. And that meant anyone. Even Rex.

'She's on a very important phone call,' said Brianna. 'I can call you when she's done.'

'Well, if it's a *very* important phone call …' came Martin's slightly sneery voice. 'I suppose I'll have to wait.'

Alex threw on her skirt and hurriedly tucked in her blouse. It wasn't wise to keep Martin waiting.

'I'm off the phone now, Brianna,' called Alex, straightening the skew-whiff skirt. 'Please show him in.'

She opened the door with a winning smile pasted to her face. 'Martin, thank you for waiting.'

He gave a little bob. 'I received your email requesting an appointment to discuss an important matter.' He used air quotes around the word *important*. 'I thought now might be a suitable time?'

Alex's heart skipped a beat. So distracted was she by the meeting with the partners she'd completely forgotten the email. Part-time work. Yes. That's what she was going to ask for, but that was before the partners' meeting. That meeting had changed everything.

'Martin. Sorry. Yes. I did send you that message, but um … I've … um, managed to work out the problem.' Alex tapped a file on her desk. 'It's all under control.'

Martin nodded. 'Very well. Still, I think it would be advantageous to confer over the precise details of the partnership arrangements at Macauley. Rex has requested that I walk you through the financial detail and his instructions are to have the contract drawn by the end of the month.'

Martin bobbed again, and Alex blinked quickly.

'All right then. Yes. That would be wonderful.'

'Excellent. 3 pm in my office,' he called over his shoulder and stole off silently down the hall.

Shit, he was talking as if the partnership was a done deal, as if there was no possibility that she would say *no*. Had no one in the history of Macauley Partners ever refused a partnership? When Alex joined the company, she'd vowed to make history, but that wasn't quite the history she was contemplating.

Her phone buzzed.

How'd the meeting go?

James! She needed to ring him and tell him the news. He'd be thrilled, wouldn't he? He knew how much this meant to her.

She dialled and her husband picked up straight away.

'So? Don't keep me in suspense …' He sounded anxious. He was worried for her. He really was the loveliest.

'Well,' Alex began. 'It didn't go quite as planned.' She took a breath. 'They've asked me to become partner.'

Silence. 'Good one, Alex,' her husband chortled. 'You nearly got me there. I've never heard you so serious. C'mon, what did they really say?'

'I am serious,' she said with irritation. 'What? You think I'm not up to it?'

'No, no. I think you run rings around those people. I just can't quite believe the timing. It's just … uncanny.' He paused. 'Did they really ask you to become partner?'

'They did! They really did.' Alex proceeded to repeat the entire boardroom palaver, recounting word-for-word Rex's comments about her work ethic and expertise and, for added authenticity, she even included the fact about her skirt button popping mid-sentence.

At that point, he believed her. No one could make *that* up.

'Holy shit,' he breathed down the phone. 'Partner? It's, like, your dream …'

'I know. It's crazy, isn't it?' Alex's voice trembled from the effort of having to keep it low. Macauley wasn't the place for wild celebrations.

Their conversation was brief. James had a patient to see. Alex said they'd talk about it more that night.

'Well done, Alex. I'm proud of you.' But there was a strained tone to the words.

He's at work, too, after all, Alex reasoned.

A minute later, her phone buzzed with a text message.

How's this actually going to work? With the baby and everything?

Poor man. This morning, she'd set out for work with a mission to insist on reduced hours, now she was looking at increasing them substantially. She swivelled in the chair and picked up the framed photo of the twins on her desk. It was a reasonable question. How would this work? When Alex had first set her sights on becoming partner, she wasn't a mother, she wasn't married, she hadn't even met James. It was easy, almost obligatory, to set lofty career goals when career was the only thing in your life and you were the only person in your family to have completed a university degree. Now, there were the twins, and James, and Noah's problems to deal with and, to top it all off, a baby on the way. How was a person supposed to juggle all of that?

Alex typed out a reply.

I have no idea, but let's talk about it tonight?

James's response was immediate.

I'll pick up some Chinese takeaway. This is something to celebrate, whatever we decide.

Alex flinched at the word *we*. He was right, it would have to be a joint decision. After all, accepting the partnership would affect James's life as much as hers. For better and for worse. It would be busy, that went without saying, and she would certainly need additional domestic help. But with the bump in earnings that came with a partnership, she'd be able to afford a full-time nanny for the children, a private tutor for Noah, meals supplied by Nourish, *and* they'd be able to pay the mortgage off the house in half the time. James could choose whether he wanted to work or not.

But that word – *we* – still annoyed her, for it implied the degree to which she, and she alone, had worked for and earned this huge opportunity didn't really matter at all.

She turned back to her computer. Forty-five unread emails in her inbox, starting with one from Martin about the take-over matter. Alex sighed. She couldn't concentrate on a multi-billion dollar acquisition right now, she was hungry. She needed to make an acquisition of her own – lunch. And she needed to talk to someone, anyone, about her confused feelings over the partnership.

'I'm taking you to lunch,' she announced, standing by Brianna's desk.

'I've already brought lunch,' said Brianna, her eyes still glued to the screen.

'I'm offering you a free lunch … Just take it.' Alex had her hands on her hips.

'You're the one always saying there's no such thing as a free lunch, especially for a woman,' said the secretary.

'There's a caveat to that – when it's being bought by another woman, especially if it's the woman you work for. This is me, showing my appreciation for all you do for me.' She shifted her weight. 'Just let me buy you a damn sandwich, all right?'

'Fine.' She stopped typing. 'But I'd actually prefer sushi.'

Alex stood at the entrance to the food court, packed with city workers on their lunch break. Sleeves rolled up. Ties loosened. A few smiles here and there.

Like prisoners on day release, thought Alex.

Her stomach grumbled like a garbage truck.

'Was that you?' said Brianna, eyebrows raised.

'It's fine. Just hunger. How about I get a table while you look around and decide what you want, then I'll order and pay. Okay?' She pointed to a nearby sushi place. 'That's where I go every day. It's good.'

She took a seat and watched Brianna weave through the crowd. She moved with composure. Head held high. Back straight as a rod. A natural confidence. Instinctively, the crowds parted for her. Men and women alike.

Alex tugged at her waistband and covered her mouth to burp. Blood and coffee. Charming.

Brianna was back. 'I'll just have two tuna and avocado sushi rolls, thanks.'

'And?'

'That's it.'

'A little boring, don't you think? This is the boss paying. Lash out. Live a little.' Alex gripped the table and leant forward.

'Well, what are you having?' Brianna frowned.

Two pieces of salmon sashimi, three gyoza and one of those inside-out type rolls with raw tuna. And maybe a friand for dessert. Eating for two, after all.

Alex stopped. Raw fish. It was completely off the menu. She didn't want to poison the poor foetus.

'Um … well … actually.' Alex looked around the food court. Burritos. They'd be fine, wouldn't they. All cooked meat. Hang on, there was the lettuce and tomato sitting around in a bain marie … Right, fish and chips then. No salmonella could survive a deep fryer. On second thoughts, hadn't she read something about high mercury levels in that type of fish. Strike that.

'I'm … ah … I'm going to have a toasted cheddar cheese sandwich.'

'So a toasted cheese sandwich now constitutes living a little?' Brianna demanded.

'Well, as it so happens …' Alex stopped and allowed herself a little smile. She always got nervous before telling people she was pregnant. It was quite an intimate thing to reveal when you thought about it. *Yes, my husband and I DO have sex and his sperm recently had a happy meeting with my eggs and now I'm KNOCKED UP!*

'I'm pregnant.'

Brianna looked at her and cocked her head. 'Again?'

Alex opened and closed her mouth. 'The usual response is *congratulations*, you know.'

'Congratulations,' said Brianna. 'Is it a boy or a girl?'

'We don't know yet,' said Alex, waving her hand dismissively. 'Anyway, it doesn't matter.' She brought her hands into the prayer position. 'I do have some other news that may interest you more. But it's a secret. The baby thing is a secret too, but I have a feeling you won't go round telling everyone.'

'No,' said Brianna. 'I won't.'

'All right, well, the second bit of news is …' She took a breath. 'I've been asked by Rex Macauley to become a partner.'

'Oh my god, that's fucking amazing.' Brianna clapped a hand over her mouth. 'I can't believe I just said that,' she whispered, eyes shining. 'But it's seriously very cool. Well done. You must be stoked. Just think about the work. We're going to get the best matters.' She rubbed her hands together. 'I can't wait.'

Again, there was that *we* word. For a promotion that was ostensibly hers and hers alone, both James and Brianna seemed to be taking an awful lot of ownership over it.

'Yes, well, I appreciate your enthusiasm. But there is the small matter of this baby to think about. And my other children. Not to mention my husband. Not quite sure when I'll squeeze in time to see him … ' She trailed off.

Brianna was staring at her. 'You're not seriously thinking of saying no are you?' Her voice was hushed and urgent. 'You can't say no. This is … this is … everything.' She raised her hands skywards and dropped them down again. 'You can do this. You *have* to do this. Otherwise, what message does it send?'

'It doesn't send any message. It's just a decision,' said Alex. 'My decision.'

Brianna violently shook her head. 'No, it's not. You're smart, you're incredibly ambitious and you can juggle a million things at once. If you can't make this work, then what hope is there for the rest of us? This is just your guilt talking.' Brianna nodded. 'Yes, it is. If you were a man, you wouldn't be talking about babies and children and husbands, you'd have already called an interior designer to deck out that fancy corner office you're going to get when you say *yes*. You owe it to women everywhere to take this job.' She tapped the table. 'And you owe it to yourself.'

Alex sat back. Who was this passionate feminist firebrand before her? And where had her efficient, unemotional secretary gone?

'Okay, well, I hadn't really thought of it that way.'

Brianna's eyes narrowed. 'You should, you really should.' She paused and stood up. 'Right, now you're going to give me fifty bucks and I'm going to order us one of those sushi platters over there.' She pointed to a plate full of raw and exotic seafood, plus a few dumplings and sushi rolls. 'And you are going to eat it because you don't get bossed around by the pregnancy police. You are Alex O'Rourke, senior associate and incoming partner at one of the city's most prestigious small-to-medium-sized law firms. You. Have. Got. This.' Brianna clenched her fist and, buoyed by her enthusiasm, Alex produced her wallet with a flourish.

Brianna was right. She could do this. There were these people called nannies. She would hire one for the twins. Maybe a live-in. Give her and James the occasional date night. She would take six weeks maternity leave and no more. Work from home in that time. Get the nanny to bring the baby in for feeds.

Alex looked in her wallet while Brianna watched her expectantly, encouragingly.

Hang on. No cash, not a cent, and she knew her credit card was maxed out thanks to all the extra-curricular activities she'd just enrolled the boys in.

Yep, she really had this.

CHAPTER NINETEEN

'So, if we factor in a kilo of mince, one bottle of passata, an onion, three carrots, maybe a zucchini just to up the vegie content …' Cara scribbled furiously in her notebook. 'And let's say that serves six people, then our per-portion cost is roughly …' She chewed the end of her pencil. 'Two dollars fifty per person, give or take a few cents. And we could provide a green salad, the dressing separate, just some oil and vinegar to shake up and emulsify.' She scribbled again. 'Does that sound right to you?' Cara paused and looked up. 'Beth? Beth? Hello … earth to Beth.' Her neighbour's eyes were fixed on some distant spot over Cara's shoulder, somewhere near the bougainvillea. She waved her hand. 'Beth? Are you listening?'

'Excuse me? Sorry. Say that again?' Beth shook her head and refocused her gaze. 'I'm ready now.' She held up her pencil. 'Still feeling the effects of that alcohol from last night. I really wish you and Alex hadn't encouraged me to drink quite so much. I nearly disgraced myself at the swimming carnival today. It was awful.' She shuddered.

Cara cocked her head. Did it matter if her recollection of the evening differed from Beth's? Probably not. The poor woman's eyes were bloodshot, her cheeks pale. 'We can take a break, if you'd like. I think we've done pretty well for today.' She ran her pencil down the list of things they'd already ticked off – a Facebook page, registration of the business name and a web domain, a basic web page, and an initial inquiry to council about what approvals they'd need.

'Oh, I forgot to mention that because the shed is already registered as a licensed food premises, the council says we can start cooking out of here straight away. Isn't that great?'

But Beth was staring off into the distance again.

Cara lightly touched her arm. 'Tell me what's going on with you. I can see there's a problem. Did something happen after I left last night?'

Beth shook it off. 'Of course not,' she said briskly. 'Just distracted and a little hungover, that's all. I'm fine. Absolutely fine. Just tell me what you said again?'

'Fine? That's the four-letter f-word that women use when everything is far from okay.' Cara felt herself colouring. 'A nurse once told me that.'

Beth sighed, and let the pencil fall from her hands. 'It's this texting business ... Max. I just can't get it out of my head.' She rubbed her temples. 'At one point today, I actually thought maybe there was something going on between Max and Charlie.'

'Charlie Devine? Why?'

'Oh, just something Talia said … and the way they act when they're together.' Beth waved her hand. 'But I can't be sure. The phone numbers don't match.'

'You've checked?'

'I asked Talia for her mum's number on the pretext of sending her a message to say I'd given her a lift, but her mother's just got a new number so I'm really none the wiser.' Beth dropped her head into her hands. 'Lying to a child like that,' she muttered. 'It's awful.'

Cara waited. It was still light in Cuthbert Close but the shadows were just starting to lengthen in the garden. Poppy was inside, watching the half hour of television that she was allowed after her homework was done. A couple of crows wheeled overhead against the amber sky.

'Perhaps it's time to ask Max about the messages. Talk to him. Tell him you're afraid,' said Cara.

Beth violently shook her head. 'No. No. I can't do that. He'll think I've been snooping. That I don't trust him.'

'But he has given you a reason not to trust him. All you're doing is asking a question.' Cara glanced briefly at her note-pad. *Oil and vinegar*, she'd written. So many people thought they couldn't mix. Not quite true. If you shook hard enough, the mixture blended eventually, not perfectly, but enough to spread tiny drops of one through the other. Emulsifying. Marrying. Oil and vinegar. Her mum and dad. Her and Pete. Opposites, in so many ways, but also a perfect marriage. It all came down to the effort. The hard work.

'Surely it's better to know the truth.' Cara took her hand and squeezed. 'You're a strong woman. You'll cross this bridge if it's necessary.'

Beth sniffed and produced a tissue from her sleeve. 'You're right,' she said, blowing.

'Hello? Anyone home?'

Cara's side gate squealed.

'You expecting anyone?' Beth sat up quickly, stuffing the tissue back into the sleeve of her cardigan.

'No, not that I know—' Cara clapped her hand to her forehead. 'Oh, wait. It's Will Parry. He wanted to check something.'

'Check something?'

'He didn't say what.'

Beth raised her eyebrows. 'Check up on his tenant perhaps?'

'It's not like that, I assure you.'

Cara took in Beth's hopeful smile. She was such a hopeless romantic. No wonder Max's behaviour was causing her so much grief. She really did believe in the happily ever after.

'Right, well, I might just slip through the fence, if you don't mind. Not really in the mood for small talk.' She rose and kissed Cara lightly on the head. 'Thank you for your wise counsel.'

'Let me know how it goes,' she called to Beth's retreating back.

'Cara, hi.' Will Parry stood in her back garden, hands on hips. 'Do you know that person crawling under your back fence?' He craned his neck and Cara followed his gaze to see Beth's feet disappearing through the small gap in the wood paling fence.

'That's my neighbour, Beth. Actually, my business partner as well. We're going into the catering business.'

'Really? Where?'

Cara laughed lightly. 'Actually, you're looking at it.' She gestured to the old shed. 'It's already approved as a commercial kitchen, for my styling business.'

'I presume you got landlord approval?'

'Oh, yes, your father said we could do whatever we wanted. He was wonderful like that.' Cara clasped her hands. 'You should come to our tasting party next Monday night. We're asking all the neighbours.'

Will grunted noncommittally and folded his arms. 'We want to get the place painted before we sell.' He produced a handful of colour swatches from his pocket. 'My siblings want me to decide on a colour.'

At the word *sell* Cara felt a flicker of fear, but she put the emotion aside and remembered her manners. 'Would you like some help?' She rose from the chair and stepped closer. 'I have a pretty good eye for that kind of thing.'

'You want to help me? Even though this is all in aid of selling your home and forcing you out of it?' Will's gaze narrowed.

'Your father was good to us.' She shrugged. 'Disrespecting his family would be disrespecting him.'

Will eyed her cautiously. 'All right then. Tell me what you think.' He held up the first colour swatch to the outside of the cottage and Cara touched the smooth painted brick, still warm from the heat of the sun.

'Too white. See how it's got these blue tones.' She tapped the card. 'The house needs something warmer.'

Will peered in closer. 'Fair enough. What about this one?' He held up a second swatch, this one a creamy off-white.

'Better, but it's quite pink, don't you think? Here, I'll hold it. You look.'

Will stepped back and tilted his head. 'Too pink,' he declared, producing a third swatch from his pocket. 'This one should do it.' He handed it to Cara and she turned the card thoughtfully.

'This is definitely closer to the current colour.' She held it up against the wall. 'See how it has some warmth, but—'

'It's not too yellow,' he finished.

'I think you're getting it.' She smiled and handed back the swatch.

'I don't think my ex-wife would agree.' He returned the swatch to his pocket.'She's a creative, like you … A graphic designer. Hated house painting. Once, we had to choose colours together, and she told me I was as creative as a tree stump.'

'That seems a bit unfair on the tree stump,' joked Cara.

Will's face tensed, then broke into a smile. 'That's exactly what I told her.' He looked about, as if ready to leave, but his feet stayed glued to the spot. 'I guess that's it then.'

'Would you like a tea or coffee? I might even have a beer somewhere …'

'No, no.' He shook his head and jammed his hands into his pockets. 'It's … ah … well—' He looked around at the garden. The sun had sunk further, bathing the cottage in honeyed rays and accentuating the already deep colours of pink and purple that littered the flower beds. 'The place … well … it actually doesn't look too bad at this time of day.' His eyes roved across the space and he turned in it, slowly.

He's searching for memories.

Cara was quiet. 'You know you don't have to sell,' she began softly. 'I'm starting this business so I can pay you more rent. Help to fix it up. Keep it in your family. It could be a wonderful investment, for the long term, and you get to hold on to a piece of your childhood,' she finished in a rush.

And I get to hold onto Pete, while Poppy gets to stay in the only home she's ever known.

Will wheeled around. His face was in shadow, dark and hardened. 'They'll never agree to it.' He shook his head.

'Who'll never agree?'

'My brother and sister.' He looked skywards. 'Half brother and sister, I should say. Same mother, different father.'

'Oh, I just assumed …'

'My mum's first husband died young. Really young. Left her with two little kids to raise alone. They were teenagers when Mum met Dad and they had me …' He paused and stared at her. 'I don't know why I'm telling you all this.'

'Please don't feel you have to.' Cara waved her hand.

'No, it's like I need to.' He threw his hands in the air. 'I don't know. Anyway, my siblings always resented me, even though Dad did nothing but love them as his own. Left us equal shares in the house. Everything he had he split evenly in the will.' He sighed. 'Anyway, the point is. They want to sell, so we're selling. End of story. I don't want to give them another reason to hate me. This place is a money pit and, thanks to my divorce, I have no desire to fight over property ever again.'

As he spoke, Will had stepped closer to her. She felt the heat off him, the same way she'd felt the warmth off the house. Residual energy. Cara flinched. A light had come on in the house and it spilled across Will's face. They both turned to its source.

It was just Poppy, going into her bedroom to get a book. She startled to see her mum and Will watching her, then waved happily before collapsing onto the bed and finding her page.

Cara felt Will resume his stillness as he watched, and then it was just the two of them on the outside, looking in at Poppy, so at ease and content in her surroundings that it made Cara's heart feel too full for her chest.

'I wish I'd had that as a kid,' said Will softly.

'Me too,' said Cara. 'She's lucky …'

And I need her to stay that way.

CHAPTER TWENTY

Beth closed the French doors behind her, relieved. The house was quiet. Ethan and Chloe were probably upstairs, ensconced in homework, hopefully.

More likely plugged into their devices.

But at least it gave her a moment to mull over Cara's advice. That comment she'd made, about Max giving her a reason not to trust him – it was absolutely true. This was mostly his fault, not hers. She deserved answers.

'That you, Beth?'

She jumped, hand flying to her chest. Max. He was home early.

'Yes, it's me. Just been over at Cara's.' She walked tentatively into the living room. Max was on the couch, tapping away at his phone, tie loosened and top buttons undone.

An idea struck her. 'Feel like going for a walk with me?'

He looked up in surprise. 'Don't you need to get the dinner on?'

'It's done. A shepherd's pie that I made and froze last week. We've got time. Just a stroll around the block, I promise.'

'Sure,' he said with uncertainty. 'Can I just get my joggers on?'

'Oh, don't worry about that.' She waved her hand airily, ignoring her thumping heart. 'Come as you are. It's not a race or anything. I just need a bit of fresh air. Blow the cobwebs away after last night.'

He peered at her. 'I thought you'd be tired from the carnival.'

'Me? Oh, no. I'm good.' She shifted her weight. 'Shall we go?'

Outside, Beth breathed deeply. The street lights blinked into life. Max followed her down the footpath and she slowed to let him catch her.

'So, that was quite the excitement at the carnival today,' she said. 'Did you get back to work okay?'

'All fine. Charlie brought me home to get a change of clothes and then gave me a lift to work. She's really quite friendly once you get to know her.'

And just how well do you *know her?*

'She seems an … interesting woman.' Beth brushed a strand of hair out of her eyes. 'Talia's a sweetheart.'

'Hm.'

The sky was soft indigo now and the moon was starting to transform from transparent tissue to white satin.

They walked on and turned the corner.

'Max,' Beth started. 'I need to ask you something.'

'Sounds serious.'

'It is.' She put her hand out to make him stop. Her heart knocked against her ribs. 'Max, I don't quite know how to ask this, so I'm just going to say it.' She took a deep breath, the air whooshing through her O-shaped lips. 'All right, here goes.' She took another breath.

'What is it? Just say it.' Max stood in the middle of the footpath, hands on hips.

Beth clasped her fingers and dropped her gaze.

She couldn't do it.

She couldn't ask the question. Putting it out there would be like releasing a helium balloon to the sky. It would never be re-caught. It would be out there, always, flying away from them out of reach. And even if it disappeared, the knowledge of it out there, floating somewhere, would always haunt them.

A question like that could damage a relationship irreparably.

If it wasn't true, it would be a crack in their nineteen-year marriage, not necessarily ruined, but certainly flawed. Their minds would worry on it, and return to it, like a tongue going back to a chipped tooth.

On the other hand, if it was true, she would find out in time. There'd already been clues. There'd be more, if there was more to find. What was Aunty Marg's favourite Buddhist saying? There were three things that could not hide for long – the sun, the moon and the truth. Then again, thanks to three divorces, Marg also believed all men were arseholes. Never mind. She would just have to be patient. Prepare herself. Get Nourish up and running, just in case she needed some back-up funds. After the anniversary party, that's when she would ask him. True, going ahead with the celebration meant it would be something of a sham. But it was just for one night, and it would certainly be a better option than cancelling on all their friends and family.

Max's pocket bleeped and he looked at Beth expectantly, waiting. 'Beth? What did you want to ask me?' The phone bleeped again.

'Oh, it's nothing.' She waved her hand dismissively. 'Answer your phone.'

He reached for his pocket, the screen casting a strange glow over his face. 'It's Charlie Devine,' he said, frowning. 'She's got a problem with her fuse box and wants to know if I can help.'

'Can't one of the junior agents help her? Or an electrician?'

I could call Adam … Wait, no. I need to forget all about him.

'I *could* get one of them,' he mused. 'But seeing as I'm here, it sort of makes sense for me to go over there. Be neighbourly and all, like you're always telling me. Probably just needs a switch to be flicked.'

'Oh, fine then,' said Beth, folding her arms.

'I can tell her to wait, if you want to keep walking?' he offered.

'No, no, it's okay. It was nothing important. But I might walk on a bit.' She gestured to the footpath leading further away from the close and into the darkness. 'I'll see you back home.'

'Okay then.'

Without another word, they went their separate ways.

ThePrimalGuy.com.au

From: The Primal Guy

Subject: Relationships

Hey Prime-Ordial Beings,

How hard is it to be away from the people you love most in the world? I'll tell you. It's frickin' hard. I miss being a family so bad it hurts. Like really hurts, in my gut.

But it got me thinking. Why? I got food. I got water. I got people around me. But something's missing. My family. But what makes us want to stick together? To commit, forever?

'Cause in the beginning, it wasn't like that. It wasn't like that at all. We were basically animals, after all, and it was all about the law of the jungle. The strongest dudes. The toughest. The meanest. They were the ones who got all the ladies and got to procreate with them.

But something changed. The weaklings wised up. They figured out that if they had something to offer the females – like better food, or shelter – then the chicks would dig them more and – here's the biggie – they'd stick with them.

Monogamy was born. It made, like, total sense, because now the mums also had a partner who'd be around to help out with the kids, instead of being out sowing his wild oats. And it was good for the tribe, 'cause kids could be hard work – couldn't walk, couldn't talk, couldn't get their own food – but now there was this thing called a family, and people were co-operating and, you know where we'd be without co-operation and new generations of kids? Nowhere!

Okay, so now it's different. Now, there's a million and one choices and distractions and it seems like it's harder than ever to make a commitment and stick to it.

It's not. It's natural. It's evolution. It's how we got here.

Peace out,
Ryan (AKA the Primal Guy)

PS Running a 50% discount for this week only on my manifesto: 'From Pen-Pusher to Primal Guy'. 384 pages on how I ditched the corporate life and claimed a new one by touching my inner homo-sapiens.

CHAPTER TWENTY-ONE

Cara stood at the doorway to Beth's kitchen and held up an empty platter. 'Have we got any more of the wagyu pies? They disappeared in two seconds flat.'

Beth slammed shut the oven door. 'Excellent,' she said through gritted teeth.

Cara stopped, tongs in the air. 'He'll be here, he's just running late, probably.'

'Then why hasn't he called? Or messaged? We all know how much he loves messaging.'

So far, everything at the launch party had gone perfectly – the food was delicious, the neighbours were loving it, and many had already placed orders on the menu sheets prepared by Cara. It had all the ingredients for a perfect party, but there was just one thing missing.

Max.

In the days since her aborted conversation about the messages things between them had been tense, but Beth hadn't had time to dwell on it as she and Cara went full steam ahead for the Nourish launch party.

'If it's any consolation, my parents are late as well.' A troubled look came over Cara's face.

Okay – so there were three things, or people, missing. Max, and Cara's parents. Only the three most important people, in terms of help and support.

'They've got a long way to come. Peak-hour traffic is always awful. I'm sure it's just that,' said Beth, injecting confidence into her voice.

'Same with Max.'

Tossing a tea towel over her shoulder, Beth took her wooden spoon and gave the saucepan a stir. 'The chicken curry's just about right. Are those boxes ready to go?'

Cara checked the line of cardboard containers. 'All filled with rice. Coriander chopped?'

'Just here.' Beth gave a nod towards a bowl on her right. 'How about you do another pass with the pies. I'll start serving out the curry and you can do the garnish when you come back.'

'Perfect.' Cara sailed out of the kitchen and towards the hubbub of voices coming from the front yard.

Beth dipped her spoon into the curry and closed her eyes as she consciously tested her tastebuds for the flavours – top notes of cumin and coriander, a little heat underneath from the ginger, a hint of tang from the tomato paste and the smooth creaminess of coconut milk. She frowned. It was all there, but it was just a little flat.

Cara was back. The tray empty, again.

'Can you try this?' Beth cleaned off the spoon, dipped it into the curry and offered it to Cara who closed her eyes as she swished the sauce about her mouth.

'Needs a pinch more salt to bring it to life.'

'That's it exactly. Sorry. Blame my absent husband for distracting me.' She took a generous pinch of salt from the bowl, stirred it in and tasted again. Perfect. Lively. Amazing how such a small intervention could completely tip the balance.

'Let's get it out while everyone's still hungry,' said Cara.

'Did someone say hungry?' Alex hurried into the kitchen. 'I am completely ravenous.' She leant against the bench and eased a heel out of her shiny black stilettos.

'You've come to the right place then. The twins here?' asked Beth.

'Outside with James scoffing pies,' said Alex, slipping her shoe back on and picking up a tray. 'Can I make myself useful?'

'Sure can. Max was supposed to be helping … but he's not here yet.' Beth started placing the filled curry boxes onto her tray.

'Hang on. Garnish.' Cara scooted over with coriander in one hand and a lime in the other. 'Makes all the difference.'

Alex stood back and watched them. 'Watching you ladies work together in the kitchen is like watching a choreographed ballet. It's bloody beautiful.'

Cara chuckled. 'I don't think anyone would pay to see it, though.'

'No, but they'll pay for the food that comes out of it.' Alex collected the completed tray. 'I'll get at least another couple of the neighbours on board with this lot.' She stopped at the door. 'Oh, hey, Cara, I think your parents just arrived. I saw them on my way into the kitchen. I'll go and say hello.'

'Oh, thank you! Tell them I'll be out in a few minutes. Just need to check some things to make sure we're on track.'

Cara faced the stove and mentally ticked off the menu list, while Beth opened the oven door and inhaled the sweet saltiness of the pumpkin and sage risotto. 'Nearly done. Just needs to absorb a little more of the stock and we're good to go.' Beth pulled on a pair of washing-up gloves and turned the tap to hot. 'Why don't you go say hi to your parents while I get started on this? We've got time.'

'That would be great.' Cara whipped off her apron and straightened her hair. 'I'll only be a second.'

Beth plunged her hands into the water and let her mind wander as she so often did while doing the washing up. Where could Max be? She'd been counting on him being home by six to help hand around the food. Now it was nearly seven.

'Would you like some help?' Talia Devine stood at the kitchen island. In her hands was a pile of letters and catalogues. 'Mum noticed your letterbox was full,' she explained.

Beth felt a jolt of irritation. Couldn't Charlie Devine worry about her own letterbox instead of poking her nose into other people's? For a woman who wanted space, she was certainly making a habit of inserting herself into Beth's life. And Max's.

Talia picked up a tea towel.

'You don't have to, Talia. I'm happy to do it,' said Beth.

'No, it's fine. Mum puts everything in the dishwasher, but I actually don't mind washing up. Beats homework, anyway.'

Beth snapped off her gloves. 'Have you had something to eat? I know a lot of our food doesn't fit your mum's diet, but I have a couple of sneaky pies here if you'd like one.'

As Talia went to answer, Alex swept into the kitchen with a very pale-looking Jasper on her hip and Noah dawdling in her skirt. 'Sorry to do this, Beth, but we're going to have to take off. Jasper feels like he's about to vomit and Noah says he's got tummy pains too. You're under control here?'

'Not the food that's made them sick, I hope.' Beth rubbed the limp Jasper's back and winked at the unusually wan Noah.

'Ha! No. More likely the bug that's been going round at school.' Alex inclined her head at Talia. 'This one's been helping me with the kids. Total sweetie.' Talia accepted the compliment with a small nod and Alex kissed Beth on the cheek. 'Beautiful food, Bethy. I convinced the architects on the corner to order a month's worth.'

Beth inhaled. 'That's wonderful. Thank you, Alex.'

'Don't thank me. Thank those amazing cooking skills of yours. Just think, all those hundreds of thousands of meals you've made for your family over the years – it was all training for this.'

Beth squeezed her friend's shoulder and stroked Jasper's hair. 'I hope your little men are okay.'

'They'll be fine.' Alex hoisted Jasper higher on her hip and turned for the door.

'Your house is very clean.' Jasper lifted his head briefly off his mother's shoulder.

'And you have lots of nice things,' added Noah, trailing behind. The boys had spent most of the party marauding around, playing hide and seek. Not that Beth had minded, it reminded her of Chloe and Ethan's noisy years when they'd filled the rooms with shouting and boisterous games. It was so much quieter now.

'Well, *we* have lots of toys,' Beth overhead Alex say defensively. 'And our house is very clean on Tuesdays after Alma has come.'

Beth gave a wry smile at the retreating trio.

'I'd better go too. Homework calls.' Talia finished drying the pot in her hand and hung the tea towel over the oven handle.

'Wait. Take these.' Beth packed two wagyu pies into a plastic container. She'd been saving them for Ethan and Chloe to take to school but Talia seemed to need them more. 'Our little secret.' She put a finger to her lips. 'And here's some risotto for later.'

'Thank you, Mrs Chandler ... uh, Beth, I mean. I'll make sure she doesn't find out.' Talia made her way slowly out of the kitchen with the containers balanced carefully.

'Talia ... shit. Sorry.' It was Max, in such a bumbling rush that he'd nearly caused the food to tumble right out of the teenager's hand.

'Max,' Beth admonished. 'Language.'

'It's all right, Mr Chandler. I'm pretty good at juggling.' Talia grinned and looked from Beth to Max. Noting their stricken faces, her smile faded. 'I better go.'

'Thanks again for the help.'

Max waited for the teenager to leave. 'I know what you're going to say—'

Beth took in her husband's slightly damp hair and casual shorts. 'Have you been at the gym?' she burst out. 'You know how important this night is for me. For Cara. For our business. And you went to the gym instead?'

'Not deliberately.' His face hardened. 'I forgot. I just forgot. Honestly. You don't have to go on.'

Beth's eyes narrowed. She picked up a tea towel and started wiping furiously. 'You think that makes it okay? That I'm so unimportant you just forgot me?'

'No, no, I didn't mean it like that.' He ran a hand through his slickened hair. 'It was just crazy at work. I didn't have a minute to think. I was on autopilot.'

'That's right, Max. You are on autopilot. And not just tonight, either. Sometimes, it feels like you've checked out of this family altogether.'

'Are you serious? I'm working my arse off for you guys.' He shook his head and his voice softened. 'I really am sorry, Bethy. I'm going to go outside and talk to the neighbours and hopefully drum up a bit more business for you.' He stopped. 'I do want this to work for you. Truly.'

Why? So the kids and I have some money to live on when you're gone?

Beth's skin prickled. 'Go then.'

And he did. Shoulders slumped, he made his way slowly into the front garden. She watched him, doing the rounds of the neighbours, shaking hands, patting kids on the head, doing the sales pitch that always came so naturally to him. That was the thing with Max, you never quite knew what was spin and what was just him – his natural enthusiasm and friendliness. He probably didn't know himself, the two blended so seamlessly together.

Shaking herself out of thought, Beth went to make space on the bench for the risotto. She picked up the pile of mail brought in by Talia. Bills, mostly. Marketing guff from real estate agents. Couple of supermarket catalogues.

Then, something different.

A plain white business envelope. No postmarks. No address at all. Beth ripped it open and removed a piece of paper, blue with pink lines. She opened it. A message, hand-written in large capital letters.

I KNOW WHAT YOU'RE DOING AND I THINK IT'S DISGUSTING. BE HONEST. TELL THE TRUTH

Her stomach rolled and she turned the page. The other side was blank. Who was this from? What were they talking about? Had someone seen her with Adam? Or was this about Max and his … messages? Who else would know about that? Cara and Alex were the only ones she'd told. And as far as she knew, no one at all had seen her with Adam.

Beth gripped the bench, her knees weakened. Sour saliva coated her mouth.

She looked at the note again. What should she do with it? Rip it into a million pieces and put it into the recycling? Or keep it?

Max was talking to someone else now. Who was it? She craned to see.

Charlie Devine, in a thigh-grazing white shirt dress.

She won't want to bend over in that.

That serious look was on Max's face again, the one he always got when talking to their new neighbour. At that moment, both of them looked back towards the kitchen window. Catching Beth's eye, Max gave her a half-hearted wave, and Charlie gave a wan smile, then shifted around, so that her back was turned and Beth no longer had a view of her husband.

Taking a deep breath, Beth turned back to the stove and carefully slipped the note into her pocket. Now wasn't the time. She had risotto to deal with first, and a business launch to nail.

CHAPTER TWENTY-TWO

'Ready. Set. Go.' Poppy swung her legs into a handstand, her head completely disappearing as her dress dropped over it. 'How long was that one, Halbi?' she demanded, returning to a standing position.

Sam checked his watch. 'Three seconds.'

'Not long enough,' Joy scolded. 'You can do better.'

Poppy nodded. Her face flushed. 'I can do better. Ready to time me again?'

'Poppy.' Cara used her warning voice. 'I don't think Halbi and Halmi want to spend their evening watching you do handstands.'

'Let the girl do her tricks, why not?' cried Sam.

'They've got nothing else to do,' said Poppy in a matter-of-fact tone. 'They're not talking to anyone.'

'Honey, why don't you go and find the other kids. I think they're playing hide and seek in the street.'

Without a word, Poppy took off.

'Say thank you to Halbi and Halmi,' called Cara.

'Thank you,' she bellowed over her shoulder.

Cara held out the tray of risotto. 'Pumpkin, sage and goat's cheese risotto?'

Joy groaned and clutched her stomach. 'I'm full! You have fed me too much.'

'Dad?'

Sam went to take a bowl, but Joy put her hand over his. 'He will burst. And he does not like this rice.' She wrinkled her nose and peered into the dish. 'Too bland.'

Cara flinched. She was used to Joy's barbs over her cooking. She'd come to realise her mother would always regard Korean food as being the world's only truly edible cuisine. What annoyed her was that the criticisms still managed to hurt.

'You're not actually leaving now, are you? You only just arrived. Maybe I could introduce you to some of the neighbours?' As she spoke, there was a tap on her shoulder.

'Cara, hi. Not interrupting, am I?'

'Will … hi.' She'd completely forgotten about asking him to the party and now here he was, business shirt undone at the collar, sleeves rolled to the elbow. She pressed her fingers to her chin.

'Sorry, I didn't mean to surprise you. Is this a bad time?' He glanced over her shoulder.

'No, no, it's fine. I just … um.'

'You forgot that you asked me.' He chuckled. 'It's fine. I really didn't plan to stay long.'

'No, please. Have some risotto.' She held up the tray and Will took a bowl.

'It needs chilli,' Joy volunteered.

Oh, goodness, her parents. Cara whipped around to find her mother's mouth set in a firm line. Her father smiled pleasantly.

'Mum, Dad, please meet Will Parry. He's … uh … he's the son of Mr Parry. Our landlord.'

'Pleased to meet you both.' Smoothly, Will put down the bowl of food and offered his hand. Joy took it suspiciously.

'Where is your father?' Joy's eyes narrowed.

Mentally, Cara face-palmed. The woman could sniff out a problem from a hundred paces. She mustn't find out about Mr Parry's death. Not yet. If she knew that Will and his siblings were planning to sell, the pressure on Cara would be immediate. Joy wouldn't just ask her daughter and granddaughter to move in with them, she'd simply expect it.

'Mr Parry is unwell,' said Cara. 'Will is taking care of things in his absence.'

She felt him looking at her strangely.

'You said Mr Parry was overseas.' Poppy was back, at precisely the wrong time, and delivered the words accusingly.

'No, well, uh—' Cara stammered.

'No, that's right,' said Will. 'He was overseas and then he got a bit sick.' He looked to Cara for confirmation. 'But he's going to be fine.'

Joy nodded knowingly. 'Airplanes are full of germs. So horrible. All that bad air and coughing,' she tsked. 'Tell your father to take ginger. That will fix him.' She looked to Sam. 'We are going now, old man.'

Her father put both hands on Cara's arms and squeezed. 'Congratulations, daughter, on a wonderful business party,' he whispered into her ear. 'We are proud of you.'

Both of you? Or just you?

Joy was already gone, standing out in the close by the car. She waved, and Cara waved back.

Will waited until they were out of sight. 'What was that all about?' he asked, hands on hips. 'Why did we just lie to them about my father, again?'

Cara clasped her hands. 'I'm sorry … It's hard to explain. I don't think you'd understand.'

'Try me.'

She took a breath. 'If Poppy and I have to leave Cuthbert Close, my parents will expect me to come and live with them.'

'And?'

'You just met my mother, what do you think the problem might be with that? Could you have lived with your parents as a grown adult?' She folded her arms.

'Okay … Okay.' Will nodded. 'But you'll have to tell them the truth at some point. Sooner or later.' He regarded her. 'You expect me to go against my brother and sister, but you don't want to face up to your own parents. That doesn't exactly seem fair.'

'I know,' said Cara. 'It's not.' She cast her eyes to the ground. He was right. She was a hypocrite, expecting him to challenge his family when she wasn't brave enough to do the same.

He cleared his throat. 'I've been thinking about what you said the other day about this area … The cottage … It could be a great investment.' He stopped. Something or someone had caught his eye. 'Is that Charlie Devine?' He moved to get a better view and Cara followed his gaze to a set of perfectly sculpted legs, topped by a tiny dress that might have looked trashy on anyone else but was enviably chic on her neighbour.

'You know her?'

'My ex was right into The Primal Guy. Bought all the powders and the pills,' he said with a slight tone of disgust. 'Such a con.'

Cara observed Charlie, deep in conversation with Max Chandler. Whatever was happening between them was a mystery, but one thing was certain – the woman had managed to distract Will Parry from whatever he was just about to say.

'The Primal Guy business has been super successful. You can't fake that.'

'Maybe,' he said, still staring.

'I think you were about to say something, about the cottage,' she prompted.

Will took his eyes off Charlie and fixed them back on Cara. 'Yes, right. What I came here to say is that I'm going to talk to my brother and sister.'

'Do you mean,' she began. 'You're going to ask them not to sell?' She held her breath.

'I can't promise anything.' He paused. 'But yes, I'll try.'

Without thinking, Cara flung her arms around Will's neck, and planted a kiss on his cheek.

'Mummy, what are you doing?' Poppy. Standing with her hands on her hips, next to Alex, with her arms folded.

'Yes, Cara. What *are* you doing?' said Alex.

'Um … I was just telling Mr Parry's son about the neighbourhood.' Cara sprang away from Will and rubbed her lips.

'Well, if all tours come with such five-star service, you might have to sign me up for one,' said Alex, giving her a wink.

'I thought you'd left?' said Cara, rubbing her cheek.

'I found this one hiding in our garden.' She tapped Poppy on the shoulder. 'In a spot where absolutely no one was going to find her, so here she is.'

'Thank you. Is Jasper okay?' she called to Alex's retreating back.

'Puking his guts up,' she called cheerfully. 'The glamour of parenting, right.' She waved and disappeared into the night.

'Poppy, can you go around and start collecting all the empty bowls. Take them into the kitchen, okay?' Cara wheeled her daughter by the shoulders in the direction of Beth's house. 'Go on, off you go. No more games.'

Poppy's shoulders slumped. 'Yes, Mum,' she said in a low voice and trudged off.

Cara turned to Will. His face was flushed and he looked as embarrassed as Cara felt. This wasn't like her. She wasn't a spontaneous hug-and-kiss person with men she barely knew. Her parents' version of *I love you* was a shoulder-squeeze and a sweet rice cake.

'Sorry … er, I mean thank you, for what you said about talking to your family. I really appreciate it.' She scuffed her foot into the grass, her lips still tingling from where they'd touched Will's cheek.

'I'm not making any promises.' He held both hands up, palms facing her. 'And I don't want to get your hopes up. They've never listened to me in the past, and I don't see that changing.' He shrugged. 'But what the hell … If they think there's a dollar in it for them, they might just see reason.' His gaze locked onto Cara's. 'There's real value here. I see that now.'

Cara felt heat rising again in her cheeks. 'Absolutely, there is,' she stammered. 'I mean, if you need any help in convincing them I'd be happy to pitch in and make the case with you. I could tell them about the terrific community here …'

'No.' He cut her off curtly. 'I think, in this case, we're better off keeping emotion out of it.'

She nodded. He was right, in more ways than one. Will Parry was her lifeline to staying in Cuthbert Close. The last thing she needed was to develop any kind of feelings for him, feelings that might only complicate what needed to remain a simple relationship between tenant and landlord.

'You're right.' She nodded. 'This is a business deal. Nothing more.'

It was settled.

CHAPTER TWENTY-THREE

Alex was in that nowhere place between asleep and awake. In her half-dream state, she saw Cara kissing Will Parry, then suddenly they were on a horse, riding up Cuthbert Close. No, wait. Not a horse, but some kind of strange half-horse, half-elephant thing, and Beth was chasing them with tongs. The twins were watching the whole thing, but they were dressed like little street urchins out of *Oliver Twist*. 'Please Mummy, can we have some more?' They held up two empty bowls.

Now there was a little ghostly voice.

'Mummy, I think I'm going to be …'

Alex's eyes flew open and she launched herself off the couch in the direction of the bowl she'd strategically placed within arm's length of her and Jasper.

Too late.

This time the vomit sprayed into her hair, down the side of the couch and a little on the carpet. Not much on Jasper. She swallowed the bile in her own mouth.

He clapped a hand over his lips. 'Sorry, Mummy.'

Alex was beyond anger. After puke number three in Jasper's bed, which exhausted their entire supply of sheets, she'd moved into acceptance mode. The kid wasn't purposely trying to ensure every square inch of the house got covered in his stomach contents, he was just very, very sick.

James emerged from the laundry. 'Another one?'

Alex nodded, her arm around Jasper's shoulder while he held the bowl mournfully under his chin.

'But this time he did warn me, which is progress.' Alex ruffled her son's hair. 'I'll get the cleaning stuff.'

James led Jasper to a non-puked-on part of the couch, sat him down and rubbed his back while Alex scrubbed at the stains.

'How about some water, Jas?' James put a bottle to his lips. 'You need to keep up your fluids when you're sick.'

Jasper took an obedient sip. 'Try to sleep now, buddy.' James took the bowl from his son's hands and cradled Jasper's head into his chest. The little boy closed his eyes.

There was something so sweet and defenceless about him when he was unwell. Vulnerable. Much like Noah. Perhaps they were more similar than Alex thought. Just different exteriors.

'I might go up and shower. Get the puke off me.' Alex rinsed out the cleaning cloths.

James nodded. Jasper was now sound asleep on his chest, his pale face finally at ease.

'Who's going to take the day off tomorrow?' said James quietly.

'What do you mean?' Alex paused at the foot of the stairs.

'We can't send him to school like this.' James looked down at his sleeping son.

'He might be better by then.'

James grimaced. 'There's no way this kid can go to school. For a start, he's probably contagious and it's just not fair on the other kids, and second of all, even if he's not vomiting, he's going to be exhausted. It's nearly midnight.'

There was an edge to his voice. This wasn't just about Jasper.

Alex sat tiredly on the stairs and tried not to breathe. She really did smell absolutely dreadful, but it was clear James had something to get off his chest. He'd been irritable ever since she told him about the partnership. They'd discussed the pros and cons, but they were still no closer to a decision and Martin said the paperwork was nearly ready.

'James, you know I would love to stay home with Jas tomorrow, but I have a court appearance and I can't just cancel. The firm's counting on me to deliver.'

'And I have a full day of patients who are also relying on me,' James snapped, then lowered his voice as Jasper stirred.

'But you can reschedule them,' said Alex. 'I can't.'

James threw his hands up. 'Isn't anyone at that law firm ever sick? Doesn't anyone have a child? There must be some kind of plan B.'

Alex shook her head sadly. 'Unless you're dying, you turn up. That's the way it is.' She clasped her hands. 'But this is actually about the partnership, isn't it.'

James avoided her gaze and focused on the sleeping Jasper. 'I don't understand how we went from talking about you cutting back on work, to now, where you're going to be spending even *more* time there, *and* with a baby. How's that going to work?'

Alex sighed. 'We've been through this, James. We'll get more help. An au pair perhaps. And it won't be forever, just five years or so, so we can pay off the house and have some real options.'

James stroked Jasper's hair. 'In five years, these guys will be nearly eleven years old. Half their childhood will be over.'

'We'll still have the baby.'

'The baby will be at school by then.'

The comment hung in the air. They both knew what that meant. All those firsts, first tooth, first steps, first foods, first words. All of those would be done, achieved, by the time Alex had time to sit down and actually enjoy them. James had already suggested he quit the practice and be a full-time stay-at-home dad again. But Alex couldn't let him do that. He'd done it for five years with the twins. His practice was just getting to its feet. She knew he'd resent her if he had to take a step backwards.

'But this is our dream,' Alex whispered, lowering her head into her hands.

'This is *your* dream.' James fixed her with his gaze. 'And I want you to have it. But I'm just not sure that now is the right time.'

'There won't be another time. They don't ask twice.'

'Can't you talk to them, and explain the situation? That while you really want the partnership, you also have young children who need you a lot right now, but probably won't so much in the future.'

Alex massaged her temples. 'A partner has to be committed. They'll interpret that as me flaking out. Besides, from what I've heard from other mums, it's not even true that kids need you less as they get older. If anything it's the opposite.'

Both Alex and James let the profundity of the statement settle over them. Was it possible for their children to require *more* of their parents as they grew? They had no more to give.

Jasper snuffled in his sleep and moaned some incoherent words.

'What did he say?' said Alex.

'Something about eagles? Or Ewoks?'

James smiled lovingly at Jasper, and gently disentangled himself so the child could lie down properly on the couch. Despite the extra space, the little boy curled his knees to his chest and made himself into a tiny ball.

Tears of love and frustration bit at Alex's eyes, but as James came closer, she wiped them away and made room on the stairs for him to sit next to her.

Why did it have to be so bloody hard? Why did being a mother and a lawyer have to mean that you could never be good at either?

James sat next to her, their arms touching. 'All I'm saying is could we at least keep talking about it?'

Alex couldn't move. She was suddenly, extraordinarily tired. 'Sure.'

She put her head on James's shoulder and even though her hair was still full of vomit, he let her put it there.

Just as she was about to start drooling, she heard the sirens. Distant at first, then louder, and louder still. Alex's eyelids flickered. In defiance, she screwed them more tightly shut. The sirens would get quieter in a minute. They'd take a turn and head off in another direction to where the real emergency lay.

Except they weren't getting softer. They were getting much, much louder.

Alex lifted her head, and James rose from the step. Both of them went to the door. Outside, two fire trucks were rolling up at Cara's door and disgorging what looked like an army of firefighters.

'You go and make sure Cara and Poppy are okay. I'll stay with Jas,' Alex ordered, suddenly very wide awake.

Without a word, James sprinted down the path. The firemen were pulling out hoses and putting on masks. Alex covered her mouth. What the hell was going on over there? Were Cara and Poppy okay? More and more of the neighbours filtered out onto the street, bleary-eyed. A few dressing gowns. Baggy boxer shorts. Charlie Devine in a plain white silk slip, holding tight to Talia at the end of their driveway.

The firefighters made them all stand back.

Inside, Alex paced up and down.

Please let Cara and Poppy be okay.

She pushed her face to the window. There were no flames. She squinted. But there, over the back. A small plume of smoke coming from the shed. Her insides twisted in knots.

Please let them be okay.

Less than a minute ago, she'd been so caught up in herself and her own future, worrying, like her job was the be-all and end-all. Now, here she was, just hoping like hell that her neighbours were still alive and unharmed. How was it that the big stuff of life – the conceiving of it, and the ending of it – happened in less than the blink of an eye, whereas the mundane things – the work, the cleaning, the shopping, the just plain living – were what took up all the time and brain space. But what did it really matter, unless you were alive for it?

Life and the people in it, that's what counted.

Alex felt a stabbing pain in her gut.

Oh shit, not the baby too …

Gently, she rubbed her stomach and tried to think calming thoughts. Maybe it was stress triggering the cramps?

Eyes closed, she breathed in through her nose and out through her mouth.

As James rushed back through the door, Alex's eyes flew open.

'Where are Cara and Poppy? Are they okay?'

Breathing heavily, James clutched her arm. 'They're fine. There was a fire in the shed, but the brigade got to it pretty quickly. It's all fine.'

Alex felt the adrenaline leaving her body, like a withdrawing tide, leaving her with nothing but a blinking emptiness. She slumped to the couch, close to where Jasper was still snoring softly, oblivious to the entire drama.

James sat next to her. 'You know, maybe you're right. He might just be okay for school tomorrow.' He stroked Jasper's leg. 'I think we're through the worst of it.'

'I hope so.' Alex looked at her peaceful son, the blue and red lights of the fire brigade flashing off his pale skin. 'Maybe,' she murmured.

ThePrimalGuy.com.au

From: The Primal Guy

Subject: Burn baby Burn

Hey Prime-Mates,

Switch your brains on, dudes! I've got a question for you.

What's the most important thing ever invented in this world? The thing that contributed most to human evolution?

Now, I know most of you will say 'the wheel', right? But dude, you are wrongity wrong wrong wrong.

It's fire.

Okay, so I know that humans didn't actually *invent* fire, but we did have to work out ways of creating and controlling it, which we did, about 600,000 years ago. Man, it was a total game changer. Suddenly, the primitive dudes had a way of keeping warm, they could move to colder places, cook food, make better tools, defend themselves, hunt for animals.

This stuff was the bomb. It still is.

From a little tacker, I've always been crazy-obsessed by fire, probably from the minute my oldies put a birthday candle in front of my face and I tried to eat it.

Fire can be friend and foe. It can be an end or a beginning. Hope or despair. All depends how you see it.

But I'll tell you one thing for free. It's never boring.

Peace out,

Ryan Devine (AKA the Primal Guy)

PS You want a little home-grown fire? Check out the online shop for my soil-scented soy candles. Seriously, it's like sitting round a campfire. Just use the promo code BURNBABYBURN.

CHAPTER TWENTY-FOUR

Cara scrubbed at the soot marks above the stove. It could have been worse. It definitely could have been worse. It was lucky she had a functioning smoke alarm, the fire brigade told her, or the shed most certainly would have gone up in flames in a matter of minutes. Cara shivered.

How could she have been so stupid?

The firefighters told her they saw it all the time. People who walked away from their stoves and left a wooden spoon just a tad too close to the heat. That's what had happened in this case, given the charred state of the spoon next to the camp stove. When they told her that, Cara had apologised profusely.

'I think I just panicked,' she explained.

After the smoke alarm pierced her sleep and she saw the shed starting to smoulder, she'd reached immediately for her phone and dialled triple zero. The lady at the end of the telephone was very kind and very calm. She asked if anyone was in danger, then told Cara to wait outside the shed until the brigade arrived. Opening the door could introduce oxygen that would only fan the flames.

And so she waited for what felt like hours but, in reality, was simply the longest five minutes of her life. When the firefighters went through the door she expected to see the entire interior of the shed ablaze. In fact, the flames were no bigger than a foot high, much like a camp fire, and it took one firefighter all of two minutes to put it out with a hand-held extinguisher.

Poppy slept through the whole thing.

Everyone in the street had been so kind, so concerned, offering her cups of tea and warm blankets.

Thinking back on it now, Cara flushed.

How could she have left the stove on?

She ran through what she remembered. They'd partially prepared the risotto for the launch party in the shed, then Cara had taken it to Beth's to finish in her kitchen. At the end of the night, they'd cleaned and tidied and Cara had put Poppy to bed, before returning her equipment to the shed.

How had she not noticed the gas flame then? Much less the spoon?

Exhaustion was her only answer. Pure exhaustion. With Nourish starting to take flight, she was burning the candle at both ends.

More like burning the spoon, she thought gloomily.

Fortunately, the damage was relatively minimal, mostly caused by the smoke. She'd need to re-paint, but she could simply add that to the long list of jobs that needed to get done around the house. The shed was still useable, provided she got rid of the awful smell. One firefighter had kindly suggested vinegar, and keeping the doors open for a couple of days.

Cara went back to scrubbing.

She'd been on such a high after the tasting party. An exhausted high. But still, it had gone incredibly well. The neighbours had raved about the food and several of them had placed orders. Will was going to ask his siblings not to sell. It gave her hope.

But the fire was a reality check.

Things, bad things, happened when you least expected them.

Knock, knock.

Cara startled and dropped the scrubbing brush.

'Sorry, Cara.' Talia stood at the doorway. 'I didn't mean to scare you.'

'It's fine. Come in.'

The teenager stepped inside the shed and wrinkled her nose. 'I thought you might like some help.'

'Aren't you lovely.' Cara picked up a second brush and handed it over. 'I won't say no.' She'd spent most of the day cleaning. Poppy had helped a little after school but her incessant complaints about the smell outweighed the value of her assistance. Cara had despatched her back to the house to do homework.

Talia took the brush and started scrubbing. 'Something similar happened to us once. Mum had been cooking, and she went to sleep without remembering to turn the gas off. Luckily my dad found it in time, so it wasn't too bad. He's good with stuff like that.'

'You must miss him.'

'Like crazy.' She went on quickly. 'He'll be here soon, I think. And I love my mum, too. She and I are just … different.'

Cara looked at the younger girl, scrubbing intently. 'I can see that.'

'She's a good person, but she's tough. Big on rules and sticking to them.'

Cara resumed her focus on the sooty wall. 'It's hard being a mum. Sometimes, you feel like it's this big test and unless you do things a certain way, you're going to fail it. Or fail your children.'

Cara felt Talia's eyes on her. 'But really, all you have to do is love them, right? Try to make them happy.'

'And feed them, and clothe them, and make sure they get to school, and do their homework, and brush their teeth.' Cara laughed. 'It's not as easy as it looks.'

'Mum's always working on the Primal stuff. I wish she was more like you. You spend lots of time with Poppy. I've seen you. All that painting and craft stuff.'

'It's only because I can, and I've got the time,' sighed Cara. 'But with this business starting to take off I seem to have less and less.'

'So it's going well?' Talia dipped her brush in the sink to clean off the cinders.

'It's going really well. Better than I imagined.'

'Yeah? Well, that's good, right?'

'Talia, it's a bit hard to explain, but this business is everything to me and Poppy right now. It has to work, or there's a chance Pops and I won't be able to live in Cuthbert Close any more.'

'Everyone seems to really love living here.'

'We do,' said Cara. 'And you will too, in time.'

'Oh, I already do like it. Everyone's great. Really friendly. I just wish Dad was here.'

'I'm sure that if he could be here, he would be.'

For the next few minutes, the two of them worked in silence, with only the scrubbing sounds of the brush against the wall to break the quiet. Eventually, from across the garden, came the filtered sound of someone calling.

'Talia. Talia. Where are you?'

Cara put her brush down. 'That sounds like your mum.'

Talia pulled a face. 'She's probably got jobs for me to do.'

'Probably more important you do those jobs than helping me.'

Cara followed her out the door, through the garden and down the side passage to the street. Charlie Devine stood at her front door, a hand shielding her eyes from the sun. As she spotted Talia and Cara, her frown deepened.

'Sorry, Charlie. Talia was just helping me clean up the shed.' Cara remained at the bottom of the Devines' drive while Talia scurried towards her mother. 'She's been terrific, actually. She's a real credit to you.'

'Thank you, Cara, but Talia knows she's actually supposed to be doing her homework. She really doesn't have the time to be playing around in the street.'

Playing around?

Cara prickled.

What was Charlie Devine's problem? Why was she so determined to refuse every kindness, every hand of friendship, every olive branch? She hadn't even asked about the fire.

Cara went to open her mouth but was stopped by the sight of Talia Devine slowly shaking her head.

She retreated down the driveway. The teenager was telling her not to push it, so she wouldn't; if a parent didn't fit in, that wasn't the fault of the child, as Cara well knew.

Back in the shed, she checked her phone. Nothing from Will Parry. Should she tell him about the fire? She thought for a second. The damage was minimal. Telling him might only deter him and his siblings from wanting to buy the property. No. He didn't need to know. Nothing could jeopardise her and Poppy's chances of staying in the Cuthbert cottage.

With a small sigh, she picked up the brush and started scrubbing again.

CHAPTER TWENTY-FIVE

'You haven't seen my engagement ring, have you?' Beth scanned the shelf above the kettle where she normally put the two-carat diamond solitaire when she was cooking.

'When did you last have it?' Max leant against the bench and sipped his coffee.

'I remember taking it off before the launch party to roll out the pastry, but then I must have forgotten to put it back on.' She started opening drawers. Her plain gold wedding band was still in its proper place on her finger, but the engagement ring was worth so much more, both in dollar value and sentiment.

'So, it's been missing for almost a week?'

Beth whipped around to face him. 'In case you haven't noticed, the last few days have been a bit of a roller-coaster.' There'd been the launch party, then the fire. Beth shivered every time she thought of just how bad it could have been.

Thank goodness Poppy and Cara were okay, and the damage to the shed more cosmetic than anything. It certainly hadn't stopped them from cooking and delivering 105 meals to fifteen different locations.

Today being Saturday, Cara wanted to capitalise on the momentum of their first week by recording a video for social media of them preparing a signature Nourish meal. Alex had agreed to play videographer.

'Well, suppose I'll be heading off now, then.' Max emptied the dregs of his coffee into the sink.

'You're not going to help me look?' Beth cursed the amount of stuff in their drawers. Batteries, pens, sticky tape and old bank books, and the chaos of it replicated what was going on in Beth's head. Her thoughts were a mess of fragments, about Max and his distracted state, the mysterious note, the kids and their lack of interest in anything else other than themselves, her kiss with Adam, and now, her determination to achieve some financial independence out of Nourish.

Max checked his watch. 'I've got to get to the gym.'

Beth closed the drawer and leant against it. 'Why?' Her gaze narrowed on him. 'What's the rush? Meeting someone?' She folded her arms.

'Ah, no.' Max felt in his pockets. 'I'm doing a class.'

Max never did classes. He hated classes. All that shouting, and waiting around for it to begin. He went to the gym to do weights. Get in, get out, go home. He said his aim was to be fitter and stronger at the age of fifty than he was at forty. Training for the charity run took care of the cardio fitness, but his doctor had told him that where middle-aged men went wrong was to ignore their strength. A few weights would take care of that.

Beth was suspicious. What man in the history of men had actually ever listened to their doctor? Only a blind person could fail to see the way in which the gym was changing Max's physique. In the bathroom last night, while Beth was brushing her teeth, she'd felt a twinge in her nether regions as Max showered, unaware of being watched. His eyes were closed, and the water ran down over his sculpted arms and torso, with its beginnings of a sixpack. The gym had uncovered muscles that Beth hadn't seen since they were in their twenties. After the shower, she'd hopped into bed and waited for Max, who slid between the sheets all soapy and fresh.

Beth couldn't help herself. She'd reached for him. What difference did it make? No feelings. No emotion. Just two bodies, doing what two bodies were made to do.

After twenty minutes of vigorous love-making, Max had lain spent and breathing heavily. 'Wow,' he muttered, closing his eyes. 'Where did that come from?'

Beth hadn't answered, and whatever small sense of satisfaction she'd felt from showing Max that this was what he'd be missing quickly evaporated into the warm night air. She rolled over and pretended to sleep. Sex with Max had always been good. Certainly, after children, it wasn't the wild, tear-at-each-other's-clothes type of sex that it had been in the beginning. After all, if someone did tear a shirt, then Beth would have to be the one who mended it the next day. They knew what each other liked. There was no need to waste time experimenting any more. A particular touch here, a lick there, a grab somewhere else and everyone went home happy and, more importantly, got a good night's sleep, which, as every parent knew, was more of an aphrodisiac than the best oysters or champagne.

What killed a sex life wasn't familiarity, it was exhaustion. At least it was for Beth, and she had been feeling even more tired lately. Was she pre-menopausal? Hot flushes and hairy lips were the last thing she needed.

'I've really got to go.' Max was looking anxious now.

Beth felt a chill in her bones. Was he meeting *her*?

'All right, just go then.' She slammed the drawer shut and Max gave her a quizzical look.

'Last night was … different.' He paused at the bench. 'Is everything okay?'

I suspect you're having an affair and if you can treat sex as just a 'thing', then so can I.

Beth couldn't meet his eye. She didn't have proof of an affair. Not solid proof. And until she did, she would say nothing, at least not until after their anniversary party. 'Of course it is. I just want to find the ring.'

He headed for the door. 'It'll turn up, and anyway, it's not the end of the world. It's just a ring. You can always get a new one,' he called over his shoulder.

As the front door closed, Beth's shoulders slumped. Was that really what Max thought? That she could just get a new one? Certainly, diamond solitaires with a plain gold band weren't exactly hard to come by, but it wouldn't carry the same sentiment. Not unless he took her up in a seaplane and presented it to her high over Sydney Harbour, the way he had all those years ago, shouting to be heard above the thrum of the propeller engine while a family of four German tourists looked distinctly uncomfortable at the wild display of kissing in the back of the tiny plane.

A new ring could never carry the significance of that moment.

Maybe this was an omen. A sign. She had lost the ring because her marriage was ending. Beth patted her chest. There was pain, real pain inside of it. A bit like indigestion, only she hadn't eaten that morning.

Beth took the iPad off the shelf and opened the screen to messages.

About to leave. You still okay for 10 am?

Absolutely. Got some hot new moves for you today!

Can't wait! See you soon.

That dirty, lying cheating rat! Beth felt an urge to smash the device to the ground, but resisted. Chloe and Ethan would need it for homework and if it broke, they would ask questions and demand a replacement.

'Hellooo. You there, Beth? It's me, Cara.' Her neighbour tapped on the glass at the back door and Beth, hands trembling, returned the iPad to its shelf before heading out of the kitchen.

As she went to pull the door open, she glanced quickly at her fingers on the handle. It occurred to her the plain wedding band now looked quite different without its companion, the diamond solitaire. It looked lost, and lonely.

CHAPTER TWENTY-SIX

'Got your make-up on?' Cara hurried past her neighbour and into the kitchen where she deposited an esky full of ingredients on the floor.

'No, no. I haven't had time.' Beth fidgeted with her fingers. 'Maybe I could stay off camera? I'm not feeling so wonderful. My engagement ring seems to have gone walkabout.'

Cara paused from unloading the food. She watched Beth, pressing her fingers into her cheekbones, as if trying to dissolve the large dark circles of fatigue under her eyes. She looked as exhausted as Cara felt. Not surprising. The past few days had been massive, with the launch, then the fire, and the rush to clean up and get cooking again in time for their first round of deliveries. At least Poppy was off her hands today at a friend's house for a play date. Cara desperately needed a moment to catch her breath, and Poppy deserved some downtime after being dragged along for the delivery run. Still, this was the nature of starting a new business. It was tough and gruelling, but for both of their sakes – Cara's and Beth's – it had to succeed.

She steered her neighbour towards the stairs. 'Go upstairs. Put some foundation and blush on and you'll feel a hundred times better.' She checked her phone. 'Alex will be here in five minutes.'

Beth trudged up the stairs as if walking to her death. Cara watched her, feeling a prick of pity. When it came to cooking and delivering the meals, Beth was an absolute superstar. Completely in her element, chatting away about the nutritional benefits of the food to their customers, most of them frazzled young working mums who greeted Beth and Cara as if they were angels sent from heaven. 'Thank you for this,' most of them whispered, ferrying the food-filled styrofoam boxes inside as quietly as if they were smuggling drugs.

'You're doing something good for your family,' Beth always assured them as they left. Cara had tried the same line, but it sounded better coming from Beth, because of her age and genuine sincerity.

But where was that confidence today? Beth looked as if she'd seen a ghost. Probably something to do with Max. Whatever it was, Cara was sure that if Beth wanted to share it, she would.

Cara pitched her esky onto the bench and continued to unload all the ingredients she'd need for the shoot. It had been Alex's idea. A way to capitalise on the success of the launch and show people that Beth and Cara were exactly who they purported to be – two mums, preparing fresh and wholesome meals out of their own kitchens for other mums.

She pulled out her phone and checked for the tenth time that morning for any messages from Will. He'd met with his brother and sister for dinner last night and promised to text her an answer.

Nothing.

She scrolled through the Instagram feed of pictures taken from the launch party. The wagyu pies had hit three thousand likes, and the chicken curry wasn't far behind. She'd also loaded some shots of the neighbours eating. Soft-focus stuff, so that no one was recognisable. She started to read through the comments.

FoodieBewdy *Looks delicious!*

FranticMum *Can't wait to place an order!*

FamilyTree *Amazing! Well done ladies.*

CarntCook *What a beautiful party!*

TessHan *Do you deliver to Melbourne?*

Cara worked her way through the list, liking and replying. Halfway down, she stopped.

TruthTeller *Don't be fooled by the photos! I heard that one of the kids at the party got food poisoning. This backyard business is DODGY!*

Cara's palms began to sweat. She scrolled further down.

YourBestSelfee *Thanks for the heads-up TruthTeller. Will avoid this sham at all costs.*

MumDoesRun *Was just about to place an order. So glad I didn't!*

FourMisses *The last thing we need is food poisoning. All four had gastro last week. #neveragain*

PlantBaysedMumma *Those pies look disgusting. No wonder everyone got sick.*

'Cara! Hey Cara! Open up!'

Cara nearly dropped the phone. The banging at the front door was loud and insistent. Typical Alex. Cara opened the door, phone in hand.

'Oh, shit.' Alex had her hands on her hips. 'I hate to say this, but you look about as crap as I feel. What's the matter?'

She held up the mobile. 'Have you seen this?'

'Seen what?'

Cara passed her the phone and Alex's eyes widened as she read through the feed. 'What is this person even talking about? No one got sick, did they?'

'I have no idea. A random hater, maybe?'

'Delete and block, babe. That's all you can do with trolls.'

'What are you doing to a troll? Did I miss something?' Beth brushed her hair as she walked down the stairs.

'This.' Cara held up the phone to Beth's face.

'Where are my reading glasses,' she muttered.

Cara started pacing around Beth's living room. 'I don't think we can delete and block. Too many people have seen the comment.'

'Come out fighting, then.' Alex flopped onto the couch. 'Who is this Truth Teller anyway?'

Beth passed the phone back to Cara. 'This is awful. Did we really make someone sick?'

'No, of course not,' said Cara. 'We tasted everything ourselves. It was made fresh. We used gloves. Fresh chopping boards. Every food safety rule, we followed.'

'Okay, so you need to deny, deny, deny. Get on the front foot against this person.' Alex crossed her legs. 'The best form of defence is attack. Question this person's credibility.'

Cara tapped away at her phone and spoke as she typed. 'Nourish one hundred per cent denies any outbreak of food poisoning from our launch party and would like to know where your evidence is for this assertion.'

Alex nodded approvingly. 'Very good. Strong. Couldn't have written it better myself.'

Beth sat next to Alex. 'Isn't this illegal? To just put lies on the internet?'

'A small business can sue for defamation, but it's pretty unusual.'

'Wait. Wait. They've responded.' Cara held her hand in the air and started to read from the screen. 'It says, *Check out the Legally_Parenting feed*.'

Alex jumped up off the couch. 'Shit, that's me. I don't get it …' She pulled out her phone and stopped. 'Oh crap, this is about Jasper. I posted something about him being sick and having to leave the party early, oh crap. Oh shit, shit, shit. No. I'll delete it straight away.'

Cara leant over her shoulder as Alex fiddled frantically with her phone.

'Wait, please. I want to see it.' Cara snatched the phone from her hands. 'Brilliant launch party for my neighbours' fab new catering business, Nourish. Shame our puking kid stopped us from sticking around for the mini bombe Alaskas, but we were dealing with explosions of a different kind at home. One too many wagyu pies, perhaps??!! Hashtag: Nourish. Hashtag: gastroparty. Hashtag: thejoyofparenting.'

Cara lowered the phone. 'How could you do this? It reads like we made him sick.'

'Oh fuck, I'm so sorry. I wasn't thinking.' Alex's eyes were wild. 'Let me fix this. I'll delete it. I'll clarify. I'll issue a retraction. He caught the bug from school, I have no doubt. The thing about the pies was only a joke.' She held out her hand. 'Please, give me the phone.'

Beth placed her hand gently on Cara's arm. 'Come on. Calm down. Alex is sorry. She made a mistake. Let her fix this.'

Cara curled her hand tightly around the phone. 'I know this is just a bit of fun to you, but for Beth and me, this business is our future. It has to work or we'll lose everything.'

'I do understand,' said Alex.

'How could you? You get a six-figure salary. You have a husband who would do anything for you. How could you really know what it's like to face losing your own home?'

'Believe me. I do know what it's like to have money, and I know what it's like to not have money.' She spoke calmly and evenly. 'I was the kid who always missed the excursions and had to say no to the parties because I didn't want to turn up with a crappy gift.' She paused. 'I know what it's like, as a kid, to worry about money, and I absolutely do not want that for my children, or your Poppy.'

Alex's eyes were reddening, and Beth looked from one woman to the other, unsure of who to comfort first. Slowly, and with one arm around Cara, she edged closer and managed to extend her other arm around Alex's shoulder so that the three were now in a close huddle.

Alex sighed tearily. 'I'm fucking up everything. My kids, my job, my marriage, your business.'

Beth squeezed her shoulder. 'Shush now. Everything will be fine.'

Cara felt her anger easing. She'd never seen Alex like this. So unsure of herself. She was always so strong and confident.

She broke away from the trio. 'Alex, what's going on? I thought the partnership was what you wanted.'

'It is. It was,' sniffed Alex. 'But the timing is all wrong. Look at me. Pregnant with baby number three and I can barely cope with the two I've already got.'

Cara softened. 'If anyone can do it, you can.'

Alex gave her a teary smile. 'But at what cost?'

Beth ducked into the kitchen and returned with a steaming pot of tea and a plate of madeleine biscuits. Light as air, but also rich with buttery goodness. 'You know, it seems to me, ladies, that who we should really be cross with is this Truth Teller person. Why would they want to cause such mischief?' She set the plate down as Cara and Alex took up position on the couch next to each other.

'Could be a random troll? I do occasionally get them. I've checked, and it seems to be a dummy account. No posts or followers.' Cara shrugged. 'Some people don't need a reason to be horrible.'

Alex reached forward for a biscuit and chewed thoughtfully. 'It seems more pointed than that. Maybe someone who was at the party?'

Beth looked aghast. 'But it was all neighbours there. No one from Cuthbert Close would do this.'

'Charlie Devine might,' said Alex, collecting another madeleine. In unison, Cara and Beth looked at her inquiringly. She stopped and took the biscuit away from her mouth. 'Think about it. She's new to the area. She doesn't seem to like us much, and her husband has a diet business which could be seen as direct competition for Nourish. Of course she wants you out of the way.'

'But ... but it's just such a horrible thing to do,' Beth burst out.

'Not to mention the fact that their business is huge and ours is tiny. They have absolutely nothing to fear from us. Our market is completely different.' Cara picked nervously at her fingernails.

'Like you said, some people don't need a reason to be awful.' Alex wiped at a crumb on her lip. 'And at the end of the day, we have no actual proof it's her so it's probably beside the point.'

'Could we just delete the comments and forget it ever happened?' said Beth.

Alex shook her head. 'Cara's right. It'll look like a cover-up and Truth Teller will just keep posting about it and become a real pest. I've had clients in similar situations and they always want to sue, but really the best thing you can do is to give your side of the story with good grace and humour. If you've got nothing to hide, then don't hide anything.'

'That sounds like the right approach. But how do we do that here?' said Cara.

Alex sat forward on the couch. 'I'll upload a photo of the note that the boys' school sent home about the gastro bug going round and explain that Truth Teller simply misunderstood my post, and you guys can share it on your feed as a bit of an LOL moment, you know, hashtag *instafail* or something like that. And if we do put up this cooking video today, then people will see just how professional you guys are.'

'You're right. If we give them new content, they'll move on from the kerfuffle about the launch,' said Cara, trying to project more confidence than she felt. As she went to get up, her phone bleeped with another message. 'Not another hater,' she muttered to herself as she swiped up to read.

They said no … We're selling. Also, they want to do a cosmetic reno to bump up the value so I'm sorry but you'll have to move out. I really am sorry. Will

Cara swallowed heavily but the words stuck in her chest like a stone. Slumping back into the couch, she let the phone spill from her hands. She buried her face in her hands.

'What is it? What's wrong? Is it the video? We can do it another time?'

Cara felt the couch dip as Beth took a seat by her side.

'Will's family said no,' she croaked. 'They're going ahead with the sale and they're going to renovate.'

'Oh shit,' muttered Alex.

'Oh, Cara, I'm so sorry.' Beth rubbed her back as Cara sat forward, elbows on knees, face still covered.

'We'll have to move,' she said. 'We won't have the shed any more, which means no Nourish. Maybe the troll has just sped up what was going to happen anyway.'

'Don't say that,' said Alex.

'There must be something we can do,' said Beth.

'Unless you've got a spare eight hundred thousand dollars lying around, I don't think there is.'

'What do you mean eight hundred thousand?' said Alex sharply. 'Do you have the other eight hundred?'

Cara took a breath. 'With Pete's super and life insurance, nearly, yes. Almost seven hundred thousand altogether.'

'You've got seven hundred thousand dollars?' squeaked Beth.

'I know it sounds like a lot but it would only get me a two-bedroom shoebox about forty-five minutes away from here, and besides, the money is Poppy's. I've been saving it for her.'

'Forget that,' said Alex. 'This *is* for Poppy.' She paced up and down the room. 'So, what you're saying is you need an investor to go halves with you.'

'Please don't suggest my parents again. They've just bought a place. There's no way I can ask them.'

Alex looked at her. 'I get that.' She nodded. 'You need someone you know. Someone who'll let you and Poppy stay in the house. Someone who doesn't already have huge debts or responsibilities, like children or some other major expense. Do you know someone like that?' She fixed Cara with a direct gaze.

'No.'

'Think again.'

Cara looked up. Everyone she knew either worked in creative industries, which meant they had no money, or they were parents of Poppy's friends, and they certainly weren't the right kind of people to ask. There were no cousins. No aunts and uncles. All of them were back in Korea.

Will Parry.

The name dropped into her head like a pebble plopping into a pond. Ripples of thought began to spread.

Will Parry.

Yes. He was single. No children. And he'd mentioned something about renting as he waited for his divorce settlement to come through. But would he want to buy into Cuthbert Close? Would the investment potential be sufficient? Could he overcome his negative memories of the place? She wouldn't know if she didn't try.

'Maybe I could ask the owner's son,' she began.

'The one you kissed the other night at the party?' said Alex.

'I was thanking him,' Cara protested.

Alex raised an eyebrow. 'Can't wait to see you show your appreciation if he goes halves in the house with you.'

Cara brought her knees together primly. 'I have no interest in Will Parry. Or anyone.'

'I hate to hear you say that. You deserve to be happy.' Beth wrung her hands.

'I *am* happy. I've got Poppy, and my parents, and you guys, and if I get to stay in Cuthbert Close ... That's enough for me. Anything else is more than I deserve.'

'You know, I do think that's ridiculous,' Alex began. 'But in this case, with Will Parry, it's probably sensible. A lovers' tiff could take you back to square one and leave you out on the street again.' She rose and started pacing the room. 'Keep it businesslike. You want him to want the property, but not you. This is no package deal.'

'I don't think that will be a problem. I have zero interest in him in that way.'

'Good then,' said Alex. 'Because you need to be on the same page. Now, ask him for lunch in the city ...' She paused. 'You're going to make a feast. A picnic feast. I'll prepare the business case. By the end, you'll have him eating out of your hand. Literally.'

Cara cocked her head. 'I thought you said I shouldn't get too close.'

'Ever heard of corporate hospitality? You wine and dine clients because you want their business, not their bodies, but it's still a seduction.'

An image slipped into Cara's mind, of tanned and sinewy forearms.

She shook her head and mentally kicked herself. 'I have no interest in Will Parry's body.'

'But are you sure that he's not interested in yours? He didn't seem to exactly hate your show of gratitude at the party.'

Cara's stomach swooped and somersaulted as she thought back to the kiss, his lovely, musky scent. No. This wasn't helpful. She snapped herself out of the memory. 'He's still getting over a messy divorce, so I think he's about as interested in another property settlement as I am in his arms.'

Beth and Alex looked at each other in confusion. 'Arms?' Alex inquired. 'Who mentioned anything about arms.' Her gaze narrowed. 'Are you sure you can do this without getting attached?'

As Cara picked up the phone and opened a new message to Will, she felt those butterflies again, having a field day in her stomach.

'I've never been more certain.'

CHAPTER TWENTY-SEVEN

Alex hurried down Beth's front steps. At the bottom she stopped. The video had taken much longer than expected and the sun had already set, casting the close into darkness. James had fed and bathed the boys but his last text had sounded a little testy. Should she cut across the pristine lawn, perfect as a putting green, or take the carefully positioned pavers that Beth had laid out specifically to stop her precious grass from being trashed? In another life, Alex would have loved to be the kind of house-proud person that cared about every blade of grass, every peel of paint, every inch of rust.

But in this life she didn't have time.

Removing her heeled sandals, Alex tiptoed across the grass and thought through all she still needed to do.

Firstly, she needed to double-check her socials accounts and make doubly sure that all references to the alleged food poisoning had been explained and responded to. What an epic fail! How could she have been so naive? Baby-brain, clearly.

Secondly, she wanted to nut out a detailed plan of attack for Cara to make sure she got that house. It was the least she could do after nearly ruining the poor woman's business. Even though it had taken hours to film, the video had at least gone well. Cara and Beth had even been able to make a little joke out of the gastro palaver, in the midst of cooking a mouth-watering Moroccan tagine.

Now across the lawn and onto the nature strip, Alex's guilt eased a little. The narrow grassy patch was public land and as such Alex felt no shame in walking freely across it. She picked up the pace.

'Oh shit. What's that?'

It was a person, that much was clear. A smallish, crying person that Alex had nearly trodden on in her haste to get home.

She leant down and squinted.

'Talia, what are you doing out here? Are you hiding? I nearly stepped on you.'

The girl got up quickly and wiped her nose with her sleeve, keeping her eyes downcast so that Alex couldn't quite see into them.

'Sorry ... I ... I didn't mean to scare you. I'll go now. Bye.' Talia turned her back on Alex, her shoulders hunched but heaving erratically.

'Wait. You're crying. What's wrong?' Alex caught up to her and touched her arm. 'Is there anything I can do?'

The teenager faced her and moonlight glinted off the passage of tears down her face. She'd obviously been crying for quite some time.

'Mum won't let me go to the movies with my friends,' she blurted out. 'At my last school she was always telling me to make more friends and be more friendly and get my head out of the books, and now, at this new school, I'm doing that and she won't let me go anywhere.'

'Did she say why?' Alex folded her arms.

'Just that, with the move and everything, we've had to spend a lot of money and she says we can't afford *unnecessary extras* at the moment.' Talia used air quotes around the words. 'But she still has her gym membership, so I guess that's a necessary extra.'

Alex's heart twinged. How many times, as a teenager, had she missed friends' parties because she either had a shift at Macca's or her parents couldn't afford the kind of gift or outfit that would allow her to hold her head up with pride? She knew that feeling, but she'd been able to survive it because her parents were always first to make a sacrifice. Yes, Alex had missed a fair few parties but her parents never went to any. She touched Talia's shoulder. 'I completely get where you're coming from and it sounds really shit.' She paused, trying to remember the things that had helped her at the same age. Not sympathy, that was for sure. But practical help. 'You know, I meant what I said about babysitting for the boys. Maybe I could talk to your mum again, and that might be a way you can earn your own money.'

'You'd do that for me?' The girl's eyes were round with hope.

'Of course I would. We are neighbours after all, and I did nearly tread on you. It's the least I can do.' She gave what she thought was a reassuring smile, but even in the gloom of the evening she could see the girl was still unsure. 'Unless you don't want to babysit, of course,' she added. 'The boys can be a handful.'

'It's not that,' Talia started. 'It's just … I need to tell you something … About your guinea pig. What really happened to her … You've been so nice to me and now I feel really bad about it all.'

Alex took a step back. 'What do you mean?'

'It was all my fault,' she burst out. The streetlight accentuated the shadows on the girl's face. Half in light. The other half in dark. She wiped at fresh tears that Alex couldn't quite see. 'When we arrived, Mum told me that if I wanted to go outside, I had to put Banjo in the cat cage because he'd run through the front door, and, anyway, she asked me to check the letterbox and I opened the door without thinking.' She swallowed hard. 'He went straight through my legs and bolted into your garden and a few seconds later he came back with your guinea pig in his mouth.' The girl shifted her weight like she needed a wee. 'It was awful, and I ran in to tell Mum but she said I shouldn't do anything because it would make a bad first impression and you'd hate us, and we could just make it look like Henny wandered into our garden when she didn't at all.' Talia buried her face in her hands.

'So when you came over to offer us help to find Henny, you knew all along she was dead.'

'Yes,' wailed Talia. 'Mum told me not to go, but I wanted you to find her as quickly as possible.'

Alex gulped at the huge ball of pity stuck in her throat. She could have been angry at the child but she wasn't. She'd never liked the guinea pig that much anyway. Talia, on the other hand … She seemed completely traumatised by the death. But she was only a kid and kids made mistakes. As for Charlie, she definitely should have known better than to make her daughter lie. If Alex was angry at anyone, it was her.

'Look, Talia, I appreciate you telling me what happened.' She put her hand on the girl's shoulder. 'But you're not to blame. If Henny was in her hutch like she should have been, then none of this would have happened. It's as much our fault for not keeping her safe as it is yours. Actually, it's probably more mine than anyone's. I knew the boys had left her outside but I was running too late for work to find her.' Alex squeezed. 'At least your mistake was entirely accidental.'

'I should have told you the truth,' the girl said miserably.

'You have now, and that's what matters.'

ThePrimalGuy.com.au
From: The Primal Guy
Subject: Taking Risks

Dear Prime-Ribs,
Okay, so all the lefty-ladies out there will want to have my balls for breakfast when I say this but I'm gonna say it straight out anyway – men are better at taking risks than women.

There, I said it, and before you hunt me down with your pitchforks, you better hear me out. I got science behind me. Evolutionary science actually. It's kind of undeniable. The men went out and risked their lives to spear the bison, while the women stayed in the cave to keep the home fires burning.

I mean, look at me. I'm here, on this mind-bending trip, taking risks, making new moves, but it's all about keeping food on the table (not bread though, right, the carbs!) while Mrs Primal Guy is keeping the home fires burning.

But change is a-comin'. Yes sir. I feel it in the wind. Women are getting out there. Sisters are doing it for themselves. They're putting food on their own tables, partly 'cause they want to, and partly because their Neanderthal men-folk have let the side down.

Here's the thing, though. What hasn't changed are the genes. The ladies just aren't programmed to take the leaps that men are, so they're always gonna be a step behind. That's if you obey your genes. You don't actually have to, you know.

So – here's my challenge. To any of the dudettes who read these words of wisdom – I want you to hear this. Take that risk. Run at it. Leap. Jump. Get the biggest air on it that you can.

It's the only way to touch the stars.

Peace out,
Ryan Devine (AKA the Primal Guy)

PS 20% discount on our 10 day detox teas for WOMEN ONLY this week. Okay, so maybe we can't actually verify if you're a woman or not in our online check-out. But there's this thing called Karma, and she can be a bitch if you lie!

CHAPTER TWENTY-EIGHT

Cara clutched the picnic basket closer to her chest as the city rushed about her. Everyone was in such a hurry, and they were dressed so smartly. Tailored suits, crisp shirts and ties, shiny shoes and bags in gleaming leather. She looked down at her floral shift dress. When she wore it in Cuthbert Close, she felt like a nineteen sixties movie star. Here, in the corporate heart of the city, she felt completely out of place.

This was a mistake. This was all a mistake. She shouldn't have asked Will Parry to meet with her for lunch. She shouldn't have made a picnic and she certainly shouldn't have worn this dress.

How could he take her seriously when she was dressed like Doris Day?

Cara went to dig out her phone. It wasn't too late to cancel. She was a little bit early after all. She would say that

Poppy was sick, that she'd received a call from the school and had to go immediately to collect her.

'Cara, hi.' Too late. It was him.

Her stomach flipped. Just nerves. Nothing to do with the way his pale blue business shirt so perfectly set off his eyes. Cara shook her head and squared her shoulders.

'Hello, Will. Thank you for agreeing to meet with me.' She went to shake his hand but he pulled her in to kiss her cheek. 'Oh, right.' She laughed nervously. He smelt good, too. Vanilla and cinnamon.

'Can I take that?' He gestured to the picnic basket.

'Oh, it's not that heavy.' She smiled through the cramp in her arm.

'Let me.'

He took the basket from her hands and gave a comedic grimace. 'Yes, it's not heavy at all. Light as a feather.'

'I really don't mind ...'

'Just kidding. C'mon. I have a feeling there's a feast in here and I'm absolutely starving.'

He started walking towards the park, keeping up polite chat about the weather and Poppy and how he'd had an awful morning at work, starting with his train being cancelled which made him late for an important meeting with a major client who'd come in specifically to talk through some *issues*. He used air quotes around the word. This was a different Will Parry. This was a man at ease in his environment – the business heart of the CBD. Where was the gruffness, the abruptness he'd displayed when he first came to Cuthbert Close?

'What is it you actually do?' Cara asked.

'I have a small project management consultancy.' He delivered the words flatly, as if the title was completely self-explanatory.

'What does that actually mean?'

He looked at her. 'Well, it means that I identify the objectives of the project, engage the key stakeholders, co-ordinate the staff, set the budget and monitor the deliverables.'

'Sounds a bit like cooking. You have a goal, and you have a recipe to follow, and it's just about executing the steps.'

'I suppose so.' He smiled. 'But I imagine your cakes don't come with a two billion dollar budget and a lot of ridiculous jargon.'

'Two billion dollars,' she gasped.

'The big ones.' He shrugged. 'But they don't let me spend all the money.'

They were in the park now. Cara stopped to admire the elaborate water fountain with its bronze Greek gods and water spouts, catching the midday light like sprays of diamonds.

'I used to bring Poppy here when she was little,' started Cara. 'The little tortoise sculptures were her favourite.'

Will followed her gaze to the static reptiles at the base of the sculpture, spitting continuous jets of water out of their mouths. 'They're pretty weird, aren't they.'

'She thought they were real. Sort of. She thought they'd died, and that's why they weren't moving. But they'd been alive, once.'

As Cara spoke, a little girl near them launched herself out of her mother's grasp and sprinted towards the fountain, shouting, 'I wannna touch the turtles.'

'Sienna. Wait. Stop. You'll fall in.' A woman raced after her but little Sienna was climbing determinedly over the low wall, the only thing separating her from the pond.

Cara sucked in a breath. The urge to run to the child's aid swelled like a wave inside of her. But she and Will were much further away than the little girl's own mother and at the last moment, just as Sienna was about to launch herself into the water, the mum managed to pluck her daughter to safety. 'Oh no you don't, you cheeky monkey.' The woman buried her daughter in hugs and kisses and the little girl shrieked in delight.

Cara breathed out and felt a pang. She missed those days with Poppy, when it was just the two of them, and they had the freedom to spend endless hours together doing whatever they pleased. Her grief over Pete's passing was still raw, but there'd also been huge moments of joy as she and Pops discovered the city together, visiting museums and parks that Cara hadn't visited since she was a child. Sometimes, it was even possible to forget, for just a moment, that Pete was gone.

'Busy little beavers, aren't they,' commented Will, as the woman returned her child to her pram.

'Last time you mentioned nieces and nephews.' Cara wandered towards a shady patch of grass. 'This spot do?'

Will nodded and set the basket down. 'Two nieces. Three nephews.'

'That's quite the tribe.'

'They're great fun to hang out with. Much nicer than their parents. But, god, they're exhausting. At least I get to hand them back. I don't know how you parents do it. And on your own.'

Cara spread the blanket. 'Sometimes, you don't get a choice.' She sat down, curling her legs under her bottom. 'Does your family ever pressure you about children?'

Will sat close to her. 'They did. But the divorce put a stop to that.'

What did that mean? That he didn't like children, or simply hadn't been in the right relationship to have them? Not that Cara cared ...

She opened the basket and was hit by the aroma of chicken marinated in kecap manis. Her mouth watered.

'I hope you like Vietnamese chicken salad.' She passed him a fork. Alex had advised her to prepare something that was thoroughly delicious to eat, but not messy, which ruled out most of Cara's repertoire of meals. Ordinarily on a picnic for her and Poppy she would have gone for sticky chicken wings, meatballs with lava-like tomato relish, a palate cleanser of chin-dripping watermelon hunks and a sweet finish of snowflake meringues that always left a trail of sweet, white crumbs on the upper lip. She and Poppy would return home, completely satisfied, with fingers that still tasted both tangy and sweet. Showering was almost a disappointment.

But that wasn't the right approach for today. She couldn't afford sticky fingers and tomato stains on her dress. Calm, cool, professional. That's what she needed to project.

'Chicken salad?' Will's face fell. 'Okay.' He nodded.

Cara held a fork in the air. 'If you're allergic or something you need to tell me. My feelings won't be hurt. I'm a professional, remember.'

He looked down at the plastic container. 'No, it's not that at all. It's just ... after we met, I looked at your social media.' A momentary expression of embarrassment flashed across his face. 'You're actually pretty talented … all those splodges and everything spilling everywhere.'

Cara laughed. 'You make it sound like a hot mess.'

'No, no. That's not what I meant.' He twiddled with the fork. 'It's decadent and luxurious, and … kind of wild, if that makes sense.' He angled his head. 'It's passionate. It's not …'

'Chicken salad?' She passed him the plastic container full of polite, mess-free food and Will peeled back the lid. 'You know what? It smells okay.' He took a mouthful and munched. 'Yep, it's not bad.'

Cara took a bite and closed her eyes for a moment to concentrate on what she was tasting. The first note was the coriander, followed by the sweet saltiness of the kecap manis, a little tang from the tamarind puree in the dressing and a small burn in the back of the throat from the chilli. She opened them. It was good. Hit all the right notes for Vietnamese food. Maybe not spectacular. But then again, Cara never felt her own food was spectacular, in the same way that a magician could never be surprised by their own tricks

'It's probably better than not bad,' said Will. 'It's actually pretty bloody delicious.'

Cara smiled and watched him eat hungrily, a splodge of dressing running down his chin. So much for mess-free food. Without thinking, she took a napkin and dabbed at it, her fingers lightly brushing his skin.

Will flinched, frowning, and Cara withdrew her hand. 'Sorry. Bit of a bad habit. Poppy's always ending up with a messy face.'

Will closed the lid on the empty container. 'Sorry for eating so quickly, but it was delicious and I was starving …

I am conscious of the time too.' He checked his watch. 'And as much as I know you love cooking, I have a feeling you wanted to do more than just feed me.' He paused, and as he did so, the sun went behind a cloud, and shadow fell across his face. 'To be honest, I thought I'd never hear from you again after my family said no to buying the house,' he said quietly. 'I do feel bad about you having to move.'

Cara cleared her throat. 'I asked you here today because I wanted to run another idea past you.' She put the salad container by her side and wiped her hands on a napkin. 'It's a proposal for you. A business one that I think you'll see can solve the problem of Cuthbert Close for both of us.'

Will nodded. 'I'm listening.'

Cara had practised her speech with Alex. Clear and direct. No bullshit. No ums and ahs. Tell him what's in it for him. *Facts and figures*, she drilled into Cara, until she felt almost frightened. No wonder Alex was so successful as a lawyer. The judges were probably scared of her.

'I get the feeling that you're open to holding onto Cuthbert Close and you know that I absolutely want to. For both of us, the reasons are personal but the investment rationale is equally sound. Over the past decade, property prices in Cuthbert Close have increased by—' She checked the inside of her palm where she'd written a figure in texta, supplied by Max. '—thirty-eight per cent in real terms, and the current rental yield is nearly six per cent, which is extremely strong.'

Will nodded. 'You've done your homework,' he said. 'But my family has already said no to keeping it so I'm not sure what you're suggesting.'

Cara looked down and twisted her wedding ring. She took a breath. 'I'm suggesting we buy it together, fifty-fifty each.'

He digested her words. 'Buy it from my brother and sister, you mean?'

Cara nodded. 'Yes. But I would also ask you for a ten-year lease on the property, meaning Poppy and I can stay there until she's at least eighteen.'

Will rubbed his lip, his face troubled. 'I don't know Cara ... It's a big ask. I'm not sure ...' He trailed off. Gone was the easy certainty with which he'd greeted her. Now, his face was one of confusion, and doubt, and something else that took Cara more than a second to work out ... Fear.

'You're worried about going against your brother and sister, I understand that,' she said.

'You make me sound like a complete wuss.' He laughed bitterly.

'Not at all. I still hold my breath when my mum tastes my kimchi.'

'But you still make it.'

'I can cope with my mother's disappointment, but I cannot live without kimchi.'

Will smiled briefly, before the shadow again returned to his face. 'I don't know, Cuthbert Close ...' he began. 'It wasn't the happiest home for me. Why would I want to hold onto that?' He fixed his eyes on her, challenging.

'The past is who we are, for better or worse.' She bit her lip. She could go on. She could tell him about the riotous birthday parties she'd hosted for Poppy in the garden, or how her daughter cried when she was stung by her first bee and her little finger swelled up like a sausage. She could tell him how Pete had carried her over the threshold, fresh from their honeymoon, or how, two years later, she'd spread his ashes around the casuarina tree house. Instead, she said nothing. Businesslike. She needed to get back to being businesslike.

Cara cleared her throat. 'I really do think this is a great investment opportunity. I'm happy to send through more information if you'd like?'

Will waved his hand dismissively. Somehow, her words had caused the shutters to go up again on his face. The abruptness was back. 'I know the area, and I know it's on the up. Everyone knows you can't go wrong buying the worst house in the best street. We'd need to get the property independently valued. My brother and sister would insist on full market value.'

'My neighbour Max Chandler is a real estate agent, and he thinks the property is worth between one point four and one point six million. But, as you say, we'd certainly need an independent valuation.'

'So, potentially we'd be up for eight hundred grand each?'

'More like three-fifty for you, given you already have a one-third share in the property,' Cara spoke quickly.

'Still, it's a lot of money. How does a single mother on a freelance income come up with that kind of dough?'

Alex had prepared her for this question and told her how to close it down.

'You don't have to worry about that. What I would propose is that we have a contract drawn up that outlines the terms of our agreement, protecting both your interests and mine.'

Will looked at her. 'You've thought of everything, haven't you?'

'I have to,' said Cara quietly.

Will didn't speak. Cara stole a glance at him. He knitted his fingers together, then released them.

Again, Alex's words rang in her ears. *Don't fill the silences. Women always make that mistake, thinking they have to fill the gaps, and that leads to compromises and apologies. Hit the ball into his court, and leave it there. Don't run around and hit it back for him.*

Will took a breath, about to speak. Cara braced herself, drawing her knees up under her chin and studiously inspecting the grass.

'I can't give you an answer right now.' The *but* hung in the air between them. 'I need to consult with my partner. She's the financial brains behind everything.'

Cara forced a smile. He was divorced and he already had a new partner? Why hadn't he mentioned her before? And why did Cara care? She had no right to be disappointed. She wasn't disappointed. Will was a potential investor. Nothing more.

'I completely understand,' she said, collecting Will's empty container and returning it to the picnic basket. 'I never expected a yes on the spot. You should definitely go away and consult your ...' she choked a little on the word, 'partner ... and let me know what you decide. If there's any more information you need, please don't hesitate to ask.'

Will nodded. 'Can you give me a week? That'll give us enough time to do the sums and talk with the bank.'

'Of course. Now.' Cara shifted to her knees. 'Moving on to more important things.'

'There's more?' Will raised his eyebrows.

'There is.' Cara opened the basket. 'Espresso donuts with salted caramel dipping sauce.'

Will looked hungrily at the container. 'The Primal Guy would be hating us right now.'

'Yes, he would. C'mon.' She put the still slightly warm donuts under his nose. 'All the more reason to eat them, right?'

Will took a bite and ran a finger under his chin to catch the dripping caramel. 'You know, when we first met, I wouldn't have picked you for a risk-taker.'

'I'm not. I'm a complete rule follower, except when it comes to food.' Cara replaced the lid.

'What about recipes? They're pretty prescriptive.'

'A recipe is just a set of suggestions. Really, there are no rules. Just your imagination.'

'You make it sound fun.' Will removed the lid. 'Can I have another one.'

She nodded. 'It *is* fun.'

'Eating's fun. Cooking, not so much.'

'So your partner does the cooking?'

Will startled, his face lined with confusion. 'My what?'

'You said you had a partner, earlier.'

The confusion lines eased. 'Tracey? Oh, no. Trace is my business partner.'

'Of course, sorry.' Relief swept over her. A sense of relief she had no interest in feeling. What did it matter to her if Will Parry had a girlfriend or not? Cara was taking enough risk inviting him to invest in Cuthbert Close – developing a personal attachment would be one risk too many. What if it didn't work out? A failed relationship might only set off another property dispute – the last thing either of them needed.

She snapped the lid back into place. The container was empty.

CHAPTER TWENTY-NINE

'Tell me again why we're going to this thing?' James stood in front of the mirror and adjusted his tie.

'Because this is what partners do. They go to events and schmooze. It's how they get clients, like I was telling Cara last week. It's a seduction, where the climax is lots of money.' Alex stood in front of James and blocked his view of the mirror. 'Could you zip me up?' She held her hair away from her neck and felt James's fingers in the small of her back.

'It's a little snug.' His voice was tight. 'I don't want to break it.'

'Just give it a yank. Sometimes you just have to force it.' Alex sucked in her stomach and pressed her hands against her abdomen. Even her tummy-sucking shapewear wasn't doing the job tonight.

'But you're not a partner. I mean you haven't actually said yes. There's no signed paperwork, is there.' He moved to the side so his face was now visible in the reflection of the mirror.

'Martin thought it would be a good idea for me to get a taste of it all – what it's like to represent the firm and tout for business.' *Because unlike you, he and the rest of the world assume the only answer is yes.*

'These corporate dinner things are all a bit the same, aren't they. Dry chicken. Expensive raffle tickets. Some kind of jazz band. I mean, if it's all about raising money for a hospital, why don't they just ask for a donation. Why the need for all this … palaver.' James gesticulated in frustration. 'This zip won't budge.'

'Yes, it will,' said Alex. 'Just keep trying.' She put her hands on her hips and tried to ignore the beat of annoyance pulsing through her body. 'It's called socialising. I know we haven't been out much in the last six years, but apparently it's what normal adults do on a Saturday night.'

'But socialising is with friends, not work colleagues.'

'Haven't you heard of mixing business with pleasure?' She tried to keep her voice light.

'This is pleasure?' More tugging. 'This zip really is stuck.'

'All you have to do is eat the food, drink the wine and dance with me a couple of times. It's not like we're being forced to go to war. It's a fundraiser. You're not even paying.'

'But Saturday nights are our family time. I'd rather be home with you and the boys, hanging out.'

'You mean fighting about what movie to watch and refereeing over who gets the last slice of pizza?'

'It's not always like that.'

Alex sighed. 'It's just one Saturday night.'

'But if you take the partnership, you'll have to go to loads of these things.'

The next yank was more violent. Alex jumped and dropped her hair. 'Ow. You pinched my skin.'

'Sorry.' The apology was terse. 'Should I keep going?'

'Yes,' said Alex in exasperation. 'Look, if I'm partner, I'll get more say in what I do and don't attend. They know I have a young family. There'll be some leeway.'

'Really? Because in the five years since the twins were born I don't recall Macauley cutting you any slack at all.'

'Yes ... no. I don't know. Maybe. How's the zip?'

'Getting there. If you could just breathe in a little more.'

Alex closed her eyes, inhaled deeply, and visualised herself sucking up all her frustration and fears until there was no more room for air. Did James have a point? Had Macauley been a one-way street? All take and no give? She opened her eyes and looked about their lovely white bathroom with its chrome tapware and deep, freestanding stone bath. Macauley had paid for that bath. Yes, Alex had worked for it, but plenty of people worked hard and weren't nearly as handsomely rewarded for their efforts as lawyers were. Like her parents. But if Alex took the partnership, then Cuthbert Close would be completely theirs within a matter of years, debt-free, and she would have Macauley to thank for it. It was a no-brainer.

'There. Got it.' James sounded relieved. Alex felt suffocated.

She stepped away from the mirror and tried to breathe out but found she couldn't. The dress wouldn't let her. This was going to be a painful night.

All good things take a little suffering.

'Are you nearly ready? I don't want to be late.'

'I'm going as fast as I can.' James fiddled some more with his tie.

'Okay, well, I'm going to check on the kids. Talia's reading a book to them.'

Alex trod carefully down the stairs. She couldn't look down. The dress wouldn't let her bend. Halfway, she stopped to listen to the voices coming from one of the boys' bedrooms. It sounded like Talia was pleading with them.

'Noah, please tell me where this ring came from? Is it your mum's?'

'I don't know. I've never seen it. Can we read another book now?' Noah sounded unconcerned, almost flippant.

With her heart sinking, Alex strode into the bedroom. 'What's going on?'

'Nothing, Mummy.' Noah sat on the bed, his legs swinging like a pendulum underneath. 'You look beautiful.'

'Thank you, sweetheart.' She bent her knees and lowered herself to kiss him on the nose. 'Now what's this about a ring?'

Talia bit her lip and looked sideways at Noah. 'I was getting a book off the shelf to read … And I found this on the floor.' She held up a small silver jewellery keepsake box, the one they put the boys' teeth in for the tooth fairy, roundly regarded as a very forgetful flibbertigibbet who tended to take at least two nights to leave a coin.

Talia continued. 'I heard something inside, so I opened it and found this.' In the palm of the girl's hand was a sparkling diamond ring.

Alex peered closely. 'It's not mine.' She picked it up. 'It's definitely the real thing, though. Where did you get this?' she said sharply to Noah.

'I don't know, Mummy.' He edged closer to Talia.

With a degree of difficulty, Alex knelt down in front of him. 'This ring is worth a lot of money and it's very important you tell me where you found it.'

'Really, Mummy. I don't know.'

She took her son by the shoulders. 'I'm not cross with you, Noah, but I need you to tell me the truth. Remember, you don't get in trouble if you're honest. Now, who owns this ring?'

Noah wriggled free and cowered into Talia. 'I *am* telling you the truth. I don't know.'

Alex stood up. 'I'm going to get your father.'

In the hallway, she passed Jasper, emerging from the downstairs toilet with a dribble of toothpaste running down his chin.

Alex wiped it away and stood before him. 'Do you know anything about this ring in Noah's room?'

'What's a ring?' he asked innocently.

Alex wanted to shake him. What was wrong with her sons? Either they were very good at pretending to be dense, or they actually were that way. Neither was good.

'Go into Noah's room, and wait for me there,' she ordered. 'James. James,' Alex called up the stairs. 'Could you please come down here? We have a problem.'

'Just a minute.'

She waited. A final slam of the cupboard door and James hurried down the stairs. Alex filled him in on the unwelcome discovery of the diamond in Noah's bedroom.

'Any idea who it belongs to?' James folded his arms.

'None.'

'I think I might be able to help.' Talia stood in the doorway. She fiddled with a thread on her cut-off denim shorts. 'Your neighbour, Mrs Chandler, has a ring like this one.'

She gave an uncertain smile. 'I have a thing for diamonds. That's one thing Mum and I have in common. Did you know Beyonce's engagement ring was 18-carat? Crazy.' Talia shook her head.

'You think it's Beth's?' Alex asked.

'You could send her a photo and see,' said Talia.

'I'll do that.' Alex went to her handbag. 'James, you go in and talk to Noah. See if you can get any more information out of him.' She snapped a photo of the ring. 'Talia, maybe you could read with Jasper?'

Alex checked her watch. They were due at the fundraiser in ten minutes and the hotel was at least a half-hour drive away. She tapped her foot. Beth could be notoriously slow in replying to texts. There was no point waiting at home for an answer because the reply probably wouldn't come until tomorrow.

Alex collected her pashmina and handbag and went back into Jasper's room to kiss him goodnight. He and Talia were curled up together on the bed and reading *The Famous Five*. Jasper was obsessed with the Blyton series and Alex had made the mistake of fanning his enthusiasm by buying the box set of all twenty-one books, the re-written politically correct version of course. For his sixth birthday, he wanted to go camping, without Alex and James, but with plenty of ginger beer and cream cakes and a dog.

'Don't let him make you read for too long, Talia.' Bending awkwardly, Alex kissed Jasper on the forehead.

'I love these books. My dad used to read them to me when I was a kid,' said Talia.

Interesting. The Primal Guy was a *Famous Five* reader. Alex wouldn't have picked that. In fact, she was a little surprised he could read at all.

'Lights out at 8 pm,' said Alex, switching on the bedside lamp.

'Okay, Mrs O'Rourke,' said Talia.

'Call me Alex, all right.' She shut the door and headed into the other bedroom where James was delivering a very solemn speech, with Noah sitting on his lap, about the importance of not taking other people's things without asking.

'Yes, it's called stealing,' said Alex, standing by the bed. 'People go to jail for that.'

'I don't want to go to jail,' Noah wailed and buried his head in James's shoulder.

'You're not going to jail, mate.' James kissed his head and gave Alex a look as if to say *What are you thinking?*

'But Mummy says I'm going to jail,' he sobbed.

'I didn't mean that you were going to jail, I meant other people. Older people. There's no jail for kids.'

'Really?' Noah looked at her hopefully, his hair all mussed and his face streaked with tears. Alex felt herself deflating like a pricked balloon – all her frustration and anger hissing gently out of her. He was just a little boy. A confused little boy.

'I promise.' She kissed him on the forehead. 'Now, we need to leave, darling, or Daddy and I will be late for our dinner.'

'I don't want you to go.' Noah leapt off James's lap and threw himself around Alex's legs. 'Please don't go.'

She hugged him close and gently peeled him away. 'If you stop crying now, I'll give you an extra fifteen minutes on the iPad tomorrow.'

Noah's face brightened. 'Really? Fifteen minutes?'

'Sure.' Before Alex could kiss him again, Noah had sped out of the room and into Jasper's, bellowing, 'I get more time on the iPad tomorrow, and you don't!'

James stood up slowly, the bed creaking. 'Well, I think he really got the message about the consequences of stealing, don't you?' He shook his head. 'iPad time, really? Is that the best you could do?'

'We're running late.' She hurried out of the room.

'Night, boys. Night, Talia,' James called from the hall-way, collecting his keys and jacket.

'Night, Dad,' they chorused back.

'See, they're happy,' hissed Alex, giving her lipstick a final check in the mirror. James didn't answer.

In the car, he drove stony-faced. It wasn't like him at all to give her the silent treatment. That was usually Alex's MO, and James tended to disregard it. He liked to talk things out. Endlessly. It was exhausting. But she realised, now, that it was far preferable to this – the silence.

Alex's phone buzzed. A message from Beth.

Oh, you found my engagement ring! You wonderful, wonderful thing. Where was it?

'So, the ring does belong to Beth. Her engagement ring.' Alex stared straight ahead. 'She wants to know where we found it.'

'Tell her the truth.' James kept his eyes fixed on the road.

'What? That our son stole it from her? She's one of my best friends. I can't tell her that. Besides, we don't even know for sure that he did do it. He's denied it outright and quite frankly it is hard to understand why a five-year-old boy would steal a diamond ring.'

'Weren't you the one threatening him with jail?'

'Yes, but only to scare him into telling us the truth.'

James looked at her hard. 'I think you know the truth, you just don't want to admit it.'

'What are you talking about?'

'Trashing the classroom at school, that picture he drew of himself, now this ring business. It's all about getting our attention. They're cries for help.'

Alex stared at the brake lights of the car in front and narrowed her gaze until her vision was filled with a blur of red.

'I even wonder if Noah had something to do with Henny's death?' pondered James.

Alex's head snapped back. 'So now our son is a guinea pig murderer? That's utterly ridiculous. And I know for a fact it's not true. Talia told me what happened. It was definitely the Devines' cat.'

'Okay, well, regardless, we've always sworn we'd never be the kind of parents who buried their heads in the sand when it came to the kids. There's a problem here and we need to address it.'

Alex wound down the window. She couldn't breathe. Between the damn dress and James's ridiculous comments, suggesting he thought their son capable of killing a pet, her body couldn't complete the most basic of functions.

Alex gulped the air. 'Noah may have some issues, but he's far from being a budding psychopath,' she croaked. 'I think you're saying all of this to make me feel guilty. You don't want me to take the partnership, why don't you just admit it?' Alex gripped the armrest. The wind rushed at her, too fast for her to breathe. Everything was coming at her so quickly. The baby, the partnership, Noah's problems. Her vision was narrowing, becoming black at the edges. It was like rushing headlong into a tunnel, and falling down, further and further, with James calling after her.

'Alex, Alex.' But his voice was distant, watery and melting away. She blinked and blinked again, tried to focus on the red light but the dark had overtaken that as well.

Suddenly, everything was blissfully black and silent.

CHAPTER THIRTY

Cara put the final spoonful of beef bourguignon into the last of the thirty-eight plastic containers laid out on the trestle table in the back of the shed. Beth followed behind, adding a sprinkling of parsley. Served on a bed of cauliflower mash, with a side of blanched green beans, the French casserole, with its flavours of salty bacon, rich red wine and fragrant garlic, was proving one of the most popular of Nourish's dishes. Overall, orders for the week ahead were up by fifty per cent. Everyone who'd ordered in the first week had ordered again, and this time more meals. Tonight, with Poppy asleep and Max out with the kids at a movie, Beth and Cara planned to crank out two of the seven dishes on offer for the week.

'There. One lot of meals. Done.' Beth wiped her hands against her apron and mopped her brow. 'Thank goodness.' Cara put the pot back on the camp stove and absent-mindedly licked the ladle.

'Did you season this?' She took a second taste.

'I think I did.' Beth frowned. 'I did it just before Alex's text message about the ring.'

'Are you sure? Because it tastes really flat.' Cara scraped again at the bottom of the saucepan and offered Beth the spoon.

She made a face. 'I don't understand. I had the salt in my hand. The phone buzzed, so I replied to Alex and then ...' She pressed her fingers to her cheek, her little finger resting on her lip. 'I'm sure I put it in. It was in my hand. Maybe I didn't quite stir it through to the bottom.'

Using a fresh spoon, Cara dipped lightly into one of the filled containers. 'This one's the same.' She tested another. 'So's this one.'

Beth wrung her hands in the apron. 'I'm so sorry, Cara. I must have forgotten. I think I was so distracted I just ... I just forgot. There must be a way we can fix it.'

'I don't think so,' said Cara. 'If we put it back in the pot, there'll be cauliflower and parsley all through it.' She dropped the spoon with a clatter back in the saucepan. 'It'll look terrible.'

'Maybe we could supply it with a sachet of salt on the side?'

'Like you get at McDonald's? You know we can't do that, Beth. This is a premium product. These mothers are paying so they don't have to lift a finger.'

Beth was quiet. 'I'm sorry. Really.'

Cara looked at the food before them. All the wasted time and effort, not to mention the cost of buying the ingredients. How could Beth make such a basic mistake? She was a better cook than that. Cara clenched her fingers and tried to swallow the ball of anger in her throat. First, the fire, then Alex's social media faux pas over the launch, and now this, a dish completely ruined, because of Beth. It was like they were deliberately trying to sabotage the business or, at least, simply weren't taking it seriously enough. It was fine for them, she supposed. After all, they had choices. They had husbands. Their homes in Cuthbert Close were secure, at least for now.

She took a breath. She remembered this anger. This sense that the world was conspiring against her. She'd felt it the day Pete's oncologist had sat them down to tell them his cancer was terminal. There were new tumours. Too many for surgery, and too aggressive to be controlled with chemo. Cara was stunned. Speechless at first. Then, the baby inside of her, Poppy, kicked, and Cara felt her anger ignite. How dare the doctor give up on them. There had to be something. A second opinion. An experimental treatment. Something. In the doctor's small, airless office, she ranted and raged until Pete put his hand over hers.

'Cara, he's trying his best. We're all trying our best.'

The admonishment shamed her. Pete was right. There was no one to blame. No point to her anger. It was just stupid, dumb bad luck that her husband was going to die, and she could either accept it with grace and make the most of their final days and months together, or she could carry on like a spoilt child. After the appointment, she went home and cooked a cheesecake and she and Pete had eaten every last piece of it.

Cara had never made another.

'I know you're sorry, Beth. I know you didn't do this on purpose.' Cara sighed. 'I'm sorry, too. For being cross.' She folded her arms. 'I just really need this business to work.'

Beth stood before her and pushed a stray hair off Cara's face. 'It *is* going to work. I'm going to make sure of it,' she said. 'Now, how about we get started on that second dish? I'll pack these up and maybe we could offer them to residents of the close at half price so we can at least get our costs back?' Beth stifled a yawn. 'Let's get started.'

'I've got a better idea,' said Cara, taking in the grey circles under Beth's eyes. 'Let's pack up these meals and call it a night. We can start the pasta dish first thing tomorrow morning.'

'Are you sure?'

'Absolutely.'

Beth gave a relieved smile. 'That sounds perfect.'

Half an hour later, the shed was back to its normal spotless self, with all the meals packed into Beth's freezer.

'Back here at seven?' Beth untied her apron.

'Can't wait.' Cara smiled and watched to make sure her neighbour made it safely through the fence. At her back door, Beth gave a wave and disappeared.

Inside the cottage, Cara checked on the sleeping Poppy. Her daughter was splayed across the bed, damp curls stuck to her forehead. Cara tried imagining her in a different bed, in a different room other than the one she'd known all her life.

She couldn't.

She didn't want to. Just thinking about it made her eyes sting.

She shifted off the door frame and went into the kitchen to pour herself a glass of wine. The flushed cheeks wouldn't matter, not when she was all alone anyway. What she needed was alcohol and the food channel. Apart from cooking, it was the perfect balm for her mournful mood.

Settling back into the couch, she aimed the remote control at the TV and fired. The sound of an angry, berating Englishman filled her lounge room. Gordon Ramsay. Exactly what she didn't need – a chef scouring other people's kitchens for evidence of poor hygiene and cooking.

'Give them a break,' she muttered at the screen. 'They're doing their best.'

Her phone bleeped with a text message and Cara nearly dived on it, relieved to have an excuse to take her attention away from the expletive-ridden angst being played out on screen.

It was from Will. Cara sat up quickly, cursing the small spill of wine that her sudden movement caused. Heart thumping, she started to read.

Hi Cara, I know it's late but I thought you'd like to know this sooner rather than later … I'm in. For the house, that is. I've done the numbers and I'm pretty confident that it stacks up as a great investment. The family doesn't mind, as long as they get their cash they don't care. I'll touch base next week to have documents drawn up.

She yelped and read the message again. Once. Twice. Three times to make sure her eyes weren't tricking her. No. It was there on the screen. The phone trembled in her fingers. He was in! Definitely in. Her mind scrambled to think through everything that short text message of less than 100 words meant. No moving. No new school. No long commute. No shoebox apartment. No living with her parents. Provided she could get a modest loan from the bank, their lives wouldn't have to change at all.

She and Poppy could stay! They could live. They could sit and breathe and laugh and play and paint and cook and work and stay close to Pete's memory, just as they'd always done.

The only thing she couldn't do was fall in love with Will Parry.

And that was fine, she told herself. Perfectly fine.

CHAPTER THIRTY-ONE

'Alex.' There was a tugging at her arm. 'Alex, Alex, wake up.' Now there were fingers on her chin, moving her head from side to side. 'Alex. Come on.'

Where was she? The last thing she remembered was poor dead little Henny the guinea pig and Noah stomping on her with a diamond ring between his teeth and a demonic glint in his eye. Wait. What the fuck?

Alex's eyes blazed open to find James approximately an inch from her face, his forehead creased with worry.

'What are you doing?' Alex clutched the seatbelt. Now she knew where she was. The car. The fundraising ball. Her big night to shine on behalf of Macauley.

'You fainted.' James took her wrist. 'Your pulse is going crazy.' He touched her head. 'And you're quite feverish. I think you're coming down with something.'

'I just fell asleep for a minute,' Alex protested, pushing James's hand away, her head spinning wildly. She blinked. And blinked again to bring the world back to a standstill. 'I'm fine,' she said through gritted teeth.

'No, you're not.' He was firm. 'And you didn't just fall asleep, you fainted. We were in the middle of a conversation and you stopped, mid-sentence.'

'I'm exhausted! I'm pregnant, don't forget.' As if to prove the point, she burped, a bilious, eggy ejection that fortunately seemed to ease her queasy stomach.

James clenched the steering wheel. 'Let's just go home.'

'No.' Alex released the handbrake. 'We are going to this ball.' She tried to lean forward, but was constrained by the seatbelt. 'Now if I can just loosen this stupid dress and breathe properly then everything will be fine.'

James watched her.

'Maybe instead of just sitting there, you could help me,' she snapped, twisting in the seat.

In silence, James undid the zipper and Alex breathed deeply, taking in blessed lungfuls of oxygen.

'There, that's better. See, I'm fine now. I just needed to, you know, breathe.'

'Life is pretty tricky without it,' said James drily, observing her.

'Well, come on then. What are you waiting for? Let's go. We're already twenty minutes late.'

'You cannot be serious.'

'I'm perfectly serious.'

'How are you going to walk around that ballroom with your dress half undone?'

Alex rummaged through her handbag. 'I've got a safety pin here somewhere so I'll just pin it and cover the back with my wrap.' She held up the pashmina. 'Never leave home without one.'

'This is crazy.' James tapped the steering wheel. 'No job could be worth this.'

Alex looked at him. 'In ten years, when we are debt-free and sitting on a very large retirement fund, you'll thank me.'

'If I'm still around,' James muttered under his breath.

Alex pretended not to hear.

At the oversized entry doors to the ballroom, under a sparkling chandelier, Alex paused. Behind the solid wooden panels, the ball was in full swing. A jazz band, as James had predicted. She twirled slowly in a circle before her husband. 'Can you tell I'm pinned in?'

James studied her. 'You wouldn't know a thing.'

'Perfect.' She took his hand. 'Thank you for doing this.'

The silence of the remaining car ride had given her time to think rationally. James wasn't trying to stand in the way of her career. He'd always been nothing but supportive. He was worried for her. For the kids, and that was perfectly understandable. She loved him for that. But he didn't understand how these things worked. He also had no idea of what it was like to go without. His mum's idea of deprivation was refusing to foot the bill for James's French horn lessons, on account of the horrendous racket. The poor woman still felt guilty. How could James understand Alex's drive to secure their family's financial future? How could he understand that a law firm gave one chance and one chance only? This was her time. All she had to do was be brave enough to take it.

She straightened James's tie and led him into the ballroom. Both of them stopped under the entry banner, emblazoned with the words *A Night of Diamonds: Helping Our Kids Shine Brighter.*

Three months ago, she'd attended a conference here about new corporate regulation and remembered the room being as boring and stale as the ginger nut biscuits served at break time.

Tonight, it was like entering a planetarium.

Gone was the beige wallpaper, and in its place were heavy swathes of black velvet. The harsh overhead lighting had been replaced by hundreds of glow-lamps on each table, projecting stars and planets about the room.

'Oh, it's gorgeous, don't you think?' Alex turned to James excitedly.

'If only the sick kids could be here to see it,' he remarked through tense lips.

Alex took his hand. 'Please. Please just go along with this. For me?'

James nodded grimly and tucked her hand under his arm as they made their way to the Macauley table, Alex being careful to make sure her wrap didn't snag on anyone's chair. The last thing she needed was a wardrobe malfunction.

She spotted Martin, sitting at the table and studying the menu. An older man sat to his side, next to a substantially younger woman who appeared to be wearing more make-up than clothing.

Alex waved to get Martin's attention, and plastered a bright smile to her face. 'Hi there, sorry we're late. You remember James, don't you?'

Martin frowned for a minute before allowing himself a nod of recognition. 'Hello, James. Good to see you again.'

The two shook hands and Martin turned to the man on his left. 'Anthony, you've met Alexandra O'Rourke, I believe. She was one of the senior associates on your acquisition last year.'

Anthony made a face and offered his hand. 'I've tried to forget all the lawyers I met last year.'

'I try to do the same,' joked Alex. 'What's *your* name again?' she said to Martin.

'She's funny,' Anthony remarked. 'Keep her.'

'Alexandra is one of our rising stars. We have big plans for her,' said Martin. 'She's also a mother of two. Twins, I think?'

Alex blinked. Martin never mentioned her children. She wasn't even sure he knew she had them.

Anthony shook his head. 'I don't know how you young women do it all. Or why you do it all.'

'Because we love to work and we love our kids,' said Alex, laughing. 'And we want both. That's not too much to ask, is it?'

Anthony sat down and leant back, his fingers playing at the base of his wineglass. 'And what does your husband think about that?'

'I think Alex doesn't know when to stop,' said James.

'I like that in a lawyer,' said Anthony. 'A tiger.'

The band struck up a new song that Alex recognised as the old Sinatra standard 'Fly Me to the Moon'.

The bejewelled and heavily made-up woman on Anthony's other side squeezed his arm. 'C'mon, this is boring. We're not here to talk shop all night.'

Oh, yes we are, thought Alex.

'Excuse me, folks. Got to perform my husbandly duties.' Anthony rose and led the woman that Alex presumed to be his wife (second, at a guess) onto the dance floor.

'Why don't you and Martin go join them?' James took a seat. 'I'll stay here and mind the table. Make sure the wine is up to scratch.' He tipped a glass at Alex and winked.

Bastard.

Martin was the last person Alex wanted to dance with, and her husband knew it. The thought of putting her hands on his neat little waist and staring straight into his squirrelly face for at least three minutes was … Ugh! It wasn't worth thinking about and she felt quite sure that Martin would feel equally disinclined. He was the kind of man who kept antibacterial wipes in his top drawer and was forever going on about how fingers were the carriers of most illness.

But, wait, shit, no. Martin was rising to his feet. 'I was actually a junior champion in ballroom dancing back in the day.'

Of course you were.

'Shall we?' He extended his hand to Alex.

'Sure.'

His palm was clammy and Alex resisted the urge to rip her hand away and wipe it down her dress, wishing very hard at that moment for Martin's box of antibacterial wipes.

Pull yourself together.

She was an adult. So what if she shared a little sweat with her co-worker? It could be no worse than Jasper's puking.

On the dance floor, Martin clicked his heels together and held his arms out wide. Alex stepped into them and saw a momentary blink of confusion as he pressed his hand into her back.

Oh shit. He's felt the pin.

But before she could worry about it any further, they were dancing. Martin's movements were smooth and precise, if lacking in flair. In other words, he danced the way he worked.

'I hope you don't mind my mentioning your children to Anthony.' Martin avoided eye contact by staring off to the side, the way professional ballroom dancers did, as if paradise lay just beyond their partner's shoulder. 'But he's about to become a grandfather and his daughter is your age.'

Alex raised her eyebrows. So his second wife was around the same age as his daughter. Charming.

Martin went on. 'Clients like to work with lawyers they can relate to, just like any business. People think the law is all about justice and fairness and applying legislation and regulations.' He stopped to dip her. 'But at the partner level, it's actually about personal connections. Most of the work of being a partner is about cultivating and feeding our client relationships.'

And sacrificing your personal ones.

'That makes perfect sense,' Alex murmured, starting to feel a little dizzy from Martin's continual twirling.

'The other critical aspect of a partner's role is to develop and guide the company's culture.'

'I'm glad you said that Martin, because I have …'

He cut her off. 'We need a working mother to join the partners.'

'Right,' said Alex uncertainly.

'Specifically, we need a working mother with *young* children. Our graduate intake this year is seventy-five per cent female and, as you well know, we invest heavily in training and developing our new recruits.' He stopped twirling and dipped her again. 'We need a return on that investment.'

'I see.'

Actually she didn't see. All the female graduates worked their arses off. Macauley more than made its money back on them.

He righted her. 'That's where you come in. We want to offer these women the chance to freeze their eggs.'

'Sorry. What?'

Martin twirled her out, and reeled her back in. 'It was my impression that you were familiar with the process of in-vitro fertilisation.'

'If you're asking if I went through IVF, then yes I did, but that was for fertility issues, not because I wanted to delay having children.'

Martin shrugged. 'The reasons don't matter. What's important is that you've done it. You can lead this program. You can show young women that they don't need to rush off and have babies.' He said this with a slight sneer. 'Pregnancy is an inconvenience, as you well know. Remember the Merrill matter?'

How could she forget. They'd been pushing for a resolution for over twelve months, and just as word came through that the other party was ready to do a deal, Alex had the temerity to go into labour with the twins and had had to hand over the reins to Martin. She'd briefed him between contractions, a fact he'd never let her forget. Alex had to concede it was a little disjointed. But still, she was having a baby. Actually, two of them. At that point, she really didn't give a shit about the Merrill matter.

'With the egg-freezing program, they can stay working. Establish themselves. Have children when *they* want to, not according to some arcane quirk of biology. We want them to *lean in* and, in so doing, ensure that all the time and money Macauley puts into them isn't wasted.'

Alex stopped dancing and dropped Martin's hand. 'So that's why I've been asked to become a partner, so I can be the poster-girl for IVF?'

'I wouldn't quite put it in those terms,' said Martin. 'You're also an excellent lawyer.' He took her back in his arms. Alex felt trapped. She'd given her life to the company. Missed school assemblies and tuckshop duty, even one of the twins' own birthday parties, to deal with a crisis. She'd assumed the partnership offer was reward for effort and excellence, recognition of the way in which she'd managed to keep her family invisible from her workplace. It was an offer made *despite* being a working mother, not *because* of it. Now, she was learning it was the opposite.

Her head spun in time with the mirror ball. Alex stopped still. 'I'm sorry, Martin, but I'm not feeling very well.'

He jumped back, as if stung by a wasp. 'You should have told me earlier,' he said, not in a kindly way.

At the table, James was chatting with Anthony. His wife scrolled through her phone.

'Anthony, I'm sorry to interrupt, but we need to leave.' Alex stood next to her husband and tapped the table.

James looked up at her in surprise. 'What's wrong? Are you feeling okay?'

'No … Yes … I'll explain later.' She took James's hand and tugged him to his feet. 'Goodbye, Anthony. It was a pleasure to meet you. Please wish your daughter good luck from me in becoming a mother. She'll need it.' Alex turned on her heel. She had the sense James was following close behind, but it wasn't until they reached the doors that he finally caught her hand.

'What's going on? Why are we leaving when we've only just arrived?'

Alex looked around. Everywhere she saw money, from the glittering glassware, to the full-to-the-brim champagne flutes, to the thousand-dollar tuxedoes and the even more expensive designer frocks being twirled about on the dance floor.

The fairy lights glittered overhead like stars.

'This is another planet,' Alex whispered. 'And I don't think I want to be here any more.'

She took James's hand, and started walking away.

CHAPTER THIRTY-TWO

Beth knew she should have a stern expression on her face, but she couldn't help a smile of encouragement at the little boy before her at the front door.

'It's all right sweetheart, I'm not angry,' said Beth.

'Noah, tell Beth you're very sorry.' Alex stood over her son with her hands on her hips.

'But Mummy, I told you last night, I didn't take it.' Noah's eyes were dark and sorrowful.

Alex exhaled loudly. 'Remember what Daddy and I always tell you. You're not in trouble if you tell the truth and apologise.'

'But I am telling the truth. It wasn't me.' Noah stamped his foot.

'Who was it then? The ring was in your room, in your tooth fairy box.' Alex folded her arms. 'Please, Noah,' she pleaded. 'Just say sorry to Beth, and we can leave.'

'No.'

'It's fine, Alex. I'm sure he understands that stealing is wrong,' said Beth, kneeling to look straight into his eyes. Noah nodded.

'Here, give Aunty Bethy a cuddle.' The little boy leant in and she felt his arms straining to reach all the way around her neck, his warm breath in her ear. For a second, Beth closed her eyes and remembered what it was like when Chloe and Ethan were this age and life was so much simpler. All a child of that age really wanted from their parents was their time – time to kick around a ball, bike ride in the park, sit down and do colouring, read with them and play snakes and ladders. Physically tiring, yes, but less emotionally exhausting when compared with teenagerhood.

She had a sudden compulsion to take Alex by the shoulders.

Enjoy this time. This is the best time.

But from the exasperated expression on Alex's face and the look of fear on Noah's, she concluded that now might not be the right time to be extolling the virtues of five year olds.

Instead, Beth took Noah's hand. 'Sweetheart, why don't you go into my special cupboard in the kitchen where I hide the lollies. There might be a jelly snake for you there.'

'Just one,' called Alex after her scurrying son, then spoke in a low voice to Beth. 'Are you sure it's wise allowing him into your kitchen unsupervised? He might swipe your wallet while he's at it.'

'Oh, Alex. Don't be silly. Noah's a good boy at heart.'

'He's a budding criminal, that's what he is,' said Alex, folding her arms. 'I really am very sorry about your ring.'

Beth looked at the diamond, sparkling up at her, back where it was supposed to be on her finger. She'd expected to feel happier at its return, but the ring felt loose, like it could fall off at any moment. She twisted it anxiously.

'Don't be so hard on him,' she began. 'You know, one day you'll look back …'

'If you're about to tell me that one day we'll look back on these years as the easy times, then please save it.'

Beth recoiled, stung. 'I'm sorry, I was only trying to make you feel better.'

'Well it doesn't, it makes me feel worse, because if these *golden days* are so fucking hard for us, then what hope do we have for the future?' She threw her hands up. 'Mothers always do this. From the minute you're pregnant and you're exhausted and enormous and you're walking round with a bowling ball in your pelvis, it's like *oh you think pregnancy is bad, wait till you actually have the kid*, then you have the baby and you're a sleep-deprived, hormonal wreck, and they say *oh, wait till it's a toddler, then you'll know what busy is really like.* Then they're at preschool and they're getting nits and viruses every second week and parents say *oh, you wait till you have to deal with homework, it's a nightmare.* At this rate, the only time that actually seems easy is when our kids are forty years old and James and I are nearly dead! I'm sick of it.'

Beth put her hand on Alex's arm. 'I'm sorry. I really didn't mean to upset you.'

She sighed. 'It's not your fault, Beth. It's me. I'm cross at myself. Have you ever heard that saying – that the definition of stupidity is to repeat the same thing over and over and expect a different result.'

'I think they use that in Alcoholics Anonymous.'

Alex nodded. 'That makes sense, actually, because I feel like I've been so wedded, almost *addicted,* to this dream for nearly twenty years, of having the big career and the nice house and saving the world through law and I keep trying to make it happen but I seem to be making things worse and worse for everyone. And I'm not even sure that it's what I want any more. I think my bosses are probably tokenistic arseholes who actually don't deserve my time and effort.'

'So maybe it's not *you* that's the problem, it's the *dream,*' said Beth.

'Maybe.' Alex put a protective hand over her stomach.

'Mummy, Mummy.' Noah half-ran, half-walked down the hallway, his hands cupped carefully. 'Look what I got!'

'What? Show me. Not another diamond, is it?'

'No. It's a ladybird. I found it in on the floor in Beth's kitchen. Look, it even has black dots and a red back.' Noah un-cupped his hands. 'It's like magic, isn't it?' He spoke with wonder in his voice.

Over his head, Alex gave Beth a wry smile of concession.

'You're a sweet boy.' Alex kissed her son's head. 'Now say goodbye to Beth.'

'Bye, Beth.' Noah set off down the path, followed by Alex, who stopped at the gate.

'Hey, have I RSVP'd yet for the party?'

'The party?'

'The anniversary party. Twenty years of your wedded bliss, remember? It's only a few weeks away and I'm pretty sure I haven't yet told you that we're definitely coming, pre-suming it's still happening, is it?' Alex raised her eyebrow.

Oh goodness, the party. In the whirlwind of setting up Nourish, and figuring out what to do about Max, she'd conveniently managed to forget that eighty of their nearest and dearest friends would be landing on their doorstep in just under three weeks' time.

'Still happening. Yes. Cara and I have a big cooking session planned for Thursday. Things we can cook ahead and freeze for the party. We could always do with another pair of hands …' She trailed off as an expression of horror slid over Alex's face. Of course. The poor woman hated cooking and she had a million and one things on her plate. 'You know what … don't worry. We'll be fine.'

As she waved at Alex, the diamond caught the sun, causing a blind spot in her eye.

Beth blinked, and blinked again before closing the door. Damn ring.

She slipped it off her finger with ease.

'I'm heading off now.' Max stood in the kitchen, dressed in his golf gear and Beth quickly slipped the ring into her pocket.

'You're playing golf today? I thought we might have gone bowling or something with the kids.' Beth couldn't hide the disappointment in her voice. As much as she'd sort of come to grips with Max's infidelity, a small part of her wanted to keep playing happy families, at least until the very end. Lying in bed that morning, still half-asleep, she'd fantasised about them all going to the beach together, frolicking in the waves, having body-surfing races, which Chloe would inevitably win. That was until she got up and discovered the day was too breezy and changeable – brilliant sunshine one minute, cool and overcast the next. Now, standing in front of Max, with his golfing gloves in one hand, she saw the vision for what it was, a silly little dream.

'Chloe's got special squad today, remember, so I'm going to drop her on the way, and Ethan's going to a mate's to study all day, and he's going to catch a lift with us as well. They're in the car, ready to go. I just came to say bye.' He smiled. 'So, you're free. You've got the whole house to yourself.'

Beth forced a smile. 'Great. Well, have fun.'

With a wink, he was gone. Beth trudged back into the living room and stood there, unsure what to do with herself. She'd gone over to Cara's early to finish off the cooking, figuring it would leave her free to spend the rest of Sunday with her family. So much for that plan. At least Cara was in a good mood, thanks to that lovely Will Parry. With such an upbeat feeling in the shed, the cook had gone well. Beth had remembered to taste the chicken cacciatore at each step, the salt grinder close at hand. There was even enough left over to bring some home for her family's dinner. If they ever returned.

Beth looked about the room. There was nothing to do. The house was clean, the washing up to date, and the fridge full of food.

She drummed her fingers against the bench top. What to do … What to do …

Read a book, perhaps?

No, a book required too much concentration.

Listen to music? Read a newspaper?

She wasn't in the mood for that either.

Emails.

She could check her emails. Clearing her inbox always gave her a small sense of achievement. Beth sat down at the computer in the study and logged in.

Ten new emails, mostly from friends and family, confirming their attendance at the anniversary party.

Can't wait for it!

We'll be there with bells on.

Twenty years! What an incredible achievement!

Beth dutifully responded with an effusive *Wonderful! So glad you can make it,* checked off their names from her RSVP list, then deleted each and every one.

There were two emails left. One from The Primal Guy, which she deleted without reading, leaving one remaining.

Dance Your Way to Fitness.

Beth clicked on it. It was from Max's gym, announcing a new Zumba class for beginners. Beth swivelled on her chair and reread the details. *Full body workout. Get your heart pumping and your booty shaking. Incredible instructors. Pay by the class. Absolute beginners welcome! 10 am Sunday.*

Beth's hand hovered over the delete button.

It was twenty-five years since she'd last taken a dance lesson, and that was a flamenco class, taken on a whim at the height of *Strictly Ballroom* mania where every second person was wearing Bonds singlets as going-out attire, and John Paul Young was cool again, thanks to 'Love Is in the Air'.

Should she?

What would she wear?

No, it was too silly.

The RSVPs had reminded her of other jobs she needed to do, like check the trestle tables and chairs that they'd need for the party. Yes, that was something she needed to do! Buoyed with purpose, she closed the email window and headed outside, down the path. There was no one in the

street and Beth tried to ignore the nagging feeling that it
was because they were all spending time with their families.

In the gloom of the garage Beth stopped to let her eyes
adjust to the lack of light.

What was that over in the corner?

She squinted and walked closer.

She touched it.

Max's golf bag. He'd left it behind. She must ring him.
Let him know. He'd feel like such a fool. Going to golf
without his golf clubs.

Halfway out, Beth stopped.

Max wasn't an idiot. Beth was the idiot.

He hadn't forgotten the clubs at all. He was meeting with
her.

Suddenly, Alex's words rang in her ear. *The definition of
stupidity is to do the same thing over and over and expect a
different result.*

Slamming the garage door shut, Beth scurried inside
where the computer screen was still giving off its ghostly
glow. Reopening the email, she scribbled down the address
of the gym. It was time to do something different. Something just for her. If Max could be a selfish pig, then why
shouldn't she do something for herself as well? Something
just to make her feel good, that didn't involve adultery, or
the children.

Dance. Yes, take a dancing lesson. It was perfect.

Realising she had nothing suitable to wear in her own
closet of chinos and knits, she went straight to Chloe's
wardrobe, which was full to overflowing with leggings and
crop tops. Admittedly, they were a few sizes too small and
no doubt her daughter would have a meltdown if she knew

her mother intended to wear them out in public. But Lycra was designed to stretch, wasn't it?

From Chloe's cupboard, she picked out a pair of the larger-looking leggings, with a subtle ocelot print, and a plain black crop top.

She stood in front of the mirror and surveyed her body dispassionately. She wasn't used to seeing herself this way. Usually, her morning mirror check was simply to make sure her hair wasn't a mess and her eyeliner in the wrong spot. She didn't pay much attention to her body because it was normally covered by her standard uniform of loose-fitting top and slim-fit-with-stretch pants. Thanks to her nutrition background, she'd never really had to worry about weight gain. She ate sensibly and walked regularly. Food was fuel and Beth liked the feeling of putting good fuel into her body.

But now that she looked at her body, with only a few swatches of Lycra separating her from total nudity, she realised it was really quite a good body, given her age and the fact of having carried two children. She still had a waist and Chloe's crop top was doing a good job of keeping her breasts in an acceptable position. The high-waisted leggings covered the stretch marks and it seemed her bottom had somehow resisted the forces of gravity and stayed in relatively the same spot as it was twenty years ago. She could claim no credit for her shapely legs, however. They were inherited from her mother.

'Not too bad,' she muttered to herself, sailing out of the bathroom with a spring in her trainer-clad step.

The gym was five minutes away by car and while Beth usually objected to the idea of driving to an exercise class, she didn't feel quite brave enough to walk down Cuthbert Close in Chloe's activewear. It had been quiet earlier, but that could change in an instant. Mrs Nelson at number eight tended to water her garden every Sunday morning, and if she was there she would no doubt want a chat. Besides, it was quite frankly too chilly to be outdoors in such flesh-baring attire. Autumn was upon them and it was one thing for a room full of strangers to observe the outline of her nipple through Chloe's overstretched crop top, but quite another for Mrs Nelson to peer at them over the reading glasses that hung at permanent half-mast off her nose. Beth grabbed her phone and keys, slung them into a recyclable shopping bag and headed back to the garage. She wasn't quite sure what type of bag people took to the gym but figured a green shopping bag would be a less appealing option for thieves, in case of there being no lockers.

'Hello, Beth.'

She jumped and the bag slipped from her shoulder. It was Charlie Devine, and she was wearing almost exactly the same outfit as Beth but in the opposite colour – white leggings and a crop top, along with the ubiquitous diamond earrings. Slung across her body was a tiny, white quilted-leather bag, giving the outfit an edge that Beth's shopper bag completely failed to deliver.

'Good morning, Charlie!' she said too brightly, overcompensating for the oily sense of unease that had settled in her stomach. 'Looks like we've got the same idea. Off to the gym?'

Charlie frowned. 'No.'

Beth waited for her to offer more but the woman just stood there. Beth couldn't bear the silence. 'Well, I'm off to my first ever Zumba class and I'm feeling a bit nervous actually. You're a dancer, aren't you? What can I expect?'

'It's a long time since I taught dance.'

'Really? That's such a shame. I'd love to have been a dancer. Didn't really have the flexibility for it, though, and my parents didn't think it was a very sensible career path.'

Charlie raised her eyebrows.

'For me,' Beth went on. 'I'm sure it was fabulous for you, but I really wasn't good enough. Does Talia dance?'

'She's not interested.'

'Ah, shame. Well, I guess you can't control what your children enjoy, or don't enjoy. They are their own people, and Talia seems a sweet girl.'

Charlie checked her watch. 'I really need to be leaving.'

To meet with my husband? No, don't be paranoid.

'Yes, of course. Don't let me hold you up.'

Charlie nodded and turned to get into her car.

'Charlie, sorry,' Beth called, and the other woman spun around. 'One more thing.' Shyly, she stepped out from behind her car. 'Do I look okay? I mean, does this look completely ridiculous on me?'

Charlie looked her up and down, with an unemotional, analytical eye, like she was appraising a turnip, or some other equally uninteresting, inanimate object. 'Your body is fine, but you look uncomfortable.'

'It's actually quite surprisingly comfortable,' Beth protested.

'No, I mean, you can tell the outfit's not you. It's like you're wearing a costume. It's obvious you're not feeling it.'

'Well … it is more revealing than what I'm used to,' Beth admitted.

'You need to own it. No apologies. And if you're not feeling it, just fake it. Square your shoulders and lift from the chest. Fake it till you make it.'

As Charlie spoke, Beth found herself automatically obeying the woman's commands. And yes, it did make a difference.

'That's better.' Charlie nodded. 'But you're still not there. Some people just can't carry it off.' With a dismissive shrug, she hopped into her car and sped off down the street, leaving Beth to cough in the wake of her sulphurous petrol fumes.

'Actually, I'll have you know I *am* feeling it, Charlie Devine.' Beth pulled her shoulders so far back she could feel it in her vertebrae. Her breasts lifted in response. 'This *is* the real me. And I feel *hot*.'

Opening the car door, she flung her shopper bag into the passenger seat, started up the engine and roared out of Cuthbert Close, just as quickly as Charlie Devine had.

CHAPTER THIRTY-THREE

'Ready for that tea now?' Cara set down the tray on the outdoor table.

'Just want to finish this little bit here.' Will carefully applied a streak of paint under the eaves. 'Tricky little spot,' he muttered before leaning back to survey his work. 'Look all right to you?'

'Looks perfect.' Cara assessed the morning's effort. Already, the cottage was looking a little more loved. Even in the weaker autumn light, the colour was delicious, like vanilla ice cream. She experienced an unexpected shiver of pleasure.

'I really thought I was going to hate doing this, but it's actually not the worst job in the world.' Will clambered down off the ladder.

'Gee, please stop with the enthusiasm. I don't think I can take it.'

Cara laughed and Will gave a rueful smile. 'Sorry … it's not personal. It's just … being here. I thought it would be harder. Bring back memories.' He looked around. 'But it's just a house. Nothing scary. Just a little, old, falling-down house.'

'No, really, you're killing me with the compliments. This is my house you're talking about.'

'Mine too.'

There was that shiver again. A breezy day, that's all.

She went to pour the tea and as Will dumped the paint pot down on the table, a small drip of it flew from the tin and landed on Cara's sleeve.

'Oh, shit, sorry. I didn't mean to …'

'It's fine.' Cara waved away the apology. 'I mean, you've only ruined my best ten-year-old tracksuit top, but that's fine.' She went to pick up the mug of tea but managed to brush against the hot teapot, causing her hand to fly off the handle and accidentally flick the paintbrush from where it had been sitting on the tin. This time the splodge of paint landed on Will's nose.

'Oh, you're going to play it like that, are you?' he said and wiped at the smudge.

'I didn't mean to … It was an accident. Honestly.'

Will picked up the brush that had fallen off the tin. 'Very convincing. Accident, huh? Like this?' He flicked the brush in her direction, landing a spatter of paint across her chest.

Cara sucked in a breath. 'Oh, now you've done it.' She picked up the second brush. 'Poppy,' she called. 'I need reinforcements.'

Her daughter came flying out of the house and into the back garden. Spying the two adults wielding brushes, she squealed. 'Paint fight. Yay!'

'There's another brush in the shed,' Cara commanded.

'Well, that's just not fair,' Will protested, while trying to move stealthily away from the table. 'Two against one.'

'Your brush is bigger.'

'You're closer to the paint.'

'I really don't think we should waste any.'

'Either do I.'

'You drop your brush and I'll drop mine.'

'Let's do it together. On the count of three. One, two—'

A car horn interrupted them, an unmistakeably tinny beep from the street.

'Halmi! Halbi!' Poppy squealed and ran.

'Who is it?' asked Will.

'It's my mum and dad.' Cara returned the brush back to the tin. 'Their idea of letting me know they're coming is to beep the horn from the street. One of their less endearing habits.'

'At least they come.' Will dropped his brush back into the pot with Cara's.

She bit her lip. She got what he was saying. At least she still had parents alive. That *was* something to savour. But couldn't they at least learn to make a phone call before arriving on her doorstep?

'Look, it's Halmi and Halbi.' Poppy dragged them into the garden. 'They've brought things.'

Her father set a large cardboard box down on the grass. 'We cleaned out when we moved.' He stretched his back. 'These are yours.'

'Dad, you remember Will Parry.'

Sam offered his hand. 'Hello.'

'And you've already met my mum.'

'Yes, Mrs ...'

'Everyone calls me Joy,' said her mother abruptly. She took a step towards the house, noticing the fresh paint. 'You are finally fixing this place up. What took you so long?'

'You can blame your daughter for that. She's very exacting when it comes to picking colours.'

'You let *her* choose the colour?' Joy's eyes widened, and Cara understood her confusion. Over the years her mother had become accustomed to landlords who would never let them bang a nail in the wall, let alone choose the colour of it.

But Cara wasn't a tenant any more. Or, at least, she soon wouldn't be.

Not that her mum and dad knew that.

'Oh, sure,' Will shrugged. 'I mean, I know we haven't signed the paperwork yet but—'

'Mum, Dad, why don't you come in for a cup of tea?' said Cara. While her parents dawdled near the front door, inspecting the paintwork, she sidled up to Will. 'I haven't told them yet, about your dad, and about us ... buying the house,' she added. 'But I'm about to. Right now.'

Will shook his head in disappointment and Cara couldn't meet his eye. He'd already done the brave thing and challenged his siblings by deciding to keep Cuthbert Close in the family, while Cara had been too afraid to do the same.

'Will Parry, are you coming in too?' Joy called at the door.

He turned his gaze on the paint tin. 'You know what, I think we need more paint. I'll head up to the shop.'

'Sounds good.' Cara ushered her parents inside with her mother still grumbling and her father holding the cardboard box. She looked over her shoulder to watch Will leaving. He roared out of the street without a backwards glance.

'You need to be careful of this man. He is strange.' Joy had seen her watching him.

'Mum, he's not strange.' In the kitchen she set about making a fresh pot of tea, while her mother took up a seat at the table and her father deposited the box on the bench. She felt their eyes on her, watching as she retrieved cups and saucers. 'There's something I need to tell you.'

'This sounds serious, daughter. Come, sit with us.' Her father gently patted the chair next to him and Cara gave a grateful smile.

'I know you think it's odd that Will let me choose the colour for this house.'

'A man does not let another person make this decision unless there is a reason.' Joy's voice had a tone of warning and her raised eyebrow hinted that she understood exactly what that reason was.

'It's not what you think ...' Cara took a breath. 'He let me choose the colour because ... well, because something very sad happened.' She took a breath. 'His father died ... Mr Parry, the owner of this place. He had a heart attack ... There was no warning.'

Joy blessed herself and kissed the crucifix around her neck. 'May his soul rest in peace. He is in a better place.' She looked skywards briefly, then back to Cara with a steely gaze. 'So Will Parry is selling this house?' She nodded. 'I understand. You and the little girl can come live with us.'

Cara cupped her hands. 'Thank you, Ma, that's very generous ... But actually, Will Parry and I, we're buying this place together. Fifty per cent each. His brother and sister have agreed on a price, and it's a fair price, and Will says Poppy and I can stay in the house as long as we like.'

Joy's eyes widened. 'You are buying this house with this man? Together?'

Cara nodded.

'Do you love him?' her mother demanded.

She vehemently shook her head. 'No, no. Nothing like that. It's an investment, for both of us. Like a business deal.'

'You cannot make a business deal out of your home.' Joy folded her arms. 'Do you know this man? How can you trust him?'

'I'm going to ask my neighbour, the lawyer one that you like, to have a contract drawn up, so everything will be set out in black and white.'

'This is very, very strange,' said Joy slowly. 'You should come and live with us. We are your family. You should depend on us, not this man who you do not know.'

'Mum, thank you.' Cara clasped her hands on the table, unable to meet her mother's disapproving gaze. 'But I need to be independent. I'm thirty-two years old and I can't live at home. You left Korea when you were only eighteen, and you never went back.' Looking up, she took Joy's hand in hers. 'Please be happy for me. This way, Poppy gets to stay at her own school with all her friends and she gets to come home to a community that she knows and loves ... I think it's the least she deserves.'

Her mother snatched her hand back. 'This is not how a daughter should behave.' Before Cara could speak, her mother had leapt to her feet and was at the door. 'Sam, come, or we will be late for church.'

'Mum, wait! Can't we talk about this?'

But Joy was gone.

'Ugh. She's impossible.' Cara jumped to her feet and flung open her pantry door. She was seething, furious. Why couldn't Joy understand? Or even *try* to comprehend Cara's position? Her eye fell on a packet of crushed hazelnuts. Perfect. She would make a meringue hazelnut torte and take out all her frustrations and anger on the egg whites, which would require a good, solid whipping. With this level of emotion driving her, she'd be done before Will was back from the paint shop. 'It doesn't matter what I do, I can never make her happy.'

'Daughter, please.' Her father touched her arm. 'She is proud of you.'

Cara stopped searching for ingredients. 'She's got a strange way of showing it.'

'She is proud of you,' he said. 'It is herself she blames.'

'Herself? For what?'

He laid his palms open. 'She left her family, everything she knew, to come with me to this country.'

'But you came for a better life, for me. There's nothing wrong with that.'

Sam shook his head with a smile. 'I was a poor farm boy. A different man would have given her a better life.'

'But she fell in love with you!'

'Some say love is a choice.' He shrugged. 'Her mother never forgave this choice, and your mother has never forgiven herself. She must always make amends. Try her best. Have the nicest house. Make sure you do not make the same mistake. Everything bad that happens … is her fault.'

'That's crazy.' Cara started sorting through her drawer for the whisk and the metal utensils clattered through her hands. 'And I'm not even sure it's right.'

The skinny beep of the Daihatsu made them both stop still.

'You should go.' She slammed the drawer shut. The whisk wasn't where it should have been. It was infuriating.

Sam stood at the door. 'Look inside the box, daughter.'

She waited until he was gone before taking the box and putting it on the floor. She would look at it later. Right now, what she really needed was to beat some eggs and let the baking absorb her anger.

CHAPTER THIRTY-FOUR

Alex shivered and pulled her coat tighter against the chill autumn wind skittering across the park. The sun had disappeared again behind cloud and she cursed the indecisive weather. Whose stupid idea had it been to enrol the boys in Sunday afternoon soccer?

Oh right, hers.

'Get in there, Noah. Kick it,' she screamed from the sideline.

But either Noah couldn't hear or he refused to, for there he was, dawdling in the middle of the field, while a pack of ten other five year olds tussled over the soccer ball, like a litter of puppies play-fighting over a chewed-up shoe.

'Why won't you try,' she muttered under her breath, as the child-puppies gambolled up the field in pursuit of the ball, leaving Noah ambling in their wake.

'Here you go. Decaf double shot. Extra sugar.' James pressed a warming coffee cup into her hands. 'Miss anything?'

'Jas scored a goal but Noah won't move.' Alex gritted her teeth. 'What is wrong with that child?'

'Jas scored? That's great.'

Alex glared at him. 'This was supposed to be about Noah.'

James sipped his coffee. 'Maybe soccer's just not his thing.'

Maybe life just isn't his thing.

Somehow, the ball had emerged from the pack of kids and it dribbled towards Noah. A little boy from the opposition team set off in pursuit.

'Kick, Noah! Kick! Stop that boy. Get him!' Alex shrieked.

Her son looked up in surprise.

'The ball, Noah. Get the ball!'

He stared at her, then back at the ball, by which time the other child had scooted past and kicked the ball clear.

Alex's shoulders slumped.

'You can't do that,' said James quietly.

'Can't what?'

'Yell at him like that.'

'Why not?' She gulped the coffee and swallowed hard, her mouth scorched by the heat.

'The other parents don't like it.'

Alex looked around. He was right. A few other puffy-coated souls were looking her way and whispering.

'But I'm only yelling at my child, not theirs,' she said. 'Theirs are probably as deaf as Noah and can't hear a word I'm saying.'

'Doesn't matter. You saw the sign.'

Ah, yes. The sign that had greeted them at the entrance to the wind-swept park.

Please remember
These are kids
This is just a game
The coach is a volunteer
The referees are human
This is not the World Cup

'You reckon they have that kind of sign for kids in Russia?' Alex spoke in a low and urgent tone. 'No wonder Australia never does any good in the World Cup.'

James set his coffee cup down on the grass. He took her by the shoulders, blocking her view of the game.

'What are you doing? I want to watch!' cried Alex, trying to look over his shoulder.

'Talk to me.' James squeezed. 'Ever since we left that silly fundraiser last night, you've been as wound up as a spring. You wouldn't say anything in the car and you stomped around the house all morning yelling at everyone and I want to know what's going on. Tell me.'

Alex dropped her gaze to the muddy grass. 'It's nothing.'

'I'm not moving until you tell me.'

'The game's going to finish in five minutes.'

James sighed. 'Just tell me.'

Out of the corner of her eye, Alex could see that Jas had the ball and was dribbling it down the sideline, while Noah stood at the other end of the field and looked up at the grey clouds overhead, scudding across the sky.

It was hopeless.

'Last night, Martin told me that Macauley is introducing an egg-freezing program, so they can get more years out of the female solicitors, you know, *don't worry about having kids in your thirties, just freeze your eggs, do IVF, build your career, have them when it suits you et cetera et cetera …* They want me to be the partner that champions it. Promotes it.' She couldn't look at her husband.

James dropped his hands. 'Shit. They really have no idea, do they.'

'I don't know …' she said. 'I mean, other companies do it, like Google and Facebook.'

'Yes, the real high bar of ethical behaviour, those two.'

Alex startled. Her darling husband didn't do sarcasm. He generally left it to her.

'You do remember, don't you … what it was like?'

'Of course I do …' She shivered again, not because of the cold, but because of what flashed into her mind. James, standing before her with a needle, chock-full of hormones to boost her egg production. He'd been so patient, so kind, while she'd been an emotional wildcat through the entire process. Manically high on the fumes of hope one minute, and curled up in a ball on the bathroom floor the next as the midwives calmly informed her that the embryo hadn't 'taken'. Ten rounds it took to get the boys. It was, without doubt, the hardest eighteen months of their lives – a period that had ended up costing them over a hundred grand, and nearly their marriage.

This was what Macauley wanted her to sell to the women of the firm.

'I'm trapped,' she whispered, tears threatening to spill out of her eyes.

Suddenly, she felt James's arms wrapped around her. His hand guided her head into his shoulder and she let the tears flow freely as she recalled everything she'd gained, and lost, in having the twins.

A little head nuzzled in between them. 'Mummy, what's wrong? Why are you crying?' It was Noah. He slipped his hand into hers. 'Please don't be sad. I'll try. Really, I'll try for the next game. Promise. You won't have to yell.' His lower lip trembled. 'I'm sorry.'

Alex felt her chest tightening as she took in her son's pale face. Oh, the guilt. Her knees wanted to buckle. Why had no one ever warned her of this? That mother-guilt was so crippling. Literally. She put her arm out to James for support and kissed the top of her son's head. 'It's not you, darling,' she sniffed. 'It's me.'

Behind them, further down the sideline, the other parents cheered.

Jasper had scored again.

CHAPTER THIRTY-FIVE

'New clothes?' Max stood before the bed. Beth had heard him stomp in five minutes ago. But instead of rushing to greet him, she'd stayed right where she was, reading the latest Liane Moriarty, and enjoying an uncustomarily lazy Sunday afternoon.

'Yes.'

After her conversation with Charlie Devine, Beth had raced up to the shops before the gym class began and bought the brightest, boldest set of leggings and matching crop top that she could find. Chloe's clothes weren't her. Charlie was right. Beth wanted something bigger and bolder than boring old black. She wanted pinks and yellows that clashed in a totally mad, yet somehow completely stylish, way. She would show that woman who she really was! An exotic, dancing bird of paradise. And she'd show Max, too, while she was at it. The old Beth might have sought to justify the purchases, or explain how she got them at a substantial discount – not that Max ever seemed to query her about the money, it was just something she felt she ought to do, given everything she spent on herself had been earnt by him.

Not the new Beth.

As she calmly put down her book and asked her husband how his game of golf had gone, she noticed his eyes lingering over her body.

'A bit off today.' Max shrugged. 'It was windy out on the course. The ball was flying around a lot.'

'Hmmm … you poor thing,' said Beth. 'Not to mention the fact you didn't actually take your golf clubs.'

Max startled. 'I just forgot them,' he muttered. 'Borrowed Angelo's.'

'I thought Angelo and Sylvia were overseas at the moment?' Angelo was a workmate of Max's and Beth knew full well that right at that moment he was on a barge, sailing down the Canal du Midi in France. Sylvia had emailed to let her know they wouldn't be able to make the party.

'Angelo came back early. Sylvia's still there, visiting family.' Max sat on the bed and grunted with the effort of bending over to undo his laces.

'So he'll be coming to the party, then?'

'Ah … no,' Max panted. 'He won't want to come on his own.'

Beth nearly snorted. Max was such a terrible liar. Surely he knew she could expose his fibs with just a couple of phone calls?

He obviously took her for a fool. Didn't even consider that she suspected a thing. Well, she would show him! But not yet. Not till after the party. Until then, she was going to have her own fun.

Max lay down on the bed and closed his eyes. 'I'm exhausted.'

'Yes, I can imagine how exhausting all that walking must be. Poor Max,' she cooed, and pressed her body into his.

'You seem happy. What did you get up to today?'

'I took a dance class,' said Beth, running her hands lightly over Max's chest. 'It was amazing.'

That part was true. The Zumba class had been loud and sexy and loads of fun. The instructor was a very hot young Brazilian guy who flirted outrageously with all the women in the class with his winks and shoulder shimmies. At first, Beth had flushed as bright as her lairy leggings at the instructor's attention. But midway through the class, Jorge took a two-minute break during which Beth spotted him kissing another man on the lips by the water cooler. Of course, gay. What a relief!

In the second half of the class, Beth flirted with complete abandon. It was incredibly liberating. She hadn't felt this free since … well, since before she had children. The music swept her up, pulsed through her body and made it come alive. It was different to the nightclub. There, she'd been so conscious of the crowd around her, and the gorgeous Adam. Here, in this class of twenty middle-aged women and one very hot, very camp instructor, she was completely free to be herself. In the mirror, she watched the way her body moved easily to the music. Sexy and sultry. Underneath those chinos and loose knits was a fiery Latina lady.

'I'll show you some of the moves if you like.'

Before Max could answer, Beth leapt off the bed. Jorge had directed her to a streaming service on her phone where they could find the music they'd danced to in class. With a few taps, Beth had the bedroom grooving to a sensual Latin American beat. She closed her eyes and started to do the moves Jorge had taught them, the slow body rolls and the hip circles – moves that in class had made Beth cringe at first with the overt raunchiness of them.

As the music came to an end, Beth opened her eyes.

'I'm impressed. You're a fast learner.' Max sat up on his elbows and narrowed his eyes. 'Why don't you come here and practise some of those moves on me,' he growled and patted the mattress beside him.

'Oh no,' said Beth pretending not to notice the bulge in Max's pants that proved exactly how *impressed* he was with her moves. 'You're tired, and I'm all sweaty.' Beth sashayed towards the bathroom, putting a little extra hip movement into her walk.

'I'm not tired, and I don't mind if you're sweaty.' Max's tone was pleading, almost pathetic.

Beth closed the bathroom door and pressed herself against it. 'Besides, you hate dancing, remember.' Locking the door, she switched on the water.

'Bethy, let me in. Please. I'm sweaty too.'

She imagined him, standing on the other side of the door, jiggling at the handle and horny as a bull.

'I can't hear you,' called Beth as she sat on the toilet seat and felt a little bit sorry for him, before remembering that in all likelihood, Max had already scored his hole in one that day. And not with her.

ThePrimalGuy.com.au
From: The Primal Guy
Subject: How to Get What You Want

Hey there, Prime-Ministers,
You know how many people like to run me down for trying to live by pre-historic principles? A shit-load. 'The world's moved on, man. You can't actually go kill a woolly mammoth. It's the 21st century.'

Dude, I know that.

What I'm about is learning from the past. Like, there's this book you've probably heard of. *How to Win Friends and Influence People*. It came out in 1936. Yup. It's ancient. But people still talk about it, because it's the biz. Okay, so it's nearly 300 pages long and I know you're a slave to the man and haven't got time to read it, so I'll give you the bottom line – if you can get people to like you, they'll do what you want them to.

Next problem – how do you get people to like you? It's not that hard. You be nice. Smile. Use their names. Give compliments. Don't insult, shame or embarrass them.

In other words, be a bit of a pussy.

Now, you know me and you know I'm no kitty-cat, but when I have to, I can suck up with the best of 'em. I'll tell you something.

Right now, I'm sucking real hard in this new place. But that's okay, because it's going to get me where I need to be – right in the sweet spot where people are going to let down their defences, and let me in. And then I can really raise hell.

Peace out,
Ryan (AKA the Primal Guy)

PS No reason you can't look hot while you sweat. Buy one 'Primal. It's Final' t-shirt and get one free. This week only!

CHAPTER THIRTY-SIX

Cara rushed down the hallway and out the front door, her daughter's backpack slung over her arm, a piece of toast in one hand and Poppy's toothbrush in the other.

Standing on the front step she called back inside. 'Poppy, where are you? We're going to be late.' She checked her watch. 8:25 am. Monday morning. The week had barely begun and Cara felt it already starting to spin out of control.

Her shoot started at 9 am and the studio was at least half an hour away, but first she had to get Poppy to school and she hadn't even finished her breakfast or brushed her teeth.

'Morning, Mrs Pope.' Talia Devine waved from the footpath and trundled past with her hands grasping each strap of her backpack like a safety parachute.

'Hello, Talia. But it's Cara, please.' She tapped her foot. 'C'mon Poppy, we don't have all day,' she called down the hallway.

Talia stopped and leant on the O'Rourkes' gate. 'I'm just waiting for the twins.' At that moment, Alex's front door opened and the boys tumbled out, followed by their harried-looking mother, also clutching toast, two toothbrushes and schoolbags.

'Snap!' called Cara to Alex, smiling and holding up her hands.

'Look at us.' Alex limped towards the gate, trying to juggle the putting-on of a second high heel, balanced precariously in the same hand as the toothbrushes. 'If only Germaine Greer could see us now. Really nailing this working mother thing, aren't we?' She grinned before handing the bags, brushes and breakfast over to the boys at the front gate. 'I think we should put a ban on Daddy going to work early. What do you both think, hmm?'

'Hey, I got some good news on the house over the week-end. Any chance you could come over later for a chat and a cuppa?' Cara dumped the backpack and began wrestling Poppy's curls into a ponytail.

'Absolutely! I'll come tonight once the boys are down.' Alex stopped and stepped into her second shoe. 'Now Talia, when the boys are done with the breakfast and the brush-ing, just put the toothbrushes into the front pocket of their bags, okay?' She gave the boys hurried kisses. 'Quickly, boys, or Mummy's going to be late.' At the car, she stopped and turned, shielding her eyes from the sun. 'Cara, Talia's walk-ing the boys to school – it's on the way to hers – I'm sure she wouldn't mind taking Poppy as well.'

Cara thought for a millisecond.

'Talia, is that all right?' she asked.

'For sure.'

'I'm not sure that's a good idea.' Charlie Devine's voice cut across the close. Where had she come from? She must have been watching from her house. Now, she stood by her daughter, her arms folded over a white satin dressing gown.

'It's fine, Mum. Really. I'll be fine.'

'Three children? That's a lot …' Charlie looked knowingly at the twins.

'Honestly, Mum. It'll be fine.' Talia sighed. 'Trust me.'

Cara stepped in. 'Poppy's very responsible, I can assure you. Talia will probably find it easier to have her tag along. The twins seem to listen to her, for some reason.'

'It's true,' Alex confirmed. 'They listen to Poppy more than they listen to me.'

'I can bring them all home too, if you like?' offered Talia. 'It's basically on my way.'

Cara clasped her hands together. 'Oh, would you? That would be amazing, Talia. I'm out this morning at a shoot but I'll be cooking in the shed all afternoon. We got flooded with orders over the weekend.' She made a face. 'Just come and knock on the door when you get back.'

'Cool,' said Talia. 'See ya, Mum.' She waved and set off down the street with the caravan of kids in tow, while Alex sped away in her car. Up front, Cara could hear Poppy chatting away to Talia about how her mummy was the best cook and she was famous because she was on the internet and everyone wanted to buy her food, and she heard Talia reply, 'Did you know that my dad is famous too?'

So sweet.

'Things are going well then, with the business?' Charlie Devine was still standing at the end of her drive, watching the kids disappear into the distance.

'Almost too well,' Cara admitted. 'I really should be staying here to cook with Beth but it's too late for me to cancel this shoot.' She checked her watch. 'I'm sorry to rush but I really better get going.'

Charlie nodded, unsmiling. 'That's the way it is in this business. You say yes to everything because you never know what's around the corner. It's easy to become a victim of your own success. But you really should take it slow. Threats are everywhere and you won't even see them coming.'

There was a strange tone in Charlie's voice and later, after they'd said their goodbyes and Cara was driving to the shoot, she mulled over the words. Was it advice Charlie was giving her, or a warning?

She shook her head. It was silly. Maybe a little paranoid.

She had everything she wanted. Will had agreed to go halves in the house, and Nourish was booming, which meant she could easily service whatever small loan she might need to take from the bank.

It was all perfect.

CHAPTER THIRTY-SEVEN

'Oh, no, no, no. No, you don't.' Seated in her office chair, Alex rolled away from her desk, and away from the envelope that Brianna had just placed on it. A perfectly ordinary, plain white envelope, unsealed and with one, simple handwritten name on the front.

Alex.

Brianna pushed it in her direction. 'Please,' she began, in a gentle voice, so unlike her normal direct one that Alex's stomach sank even further.

'Nope. Not today, Brianna. I cannot deal with this today. Come back tomorrow. Or not at all, ideally.' Alex shuffled files on her desk. 'I cannot afford to lose you. Not now.'

Calmly, Brianna took a seat while Alex continued to rearrange papers on her desk, sensing her assistant's eyes on her.

'My mother is sick.'

Alex stopped and put down the files, her stomach plummeting. 'How sick?'

'Pretty bloody awfully sick.' Brianna broke eye contact. 'It's lung cancer. Stage four.'

Alex's hand flew to her mouth. While she wasn't exactly au fait with the precise stages of cancer, she knew enough to understand there was no stage five. 'Oh, Brianna. I'm so sorry.'

Brianna accepted the condolences with a nod of her head.

'What can the firm do? What can I do? I think you're entitled to some type of personal leave … it's probably written down in your contract somewhere.' She started shuffling papers again, knowing full well the answer didn't lie in them. 'Not that anyone ever takes it,' she muttered under her breath.

'Alex,' Brianna began, 'I'm resigning.' She pushed the letter forward again. 'I need to be with her.'

Alex pushed it back. 'But you don't need to resign. We can make this work. More flexible hours. The occasional work-from-home day.' She leant forward in her chair. 'You're about to become assistant to a partner. Do you know what that could mean for your career? You don't need to throw it all away. Remember that pep talk you gave me, about owing it to women everywhere to take up the challenge?'

'This is different … My mum's dying, and I owe it to her right now to be by her side.' Brianna gave a weak smile. 'I'm going to keep studying and I'll be back, but when I do come back it'll be with a degree under my belt.' She paused. 'I'm good at what I do, and I need to back myself on this one. It's not like this place is going anywhere.'

The unspoken words hung in the air. Work would always be there. Her mother would not.

Alex placed her palm over the envelope and slid it closer. 'All right.' She exhaled. 'I accept your resignation. Reluctantly.'

Brianna stood. 'Thank you, Alex.'

'When do you plan to leave us?'

'Friday, if possible.'

Alex blanched. 'This Friday?'

'Mum starts intensive chemo next week.'

The timing couldn't be worse. She had a manic schedule of meetings booked up for weeks over the takeover matter. She was counting on Brianna to keep all of her other matters ticking along. A new assistant would take at least a couple of months to be brought up to speed, and that's presuming HR could be bothered to get off their arses and hire one in a hurry.

Brianna paused at the door. 'She's very grateful, you know.'

'Who?'

'My mum. I know you've never met, but I've told her about you, and your family ... The twins and everything. She thinks you must be some kind of miracle worker to handle everything you do. She doesn't want me to quit.' Brianna's voice dropped to a whisper. 'She says I won't find someone else like you who doesn't care about where I went to school, or that my clothes aren't the latest and greatest.'

Guilt smacked Alex in the mouth. Here she was, worrying about how she'd handle her work schedule, when her assistant's dying mother was expressing gratitude to her, for giving her ridiculously talented and efficient daughter a go!

'I'm the lucky one,' said Alex. 'And as long as I'm at this firm, you'll have a job here whenever you like. No question.'

The phone on Brianna's desk started to ring and, as always, she went to answer it within the first few trills.

'Wait.' Alex held up her hand. 'Leave that for a moment.' She rose from her desk and walked round to the other side, while Brianna stood in the doorway. 'I know you've always said you don't want children, but is that the honest truth?'

Brianna made a face. 'One day … If the right person comes along.'

'Okay, okay.' Alex folded her arms and leant against her desk. 'If Macauley offered you ten thousand bucks to freeze your eggs in your thirties so you could consolidate your career and have kids later, would it make you want to work here? More than another company?'

Brianna's eyes shot to the ceiling. 'No. But if there was on-site childcare I might. The tech firm across the street has one. Seems pretty good.'

Alex stared at her. How did a twenty-three year old know so much about kids? About life?

'My sister has a two year old,' Brianna explained, as if reading her mind. 'No point taking the ten grand unless you can figure out a way to look after the kid.' The phone was still ringing, and she pointed at it. 'Can I get that now?'

'Of course.' Returning to her chair, Alex stopped in front of her framed university degrees, hanging on the wall. Her Bachelor of Arts, her Bachelor of Laws, and her Masters. All that work, crammed into three pieces of gold-framed parchment and funded off the back of pulling beers at shitty pubs, and shovelling fries at greasy spoons.

She sat heavily and rotated in the chair to look out the windows and down onto the busy CBD streets. From this vantage point, twenty storeys high, the vehicles were like Matchbox cars and the people like ants, marching with focus and determination, as if it was actually really important.

Alex swivelled back to her desk. Putting Brianna's envelope to one side, she opened up a new document on her computer and started typing.

The Macauley Egg-Freezing Program: Why you can't bribe women into staying

'A bit too punchy,' said Alex under her breath. She pressed delete and poised her fingers over the keyboard.

Ten ways Macauley can make itself family friendly that don't involve injecting women with hormones

'Passive-aggressive much?'

Delete.

She started again.

A Family-Friendly Macauley: The vision and the business case

Yes, that was more like it.

'Hey, Bree,' Alex called through the door. 'Could you call Rex's PA and get me an appointment for this afternoon?'

'Sure.' Brianna came to the door. 'What do I tell her it's about.'

'Tell her—' Alex paused. She picked up the framed photo of the twins – the one from the professional shoot where they'd had to bribe the boys into smiling with the promise of a Ninja Turtle each. 'Tell her it's important, and that I'll meet him in the cafe downstairs.' She ran her thumb down the side of the frame.

'Tell her that it's about the future.'

CHAPTER THIRTY-EIGHT

Beth read through the recipe for pork and sausage cassoulet that Cara had left pinned to the door of the shed. Thanks to the big influx of orders over the weekend, today promised to be a huge day of cooking and Beth couldn't wait to get started. Cooking would clear her mind and help put the events of the weekend behind her. Thank goodness for Nourish. It was saving her bacon in more ways than one, giving her a distraction from Max and a very tidy nest egg that would grow into an ostrich egg if the orders kept up like this.

First things first. Music. Though Cara tended to play music through her phone, Beth knew she had an old radio in here somewhere. Ah yes, there on the shelf. Beth turned the dial to the classical station and allowed Vivaldi to fill every corner of the tiny room. Next she put on her apron and set about sharpening Cara's biggest knife. The cassoulet required her to break down three pork shoulders into four-centimetre cubes.

Normally, she would have been less than thrilled to undertake such a messy and fiddly task; butchery was not exactly her forte. But that was the old Beth. Today, the new active-wearing, Zumba-loving, unemotional-sex-having Beth positively grinned with murderous glee as she set about slicing through the fat and flesh.

Max's golf bag was made of pig skin.

Beth brought the knife down hard against the chopping board.

Bloody Max. How dare he damn well do this to her, and to Ethan and Chloe?

She prepared to bring down the knife hard again but paused.

There was a knock at the door.

She grunted in irritation. Cara wasn't due back till after one and it was far too early for the kids to be home from school. It was probably a tenacious door-to-door salesman or some other annoying type of creature.

Beth stomped over to the door and wrenched it open, knife in hand.

'Yes?'

The man before her took a step back. He was small, and everything about him was little, grey and gloomy, from his hair to his pants. He reminded Beth of a little teardrop.

'Is this Nourish – the catering business?' he said, eyeing Beth's knife.

'Yes, and who might you be?'

'My name is Terrence Mooney and I'm a food safety inspector with the local council. And you are?'

'Beth Chandler, one of the co-owners of the business.' She lowered the knife. 'How can I help you, Mr Mooney?'

He shuffled uneasily and tucked a clipboard under his arm. 'Well, there's been a complaint.'

Beth kept her face neutral even though her pulse had moved from a trot to a canter. 'A complaint? What about?'

The inspector consulted his clipboard. 'We've been alerted to a possible outbreak of food poisoning caused by items prepared on these premises, and I'm here to investigate.'

Oh, bugger that silly message that Alex posted.

'Of course, Mr Mooney. Please come in and I'll explain everything. Can I get you a cup of tea?' It was a good thing she hadn't entirely erased the old Beth – the one who was conciliatory and obliging and offered cups of tea to little men with nothing better to do with their time than follow up vexatious, time-wasting complaints.

The pork would have to wait, but she would get to it eventually, and dice that flesh to perfection if it's the last thing she did.

New Beth wasn't going anywhere. Not really.

CHAPTER THIRTY-NINE

Alex sat at the table, fidgeting. She checked her phone. Took a sip of water. Watched the comings and goings in and out of her building and wondered, not for the first time, at the strangeness of ties on men. Who exactly decided their necks needed a strange little knotted strip of material, she pondered. Anything to keep herself from thinking about what she was about to do.

'Alexandra. This is an unexpected invitation.' Rex sauntered across the foyer and went to take a seat at her table.

'Don't sit,' she ordered.

'Pardon?' Her brusque tone wiped the confident smile from Rex's face. He wasn't used to being bossed around, especially by wannabe-partners.

'I mean,' she stammered. 'We're going across the road. I ... I need to show you something.'

Rex regarded her. 'Are you going to tell me what it is?' His gaze narrowed. 'First rule of law school – never allow yourself to be led down the garden path. By anyone.'

Alex squared her shoulders. 'I think you'll find this interesting, and useful.' She started walking, and motioned for Rex to follow. 'Martin told me about the fertility assistance program you're planning to introduce.' She stopped at the curb.

'I read about the concept in the paper. All the big tech companies are doing it,' said Rex with a self-satisfied smile. 'Seems a neat solution to our woman problem.' He stepped into the traffic and Alex resisted the urge to push him in front of a bus.

'I'm not sure if you're aware,' said Alex, directing Rex into the foyer of another glass-walled high-rise. 'But the live-birth rate using frozen eggs is just nineteen per cent per embryo. In other words, you'd be encouraging women into a process that either may not work at all, or at the very least, will probably take several rounds to succeed. At worst, that could be seen as unethical, at best, it could be seen as the company offering a ten thousand dollar discount on a fifty thousand dollar process – hardly enough of an incentive to keep women engaged with the firm. You have to ask yourself, would this be a cost-effective solution for Macauley at all?' Alex swallowed the bile in her mouth and silently apologised to the little being in her stomach. After this conversation with Rex she planned to never again discuss a baby as a commodity.

'You think there's a better way?'

'I know there is.' She ushered Rex inside the lift and pressed the button for level two.

'I'm intrigued.'

Alex produced the file she'd been keeping tucked discreetly by her side. 'I've compiled a few ideas – by no means exhaustive, just some suggestions around best practice at other corporates and the return these companies have achieved by investing in family-friendly work practices.'

The lift pinged. As the doors opened, a wall of high-pitched squeals and shrieks flooded the confined space of the elevator. Rex recoiled and Alex took his elbow.

'It's fine. They're just playing,' she reassured him.

Behind frosted glass emblazoned with a rainbow, blurred shapes ducked and weaved. Alex pressed the intercom and gave her name. 'We spoke on the phone earlier. Alex O'Rourke, from Macauley across the road. Just here to have a quick look round.'

The door opened with a smiling young woman in jeans and trainers standing beside it. 'Lunchtimes are a bit of a madhouse here.' She stood aside and ran a hand through her fantastically wild curls. 'It's when a lot of the parents drop in, which is great, but it does raise the energy levels.' She outstretched her hand. 'Ginny Taylor. Director of the centre.'

'Rex Macauley, chairman of Macauley Partners.' But as he shook Ginny's hand a strange look came over the older man's face and he withdrew his hand quickly and held it up.

There was a slash of red across his palm.

'Oh gosh, sorry. Mustn't have got all the paint off after I finished with the kids. I'll show you the bathroom and you can wash off there.' Ginny turned on her sneakered heel and walked efficiently down a hallway, off which led a number of doors.

'This one?' Rex went to open the first door.

'Ooops, not that one.' Ginny gently directed him away. 'That's our breastfeeding room.'

Rex jolted, as if zapped by electricity. 'Best not go in,' he muttered.

'It's empty now.' Ginny laughed. 'But we have mums coming and going all the time.' She directed him to another door. 'Bathroom's in that one.'

He nodded.

'I'll wait here,' said Alex.

'Feel free to take a look around.' Ginny's eyes went to two little boys scuffling over a truck. 'I'll be right back,' she murmured.

'Take your time.' Alex leant against the wall and, for the first time since coming into the centre, she took it all in. The scattering of small chairs and tables, the buckets and buckets of Lego, a corner for dress-ups and another filled with books and beanbags. It was exactly like the twins' preschool, the one she used to race into on the rare occasion when James wasn't available at five minutes to six to avoid paying the late pick-up fee and facing the pissed-off carers. If she closed her eyes, it even smelt the same – craft glue, paper and crayons.

But there was something that was different.

There were parents around. They had to be parents, unless the carers had taken to wearing sharp suits, high heels and ties. There weren't many. Maybe five or so, either reading or playing Lego or colouring in. Just doing the normal things parents did when they weren't working.

Ginny was back, the contested truck in hand. 'We get quite a few parents coming down during the day,' she said, as if reading her mind. 'For some kids, it's a bit unsettling and the parents drop it after a while. For most, it's just about knowing they could be here in two minutes if they needed to.'

Alex thought of all the times the twins' preschool had called her at work, with one of the boys either sick or injured, even though she'd told them, repeatedly, that James was the one to contact – he was at home, after all. It was impossible for her to drop everything and run, much as she wanted to. 'Must be reassuring for the parents, to be so close.'

'That's what they say.' With that, Ginny darted off in the direction of a little girl poised to demolish a carefully constructed tower of blocks, completely unbeknown to its proud builder, a small boy with sandy hair.

Alex held her breath. Ginny was just out of reach. The girl nudged her toe against the bottom block. The whole thing teetered and crashed to the ground. The boy wailed and buried his head in the carer's legs.

'Now, come on, Marcus. You did have a good long go with the blocks and Isla had asked you several times if she could join in but you wouldn't let her. I'm not saying she should have knocked them over, but this is what happens when we don't share.'

Calmly, Isla had picked up the blocks and started rebuilding.

'Alexandra, I think it's time for us to leave. I have a two o'clock.' Rex was back, his hands clean but empty.

'Where's that vision document I prepared?' she asked.

'Oh, it got wet in the bathroom. Send it to Ava. She can print it again,' he said and glanced around. 'I think we're done here. You've made your point, Alexandra, but a child-care centre? I really think that's beyond our resources.' He went to leave.

'Wait, Rex, this is important.' She raised her voice over the din of children. 'There are other things Macauley can do – job sharing, more part-time roles, working from home, more generous maternity leave. That's how you get women to stay.' Alex hated the pleading tone in her voice. 'Are you really not even going to have a look around?'

It was only at the door that Rex stopped and waited. 'Alexandra, come on. You sound hysterical. Let's talk about this in the office.' His voice was soothing. Gentle. Like he was talking to a five year old. Like he was lying, because he wanted the child to obey.

'I'm not taking the partnership.' Alex lifted her chin.

'Pardon?' Rex flinched.

'I. Refuse. Your. Invitation.' She enunciated the words clearly.

His expression darkened. 'But we need you. We need a working mother. We're losing all our talent. You need to help us.' He shifted his weight onto the other leg and cocked his head. His tone made her want to scream. She hated whining.

'I'm leaving the firm.' She reached into her handbag and produced an envelope with Rex's name handwritten on the front. 'If you can't take this seriously, then I can't work here any more.'

'I'll have you know, I don't respond well to blackmail.' His voice took a darker edge.

'It's not blackmail, it's a simple reality. I can't continue to juggle my life the way I have been, and I'm not alone.'

'You can't leave,' he exploded. 'People don't get offered partnership and leave. What do you think you're doing?'

Alex pressed the envelope into Rex's chest. 'I'm backing myself,' she said. 'I don't need you. I need this.' She looked around at the children, the carers, the mums and dads, some of whom she sensed were now listening. 'I quit.'

With that, she brushed past Rex and didn't stop. Behind her, she heard the sound of blocks, tumbling and falling, scattering and cascading. Another tower had tumbled and a little girl shrieked with delight.

Alex smiled and kept walking

CHAPTER FORTY

With a screech of tyres, Cara pulled into Cuthbert Close. Beth had sounded frantic on the phone, though in the hubbub of the photo shoot it had been difficult to decipher exactly what she was saying. The only clear part of the message was that Cara had to get back to the shed. Quickly.

She slammed the car door and hurried in. From the outside, everything *looked* calm. Cuthbert Close was at its quietest in the middle of the day, with little more to be heard than the breeze in the trees.

She found Beth at the door of the shed, wringing her hands.

'You just missed him,' she said. 'I tried so hard to keep him here because I knew you would be able to explain everything so much better than I could, but he wouldn't listen, and now he's gone, and I feel like it's all my fault.'

The woman was ashen-faced.

'Calm down. I'm sure everything's going to be fine. Now, come and sit down and tell me who came to the shed?' Cara led her to the table and chairs under the she-oak.

Beth took a deep breath in through her nose and out through her mouth. 'It was the food safety inspector from the council. At first, I thought he was here to do a random inspection, but then he told me there'd been a complaint.'

'About Nourish?'

Beth nodded. 'He said someone had called them about a food poisoning outbreak.'

'Jasper's virus,' Cara breathed.

'Yes, exactly, and I explained how it had all been a big misunderstanding and showed him Alex's post, and how she clarified that Jasper had a virus and not food poisoning. I said he could even check with the school about other reported cases of gastro. But he just wouldn't listen.'

'Why not?'

Beth's frown deepened. 'He said that any complaints of food poisoning caused by a business had to be taken extremely seriously and required a thorough inspection of the premises.'

'I'm sure he didn't find any problems there.' Cara prided herself on keeping an immaculate kitchen.

Beth flushed. 'There were a couple of minor issues.'

'Like what?'

'Apparently we're supposed to have a thing called a digital probe thermometer so we can check the temperature of the fridge.'

'The fridge is barely a year old!' Cara exploded. 'It works perfectly well.'

'The inspector said we should be keeping a record of the temperature history of all perishable products, like a logbook.'

'I've never heard anything so ridiculous. We're experienced cooks. We have forty years of cooking experience between us and not once have we ever made anyone sick.' Cara sat back and looked up to the sky. So clear and blue, completely at odds with the turmoil going on in her mind.

'He's shut us down,' said Beth timidly.

'He what?' Cara's head whiplashed around.

'He says we can't operate until they've investigated the complaint and we've fixed our *issues*.'

'You mean gone out and bought a thermometer,' Cara snapped. She closed her eyes and shook her head. 'I can't believe this is happening. All those orders. How are we ever going to fulfil them? People have paid for their meals. They're expecting us to deliver. They'll never use us again if we can't provide what they've paid for. This could kill the business.'

'I'm sorry,' said Beth.

'This is not your fault.'

Beth pursed her lips. 'When the inspector arrived, I was cutting up the pork and I left it on the chopping board to answer the door, so when he came in, it was just sitting there. He didn't like that. He said I should have covered it and put it back in the fridge before answering the door.'

'He sounds like a real piece of work,' said Cara, before taking her friend's hand. 'I'm sure it wasn't the main reason he closed us down. Don't blame yourself, blame the person who dobbed us in.'

'Who would do such a thing?'

'The same person who tried to make mischief out of Alex's Instagram post, I suspect. A random troll with nothing better to do than spread misery.'

Beth looked at her, as if deciding whether to speak. 'The inspector said the complaint had come from someone in the street.'

Cara did a double take. 'A neighbour? No.' She shook her head. 'I don't think so.'

'That's what he said.'

'Hey, ladies.' Beth and Cara's heads turned in unison. It was Alex, clambering through Cara's back fence, still dressed in her work clothes.

'You're home early,' said Cara.

'Is everything all right?' asked Beth.

Alex flopped into a chair beside them. 'I just quit my job.'

'You what?' said Beth and Cara together.

'You two should see your faces.' Alex grinned. 'It's like I just told you that I'm planning to cook up my placenta and eat it.'

Beth's nose wrinkled. 'Please don't do that.'

'I don't understand. I thought you were going to take the partnership,' said Cara.

'Turns out it wasn't what I wanted. You were right, Beth. It wasn't me that had to change, it's the dinosaurs in charge.'

'But I didn't mean you should resign. What will you do?'

Alex's face darkened. 'James and I have spoken about it and we might have to leave Cuthbert Close.'

'Alex, no,' gasped Beth.

'You can't leave us,' said Cara. 'No one leaves Cuthbert Close unless they're dying—'

'Or divorcing,' Beth cut in.

'Or drowning in debt,' said Alex. 'Which is basically what we are.' She looked around. 'I love this place, and I love you guys, and I love our home.' She paused. 'But I'm not sure I like the person I've become here. I've never really had the chance to sit back and enjoy it. It's always been work, work, work, to earn enough to pay the mortgage. It's madness, really. Why do we do this to ourselves?'

'For our children?' Cara ventured.

Alex snorted. 'My boys would be happier living in a tent.' She flicked a leaf off her lap. 'It's made me realise that having less actually isn't the worst thing in the world.' She looked up at the trees, waving gently in the breeze. 'It's like money has a tipping point. Too much of it, and you're miserable, and the same goes for having too little. I think there's a happy medium there, but I just need to find it. The boys don't need a ducted sound system. They just need to feel safe and loved and secure. I'm lucky, when you look at it. My mum never got to choose.'

'I think that's very wise,' said Beth.

Cara nodded. 'That's all I want for Poppy.'

Her voice cracked and Alex reached out to pat her knee. 'And you're going to have it. I gather Will Parry is coming to the party with his eight hundred k. That's fantastic!' She looked at Cara. 'So why do you look like your cake just went flat?'

Cara sighed. 'The council has shut down Nourish.'

'Oh, shit. Why?'

Cara and Beth exchanged glances but neither spoke. Alex looked from one woman to the other. 'Not the food poisoning thing?' Her eyes widened as Cara nodded. 'Oh, no,' she groaned. 'That stupid fucking photo. I can't believe it. There must be something we can do. Did they leave you with some kind of orders or notice? Maybe we can challenge it?'

'He did leave us with something.' Beth ducked into the shed and returned with a letter, which she passed to Alex.

'Okay, so it says here that the order is valid for one week while they investigate.' She lowered the notice. 'How about I ring him and explain. See if there's a way to get it lifted sooner?'

'We've got fifty orders due for delivery on Wednesday, so even if we got it lifted tomorrow, it still wouldn't give us time to complete.' Cara rubbed her temples where a dull ache had set in. 'It would be the end of the business.'

'All right, so we need to get this lifted today.' Alex pulled out her phone. 'I'll ring them now.'

Cara and Beth watched as Alex wandered deeper into the garden, too far away for them to hear the conversation.

In a minute, she was back. 'Okay, so there's a glimmer of hope here.'

'What is it?' Beth leant forward.

'The only way you can get up and running again before the week is up is if the original complaint is withdrawn. So what we need to do is find that person. Any ideas who it might have been? The inspector wouldn't give me a name.'

'All he told me was that it was someone from Cuthbert Close,' said Beth.

Cara thought for a moment. Which neighbours? The architects? Surely not. They wanted Nourish to cater for their wedding reception. Mr Atherton at number fifteen? She hadn't seen him in weeks, and the chances of him using social media were slim to none. Mentally, she worked her way down the close, discounting each resident one by one until she reached number twenty-five – the Devines.

Threats are everywhere, and you won't even see them coming.

Now it made sense. Cara snapped her fingers. 'It's Charlie Devine.'

'You really think she would do such a thing? It's so horrible.' Beth was incredulous.

'I believe it. I never liked the woman. From the moment she shut down our street party, I knew she was trouble,' said Alex. 'And you can't deny you've had your suspicions.'

'But why would she do it? We've done nothing to her,' said Beth.

'Think about it. Her husband has this hugely successful business selling meal-replacement shakes and supplements. Now what's the worst thing that could happen to that business?' said Cara.

'People decide they want to eat real food again?' said Alex. 'Made by real people in a real kitchen.'

Cara pointed at Alex. 'Precisely. We're a threat. A small one, but a threat nonetheless. She was at the party. She saw Alex go home with poor Jasper, and bang! There's your food poisoning conspiracy. Goodbye Nourish.'

'It's genius,' said Alex with grudging admiration.

'It's evil,' said Beth.

'So what do we do?' said Cara.

'We go and confront her and force her to withdraw,' said Alex.

'Face to face? I'm not sure that's a good idea.'

'Beth, this is our future on the line. You need this business as much as I do,' said Cara.

'I'll come with you,' said Alex. 'Even if I can't live in Cuthbert Close, I want to make sure you two can.'

ThePrimalGuy.com.au

From: The Primal Guy

Subject: Moving in for the Kill

Hey Prime-Examples,

Soz, gotta keep this one short.

Things are really heating up round here. I'm getting so close to the end, to getting what I want, that I can almost taste it. This journey has been my Everest. I got nearly all the steps behind me, and if I can just nail these last ones, I can be done with this place and get back to my family.

But I know I gotta be careful. 'Cause this is where it can all go bad.

When you've got the spear in your hand, and your prey is there – sad and defenceless – sometimes you get the feeling like you want to pussy out.

All I can say, man, is that you gotta keep your eyes on the prize. You know what you need. You gotta eat, after all. You know that blood will have to be spilled if you want to get it.

But it won't be yours. Not unless you take the damn shot.

Peace out,

Ryan (AKA the Primal Guy)

PS No PS this week. Too much happening!

CHAPTER FORTY-ONE

There was no sign of life at the Devines' house. Plantation shutters firmly closed. No car in the drive.

Alex rapped on the door and stood aside.

'Maybe no one's home?' said Beth hopefully.

The door opened. Charlie looked pale. Dark circles shadowed her eyes. She wore no make-up. Usually, her all-white wardrobe was like a highlighter for her tanned skin, but today, the simple oversized white linen shift dress gave her an ethereal, slightly vulnerable presence. The tan – obviously fake, Beth now realised – had faded.

'Hello Alex, hello Cara … Beth.' Charlie had to lean to see her, hiding behind Cara. Beth gave a little wave.

'Could we come in? There's something we need to discuss with you,' said Cara.

Charlie frowned and gripped the door handle. 'It's not a good time.'

'It's quite important, please,' said Cara.

'Can we discuss it here?'

'Not really,' said Cara, holding her ground.

'All right.' Charlie stood aside to let the women through.

It was years since Beth had been in the house. Was it Christmas drinks one year that the Pezzullos had hosted? Anyway, she remembered it as a gleaming white modern box inside, with blond-wood furniture and fresh white lilies at every turn.

It wasn't like that any more. There was a sense of weariness about the place, maybe because it had been empty for all those months? Or was it the mess now scattered about the place, towers of still-taped packing boxes, and piles of paper and magazines strewn about everywhere? It was not what she had expected of Charlie Devine. Not at all. Three weeks should have been enough time for anyone to unpack their belongings and get a house in order. Her eye was drawn to a notepad, sitting on top of a particularly large pile of papers. Her brain pinged with recognition. There was something familiar about it …

'I wasn't expecting visitors,' said Charlie, as if reading her mind. 'We're still getting sorted. All I can offer you is a green tea or an acai juice.'

'No, thank you,' said Cara. 'I wanted to talk to you about what you said this morning, about Nourish, and the unforeseen threats we might face.'

A look of surprise scudded across Charlie's face. 'I didn't mean anything, really, just that being in business is difficult and you need to keep your wits about you.'

'But why would you say that?' Cara insisted. 'Why this morning?'

'No particular reason,' said Charlie. 'I was just making conversation. Being friendly. That's what people do in this street, don't they?'

Her voice was even and unreadable. That Cuthbert Close was a friendly place was surely a positive? But Charlie's tone gave it an air of criticism. Seemingly it wasn't just Beth she needed distance from, it was everyone in the street.

'You see, Charlie,' said Alex, 'Cara and Beth here had a visit from the food safety inspector today, and he's shut down their business because of a complaint from a neighbour.'

'Oh, I see.' Charlie's fingers went to her chest.

Cara, Beth and Alex waited. Charlie's eyes moved from face to face.

Alex cleared her throat. 'We think maybe the complaint came from you.'

Charlie's eyes widened and she blinked quickly. 'It wasn't me. I have no interest in seeing your business close down.'

'C'mon, Charlie, it's obvious. You see Cara and Beth as a threat. You basically said as much. Now, all we're asking is that you ring the council and withdraw the complaint,' cajoled Alex.

'I don't know what you're talking about, and I think it might be time for you to leave,' said Charlie, sounding defensive.

Beth went to stand. She wanted nothing more than to leave. Something was ... off. 'Yes, of course. Sorry to disturb.' As she rose the front door to the Devines' house swung open, bringing in a blast of cooler air from outside.

'Mum! Mum!' The voice was quavering, panicked.

All four women stood, with Charlie leading the rush towards the doorway. It was Talia, and she was holding something in her hand. Something that looked like … like hair. Human hair. Curly human hair.

Beth gasped.

'I'm so sorry,' Talia whimpered.

Cara stepped closer.

'It's Poppy's,' she said, her voice high and strangled.

CHAPTER FORTY-TWO

'Talk me through it again,' said Alex tersely. 'Step by step.'

Talia gulped. 'We got to your house, but no one was home, so we went across to Cara's to wait in her back garden. Then Poppy said she wanted to play hairdressers, so I got some scissors out of the shed and gave them to the boys. I made them swear on their lives that they wouldn't actually cut any hair. They were just supposed to pretend. I'm so, so sorry.'

'Then what happened?' Alex demanded.

'I went back into the shed because the kids were hungry and I thought there might be some food. When I came back out, Poppy's ponytail was on the ground, so I just picked it up, grabbed the scissors and ran home.' The stricken girl looked at the boys, sitting on the couch with their feet dangling six inches off the floor.

'So you didn't actually see who did it?'

'No.'

'All right, Talia, you should probably go home now.'

'I think I'll go check on Poppy. Make sure she's okay.' The girl slipped out Alex's front door and into the arms of her mother waiting outside, grim-faced. Talia gestured in the direction of Cara's house. Charlie shook her head.

Alex's stomach heaved. What must Cara think of *her*? The twins? She turned to the boys, who sat still and stony-faced.

'Noah, Jasper.' Her voice was steely. 'I'm going to give you one chance and one chance only to tell me the truth. Which one of you cut Poppy's hair?'

The boys looked at each other and spoke in unison. 'I did.'

CHAPTER FORTY-THREE

Cara sat and stroked her daughter's hair, the little that was left of it. She buried her head in the soft curls as tears bit at her eyes.

'Mummy, please don't be sad.' She felt her daughter's sweet breath on her neck. 'Please, it's only hair. It will grow back.'

'Pops, I don't understand. How can you not have seen who did it?'

Her daughter stiffened. 'I didn't see. I promise, Mummy.' Now her lip was trembling. 'It was one of the boys, but I didn't see which one, honest.'

Cara looked at her daughter. Her strong, brave, sensible child. She cleared her throat to get rid of the tears. 'You're not in trouble, sweetheart. I'm sorry . . . I just can't help feeling a bit sad. It was such lovely hair. You had that hair since you were a baby.'

'I still have *some* hair and think how much easier it will be to brush in the mornings.'

Using her little thumbs, Poppy pressed Cara's cheek. 'Really, Mummy, I don't mind. I think this hair actually suits me.' She flicked her head back and forth the way a hair model would in a television commercial.

Cara couldn't help but laugh and Poppy kissed her on the lips. 'Please don't be cross.'

'I'm not cross with you. I'm cross with whoever did this to you!' She drew her in tightly. She hated Poppy seeing her cry. She'd never seen her own parents cry. Ever. They were strong, and resilient, and that's what had made Cara strong and resilient too. If Pete's death had taught her anything, it was that she was far more adept at giving comfort than receiving it.

She checked her watch. 'Sweetie, it's time for PJs, so how about you go inside? I've got a couple of things to clear up in the shed.' Gently, she stood and pointed her daughter's shoulders in the direction of the house. 'I'll be there in a few minutes.'

At the door, Poppy stopped and waved. Cara grinned, but as the little girl disappeared inside, she let her face, and the tears, fall. She started stumbling towards the shed where she'd be able to cry in peace.

'Um … Hello? Cara?' It was Talia.

Cara stopped, and wiped her face hurriedly. 'Sorry, Talia … hi.'

Talia stopped. No doubt she'd seen Cara's reddened face and knew what it meant. She stood in the garden, shame-faced, with one hand jammed in her pocket and the other clutching a plastic bag. 'I just wanted to bring these over for Poppy.' Nervously, she held up the bag. 'It's just some hairclips and bands. My dad got them overseas and I've never worn them.' She made a face. 'He still thinks I'm into pink. But I thought Poppy might like them … for her new hairstyle?' Talia stepped tentatively into the garden.

'That's very kind.' Cara blinked quickly.

'I'm so sorry about what happened.' The teenager let the words out in a rush, shifting her weight uncomfortably. 'Really sorry. I can't believe I didn't see what happened.'

Cara swallowed the stone in her throat and waved her hand. At fourteen, Talia was only a child herself. Maybe Charlie had been right – three children was a lot to handle. Too much. Cara felt a wave of guilt sweep over her. How could she have let herself get so busy with work that she forgot the one person who she was supposedly doing it all for – her daughter.

Now she really felt like howling. 'It's not your fault, Talia.' She gave what she hoped was a reassuring smile. 'Poppy's gone inside. Why don't you take those things in to her. I just want to lock up out here.'

'Okay.' Talia turned for the house and Cara headed to the shed.

At the door, she stopped. It was a mess. Drawers pulled out. Half-eaten packs of biscuits on the benchtop. Plastic containers strewn about the floor. Even the curtain on the window had been pulled skew-whiff. What had gone on here? The kids must have arrived home and decided to trash the place. Those twins were completely out of control! Cara felt anger rising in her belly, overtaking the shock and the guilt. She would have to say something to

Alex. It was unacceptable. At a stretch, she could maybe, maybe understand the chopping-off of Poppy's ponytail as play-gone-wrong, but trashing the shed? It was just wilful and wanton destruction that made her think the 'accident' wasn't as accidental as she'd wanted to believe. Maybe those little terrors had set out to deliberately hurt Poppy?

A vision popped into her head of Talia, holding the ponytail.

Cara shivered. She would never forget that image. Maybe it wouldn't be such a bad thing for the O'Rourke family to move on, after all. Alex had been a good friend, yes, but those boys were clearly beyond her.

Picking up the baby monitor, Cara wiped a red splodge of what looked like tomato sauce off the volume control. The speaker crackled, and before she could turn it off again, a voice came through.

'How about we try this blue one? Look, it matches your eyes.' That was Talia. Sweetly cajoling.

'No.' The voice was firm. Almost rude.

Cara startled. That wasn't like Poppy.

'C'mon, Poppy. Please. Just try?'

Cara held her breath.

'No. I don't want to.'

Cara flinched. Her daughter was being straight-out obnoxious. This wasn't how she'd raised her.

'Well, I don't think your mum would be too happy if she heard how rude you were being right now.'

The cloth dropped from Cara's hands. It was as if Talia could read her mind.

'Please don't talk to her.' Now Poppy's voice was fearful. 'You don't have to tell her anything.'

Right, that was it. This was all too odd. Her daughter was acting like a stranger. She strode to the door and nearly ran straight into Alex, coming in the other direction.

Cara raised her hand. 'If you're coming here to apologise again, please don't. I don't have the—'

'Actually, that wasn't what I came to talk to you about.' Alex held up her phone. 'I just got off from speaking with the council inspector. The complaint's been withdrawn.' She gave a grim smile. 'Nourish is back in business.'

Cara startled. It wasn't what she'd expected Alex to say. 'Straight away?'

'They'll come back to check next week that you've addressed the issues highlighted in the assessment. But yes, you can start up again.'

'So it must have been Charlie Devine who made the original complaint.'

'Seems that way.'

Cara frowned. 'But she was so adamant it wasn't her.'

The day couldn't get any stranger.

CHAPTER FORTY-FOUR

Beth stopped at her bedroom window. It looked as if Alex and Cara were making their peace, given the quiet conversation happening between them outside the shed.

Good. She couldn't bear the idea of their friendship being torn apart by something silly the boys had done.

Poppy's hair had been delightful long, but somehow the short do accentuated the lovely elfin features of her face. No real harm done.

She leant against the window frame and allowed her muscles to slacken with fatigue, not surprising given the emotional roller-coaster of the day.

She needed a bath. Yes, a bath would soothe her nerves. Everything looked better after a soak in Epsom salts. She headed into the bathroom and opened the drawer where she kept her toiletries.

But when she extended her hand into the far reaches, something else fluttered out along with the salts. She picked it up off the ground. A piece of paper. *The* piece of paper. The one threatening to tell Beth about Max's affair. Or was it threatening to tell Max about Beth's kiss with Adam?

She coloured as she scanned the words again. She'd managed to put that night out of her head. The brain was good at doing that, blocking out shameful events, and given everything else that had happened since, the kiss had simply folded into the recesses of her mind. Actually, it seemed almost inconsequential now. She studied the paper. Blue, with pink lines.

Blue, with pink lines. She knew that paper.

Beth turned off the tap.

CHAPTER FORTY-FIVE

'It's the exact same paper I saw in the Devines' house. It must have been Charlie who sent the note, who was spying on me, involving herself in my marriage. She's always acted a little strange around Max and this explains it.' Beth sat at the table in Cara's shed, folding and unfolding the piece of paper before her.

'From the moment she crashed our street party, I think Charlie Devine has been hell-bent on sabotaging all of us. Your marriage.' Alex looked at Beth. 'And your business.' She looked at Cara.

'And what about you? What of yours has she ruined?' asked Cara.

'I'm still working that out,' muttered Alex.

'I still don't really understand why she would hate us so much. We've really done nothing to her,' said Cara.

'Who knows why people do anything?' Alex shrugged. 'The question is, what do we do about it?'

The women stood in silence. The normal sounds of Cuthbert Close filtered through the open door of the shed: the wind whispering through the trees. A whip of birds taking flight. The woody music of a bamboo wind chime. A leaf blower squealing in the distance. The muted beep of a truck reversing, several streets away.

A car door being banged shut.

Slammed. Too firmly.

Beth flinched. 'Who's that, I wonder?'

In a neighbourhood like theirs, there was a distinct difference between a car door being shut, and one being shut *in anger*. There was a pitch to it that made you stop and listen for what would come next.

This one was heavy and angry.

Cara, Alex and Beth were still. Next came hurried footsteps, raised voices, and not happy raised voices. Frightened ones. Panicked.

'What the hell's going on now?' groaned Alex. 'Haven't we had enough trouble for one day? This is Cuthbert Close. Nothing ever happens here!'

'I think we'd better go investigate,' said Cara grimly, leading the way out of her garden and into the street.

The first thing that hit Beth was the stricken look on Charlie Devine's face, and, in contrast, the sheer joy on her daughter's as she hugged a man Beth had never seen before.

'Looks like Daddy's home,' said Alex, under her breath.

'*That's* the Primal Guy,' said Beth in disbelief.

After all the newsletters, and everything Cara and Alex had told her about the man, Beth anticipated a Chris

Hemsworth-style man-mountain, not this slightly dishevelled and puffy-looking fellow, with his shirt half untucked and nothing more than thongs on his feet.

'I've missed you so much, Daddy.' Talia clung to him tightly.

'Me too, baby girl. Me too.' He kissed her head and they rocked together in the middle of the Devines' front garden.

'Ryan, you know the deal. You need to leave now.' Charlie Devine stood with her arms folded, her lips set in a line. 'I'm serious. You need to go.'

'Mum, no!' cried Talia. 'He's only just arrived.'

'Talia, we've been through this.' Charlie's voice was steely.

'Why can't you give him a second chance? Why do you have to be such a bitch?'

Beth's hand flew to her mouth.

'Talia,' said Charlie. 'Come inside. Ryan, I'm going to call the rehab centre to let them know you're here. But you have to go back. You know that.'

'No need, baby-cakes. Look at me. Perfectly fine.' Ryan spread his arms and started to put one foot in front of other. Two feet from his wife, he stumbled and fell towards her. Instinctively, Charlie's hands rushed to shield her face.

'Look, mate.' Alex strode over the grass. 'I think you better leave, or I'm going to have to call the police.'

'Whoa, whoa, whoa. Who are you?' slurred Ryan. Up close, Alex could see his pupils were like pinpricks, his eyes riven with angry red veins.

'My name is Alexandra O'Rourke and I've spent more time in a courtroom than you have in a gym. If this woman is asking you to leave her property, then you must, or you'll be charged with trespass.' She held out her phone and made a show of starting to dial.

'Please, Alex. Don't. I want my dad to stay. I need him.' Talia clung to her father.

'Talia, I'm sorry but your mother has asked him to leave and I think she knows best,' said Alex.

'She has no idea,' spat Talia. 'I hate her.'

Cara stepped closer to the teenager and was about to speak when she felt a tug on her arm.

'Mummy, stay away from her.' It was Poppy. Where had she come from? She must have followed Talia onto the street when she heard the commotion.

'Darling, it's fine. Just go back inside.'

'Don't go near her,' Poppy whispered.

'Who? Charlie?' Cara took her daughter's hand.

'No. Her.' Poppy pointed and Cara followed the direction of her finger … straight to Talia, who was now speaking quietly and urgently with Charlie and Ryan.

'What do you mean?'

But Poppy's lips were clammed shut.

Suddenly, it clicked. It was shocking and almost incomprehensible but it somehow made sense.

Cara knelt down. 'Did Talia cut your hair? Did she threaten you?' She clasped her daughter's hands. 'Don't look at her. She won't hurt you. Look at me.'

Poppy's eyes were troubled. 'She told us that she'd made her cat kill Henny and that if we told anyone what happened, she'd get her cat to kill all the pets in the street.' The little girl's voice wobbled.

Cara felt winded. There was a pressure in her chest. Her mind was a storm of thoughts and feelings. How? How could Talia do such a thing? And why?

Cara squeezed her daughter's hand and rose to her full height.

'Talia,' she called, and the teenager turned to face her, releasing her grip on her father's arm. 'I think there's something you need to tell us about Poppy's hair, about what happened earlier.'

Talia's eyes narrowed. 'I told you what happened. I didn't see anything.'

'I heard you on the monitor. Poppy didn't want you to touch her. She was scared.'

'Talia.' There was a tone of warning in Charlie's voice, but also something else … fear. 'Talia, what happened to Poppy's hair? You need to tell the truth.'

'The truth?' Talia turned on her mother and the look on her face was one of pure loathing. 'You know the truth.'

Charlie inhaled and took a step back. 'Oh, Talia, you didn't, did you?'

'I've always thought I'd make a good hairdresser, and I think little Poppy agrees with me. Short hair suits her, doesn't it.' Talia folded her arms, triumphantly.

'But you let the boys take the blame,' said Alex. 'That's just horrible.'

Talia wheeled around. 'What would you care?' she burst out. 'You're never around for them anyway. Why did you even become a mother? That poor little Noah. I feel sorry for that kid. Even when he's telling the truth, no one believes him. I mean, think about it, what would a kid want with a diamond ring? Did you even stop to think about that for one minute?'

'Talia, stop,' said Charlie.

'That was *you*,' said Beth. 'You took my engagement ring and planted it in Noah's bedroom?'

'Well, let's face it, Beth. It's not like you'll be needing it for much longer. I saw you kiss that young guy. It's disgusting. You're old enough to be his mother,' she hissed.

'And that's why you sent the note ...' said Beth.

So it wasn't about Max after all. It was about me.

'I sure did.' Talia nodded with satisfaction. 'I mean, how could you do that to your family? To your kids? Your poor family, having to eat those disgusting quiches every night. I loved putting that thing in the bin.' She turned to Ryan. 'Seriously, Dad, you would have puked.'

Beth recoiled. 'I don't understand, Talia. Why would you take it if you didn't want it?'

'Because I knew it would make you feel good. I had to get you to like me so that you would hate her. And you fell for it, hook, line and sinker. My dad's the Primal Guy! Of course I wasn't going to eat the stupid quiche.' She shook her head at Beth. 'You did it for you! Seriously, all you women think only about yourselves. You don't give your kids a second thought, do you.' She whipped around to face Charlie. 'Do you, Mum. You really don't give a shit about me.'

'That's absolutely not true,' said Charlie, her voice breaking. 'I moved here for you. For us. To give us a fresh start. To get away from all the chaos ...'

'That's such bullshit,' Talia exploded. 'You never even stopped to think twice about me.'

'That's totally unfair,' Charlie cried. 'The way we were living was so toxic. It was a complete lie. Your dad was out of control, and I had to get you out of there, away from him ... You were getting caught up in it too.'

'But he's my dad.' Talia flung herself into her father's arms and sobbed into his shoulder, causing him to stumble backwards. 'Daddy, I want to come with you. I've been working so hard to make you proud of me. I did it all for you.'

'Did all what for me, baby girl?' He took her chin in his hands.

'Got rid of them for you, Daddy.' She thrust a look in the direction of Cara, Beth and Alex. 'They were moving in on our turf, and you know what we always say, the main threats are the ones you never see coming, except I did see this coming, so I did something about it.'

Cara felt winded. What was Talia talking about now? Surely not … 'You lit the fire in the shed, didn't you? You could have killed someone.'

Talia gave her a disdainful look. 'To be honest, I'd hoped for a little more damage. But, whatever.' She shrugged. 'My friendly local council was more than happy to talk to me … They take food poisoning extremely seriously.'

'So, the complaint to the council came from you too?' said Alex.

Talia folded her arms. 'For a lawyer, Alex, you're not exactly careful with your words, are you now? The internet is forever, didn't you know. That's what you adults are always telling us.'

Charlie took a step towards her daughter. 'Talia, I understand that you're upset with me, but I want you to apologise now. These women are not our enemies. They've done nothing wrong.'

Talia turned to her, eyes streaming with tears. 'And I did nothing wrong either—' her voice broke '—but I lost everything.'

CHAPTER FORTY-SIX

Apart from the sound of knife on board and the bubbling pot on the stove, Cara's shed was quiet, with a kind of stunned silence sitting over it like a cloud of steam.

'I still can't quite believe it,' said Beth in wonder.

'I believe it,' said Alex. 'There was something about that family that was off from the start.'

'But you thought it was Charlie, not Talia. You asked her to babysit the boys. You trusted her,' Cara pointed out.

'Yes, well. We all make mistakes.' Alex hacked away at a carrot for the next batch of cassoulet.

'We all trusted Talia, really,' said Beth.

Alex shook her head. 'And she turned out to be a psycho.'

'I don't know about psychopath ...' Beth turned down the hob on the stove. 'She's definitely a very mixed-up, sad little girl. And it makes sense, really, when you think about everything she's gone through. I mean, who'd have thought the Primal Guy was a total fraud. All this time he was preaching clean living to his followers, when on the side he was partying like a madman.'

'Sniffing too much of his own protein powder,' said Alex.

'It's funny, isn't it, how you can live less than twenty feet from someone else's front door and yet never really know what goes on behind it?' remarked Cara.

'I'm not sure if it's funny or depressing,' said Beth. 'I thought Cuthbert Close was different, special somehow. We do all like each other, don't we?'

'Well, *we* do. I can't speak for the rest of the street. But you ladies are like sisters to me,' said Cara.

'I feel the same,' said Beth.

'Ha! Sisters and neighbours – you don't get to choose either of them!' said Alex.

Beth stirred slowly. 'The one I really feel sorry for is Charlie. I mean, where do you go from here? A business that's obviously in trouble, a drug-addicted husband in rehab and a daughter who needs urgent psychological treatment. Maybe there's some way we could help her?'

'Are you kidding? Her daughter nearly killed your business, and you want to help her? For a minute, you thought she was having an affair with Max. What about that?'

Beth reddened. 'I was wrong. I still think he's up to something, but not with Charlie. She's too ... wounded, and dealing with too many other problems to be messing around with Max. Look at how ashamed she seemed to be, and she *did* manage to get the council to lift the shut-down order. I think she had a sense all along that Talia was troubled, and that's why she tried to keep her distance. She obviously worked out straight away that

Talia had made the complaint and rang the council to withdraw it.'

'It was the least she could do, given all the dramas her daughter's caused,' grumbled Alex. 'Besides, look at us now, nearly midnight and we're still here cooking another bloody cassoulet.'

'Go home. Please. You really don't have to be here.' Beth placed her hand on Alex's arm.

'I'm not sure I could sleep.'

'I'm a bit the same,' said Cara. 'I feel like I should be relieved, or something.' She dipped a spoon into the cassoulet and tasted. 'But … I don't know. I get this sense that something's still not quite right … It's silly.'

'Nope. I get it,' said Alex. 'Noah might not have stolen Beth's ring or cut Poppy's hair, but he did trash his classroom at school, and now I have no job, and everything's pretty shitty.' She patted her stomach. 'Sorry, baby.'

'And my husband is still, possibly, having an affair, even if it's not with Charlie,' said Beth. 'Nothing Talia has done changes that at all.'

'And your anniversary party is only a few weeks away, isn't it. Are you still planning to wait till then to confront him?' said Alex.

'I think so,' said Beth.

'Look at us. Bunch of sad sacks if ever I saw one,' said Alex. 'Let's look on the bright side. We're here. We're healthy. We still live in one of this city's nicest streets, at least for the moment. We're making beautiful food that's going to nourish dozens of families. And we have each other. I say that calls for celebration.'

She looked at the other women for confirmation.

'Maybe,' Beth said with uncertainty.

'I could open a bottle of wine or a block of chocolate or something,' said Cara, looking about the shed. 'On second thought, why don't we try some of the pork cassoulet? We've made a mountain of it and I'm completely famished.'

As she stood, there was a knock at the door.

'Probably James or Max coming to check up on us,' yawned Alex.

Cara opened the door. 'Charlie,' she said in surprise. The last she'd seen was Charlie hustling Ryan and Talia inside the house and closing the front door firmly as Cara, Alex and Beth stood open-mouthed on the street, trying to digest everything that had happened.

'I've come to apologise,' said Charlie, her head hung low, shoulders hunched under an oversized grey hoodie and loose tracksuit pants. Her fingers clutched nervously at her earlobe. No earring, Cara noticed with a start.

'Oh, hey, you've lost one of your diamonds. Must have fallen out,' She gestured to Charlie's left ear, the naked one.

'These?' Her hand went to the other earlobe, the one that still sparkled. 'They're fake … Junk jewellery. Don't worry about it.' She waved a hand wearily.

'Oh.' Cara was still. What exactly about this woman was real? She had a sense they were about to find out. 'Please, come in.'

She stood aside and Charlie shuffled in, acknowledging Beth and Alex with a small nod.

'I'm not sure where to begin.' She sighed, defeated.

'You don't have to explain,' said Beth.

'Let her speak, Beth … Some of us are interested.' Alex gestured for Charlie to sit.

'I don't blame you for being angry.' Charlie looked down and took a seat. 'I thought Cuthbert Close would be a fresh start for us. Get away from the craziness of everything in Brisbane. I just wanted peace and quiet …'

'And to be left alone,' added Beth.

'Yes.' Charlie gave a weak smile. 'You were all so kind and welcoming, and I appreciated it, I truly did.' She looked at them earnestly. 'But I was afraid about you getting too close to us. I knew Talia wasn't … Well, she wasn't herself. She adored her dad and when he went into treatment, she just sort of … fell apart. Got mixed up in a bad crowd. Started dabbling with drinking … At the same time, I was trying to sell the business so that we could cover the costs of Ryan's treatment … I just thought it would be safer for everyone if we got away, came somewhere new and kept to ourselves.'

'But Talia thought otherwise,' said Alex.

Charlie looked troubled. 'She's so like her father. So determined. I knew she didn't want to come here, I just didn't realise how much. She was so angry and I guess she thought that if she created enough chaos I'd have no choice but to take her back to Queensland. I'm so sorry you had to get caught up in it.'

As Charlie spoke, there'd been a thawing in the tense atmosphere of the shed. Beth, Alex and Cara had all leant closer as she spoke. Now, Beth rose and put her hand on Charlie's shoulder. 'None of this is your fault. You were trying to do the right thing, and you *were* doing the right thing. But teenagers don't always appreciate that.'

'Thank you, Beth,' said Charlie. 'That's very sweet.'

Alex sighed in exasperation. 'Why does parenting have to be so bloody hard. It would be so much easier if someone just told you what to do.' Her eyes locked onto Charlie.

'You know what? I actually owe *you* an apology. When you came to Cuthbert Close, I assumed you were a bit stuck-up because your husband was famous and you thought you were better than all of us.'

Charlie shook her head but said nothing.

'I judged you and I'm sorry.'

'Really, there's nothing to forgive.' Charlie raised her eyebrows. 'You had a right to be wary. And, for the record, I don't think you're a bad mother. I think you're amazing. You're a self-made woman, something I've never been.' She turned. 'And you too, Cara. I think Nourish is a fabulous idea, and I have a feeling it's going to be a wonderful success for you and Beth.'

'Thank you, Charlie, and speaking of Nourish, we were just about to have some pork cassoulet, if you'd like some too?' Cara stopped herself. 'Sorry, wait, no. You don't eat meat, do you.' She started opening cupboards. 'You know, I might have some crackers here somewhere.'

'Actually, pork cassoulet would be lovely,' said Charlie.

'Wonderful,' enthused Beth, pulling out an extra bowl. 'If this doesn't make you feel a little better, nothing will.'

Alex was first to dip her spoon in, and she moaned as it went into her mouth. 'This is so good. I can't believe I helped make it.'

Charlie sniffed appreciatively and chewed thoughtfully. 'I'd forgotten just how delicious pork could be.'

'Why did you stop eating it then?' asked Alex.

Charlie made a face. 'Ryan was always the strict one about eating. He was so persuasive, in all areas, really. I guess I fell under his spell. Focused on the business side of things while he had the big vision.' She paused. 'But being away from him for this past month has opened my eyes to just how insane it all really was.' At that moment, Charlie's pocket bleeped. She pulled out her phone and a frown returned to her forehead. 'Sorry, it's Talia. I'd better go.' She took the empty bowl to the sink. 'Thank you. That was totally delicious. And unexpected,' she added.

Cara walked her to the door of the shed. 'What will you do now?'

'I'm not sure.' Charlie stopped. 'I don't think we can stay here. Maybe we'll go back to Queensland.'

'Don't feel you have to leave on account of us. I meant what I said about you having nothing to apologise for,' said Beth, clearing the other bowls.

'I know, and I don't want Talia to think she's gotten her way … but I do think she needs help, and I have family there. I could supervise visits with Ryan.' She looked into the distance, where their house was. 'To me, home is wherever Talia is, and she's made it pretty clear that it can't be here.'

'That makes sense to me,' said Cara, as Charlie gave her a grateful smile.

'Thank you … all of you. You've all been very generous, and kind.'

Cara watched after her and only once the small grey figure had disappeared did she shut the door. 'Do you think we'll ever see them again?'

'Who? Talia and Charlie? They can't just disappear overnight, can they? They'll need time to pack and get removalists,' said Beth.

'They never really moved in though, did they? I mean, you saw all those boxes in their house,' said Alex.

Beth shuddered. 'I just don't like the idea of people disappearing out of this street without us all having a proper goodbye.'

'I'm not sure Talia will want a going-away party. Or Ryan, for that matter,' said Alex.

The shed was silent.

'I've got an idea,' said Cara. 'Let's take a photo.'

'A what?' said Alex. 'A photo? Why? I'd rather forget this night ever happened.'

'I disagree.' Cara shook her head firmly. 'Five years from now we'll look back on this crazy night and laugh about it and we'll remember how it bonded us forever. Chaos has a habit of doing that.'

'I wonder where we'll all be living then?' mused Alex.

'Who knows, so let's just do this now.' Cara set the pot of cassoulet on the table. 'Now, let's make sure this delicious food gets in the shot.'

'Yes! It might be the first and last time I make cassoulet and I may need photographic evidence that it ever happened at all,' said Alex.

The women sat at Cara's small wooden table and put their arms around each other.

'Ready? One, two, three.' Cara held out the phone, then studied the image and tapped it. 'We look a little ridiculous, but the food looks incredible.'

Alex studied the photo. 'You know, you ladies should put this on your Instagram for Nourish.'

'Goodness, no. I look like a wreck.' Beth clutched her throat.

'I don't think I have any time to photoshop it,' said Cara. 'We've got to get these meals packed.'

Alex shook her head. 'No photoshop. No filters. There's so much bullshit out there.' She pointed to the photo. 'This is life. Three mums, working their arses off at midnight, looking like shit, but doing it for our families, and for each other.'

Cara nodded. 'I think you're right,' she said slowly. 'We're about real food. So why don't we show our customers a bit of real life to go with it.'

'Exactly.' Alex clapped her hands.

'Are you sure you couldn't add just a little bit of colour to my lips,' said Beth. 'I look terribly washed out.'

'You look fucking amazing. You always do, and I wish you could see that.' Alex patted her hand.

Beth beamed. 'All right then. Go for it, Cara.'

She started tapping away and, after a couple of minutes, held up her phone to show Alex and Beth.

Real food. Real friends. Real life. #nofilter #nourish

CHAPTER FORTY-SEVEN

Alex stood over Noah and Jasper and the ball of fluff that was licking them to death. 'Guys, come on, stop letting the dog bite you and put your shoes on. The party's already begun.'

'Mummy, can we bring Bailey?' Jasper pleaded.

'Yes, please Mummy,' said Noah, bringing the little labradoodle up under his chin.

Six big brown eyes beseeched her. 'No! She'll chew everyone's shoes and eat all the party pies. Absolutely not.'

The puppy was the twins' top pick of sixth birthday gift and came highly recommended by the psychologist. It was proven, she said, that dogs (not guinea pigs) tended to reduce stress in anxious children. Pity she forgot to mention the additional stress that having a poo-producing and shoe-munching machine in the house would cause the parents.

Last night, when they'd woken to hear the puppy crying and been forced to bring it into the bedroom, James had remarked to Alex that it was good practice for having a baby in the house again, for the two were remarkably similar.

Yes, when the baby comes we'll rub its nose in its own wee and feed it nothing but dried pellets for dinner.

She knew he was just trying to make her feel more positive about the dog, and in fact, after only one week, Alex needed little convincing.

Noah adored Bailey. He chatted to the puppy like a friend, and when the two of them curled up on the couch together, he relaxed in a way that Alex had never witnessed before.

Of course, it wasn't just the dog. Alex couldn't fail to notice how much Noah and Jasper had revelled in her being around more.

Already, in the few weeks since Alex had quit Macauley, Noah's teacher had reported a marked improvement in his behaviour at school, not to mention his academic work. *It's been quite remarkable ... I'm not quite sure what you're doing, but whatever it is seems to be working.*

Alex mentally had fist-pumped the air.

One day she would go back to work. She'd be partner at a firm that understood that flexibility meant giving options to staff, and wasn't about stretching them to breaking point. But right now, a partnership of any kind wasn't convenient. She needed to be with her boys and to enjoy her pregnancy. James had done his bit and now it was her turn to be there for them – and she was bloody lucky to be able to make that choice, one her parents had never been able to make because of the financial pressures.

'Unless the dress code for this party is shoes-optional, then we seem to have a slight problem here.' James approached with a smile and slung his arm casually around Alex's waist while the boys continued to gambol on the lawn with Bailey.

'I don't suppose you've seen the matching one?' Alex held up her black sandal.

'Have you checked Bailey's hidey-hole?'

The puppy had taken to collecting an odd assortment of household objects and placing them at the bottom of the garden in a specially dug hole. So far, random inspections had turned up the TV remote, a therapeutic neck pillow, an eye mask, a few odd teabags and a tube of moisturiser.

He's a dog that likes to be pampered. What can you do, James had shrugged.

Half with hope and half with dread, Alex crossed the lawn to see if her sandal had made it to Bailey's not-so-secret hiding place.

It had. She held it up. Only a few minor bite marks. A bit slobbered on. All in all, not too bad. She'd dealt with worse bodily fluids from the boys, and no doubt would again when the baby came. The thought of it made her smile. A new little human being to have and to hold. This time she'd get it right.

Alex slipped the sandal on and returned to find James helping the boys into their trainers.

'Right, I think we're ready.'

'Wait.' Alex held her hand up. 'The pastries. You put Bailey in the laundry and I'll go get them.'

She hurried inside, pausing for a second to admire her immaculate kitchen. House inspections were undoubtedly tedious but they were an incredible motivator when it came to cleaning. The house could not have looked more beautiful, if a little soulless with all their family photos removed from the walls – the ones from the professional shoot where the four of them frolicked naturally on the beach, hugging and holding hands, even though Noah had thrown a major tantrum midway through because Jasper kicked sand in his eye. #blessed. Alex wasn't too sorry to take down those sham photos. The agents called it 'de-personalising' and she supposed it was part of the process of moving on. Already, the house didn't really look like theirs any more. It was like a showroom. Max was confident it would sell easily, and at a price that would allow them to buy, debt-free, something suitable in a slightly less desirable suburb further away from the city.

Alex went to collect the tray of pastries from the oven and noticed her phone on the bench. Four missed calls and one message. Not surprising. She hadn't checked it since yesterday. Without a job, she didn't really need to bother.

Casually, she picked it up and dialled the number for voice messages and waited.

Alexandra. Rex Macauley speaking ...

Holy shit. Macauley was ringing her? In surprise, she nearly dropped the phone before juggling the device back to her ear.

I've ... well, I've had a chance to read through that file you gave me, and, well ... even though you've left us, I'm wondering if you might like to come in and discuss what's in it ... Martin seems to think the place is falling to pieces without you ...

His voice had gone quiet and Alex pressed the phone to her ear.

Anyway ... he boomed, causing her to jump and nearly drop it again. *Please call my assistant to set up the meeting ... If you're interested.*

Trembling, Alex hung up, put the phone down and collected the tray of pastries from the bench.

'Who was that on the phone?' James was back from the laundry. 'You look a bit weird.'

'It was no one, nothing important.' Alex shrugged. She would think about Rex's offer later. Would she take it up? Maybe ... Maybe not. What mattered was that she'd got them thinking.

'Okay, fellas, let's go before this lot goes cold.'

James, Noah and Jasper all peered at the tray.

'What are they?' said Jasper, pointing.

'They're Lebanese spinach pies,' said Alex proudly.

James sniffed. 'They smell good. Where did you get them?'

Alex feigned offence. 'I'll have you know that I made these, I didn't buy them. Beth gave me the recipe.' When it came to cooking, Alex was still finding her feet, like a day-old foal, but she was starting, slowly, to understand the joy in it, the pleasure in providing sustenance and comfort to loved ones. Not that every dish was a success. She'd had a go at making scones with the boys and they'd had tremendous fun covering each other in flour and kneading the dough. But the end product wasn't quite right.

Rock cakes, right? James had asked innocently, chewing at the biscuit like it was a piece of ancient mutton. Seemed scones didn't appreciate over-zealous kneading from six year olds. *A light touch,* Beth had told her later, *and self-raising flour, not plain.*

'I think the spinach pies look absolutely terrific.' James kissed her forehead and took the tray off her hands. 'I'm sure you won't poison anyone.' He winked and led the way down the garden path, past the large 'For Sale' sign. She glanced briefly at the Devines' – shutters closed, mail piling up in the letterbox, weeds growing out of the driveway – and felt a tinge of regret.

Maybe if they'd left them alone or given them space like Charlie had wanted, maybe … Oh, it was stupid. Last she heard, Charlie had enrolled Talia back in her old school in Brisbane and was planning to let her see Ryan on the weekends. She'd read a couple of snippets in the news, that the business was being wound up. *The Tribe Has Spoken* was one of the headlines and, reading between the lines, it was apparent there'd been ongoing financial problems in the business well before Ryan started snorting all the profits up his nose.

'C'mon, boys, let's go,' said Alex, extending her hands. First, Noah slipped his fingers into hers, then Jasper followed. Alex squeezed and felt their tiny knuckles under her palm.

'Mummy, can Bailey sleep in our room tonight?' Noah looked at her, eyes pleading.

'Yeah, Mum. Pleeeeease.' Jasper tugged her arm.

She looked at them both, her heart so full of love for the two little boys who'd reminded her about what really mattered. Wherever they moved to next, this was what they would take with them. Love, and memories. Happiness didn't exist in fancy ovens and expensive baths. It was in their hearts and hands and their mum and dad.

In two weeks, when the house went up for auction, she'd be taking them to Perth for a holiday, to show them where she grew up and to spend time with the grandparents.

'Yes, Bailey can sleep in your room tonight.'

Together, the twins whooped with joy.

CHAPTER FORTY-EIGHT

'Mmmmm, these dumplings are absolutely wonderful. You'll have to give me the recipe,' gushed Max's work colleague Marita. 'Max is such a lucky man.'

Beth murmured agreement and moved on. Never had she wanted a party to end more than this one. It was excruciating, having everyone congratulate her on the milestone that she and Max had achieved together. Twenty years of wedded bliss!

If only they knew.

They would, soon enough. If she and Max parted ways, the news would spread like wildfire throughout their friendship group. Bad news always did. Whose side would they take? In Beth's admittedly limited experience of divorce, it was all but impossible for a friend to remain on good terms with both husband *and* wife. A choice would have to be made, but how? Was it the one you liked more? The one you'd known the longest? Did men go with the men, and women with the women?

Maybe it would be a relief to cut her friendship circle in half. Thanks to Nourish, she didn't really have time any more for coffee dates and dinner parties and book-covering bees. The business was flying, to the point where she and Cara had started looking around for cheap commercial kitchens to rent. The volume of orders rolling in was too much for a domestic kitchen to handle, which was a lovely, albeit slightly frustrating, problem to have. For the first time in nearly twenty years, Beth had her own money. Not a fortune, but certainly enough to put down a bond for a flat if Max refused to move out. Who knew what he would do? She'd seen very little of him in the past few weeks. If he wasn't at work, he was either at the gym, or golf, or driving the kids about the place. Bed was now the only place she got to actually see him. Last night, she'd watched him sleeping. His eyebrows fuzzed in all different directions. A smattering of stubble. The gentle wheeze of air in and out his lovely strong nose.

She would miss him. She already missed him.

Beth felt her eyes filling with tears. This was more like a funeral than a party.

'Mum, what's wrong?' Chloe sidled up and slipped a hand through her mother's arm. She was growing so tall. Nearly up to Beth's shoulder.

'Nothing, honey,' Beth pressed a pinkie into each corner of her eye. 'These are happy tears. I mean, look …'

The backyard was a twinkling sea of tea lights and candles, and a few larger flaming torches. Max and Ethan had set up a lovely, large white marquee, in case of rain. There was even a dance floor, which Beth had originally insisted upon but now felt was a complete waste of time. She didn't feel like dancing, and she knew Max wouldn't. Maybe their guests would get some fun out of it when the DJ started up.

'Where's Dad?' asked Chloe, as Ethan came to join them.

'I dunno. I saw him around here a second ago.' He bumped her shoulder. 'Great party, Mum. Awesome food.'

'Thank you, Ethan.' She pulled both her children in tightly. 'I just want you to know that, whatever happens, your father and I love you very, very much and you are far and away the two best things to come out of our marriage.'

She clung to Ethan and Chloe, feeling their bones beneath her hands.

'Mum, you're freaking me out.' Chloe pulled away.

'Yeah, what's going on?' said Ethan.

Beth was about to speak but a squeal from the microphone interrupted her.

'Ah, testing, testing, one, two, three,' boomed Max's voice through the audio system.

'I thought we were doing speeches later.' Beth checked her watch. 'After the cake. I haven't even put the candles on yet. What's your father doing? Why is he always in such a rush?' Panic rose in her chest. She wasn't ready at all. Bloody Max! Never paid attention.

The kids shrugged. 'Just listen, Mum,' Ethan urged.

'On behalf of Beth and myself, I'd like to welcome everyone here tonight.' He searched the crowd until his eyes landed on her. 'Now, my wife is probably wondering right now what the hell I'm doing because the speeches aren't due for another hour and she still has to put the candles on the cake.' Max paused. 'But I've actually organised a little entertainment for tonight. Beth? Can you come to the dance floor?'

Applause rippled through the guests.

'Go, Beth!' came a call from the crowd.

Beth flushed. What was Max up to? Surely he hadn't organised anything embarrassing, like an exotic male dancer. She'd kill him if he had.

'Beth, come here.' He held out his hand. 'I couldn't think of what to buy you for our anniversary. I mean, how do you thank the love of your life for being such a brilliant mother, wife and friend for all those years. I could never have asked for better. You have made this house a home. In fact, you are home, to me.' He kissed her hand and Beth felt her eyes growing hot and itchy. Why did he insist on making it such a charade!

'But then I did think of a gift. Something I've never given you.' Max turned to her. 'In the twenty years that we've been married, how many times have we danced together?' He spoke through the microphone.

'None,' said Beth quietly.

'Did you hear that, ladies and gentlemen? My wife and I have danced together approximately zero times.' He made an O with his fingers.

The crowd jeered.

'Mostly because I am a terrible dancer. But if any of you know my wife—' he fixed her with his gaze '—truly know my wife, you'll know that what she loves more than any-thing else in the world, with the exception of Chloe, Ethan and possibly myself, is dancing. And for twenty years, I've deprived her of that joy.'

More booing.

'But tonight, ladies and gentlemen, I plan to make up for lost time.'

From the corner of her eye, Beth saw a woman dressed in a gorgeous flamenco dress, tiered with layers and layers of red ruffles, quietly speaking with the DJ and moving into position on the dance floor.

'Ever since Beth started planning tonight's extravaganza, I have been taking dance lessons under the tutelage of the amazing Serena Fernandez who, if you're ever in the market for dance lessons, has a terrific studio right near my office. Every lunch hour, every weekend, Serena has worked her backside off to transform these two left feet into a left foot and a right foot.'

Beth swallowed heavily. Dancing lessons? Mentally, she rewound through the text messages, about hot moves and getting down and dirty. Dancing! Of course, it could have all related to dancing. Not doing the horizontal mambo, but the actual mambo.

'Enough with the plugs, start dancing, ya big mug,' came a voice from the crowd.

This time Beth laughed for real.

'All right, all right.' Max patted the air. 'First things first.' He passed the microphone to Serena, and turned to face Beth. 'Would you do the honours?' Max undid his top button and motioned for Beth to do the rest.

Behind them, the crowd hooted and Beth imagined her cheeks going the same colour as the dancer's skirt. With his shirt completely undone, Max took it off and handed it to her. His chest was now completely bare, and Beth couldn't help but shiver at the frisson between them. He extended his arms and Serena slipped a heavily beaded bolero jacket over them.

Beth clapped her hands. 'It's just like the one from *Strictly Ballroom*!'

Max nodded. 'Paul Mercurio, eat your heart out,' he smirked and set off with a flourish to take up position. Serena shepherded Beth into a seat at the edge of the dance floor, then nodded at the DJ and struck a pose.

Through the speakers came the waterfall sound of castanets. With slight uncertainty, Max raised his hands above his head and curved them into an arc while Serena clicked her heels and began twirling her wrists in ever more elaborate circles that unfurled like flower petals.

'Olé!' shouted someone in the audience and Max flashed a grin.

As the music picked up tempo, Serena became a swirl of skirts and heels, flicks and kicks, and to Beth's great shock, Max kept up with her, striding manfully about the dance floor and stopping every so often to stamp his feet, click his fingers and clap his hands.

This was Max?

The dance ended with him dipping Serena to the floor, her back arched and her dark hair grazing the ground, but instead of looking into her eyes, Max locked his gaze on Beth and mouthed 'I love you'.

The crowd erupted and Beth leapt to her feet to join in the rapturous applause. Serena curtsied with a flourish, then drew Beth towards her husband. 'Now, the lovers,' she said in a deeply accented voice, joining Beth's hand with Max's before giving further instructions to the DJ.

As Max took his wife in his arms, the strains of 'Love Is in the Air' played out across the garden, and soon they were surrounded by all their friends and family, holding each other close and dancing to the old classic.

'What do you think?' Max's brow was furrowed. 'Did I make a complete fool of myself?'

'No,' cried Beth. 'I'm the one who's been the fool. I thought you were having an affair.'

Max's eyes rounded in surprise. 'You what?'

'All those text messages about hot moves, and how you kept disappearing all the time, I just assumed you were having an affair. I even suspected Charlie Devine of being somehow involved with you.'

Max threw his head back and laughed. 'Charlie? Oh, Beth, no. You got it all wrong. Charlie was helping me. She knew Serena from her dancing days, and when I told her what I was planning, she put me in touch and gave me an exercise and diet program to follow so that I wouldn't look like a jelly blubber when I danced.'

'Oh, goodness, now I really feel awful. That poor woman. I completely misjudged her.'

'I can't believe you thought there was something happening between us.' He shook his head, chuckling.

'Don't laugh, it was awful ...' She dropped her gaze. 'But even before that ... I felt like we were growing apart. You were so distant. Even before those messages.'

Max's expression grew serious. 'You're right ...' He nodded. 'I was feeling ... left out. The kids didn't seem to need us as much, and I could sense that you weren't quite satisfied at home any more. I just wasn't sure of my place. How I fit in. But then I realised that, with the kids being more independent, this was our time ... To do something just for us. Reconnect.' He kissed her on the nose. 'Learning to dance seemed a good way for me to do that.'

'Thank you ... it was. It is ... I just wish you'd told me.'

'Then it wouldn't have been a surprise.'

'No ... but ... I did something really silly and I feel I have to tell you the truth.' Beth closed her eyes and clenched her teeth. 'I kissed a twenty-four-year-old electrician, to get back at you. Because I thought you were having an affair.' She opened her eyes. 'Do you hate me?'

Max's face was serious. 'Just a kiss?'

'Yes. And it didn't mean anything. I was just so upset and angry with you. Please, I'm so sorry.'

He grinned. 'Well, that explains why you've been acting so strange lately. You were like a different person. More ... assertive. Independent. All that work you're doing with Cara, and those new clothes you bought ...'

'I'll take them back,' said Beth. 'They're really not me.'

'Oh, no,' said Max. 'You should keep them. I like the new Beth Chandler.' He kissed her softly on the lips. 'I meant what I said in the speech. I love you so much. I love our life together and I can't wait to see what the next twenty years bring us.'

'I think it'll be wonderful.' Beth smiled up at her husband. 'And hopefully, with no electrical problems.'

CHAPTER FORTY-NINE

Beth's backyard now had the feel of a party in wind-down mode. Jackets slung across backs of chairs, collars loosened, empty glasses, lipstick long gone from lips.

Cara shifted slightly in her chair and Poppy snuffled.

'Shh, baby girl. It's all right. Go back to sleep,' she murmured, which her daughter promptly did, resting her head into the crook of Cara's neck. There was now a wet patch where Poppy had drooled, but Cara made no attempt to wipe it away. It was years since her daughter had fallen asleep on her like this and she had no intention of doing anything that would interrupt the overwhelming closeness she felt right now with her little girl, warm and heavy in her arms.

On the dance floor, Max and Beth clung to each other and moved slowly side to side in time with the breezy jazz music that the DJ had switched into. His chin rested comfortably on her forehead and occasionally one of them would withdraw to offer a smile or a comment. Even at this distance, it wasn't difficult to lip-read the words *I love you.* Their mouths formed the words much like a kiss.

Chloe and Ethan sat at nearby tables, chatting and stealing glances at their mum and dad. Every so often they'd shake their heads, feigning embarrassment to their friends. *Oldies dancing, so lame!* But there was also a glow in their eyes that spoke of comfort and reassurance. Their parents not only loved them, they loved each other. The heart of the family beat loud and strong.

The only people to have not received the memo about the party being in wind-down mode were Alex's twins, who appeared quite drunk thanks to their current game of spinning on the dance floor for as long as possible before stopping and trying to stand on one foot. James was judge and referee, while Alex filmed the whole thing on her phone. At one point, Noah staggered sideways and nearly fell flat on his face, except that Alex caught him in the nick of time. She threw her head back and laughed, and James simultaneously scooped up Jasper before the pair wriggled out of their parents' arms and demanded they do it all over again.

Cara would miss them terribly when they left, but Alex had promised that nothing would change. 'You think I'm going to want to sit around all the time in whatever shitty new suburb we can afford? I'll be back in Cuthbert Close every chance I get. And if you want to come and see how the other half live, you're always more than welcome.'

She was exaggerating, of course. Alex would never settle for anything truly horrible, and the compromise would be worth it, in terms of the financial burden it would relieve. Part of Cara envied her. New home. Baby on the way.

No mortgage to stress over. It was a new beginning and, watching Beth dancing with Max, she felt a similar sense of renewal. After twenty years of marriage, was it possible to venture into the next twenty years with more love and enthusiasm for your partner than you'd had on the day you married?

Cara felt a tap on her elbow.

'Hi,' said a familiar voice.

'Hey, what are you doing here?'

Will Parry slid into the seat next to her and placed a large envelope on the table. 'It's the ownership agreement. I was in the area and just thought I'd drop it in your letterbox.'

'Just passing? At 10 pm on a Saturday night?'

Will gave a sheepish grin. 'If the lights were on, I was going to knock on the door. But then I saw Beth's house lit up like a Christmas tree and I remembered you saying something about how you'd been cooking for their party, so I thought I'd drop in and say hi. You don't mind, do you?' His forehead was creased.

'Not at all. In fact, I might get you to give me a hand getting this one back home. She's too heavy for me to carry and I don't want to wake her. Would *you* mind?'

'Happy to help.'

Gently, Cara transferred Poppy into his arms, causing the little girl to rouse momentarily and say a sleepy *Hi Will* before crashing straight back to sleep with her head slumped on his shoulder.

Over the past few weeks, they'd both got to know him. The painting done, they'd made a list of the most pressing maintenance problems with the cottage and had begun working their way through them. He was easy company and though Cara was far more comfortable in an apron than overalls, she began to look forward to their weekly DIY sessions.

Cara set about saying her goodbyes.

'Such a beautiful celebration. I'm so happy for you both.' She kissed Max on the cheek and gave Beth a tight, fierce hug.

'So am I,' said Beth, her eyes shining. 'And don't think that just because, well, you know ...' She looked nervously at Max.

'I think that's my cue to leave and get a drink. Night, Cara, and thank you for all the terrific food. Those rice paper rolls were fantastic,' said Max.

'My pleasure, and thank you for a wonderful night. Congratulations.'

As Max departed for the bar, Beth pulled Cara aside. She frowned and Cara's heart sank. *She's pulling out of Nourish. Now she knows Max wasn't cheating, there's no need for her to earn the money.*

Beth leant in. 'I was going to say that, you know, with Max, and what I thought ... Well, just so you know, I still want to keep working on Nourish ... with you. I love it.'

Cara exhaled. 'I'm relieved to hear you say that.'

'Because it's more than just the money. It's a new start, and I think Max probably realised before I did that we'd become too set in our ways. Things were changing, but we weren't. We were living on past glories.' She pulled her in more closely. 'You know what they say – the past is a different country and you don't want to live there. I have to believe there are just as many exciting and new challenges ahead of us as there are behind us. Who knows?' She looked around the garden wistfully. 'Maybe in a few years when the kids are older we might even move out of Cuthbert Close.'

Cara clutched her hand. 'You and Alex can't both leave me!'

Beth laughed. 'You can take the women out of Cuthbert Close, but you can't take the close out of the women. We'll always be friends, don't doubt that.' She glanced over to where Will was holding Poppy. 'You know there's also a line from *Strictly Ballroom*, which I'd forgotten until Max whispered it to me a second ago.' Beth spoke with urgency. 'It's something about living a life in fear is a life half-lived.' She paused. 'Pete … Your parents … they would want you to be happy, whatever that means.'

Cara kissed her on the cheek. 'You're a good friend, Beth Chandler.'

'Always.' She touched her shoulder and went back to her husband.

Cara, meanwhile, manoeuvred between the pinballing twins and managed to land a kiss on Alex's cheek.

'I'm off. Poppy's crashed and Will's giving me a hand to get her home.'

'He's turning out to be quite the handyman, isn't he?' remarked Alex, gazing in Will's direction. 'I wouldn't mind seeing him in a tool belt.'

Cara gave her a gentle dig in the ribs. 'You can't say things like that.'

Stealing up behind them, James circled his arms around Alex's rapidly growing waist. 'Can't say things like what?'

'I just told Cara that I thought Will Parry would look hot in a tool belt,' said Alex, with no hint of apology in her voice.

'Don't I look hot in a tool belt?' protested James.

'I never said you didn't. All I said was—'

'I know, I know.' Admonished, James disentangled himself and started off towards the Chandlers' garage.

'Where are you going?' called Alex.

'I think Max has a tool belt here somewhere,' said James over his shoulder. 'Night, Cara.'

Alex rolled her eyes. 'Idiot,' she said affectionately.

'Will's brought the ownership agreement for me to sign,' said Cara.

Alex nodded briskly, suddenly in lawyer mode. 'Yes, I sent the final documents to his solicitor earlier in the week and there should be two copies. One for each of you. I recommend you keep it in a safe spot.' Her face softened. 'So, I guess it's official. You and Will Parry are really doing this.'

'I guess so.' Cara tried to inject brightness into her voice.

Alex's eyes narrowed on her. 'You know, it's okay to change your mind, at any stage. Look at me. For twelve years, I thought I wanted to be a partner at Macauley, but when I got the chance, I realised it wasn't right at all.'

Cara laughed. 'You and Beth must have both been drinking from the same philosophical punchbowl tonight because she's been spouting lines from movies at me, and now you're sounding more zen than a Buddhist monk.'

Alex clasped her hands in a praying pose and bowed. 'Namaste, my child.'

'That's Hindu,' laughed Cara, kissing her friend on the cheek. 'Night, Alex.'

Side by side, Will and Cara made their way silently back to the cottage with nothing but the occasional flapping of bat wings to disturb the quiet of Cuthbert Close. Inside the cottage, Will trod carefully down the darkened hallway with a limp Poppy in his arms, and stood aside while Cara opened the door to the little girl's bedroom.

The covers pulled back, Cara motioned for Will to lay her down.

As they left the bedroom, he stopped at the door to look back at her, splayed like a star and snoring softly.

'Such a lady,' he whispered, and Cara playfully punched his arm.

'That's my daughter you're talking about.'

Will rubbed his elbow, feigning injury. 'Ow.'

Cara went to shut the door but he grabbed her hand. 'Just another minute.'

She closed her fingers around his, and together they watched Poppy sleep, the rise and fall of her chest. Cara's whole body tingled. Alive, as if the warmth from Will's hand was transferring energy straight into her veins. With every pore, she was aware of him next to her. The heat off his body. His spicy, musky scent. In her other hand was the ownership agreement, stiff and cool in her grasp.

Eventually, Will shifted his weight and Cara let go, closing the door on her sleeping daughter. In the kitchen, she switched on an overhead light and placed the envelope on the table. Her future. Poppy's future. It was right there on the table. Hers for the taking.

'So I guess that's it then.' Will gestured to the agreement and took a seat. 'Signed and sealed.'

'I guess so.'

'Is it okay if I move this stuff?' He gestured to the cardboard box at his feet, the one that her father had brought over several weeks ago and she still hadn't had time to go through.

'I think it's just old recipe books.'

He picked out a scrapbook and started leafing through it.

'Looks like they're really proud of you.' He held up a page and turned over to the next. They were all cuttings of her work from magazines, each picture carefully clipped and glued in, along with a handwritten date and the name of the publication.

'Must have been something Dad did.' Cara stepped closer and Will laid the scrapbook on the table. She turned to the front page where there was a note, handwritten in hangul.

'Can you read it?'

Cara held it up. 'A little … Um … Let me see.' She studied the shapely dashes and circles. 'Dear Umma …' she began. 'I thought you might be … interested to see the work of your granddaughter, Cara … She is very successful here in Australia and makes beautiful photos for food magazines. Forgive me. Your daughter, Ji-yoo.' On the final words, Cara's voice cracked.

'Hey, are you okay? I'm sorry, I shouldn't have gone through your things.'

'No.' Cara swallowed the knot of tears in her throat. 'No, I'm glad you did. That was … important.'

She is proud of me. Dad was right. She has never forgiven herself for falling in love.

'Such a waste,' Cara murmured to herself.

'What's a waste?' Will's face was a road map of worry lines.

'Nothing.' Cara took a breath and, fingers trembling, picked up the envelope. 'Will, I need you to tell me the truth. Do you love this place?'

He shifted. 'It's complicated ...'

'Tell me honestly.'

'Okay ... okay.' He looked her directly in the eye. 'I like it when you and Poppy are here and the place is ... alive. But when you're not, no. I don't like it. It just makes me think of the past.'

'Okay.' She nodded. 'Okay.'

Holding the envelope in front of Will, she tore it in half, straight down the middle.

'Cara, what are you doing?' He sat up, taking in her stony expression. 'What's wrong? Don't you want the cottage any more? Please, talk to me. It doesn't matter that I don't love this place, you do, and I want you to be happy.'

Slowly, she took two steps towards him and gingerly sat on his knee. Will's eyes widened, confused. His hands wavered in the air with uncertainty.

'I want the house,' she said carefully. 'But I want you more.' She cupped his chin. 'Will Parry, you are a kind and decent man, and I would be a fool to let you go.'

'I don't understand ...You're not letting me go. Whatever happens, this agreement gives you a secure future.'

Cara shook her head. 'It ties us all to the past. I loved Pete, but I don't have to live with his ghost around me to keep that alive. I need a fresh start. Somewhere new, with someone new.' She took a breath. 'I think it's okay for me to be happy. The past is the past, and that's where it must stay.'

'But what about Poppy? She loves this place. Don't you want her to have that stability?' Will stroked a hair out of Cara's eyes.

'A home is about being surrounded by the people you care about, it's not the bricks and mortar. They're just what holds the love.'

'Okay.' Will nodded. 'Okay.' He took a breath. 'That's lucky,' he said huskily. 'Because I am falling so hard for you, Cara Pope, that I don't know what to do.'

'It's easy.' She smiled. 'Kiss me.'

He took her face in his hands and met her lips with his. As the kiss deepened, Cara felt warmth spreading all over her body and she knew that, in Will Parry, she had found what she was looking for.

Home.

ThePrimalGuy.com.au
From: The Primal Guy
Subject: The End

To all my supporters,
As you may have read in the media, my business is in the process of being wound up, and as of next week will no longer exist.

I want to take this opportunity to thank you, my supporters, and also my family – my beautiful wife, Charlie, and my awesome daughter, Talia, who have both worked so hard behind the scenes to keep The Primal Guy going, while I dealt with some serious health issues.

First, to Charlie. The saying goes that behind every successful man is a woman. But imagine how much more amazing the world would be if it was the other way round? You were the brains and the inspiration. I'm sorry I let you down.

To Talia. How lucky am I to have a kid who's already so much smarter than me! Those newsletters you wrote on my behalf while I was away were so, so good. You nailed it, kiddo. And you're absolutely right – chaos can be the best! Sometimes we all need a butterfly to flap its wings and throw us a storm. 'Cause look, here we are, headed for calmer waters with a future so bright, I think I need sunglasses.

Peace out,
Ryan (formerly the Primal Guy)

PS If you're still interested in food and nutrition, why don't you check out Nourish.com.au. I hear their stuff is delicious, AND good for you, AND it's real, just like our forebears used to eat.

Now, why didn't I think of that.

ACKNOWLEDGEMENTS

Writing acknowledgements is a bit like staggering over the finish line at the end of a marathon. Your heart is full, your brain is so fried that you're fresh out of words, but you're so damn grateful because you know you could never have made it without the team behind you.

Therefore, to all the 'shoulders' who helped me and this book to reach the publication finish line, I offer my warmest hugs, lip-smacking kisses and victory salutes. We made it!

Special thanks to:

Jo Mackay – I could not ask for a more enthusiastic and supportive publisher. You are the ray of sunshine among the clouds of self-doubt. Thank you, thank you, thank you. And for the brilliant cover concept, thank you again.

Annabel Blay – a wise and witty editor, whose margin notes have the most delightful voice. Who knew that editing could be fun??! You are wonderful.

Sarah JH Fletcher – your attention to detail is extraordinary and I'm in genuine awe of your proofreading brain. Thank you for your close attention to every word in this book.

Natilka Palka, Johanna Baker and Adam Van Rooijen – what a crew! You are the experts at getting books into the hands of readers, and you are terrific fun to be around. What more could an author ask for?

Jenny Kremmer – you read this book in its first draft (you poor soul) and helped me to take it to the next level. Many thanks.

The Bundanon Trust – for the most productive two weeks by the banks of the beautiful Shoalhaven River. Thank you for the gift of peace and quiet – albeit interrupted by the occasional wombat and kangaroo.

To all the bloggers, podcasters and authors who help to spread the word about my books and, of course, to the booksellers who provide that crucial link to readers – I've been blown away and humbled by the support. The community of readers and writers in this country is genuinely wonderful – a beacon of kindness in what can sometimes feel like a slightly brutal world.

To my friends and extended family – you have shown up for me, literally and metaphorically, time and again over the past year and, for a new author, that means everything.

To the Hamer/Davis crew, Sade, Muz, Tim, Jacks, Felic, Zoe, Elliot, Jess, Mims and Jack – our times together are always the best. But can we agree to freeze time so everyone can stop getting older? In particular, to Muz and Sade for enduring my author talks more times than most, and never once expressing anything other than positivity. And also to Jen, for your ongoing interest and support.

Mum and Dad – if you need or want a new career in book publicity, it's yours! You have pushed my books into the hands of more people than I can count. When it comes to me and my writing, you are completely one hundred per cent biased, and I love it. Every child should know such love in their lives.

Ruby, Sasha and Lucy – this book is, rightly, dedicated to you. In the last book, I said I hoped you were proud of me. Now, I know for sure that you are and it is the best feeling in the world. I'm proud of you, too.

Sam – every night before we go to sleep I tell you I love you and in your dry way, with the humour that brought us together, you joke back, 'No you don't.'

But I do. A thousand times over I do. This whole caper could not, and would not, happen without you.

Turn over for a sneak peek.

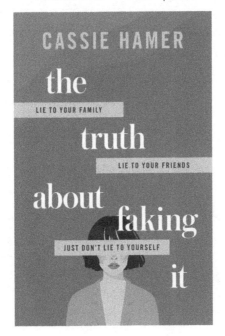

by

CASSIE HAMER

Available May 2022

CASSIE HAMER

CHAPTER ONE

Ellen Trainor put on her reading spectacles and allowed her eyes to zero in on the phallus, displayed in all its sausage-like glory before her. Yes, thoroughly delightful. Not to mention large. More kransky than cocktail frank. Spectacles completely unnecessary.

She took them off and her hand began to move.

After a few seconds, she stopped. It was no good. Her fingers were virginally tentative. The strokes meek and uninspired.

You're mature and fabulous, she chanted silently. *Own it.*

Pushing back her chunky turquoise bangle, she tried again. The following stroke was far bolder and more decisive than her limp, first attempt.

'That's more like it,' she murmured as the object of her focus started to spring to life beneath her hands. Her fingers moved at a faster pace. Yes, this was it. She'd found her rhythm. It was, as they say, like riding a bike. Her hands flitted and danced. Skittered and brushed. Almost frenzied. *Yes, yes, yes*, pumped the beat of Ellen's heart. It was glorious and liberating. She was young again. It was, dare she say it, better than sex. Or, at least, better than sex with Kenneth.

Two minutes later the job was done. Ellen let out a sigh of satisfaction and rolled her right shoulder to relieve the pinch. This was one of her best efforts, even if she did say so herself. Her gaze swung between the sketchpad on her knees and the gorgeous nude model standing six feet away looking soulfully through the window at the lilac blooms of the just-flowering jacaranda. Blades of late afternoon November sunlight shone through the lead-light windows of the art studio and fell like soft fingers on his finely sculpted torso. The model was new and thanks to her side-on view, she'd captured both his penis and left buttock perfectly.

Where was Suzie, their usual model for Monday afternoon life drawing?

Snorting hormones, hopefully. The woman was moody as a stormy sky and her droopy facial expressions about as inspiring as a tea bag. Too often, when Raphael the drawing teacher had surveyed Suzie's pose and said, 'I think there's something missing …' Ellen had been tempted to shout, 'HRT!' Life drawing was supposed to be an escape, not a reminder of the decrepitude of ageing. Women of certain years (and men, for that matter) had no business being nude in public. Ellen herself took a Victorian-era approach to dressing: the display of a delicate wrist or an ankle was acceptable, but nothing else. Occasionally, she had the misfortune to catch a glimpse of herself naked in front of a mirror. Who *was* that prune-like person with a décolletage

as wrinkled as the bellows of a piano accordion and knees
that reminded her of two sad clowns commiserating with
one another?

Oh god. It was her.

The physical act of ageing was a heinous crime against
the body and dressing was now an exercise in concealing
the evidence. Buttoned shirts, turtlenecks and pants were
Ellen's daily disguise, but she had a trick up her (tailored,
naturally) sleeve. That was to top the boring pieces with
elaborate (and cheap) beaded necklaces, chunky bracelets
and a chic, short hairdo. These she called her 'red-herring' or
'look-over-here' pieces: the ones designed to show the world
that although Ellen's skin had become more sultana than
grape and her entire body tended to ache after a few minutes
in the same position, she was still utterly fabulous.

Because she was, wasn't she?

'Ten seconds everyone.' Raphael stopped at her shoulder.
'Excellent, Ellen.' He touched a hand to the paisley scarf
around his neck, which was what he did when he approved
of something. 'The energy is … exciting me.'

From the flutters in her chest, Ellen could tell it was exciting her, too. She pulled out her phone, typed in B for boyfriend and tapped out a message telling Kenneth to take
one of his little blue pills. The reply was almost instant: a
thumbs-up emoji.

'All right, artists. I want you to take your work and
hold it up.' Raphael tossed one end of his scarf over his
shoulder. He was a nice enough fellow, but quite mad. In
five weeks of life-drawing classes he hadn't once talked
about technique or pencil grip or any of the things she had
expected. 'Ego!' he yelled at them. 'Or a lack thereof, is the

key to great art.' So extensive were his shouty lectures on the shedding of ego that Ellen considered Monday afternoon life drawing more counselling session than art class, not that *she* needed her head read. She was perfectly functional. Her ego was one of the few things that had escaped the vagaries of ageing and she wasn't of a mind to let it go. She didn't need life advice, she needed tips on shading and composition, how to inject light and dark into her pencil drawings.

'Now, I'm going to tell you how to make your work one hundred per cent better.' Raphael paused at the end of the room, beneath the portrait of Queen Elizabeth. Dust motes swirled about him. At long last! This was it, the tip she had been waiting for. The drawing advice that would revolutionise her artwork. Ellen tensed, pencil poised.

'My friends.' Raphael clasped his hands together. 'I want you to rip up your work. Tear it in half! Right through the middle.'

Rip it up? She'd spent half an hour on the model's left buttock alone. And it was excellent. Like a plump marshmallow aching to be squashed between fingers. She'd be blowed if she was going to tear it up.

What was everyone else doing? She met the gaze of the younger woman next to her, who gave an apologetic smile before gingerly tearing through her drawing, which, Ellen noted with a pang of envy, was even better than her own. Buttocks like plums.

'Ellen.' Raphael was at her side. His tone, reproachful.

'You said it was good. And I want to take it home.' *And tomorrow morning, I'll feast my eyes on that buttock while I eat my toast and marmalade.*

'Ellen, I'm disappointed in you.' He spoke with condescending patience, like she was a four-year-old caught with her hand in the biscuit tin. 'We've talked about this before. You are here to cast off your ego. Shed it as a snake sheds its skin. You are worried what people think of you. What *you* think of you. I tell you, none of this matters.'

She flinched, then squared her shoulders. *Oh, rack off Raphael, you poncy, paisley-wearing, pop psychologist.* 'I like this drawing and I'm going to take it home with me.' She held the paper to her chest. 'It's good. You said so yourself.'

'It doesn't matter what I think.'

'Of course it does! You're the teacher.'

'I'm your guide. This is a journey, remember. Not a destination. We are unlearning everything we have learnt before. We are harnessing the inner child. Shedding our inhibitions. Rediscovering our truths. You have so many walls you cannot even see them any more. You must look inside yourself.' Raphael clutched his (not to be cruel but Ellen believed in frank honesty) terrifically oversized gut.

The man was delusional. The only thing wrong with Ellen was her bank balance. The chief humiliation of this whole experience was that even if she wanted to come back to this madman's class next term, she probably couldn't afford to.

Ellen tore a tiny piece from the corner. 'There, it's ruined now. Happy?'

Raphael shook his head and moved on. 'Tex!' he called to the model. 'New position, please. Sitting this time.'

There was a rustle of paper as the class of ten or so prepared themselves for the new pose. Fools. Treating this Raphael like some Svengali, when in real life the all-knowing, all-seeing Raphael the great was, according to his website, an 'emerging artist'. Emerging? At the age of fifty-one? That spoke of tardiness in the extreme. Raphael's 'pieces' (more like childish scribble) sold for less than a thousand dollars a pop, a price that somehow alleviated Ellen's annoyance at being unable to afford one. Artwork that cheap had to be a bad investment.

Tex flexed his muscles and stretched and Ellen's groin fluttered in appreciation. He really was a fine specimen. Gosh, now he was looking in her direction. Ellen inhaled. A younger man. Hmm. Perhaps it *was* time to give Kenny the flick and try online dating, as her granddaughter, Georgie, had been suggesting for months: 'Everyone's doing it, Grandma. Even old people like you.'

Charming.

But at least the girl could acknowledge Ellen's needs. Natasha—her daughter—was in complete denial. Couldn't even bring herself to describe Kenneth as a 'boyfriend' but simply referred to him as 'your friend'. Natasha was dead against online dating and on that point, she and Ellen were united. Who could be bothered with all that typing and swiping? Not Ellen. Kenneth gave her companionship, affection and mildly satisfying sex. For titillation, there was life drawing. What more could she want? Online dating. She shuddered. Who knew what you could end up with, except for a nasty dose of the clap. Only yesterday she'd read a news article about over-fifties contracting STIs in record numbers. Honestly, how was it that these old biddies knew how to wrangle those dating-app thingies but not buy a condom? Ellen had no sympathy.

She held up her pencil, ready to draw again, and the male model's glance shifted away to the younger woman beside her. He gave a lazy smile and winked.

The cheek of him! Now there was a flush spreading up the poor girl's neck and she looked like she might cry.

Ellen raised her hand. This was unconscionable.

'Yes?' Raphael sounded bored.

'There's something you need to know.' Ellen eyeballed Tex, now seated with one leg crossed over the other to cover his penis. 'It's about the model.'

Oh, crumbs. Now everyone was looking at her. What was she actually going to say? That Tex had *winked* at a class member? Hardly a sackable offence, whatever those modern feminists would have you believe. As an eighteen-year-old legal secretary in the sixties, Ellen had suffered far worse and it hadn't bothered her a bit. A misplaced hand got a smack. Problem solved. No, it wasn't the wink itself that was the issue, it was that he hadn't winked at *her*. She paused, playing out the complaint in her head, how it might sound to the class.

He should have winked at me! *At least I would have winked back.*

Oh, how they would chortle. At *her*. What a daffy old duck. What a funny old sausage. No one else in this class was a day over thirty-five. They wouldn't understand how a woman of sixty-nine (such a lascivious-sounding age!) had needs and was, in her own mind, not a day over thirty-five.

'What about the model?' Raphael raised his eyebrows.

'I don't like the pose.' She sniffed. 'I think it's too … egocentric. He's hiding something. I want to capture him more … openly, if you will.'

Raphael nodded. 'Interesting feedback. Tex, could you interpret Ellen's thoughts?'

Tex froze. 'Actually, if you don't mind, I'd like to take a break thanks,' he muttered, uncrossing his legs and placing a protective hand over his nether regions. A small titter rippled across the class as the source of Tex's embarrassment became apparent.

'Don't be embarrassed, dear,' called Ellen. 'You're only a man, after all.'

Shooting her a look, Tex flung a dressing gown around his finely sculpted muscles and flounced off the podium.

'Was that my fault?' whispered her neighbour.

'Course not, darling,' said Ellen. 'Men are weak and can't control themselves. Not like us.'

'All right, people. Ten-minute break,' Raphael called.

Ellen stood carefully to give the blood time to flow to all corners of her body, though 'rush' wasn't quite the word. At her age, it was more like a slow amble. She bent left, then right, and was about to try forward when there was a small commotion at the door—two policemen.

Or were they? In the first week of life-drawing class there'd been something of a scandal when a group of six giggly, liquored-up young women arrived at the class with tulle veils on their heads, champagne under their arms and a substantial dose of pre-marital mischief on their minds. Raphael soon set them straight—this was *serious* drawing, not drinks and giggles—and sent them off into the night, clouds of tulle flying behind like jet stream.

Was that what was happening here? Were these 'policemen' in fact exotic male dancers in disguise? She hoped so and it seemed a distinct possibility, given the unhappy expression on Raphael's face. Then again, one of them was quite old and chubby. She did not want to see him nude.

'Ellen.' Raphael turned and beckoned. 'Could you come here for a moment?'

Her? The exotic male dancers were for her? Was Georgie up to mischief again? The girl was incorrigible.

The chubby policeman extended his hand. 'Ellen Trainor? I'm Sergeant Tom O'Hare of the Kings Cross police. Could we have a word?'

'Certainly.'

He gestured to the hallway and, as the three of them trooped into it, she glimpsed their expressions of concern. Not strippers, then.

A small flutter of worry flitted through her chest. What could the police want with her? It wasn't the small marijuana stash she kept in her cutlery drawer for special occasions, was it? Or that little bottle of perfume she'd 'accidentally' forgotten to pay for at the chemist last week? That was one upside of ageing: no one ever suspected little old ladies of anything.

'Apologies for interrupting your class, but we felt it was a matter that couldn't wait. Your neighbour told us we'd find you here.'

Maisie. That busybody. She would have wet herself at the sight of two uniformed officers banging on Ellen's door. Apartment living was so crass.

'How can I help, sergeant?' Ellen asked.

The officer removed his peaked cap. 'It's about your husband.'

talk about it

Let's talk about books.

Join the conversation:

 facebook.com/harlequinaustralia

 @harlequinaus

 @harlequinaus

harpercollins.com.au/hq

If you love reading and want to know about our
authors and titles, then let's talk about it.